Charlie's Children: Guardian of the Lost 2

Charlie's Children

Katlyn Rose

Published by Katie Rose, 2024.

This is a work of fiction. Similarities to real people, places, or events are entirely coincidental.

CHARLIE'S CHILDREN: GUARDIAN OF THE LOST 2

First edition. November 2, 2024.

Copyright © 2024 Katlyn Rose.

Written by Katlyn Rose.

To all the lost souls that are discarded, without family, feel alone, wandering the streets, and looking for love. We know you are there and are trying to help.

In the shadows of the city, where the lost and forgotten dwell, the smallest voices echo with the greatest truths. To survive is to be brave, but to hope is to defy darkness.

Katlyn Rose

PROLOGUE

I don't remember when I first found myself on the streets. Time is funny like that, slipping away like the rainwater that runs down the gutters, disappearing into the cracks of the city. The streets have become my world, a place where shadows are friends and enemies, where the cold bites and hunger gnaws at you until you forget what it was like to be warm and full.

My name? I'm not sure anymore. Names are something you lose when you're out here. They're heavy, tied to people and places that don't exist for you anymore. I think I had one once, something soft and sweet, like the lullabies my mother used to sing. Those memories are like the sun, warm but distant, something you see in dreams but never really touch.

Now, I'm just a shadow, drifting between the cracks of the city. I've learned how to hide, how to slip through the alleys and disappear when the grown-ups start yelling or when the men with hard eyes come looking. It's safer that way. The city is full of dangers, things that make your heart pound and your breath catch, like the loud bangs at night or the rough hands that grab and pull.

Sometimes, when the night is quiet, and I'm huddled in my little corner, I let myself think about the before. Before the streets, before the hunger. I used to have a bed, a soft one with warm blankets that smelled like sunshine. I had toys, too, little cars and dolls that I used to line up and talk to. They were my friends, and they never hurt me. I had a mother, too. She had soft hands and a smile that made the world feel safe. But she's gone now, like the bed and the toys. Everything is gone.

The streets don't care about what you had before. They're harsh and unforgiving, full of people who are too busy with their own lives to notice a small child hiding in the shadows. I've seen others like me, kids with dirty faces and sad eyes, kids who have learned to survive the hard way. We don't talk much, it's safer not to. But we watch out for each other, in our own quiet way.

There's a place I go sometimes, an old alley behind a broken-down building. It's my hiding spot, my little piece of the world where I can curl up and pretend that the walls around me are safe. It's cold and damp, and the smell isn't great, but it's mine. No one bothers me there. I found an old blanket in a trash bin once, and I keep it tucked under a pile of rags. It's thin and full of holes, but it's something to hold on to when the night gets too dark and the city feels too big.

The hunger is the hardest part. It's always there, gnawing at my insides like a rat, never letting go. Sometimes, I find scraps in the trash bins behind the restaurants. If I'm lucky, there's something good, half a sandwich, maybe, or a piece of fruit that's not too rotten. Other times, it's just bits of bread or cold fries. But you learn to be grateful for whatever you find. You learn to eat slow, to make the food last, because you never know when you'll find more.

I've tried begging, but it's hard. People don't like to look at you when you're small and dirty. They pass by quickly, their faces turned away, like if they don't see you, you don't exist. Sometimes, someone will toss a coin in my direction, not enough to buy a meal, but enough to remind me that I'm still here, still part of this world, even if only on the edges.

Nights are the worst. The city changes at night, becoming something darker, something scarier. The shadows grow longer, and the noises get louder, shouts, sirens, the sounds of things breaking. I don't sleep much at night. It's not safe. Instead, I curl up in my corner, pulling my blanket tight around me, and wait for the sun to come back. It's always cold, and I shiver so hard that my teeth chatter, but I keep still, keep quiet. I've learned that quiet is safe.

I dream sometimes, when I do manage to sleep. I dream of warm places, of soft beds and kind voices. I dream of my mother,

her face blurry and fading, but her smile still the same. In my dreams, we're together again, and she's holding me close, whispering that everything's going to be okay. But then I wake up, and the cold is still there, and the streets are still dark, and she's gone. The dreams hurt more than the hunger, more than the cold, because they remind me of what I've lost.

I've seen things, too, things that make my stomach twist and my heart pound. Men with hard eyes and sharp voices, grabbing kids like me, pulling them into cars that don't come back. I've learned to stay hidden, to melt into the shadows when I see them coming. I'm small, and that's my advantage. I can slip away, disappear where they can't follow. But not everyone is as lucky. I've seen other kids disappear, and I wonder if they found somewhere better, or if the darkness swallowed them whole.

I miss my mother. I miss the way she used to tuck me in at night, the way she used to sing softly until I fell asleep. I miss the warmth of her hand in mine, the way she made me feel safe, even when the world was scary. I don't know where she is, or if she's even alive. Sometimes, I imagine she's out there somewhere, looking for me, trying to find her way back to me. But deep down, I know that's just a dream, like the ones I have at night.

The city is my home now, the streets my bed. I've learned to survive, to take care of myself. But there's a hole inside me, a hollow place where love used to be. I try to fill it with scraps of food, with the warmth of the sun when it breaks through the clouds, but nothing really fits. The hole just gets bigger, swallowing up everything I try to hold on to.

I don't cry much anymore. Tears are a luxury I can't afford. They won't bring back my mother, or make the streets any warmer, or fill my empty belly, so I keep them inside, like everything else. I keep my head down, keep moving, keep surviving. It's all I know how to do.

Sometimes, I wonder if there's another life out there for me, a life where I'm not alone, where I'm not scared all the time. But those thoughts are like the dreams, they come and go, leaving me emptier than before. This is my life now, and I've learned to accept it, even if it's not what I want. Even if it's not what I deserve.

I hear stories, sometimes, from other kids, about people who come and take them away to better places. Places where they can be warm and safe, where they don't have to hide or be afraid. But I don't believe in those stories. They're just another kind of dream, another kind of lie. No one's coming for me. No one even knows I'm here.

I keep going, day after day, because that's what you do. You don't stop, you don't give up. You keep moving, keep surviving, because maybe, just maybe, there's a reason you're still here. Maybe there's a place for you in this world, even if you haven't found it yet.

But the nights are long, and the cold is deep, and the hunger is always there, gnawing away at the edges of my thoughts. And sometimes, when the darkness feels too big, too overwhelming, I let myself dream. Just for a little while. I dream of warm beds and kind voices, of a world where I'm not just a shadow, not just a small child trying to survive on the streets.

And then I wake up, and the city is still there, and the streets are still hard, and the hunger is still gnawing at me. But I keep going, because that's all I can do. I keep moving through the shadows, waiting for the day when the dreams might become real, when the world might be something more than this cold, empty place.

But until then, I'll stay hidden, I'll stay quiet. I'll be a shadow in the city, surviving as best I can. Because that's what you do when you're small and alone. You survive.

CHAPTER 1

The streets of Houston hummed with an eerie intensity as Kit and his team of rescuers moved stealthily through the shadowed alleyways. The air was heavy with the stench of trash, mingling with the distant sounds of sirens and the low murmurs of the city's downtrodden.

Kendrick Thorne, aka Kit, a tall figure cloaked in darkness, led the group with caution etched into every line of his face. His eyes, sharp and alert, scanned the surroundings as he communicated silently with his team through a series of hand signals and nods.

"Any sign of them?" Kit murmured, his voice barely audible above the din of the city.

Sofia shook her head, her lips pressed into a thin line. "Not yet," she whispered back, her voice filled with apprehension. "They've got to be close. Keep your guard up."

Kit nodded, his jaw clenched tightly as he motioned for the team to continue moving forward. The group crept through the narrow alley, their footsteps muffled by the soft crunch of gravel and trash beneath their feet.

The team's footsteps echoed softly against the cracked pavement as they approached the decrepit warehouse, it's worn exterior stands in sharp contrast to the busy, colorful city street outside its door. Kit's gaze swept over the building with a steely intensity, taking in every detail of its dilapidated exterior, the boarded-up windows, the graffiti-splattered walls, the rusted metal door that stood as a barrier between them and the unknown dangers that lurked within.

"This is it," Kit murmured, his voice barely audible above the hum of anticipation that surrounded them. "Stay sharp, people."

The team nodded in silent agreement, their eyes lit with a mixture of excitement and apprehension. They knew the risks in front of them, the potential dangers that awaited them behind those crumbling walls, but they also knew that they had a job to do, a mission to rescue the innocent souls trapped within.

Kit took a deep breath as he went through their plan of action. With a swift hand gesture, he signaled for the team to gather around him, their movements fluid and synchronized as they huddled together in the shadow of the warehouse.

"All right, listen up," Kit said, his voice low but commanding. "We know the traffickers are holed up in there with the teens. Our priority is to get the kids out safely, be prepared for anything. Stay sharp, and keep your eyes peeled for any signs of trouble."

The team nodded in understanding, their expressions set in stone as they prepared to face whatever lay ahead. With one final glance at each other, they broke apart, each member taking up their assigned position with practiced efficiency.

As they neared the entrance, Kit raised a hand, signaling for the team to halt. Jack and Miguel took up positions on either side of the door, their muscles tense with anticipation as they prepared to breach it. Calista stood ready with her electronics, her fingers poised over the keys as she waited for Kit's signal to hack into any security systems the traffickers might have in place. And Dr. Jane remained on standby, her medical kit at the ready in case any of the rescued teens were injured in the chaos that was sure to follow.

With a nod from Kit, Jack and Miguel moved forward, their movements swift and precise as they forced the door open with an unusually silent crash. The team moved forward, their senses on high alert as they prepared to confront whatever dangers waited for them inside the warehouse's shadowy depths.

Sofia, her features illuminated by the faint glow of the streetlights, followed closely behind Kit. The young social worker's expression was tense, her eyes darting nervously from shadow to shadow as she clutched a walkie-talkie tightly in her hand.

As they rounded a corner, the scene before them came into view, a small group of teens huddled together, their faces pale and frightened, surrounded by a gang of traffickers. The air crackled and Kit felt a rush of adrenaline course through his veins.

"Let's move," Kit said quietly, his voice firm and commanding. "Stay close and watch each other's backs."

With silent precision, the team fanned out, encircling the traffickers, closing in on their prey. The traffickers, caught off guard by the sudden appearance of Kit and his team, tensed visibly, their hands shooting toward the weapons concealed beneath their jackets.

"Nobody move!" Kit called out, his voice cutting through the tense silence like a knife. "You're surrounded. Surrender peacefully, and nobody gets hurt."

The traffickers hesitated for a moment, their eyes flickering nervously between Kit and his team. But before they could respond, chaos erupted.

Gunshots rang out, shattering the stillness of the night as the hidden traffickers opened fire, their bullets whizzing through the air with deadly precision. Kit and his team dove for cover, their hearts pounding in their chests as they returned fire with equal ferocity.

"Stay down!" Kit shouted, his voice strained with urgency as he exchanged gunfire with the traffickers. "We've got to keep those kids safe!"

Bullets ricocheted off the walls, sending showers of sparks cascading through the warehouse as Kit and his team fought desperately to hold their ground. Sweat dripped down Kit's brow, his hands trembling with adrenaline as he fired round after round at the spots he saw flashes of light from the trafficker's guns.

There was a pause in the shooting, the traffickers hesitated, their eyes darting nervously between Kit and his team, fear etched on their faces at being caught and apparently cornered. Kit's steely gaze, bore into them with a silent warning, while his team remained poised, ready to spring into action at a moment's notice.

But before anyone could react, chaos erupted with the deafening roar of gunfire again. Bullets sliced through the air, tearing holes in the darkness and sending shards of brick and concrete flying in every direction. The sharp crack of gunfire mingled with the panicked shouts of the traffickers, their movements erratic as they unleashed a barrage of bullets in a desperate bid to hold their ground.

"Get down!" Kit's voice cut through the chaos, his command echoing off the walls of the room they were in. With lightning reflexes, he threw himself behind a rusted dumpster that was inside the room for some reason, the metallic clang of his body hitting the ground drowned out by the deafening cacophony of gunfire.

His heart pounded in his chest like a drumbeat, the rush of adrenaline coursing through his veins as he returned fire with equal ferocity. Sweat ran down his brow, stinging his eyes as he squeezed off round after round, each shot a silent prayer for the safety of the innocent lives caught in the crossfire.

"We're pinned down!" Sofia's voice rang out from somewhere to his left, her words a desperate plea for help. Kit spared her a quick glance, his eyes meeting hers in silent understanding before he turned his attention back to the task at hand.

"We need to flank them," he shouted over the roar of gunfire, his voice strained with urgency as he gestured for his team to move into position. "Cover me!"

With a nod of ready to his team, Kit broke cover, his muscles tense with anticipation as he sprinted towards a nearby stack of discarded crates. Bullets whizzed past him, their deadly intent a reminder of the stakes at hand, but he pushed forward with a single-minded goal.

"Go! Go! Go!" he shouted, his voice a fierce battle cry as he signaled for his team to follow suit. Together, they moved as one, a well-oiled machine fueled by adrenaline and the belief that they could take the traffickers out.

Suddenly, there was a deafening roar as a series of explosions echoed through the warehouse, sending shockwaves rippling through the air. Kit's heart leaped into his throat as he saw one of the traffickers go up in flames, his screams drowned out by the cacophony of gunfire and chaos. Whee the hell had it come from?

"Move! Move! Move!" Kit shouted, his voice barely audible above the din. "We've got to get those kids out of here!"

Kit and his team sprang into action, their movements swift and purposeful as they fought their way through the chaos. Bullets whizzed past them, their bodies aching with exhaustion as they pushed forward, driven by the knowledge that innocent lives hung in the balance.

And then, just as suddenly as it had begun, the gunfire ceased, replaced by an eerie silence that hung heavy in the air like a shroud. Kit's heart pounded in his chest, his breath coming in ragged gasps as he scanned the alley for any sign of movement. His team had formed a circle around the teens, anticipating more gunfire.

But there was none. Only the sound of distant sirens and the faint echo of their own labored breathing filled the air, a reminder of the violence that had erupted in the darkness.

"We did it," Sofia's voice broke the silence, her tone a mixture of relief and disbelief as she emerged from her hiding place, her eyes wide with wonder. "We actually did it."

Kit allowed himself a moment to savor the victory, but even as he basked in the glow of their success, he knew that their work was far from over. They had to get the kids out of a burning building.

"We did," he replied, his voice weary. "But we've still got work to do. Let's get these kids to safety."

They turned toward the group of teens, their faces pale with fear as they huddled together near a box by the wall. Kit's heart swelled with relief as he stood close, his arms aching to want to envelope them in a protective embrace.

"You're safe now," he whispered, his voice hoarse with emotion. "You're going to be okay."

The teens looked up at him with wide eyes, their expressions a mixture of disbelief and gratitude as they realized they had been rescued from the jaws of death. One by one, they clung to Kit or one of the team members, their trembling bodies finding comfort in the reassuring embraces.

"Thank you," one of the teens whispered, her voice barely audible above the din of the city. "Thank you for saving us."

Kit smiled, his eyes shining with unshed tears as he looked down at the young girl. "You're welcome," he replied, his voice choked with emotion. "Just remember, you're never alone. There's always someone who will help you."

And as the smoke cleared and the sounds of distant police sirens came closer, Kit realized the explosion was probably an old oil drum that sparked from a bullet. He couldn't help but feel a sense of pride in what they had accomplished. It was his hope that these kids would survive their ordeal and live a stronger, safer life.

The team walked them outside, waited until the police were close enough to see, then disappeared into the night, telling the kids they would be okay and he would be watching out for them.

CHAPTER 2

Kit's team was a patchwork quilt of seasoned individuals, each carrying their own unique experiences and skills like badges of honor.

Kit's oldest friend and sounding board, Jack "Pop's" Thompson, a weathered veteran of the military and streets whose grizzled countenance belied a sharp mind, and keen instincts honed by years in the military and on the police beat.

Pop's was a man made in the fires of battle and honed on the tough streets of the city. Born and raised in a working-class neighborhood, Jack learned early on the value of discipline and toughness. He enlisted in the military at 18, serving as a sergeant in a special forces unit where he saw action in several conflict zones around the world. His experience in the military made him a skilled tactician and leader, qualities that served him well when he transitioned to a career in law enforcement after leaving the service.

As a police officer, Jack spent most of his career in San Francisco's toughest neighborhoods, where he earned a reputation as a no-nonsense cop who could handle the most dangerous situations with a calm, steady hand. His years on the force brought him face-to-face with the darkest aspects of humanity, but they also fueled his desire to protect the vulnerable and seek justice for those who couldn't fight for themselves.

Jack met Kit during one of his early cases as a police officer, when Kit was just a young boy trying to learn the streets and got in trouble in a rough neighborhood. The two formed an instant bond, with Jack becoming a mentor figure to Kit, guiding him through the turbulent waters of life and offering wisdom drawn from his own experiences. Jack even helped Kit find a family that would raise him as their own.

Jack is Kit's oldest and closest friend, a bond that has deepened over the decades. He saw Kit as the son he never had, and Kit, in turn, viewed Jack as both a mentor and a father figure. Their relationship was built on street knowledge, trust, and a shared understanding of the darkness in the world. Jack was been there for Kit through his toughest challenges, offering advice, support, and the occasional tough love when needed. Despite their age difference, the two share a deep camaraderie, often exchanging banter and jokes, but always with an underlying current of genuine affection.

Jack's wisdom and experience are invaluable to Kit, especially in their shared mission to rescue those in need. While Kit may be the leader, Jack is the rock upon which he can always rely, providing the steady guidance and tactical knowledge that have saved them both more times than they can count.

Although officially retired, Jack was far from inactive. He played a crucial role in Kit's underground network, providing strategic oversight, training new recruits, and occasionally stepping into the field when his presence was required. His deep knowledge of both military and police operations made him an indispensable asset to the team, and his mentorship continued to shape Kit's approach to their mission.

Jack's presence in the team offers a sense of father-like stability and reassurance, particularly in the most chaotic and dangerous situations. Even as he neared 70, Jack remained a strong force, driven by a relentless commitment to justice and the desire to protect the innocent.

Kit's next team member was Calista "Techie" LeBlanc, from New Orleans. Born and raised in the vibrant and culturally rich city of New Orleans, Calista was minature sized force to be reckoned with. Growing up in a city known for its music, food, and colorful characters, Calista learned early on how to work the streets and loved the noisy life surrounding her. Her parents, both musicians, nurtured her creativity, but it was her older brother, a computer programmer, who introduced her to the world of technology. By the age of 10, Calista was already hacking into local networks and creating her own rudimentary programs.

Despite her small stature, Calista refused to be underestimated. She began training in martial arts at a young age, quickly mastering various disciplines, including Brazilian jiu-jitsu and Muay Thai. Her skills in combat became as formidable as her abilities with a keyboard, earning her the respect of her peers and the nickname "Techie" for her dual expertise.

Calista's path crossed with Kit during a mission in New Orleans. Kit, seeing her petite frame, initially mistook her for a victim needing rescue. But that assumption was quickly shattered when Calista single-handedly took down two attackers with swift, precise movements that left Kit both impressed and intrigued. It was only after the encounter ended, that Kit realized they were both working towards the same goal, rescuing a group of trafficked children from a dangerous gang. The mission was a success, and Kit knew he had found a powerhouse techie in Calista.

Calista and Kit's relationship started with a shared mission and quickly evolved into a brother sister fellowship. Kit was initially drawn to her because of her fierce independence and unmatched computer and fighting skills, seeing in her a younger female version of himself. Over time, their relationship grew strong. Kit valueed her sharp mind and her ability to see things from a different perspective, relying on her for technological advice and assistance.

For Calista, Kit became a brother figure, someone who helped her transition from working solo to being a crucial part of a team. Despite her initial reluctance to fully integrate, she's come to see Kit not just as a leader, but as a trusted friend.

Despite people initially thinking Calista is an uneducated country hick because of her accent, she was the team's go-to expert for anything related to technology. Whether it's hacking into a trafficker's communications, disabling security systems, or gathering intel on a high-profile target, she's the one they rely on to get the job done. In the field, she's also a formidable combatant, often surprising enemies who underestimate her due to her size. Calista's quick thinking and technical prowess have saved the team on numerous occasions, making her the brains behind the scenes.

Her New Orleans roots also give her a unique perspective and an array of contacts that the team often taps into when missions take them into the American South. Despite her somewhat brash demeanor, her teammates know that Calista is always looking out for them and will do what it takes to keep them safe.

Miguel "M&M" Escarra grew up on the rough streets of Miami, where survival meant being tough, smart, and always ready for a fight. From a young age, he was drawn into the world of street gangs and underground fighting, learning the hard way how to defend himself and those he cared about. Despite his rough upbringing, Miguel was determined not to become a statistic. He put himself through school, earning a degree in business management as well as homeland security, while continuing to hone his physical prowess.

His unique combination of street smarts, business acumen, and physical intimidation made him a sought-after bodyguard in Miami's high-stakes corporate world. Miguel quickly rose through the ranks, becoming the go-to security consultant for the upper echelon of business elites. He listed carefully to conversations and learned the inside workings of many types of businesses, but also trading, which had made him a relatively wealthy man.

His reputation for being fiercely protective, combined with a tendency to use violence as a tool, earned him the nickname

"M&M" short for Muscle Man, a moniker that stuck and became synonymous with fearlessness and loyalty. Per his words, "I have no trouble stomping the crap out of people."

Miguel's knowledge of the darker side of the world, particularly human trafficking, came from his time living in the Miami underworld. He knew how these networks operated, who the key players were, and could dismantle them from the inside out if asked. He met Kit at a corporate meeting where his client was a not so nice guy, who ended up sitting in a chair trying to figure out what gorilla slugged him when he called one of the secretaries a nice piece of... Kit had risen to deck the man as well, but Miguel moved a little quicker.

With their similar backgrounds, the two men immediately recognized each other's strengths and formed a bond based on their sense of justice and treating people with respect. Until it was time not to.

Kit admired Miguel's undying loyalty and his fierce protectiveness of the innocent, even if he sometimes had to rein in Miguel's more violent tendencies. Miguel, in turn, respects Kit's leadership and strategic mind, trusting him implicitly in the heat of battle. Their friendship is a partnership built in the heat of a moment, a shared understanding to protect those who cannot protect themselves.

Miguel often served as Kit's enforcer, the one who took on the dirty work when diplomacy failed. However, Kit also valued Miguel's input on more than just physical matters, frequently seeking his advice on security protocols and the logistics of their operations. Miguel saw Kit as a leader worth following, and Kit knew that with Miguel by his side, he had an ally who would stop at nothing to see their mission succeed.

Miguel was the team's muscle, the one who handles the heavy lifting, both literally and figuratively. His role went beyond just physical protection, he was also involved in planning and executing operations, especially those that involve taking down trafficking rings. His knowledge of the criminal underworld was invaluable in those missions, providing the team with the intel they need to strike at the heart of the enemy. While his tendency toward violence was a double-edged sword, Kit and the rest of the team knew that when things get tough, there's no one better to have in your corner than Miguel "M&M" Escarra.

Dr. Jane "Bones" Johnson grew up in a family of medical professionals, with her father being a respected surgeon and her mother a compassionate nurse. From an early age, Jane was fascinated by medicine, often spending time in her parent's workplaces and absorbing everything she could about the human body and its vulnerabilities. However, while her path could have easily led her to a prestigious, high-paying surgical career, Jane's heart lay elsewhere... on the front lines of the war in the streets.

After completing her medical degree and surgical residency, Jane made a deliberate choice to work in one of the busiest trauma emergency rooms in Georgia, where the harsh realities of life and death were ever-present. She thrived in the fast-paced, high-stakes environment of the ER, where her skills as a surgeon were put to the test daily. She earned the nickname "Bones" from her colleagues, both for her skill in setting bones with quick precision and for her unflappable demeanor in the face of even the most gruesome injuries.

Jane was skilled as well, with both guns and knives, able to use them with deadly precision when necessary. Her training in these areas was a result of her desire to be able to protect herself and others in dangerous situations. She does not miss.

Jane first met Kit Thorne at a hospital function for corporate sponsors, where she initially dismissed him as just another ostentatious rich boy flaunting his wealth. But her perception of him changed dramatically when a gunfight erupted outside the function, and a young street kid was shot. Kit immediately jumped into action, helping to stabilize the child while Jane worked frantically to save his life. Despite their best efforts, the wound was fatal, and the loss weighed heavily on both of them. The incident sparked a conversation that night, leading to Kit revealing his true mission and eventually inviting Jane to join his team.

Though she was initially hesitant, Jane saw in Kit's work a chance to make an even greater impact, helping those most in need before they even reached the ER. Her decision to join Kit's team was driven by a desire to prevent the kind of tragedies she had seen far too often, and to fight for the vulnerable on a different kind of battlefield.

Jane and Kit shared a commitment to saving lives first, ask questions later. Initially skeptical of Kit's motives, Jane came to see the depth of his dedication during their first encounter, which set the foundation for their partnership. Kit respected Jane not only for her medical expertise but also for her quiet strength and her ability to remain calm in the face of chaos. Jane, in turn, admires Kit's strong leadership, finding in him a partner who understands the responsibility they both carry.

Their shared experiences, particularly in life-and-death situations, have created a strong bond between them. While Jane may not always agree with Kit's methods, she trusts his judgment and knows that they are united by a common goal, to protect the innocent and bring justice to those who prey on the vulnerable.

Sofia Malone grew up in the poorest of Mexico City's violent streets, something she faced after running away from a poor and abusive home at a young age. For years, she survived by her wits, living through the dangers of street life, hiding from gangs to traffickers. Sofia never lost her innate sense of empathy and her desire to help others, especially the younger children she encountered who were in even more precarious situations than her own.

Determined to change her life, Sofia sought out education opportunities, eventually earning her way into social work. Her firsthand experience of life on the streets made her particularly effective in her role, as she could relate to the children and teens she worked with on a deeply personal level. Fluent in English, as well as learning to speak her native language properly, Sofia also took the time to learn several Chinese dialects, recognizing the growing number of vulnerable immigrant children in need of support.

Sofia first crossed paths with Kit after she discovered one of his hidden posts on a social media site, where he discreetly offered help to those in need. Sofia, desperate to find a group of street kids who had recently disappeared in Mexico, reached out to Kit. Impressed by her ability to find his post and her genuine concern for the missing children, Kit agreed to help.

When they finally rescued the children, Kit was struck by Sofia's natural ability to comfort and calm the scared and anxious kids. She, in turn, was moved by Kit's skillful and tender approach to rescuing the children. The mutual respect they developed during that mission led to Sofia joining Kit's team, where her skills have been invaluable ever since.

Sofia's relationship with Kit is built on the need to rescue vulnerable children from dangerous situations. Kit saw in Sofia, someone who understood the darkness they were fighting against and who brought her skills easily to their table. Sofia saw Kit's dedication and his ability to stay calm and composed under pressure as qualities that mirrored her own.

Their partnership was marked by a strong sense of trust, with Sofia often took on the role of calming the rescued children while Kit handled the traffickers, making sure they could not continue their work. He was often seen holding a small child as he directed his team to complete their work.

As part of Kit's rescue team, Sofia served as both a cultural liaison and a mentor to the children they saved. Her role was crucial in helping these kids transition from the trauma of their past to a safer, more stable future. She provided emotional support, helping them understand their feelings and fears and uses her language skills to ensure that every child felt heard and understood.

Sofia was also involved in the planning of rescue missions, using her knowledge of the streets and the best hiding placed, and her ability to communicate in multiple languages to gather information and build connections. She ensures that the rescued children receive the care and support they need to start rebuilding their lives.

And last but very much not least, Zara "Poly" Dunkirk. From an early age, she was fascinated by the myriad of languages spoken around her and found that she could quickly learn and understand them. Her passion for languages led her to study linguistics at university, where she excelled and eventually became a respected expert in the field.

Zara was born and raised in Port Moresby, Papua New Guinea, a place where languages and cultures are as diverse as the people themselves. Her mother was a citizen of Paupa New Guinea, her father was a visiting doctor from Ireland who ended up staying. Growing up in a multilingual environment, Zara developed an early fascination with languages, a passion that would shape the course of her life. By the time she was in her teens, she was already fluent in several languages, including English, Tok Pisin (a creole language spoken in Papua New Guinea), and Hiri Motu.

Zara pursued her love of languages academically, studying linguistics at a prestigious university and eventually earning a doctorate in the field. Her expertise in language acquisition and cultural studies led her to a career as a translator and interpreter, where her skills were in high demand across the globe. Zara became fluent in English, Spanish, German, French, Mandarin, and several other languages, making her a true polyglot.

Her work took her to various parts of the world, where she bridged communication gaps between people from vastly different cultures. Zara's ability to connect with others on a personal level, coupled with her linguistic skills, made her an invaluable asset in diplomatic and business circles.

Throughout her career, Zara traveled extensively, working as a translator and interpreter in some of the world's most challenging environments. Her work often brought her into contact with people from diverse backgrounds, and she developed a deep understanding of the importance of communication in bridging cultural divides.

Zara met Kit when she was hired as a translator for him during a business trip in Papua New Guinea. Initially, their relationship was strictly professional, but a chance conversation over dinner revealed a shared passion for helping vulnerable children, particularly those who had been displaced or were living on the streets. This mutual interest sparked a deeper connection, and Kit, recognizing Zara's invaluable skills, invited her to join his team.

Zara was struck by his genuine interest in understanding the local culture and his respect for the people. During a dinner, their conversation shifted from business to more personal topics, and they discovered a mutual passion for helping homeless children. This shared interest sparked the beginning of a strong partnership, with Zara eventually joining Kit's team to help rescue vulnerable children around the world.

Kit valued Zara not only for her linguistic skills but also for her deep empathy and understanding of different cultures. Zara often served as Kit's confidante and advisor. She provided valuable insights into the cultural and linguistic aspects of their missions, ensuring that they approach each situation with the appropriate sensitivity and respect.

Zara was the team's translator and interpreter, responsible for facilitating communication between the team and the various groups of people they encountered. Her linguistic skills were vital in helping to understand the different languages and cultures, ensuring that the voices of the rescued children were heard and understood.

Zara played a key role in building trust with the children they rescue, helping them to feel safe and secure in their new environment. She added a layer of cultural awareness and sensitivity, making their operations more effective and respectful of the communities they serve.

Zara's contributions went beyond just language, she was a mentor, a guide, and a bridge between worlds, helping to connect Kit's team with the people they sought to protect. Her wisdom, empathy, and deep understanding of the human experience made her an irreplaceable member of Kit's team. Zara and Sofia often worked side by side to ease the stress of the children they rescued and keep them safe and calm until their families were found or they were rehomed.

Together, these uniquely different people formed a unique team, their diverse skills and desire to help those unable to help themselves, served as a light of hope in the darkness that filled the alley ways and back streets. As they stood united against the forces of evil, each one ready to sacrifice everything for the greater good, they knew that no obstacle was too great, no challenge too difficult for the guardians of the lost.

CHAPTER 3

Born into a wealthy family in Paris, Alexandre DuBois grew up surrounded by privilege and opportunity. Educated at some of the finest institutions in Europe, Alexandre quickly developed a sharp mind for business and an unquenchable thirst for power. He inherited his family's import/export business, DuBois Global Trade, and under his leadership, the company expanded rapidly, gaining footholds in ports all over the world.

While Alexandre was known as a shrewd businessman in the public eye, his true nature was far darker. His foray into human trafficking began as a means to exploit his global network for greater profit. The allure of easy money and the twisted satisfaction of exercising control over others drove him deeper into this illegal enterprise. Alexandre justified his actions with a twisted logic, that he was cleansing the streets of beggars and delinquents who served no purpose in society.

Gero Meyer grew up in the bustling port city of Hamburg, where he was exposed to the world of shipping and logistics from a young age. His father owned a small logistics company, and Gero took over the business in his twenties, rebranding it as Meyer International Logistics. Under his leadership, the company expanded significantly, gaining contracts with some of the world's largest corporations.

Much like Alexandre, Gero's success in the legal business world was not enough to satisfy his darker inclinations. His involvement in human trafficking began as a way to maximize the use of his global shipping routes, but he soon became deeply entrenched in the criminal enterprise. Gero was motivated by the thrill of the hunt, viewing the trafficking of street children as a game where the stakes were high, and the rewards are immense. He shared

Alexandre's twisted belief that these children were disposable, their lives worthless except for the profits they could bring.

Alexandre and Gero were more than just business partners, they were kindred spirits bound by a shared darkness. Their partnership was built on mutual distrust of everyone, and a shared vision for their trafficking operations. Alexandre valued Gero's cunning and business acumen, seeing him as a necessary and trustworthy ally in their illicit ventures.

Gero and Alexandre share a symbiotic relationship, each bringing their unique skills to the partnership. While Alexandre handled the strategic planning and high-level networking, Gero took care of the operational details and enforcement. They trust each other implicitly, bound by their shared greed and disdain for the lives they exploited. Their partnership was as much about business as it was about their shared enjoyment of the power they wield over the most vulnerable.

The low hum of the private jet's engines was a constant backdrop as Alexandre DuBois leaned back in his leather seat, swirling a glass of whiskey in his hand. The cabin's dim lighting reflected off the polished wood and chrome finishes, casting a warm glow over the luxurious interior. Outside, the vast expanse of the Atlantic Ocean stretched out beneath them, but Alexandre's mind was far from the serene view. His thoughts were dark, brooding, caught in the web of frustration that had been building for months.

Gero Meyer sat across from him, his laptop open on the small table between them. His fingers moved quickly over the keys, his sharp blue eyes focused on the screen. The German's expression was one of concentration, but beneath it, a barely concealed anger simmered. Both men were accustomed to success, to control, but the events of the past few months had shaken their operations to the core.

"It should have been an easy transaction," Alexandre muttered, breaking the silence that had settled between them. His voice was smooth, laced with the controlled irritation of a man who was used to getting what he wanted. "One auction, a few hours, and a clean profit. Instead, we're left with this mess."

Gero glanced up from his laptop, his jaw tightening. "It wasn't just the auction," he replied, his voice carrying the clipped precision of his native German. "It was the exposure. They were too visible, too bold. And now, we're paying for it."

Alexandre's gray eyes narrowed as he took a sip of his whiskey, the liquid burning down his throat. "Paying for it, yes. But it's taking too long to re-establish our operations. The industry should have bounced back by now."

Gero leaned back in his seat, closing the laptop with a soft click. "We underestimated the authorities," he admitted. "They hit us harder than we expected, and too many of our contacts were compromised. Rebuilding the network isn't something that can be rushed. We need to be patient."

"Patience," Alexandre echoed, the word dripping with disdain. "We've already been patient, Gero. Months have passed, and we're still not where we need to be. The longer we take, the more ground we lose to these new players who are popping up. They're eager, reckless even, and that makes them dangerous. If we don't assert our dominance soon, we risk being edged out of the market entirely."

Gero's lips curled into a slight smirk, the only sign of amusement in his otherwise stern demeanor. "You're worried about competition?" he asked, arching an eyebrow. "From a few upstarts who think they can step into our shoes?"

"I'm not worried," Alexandre shot back, his tone cold. "I'm realistic. These 'upstarts,' as you call them, have nothing to lose. They're hungry, willing to take risks we can't afford right now. If we don't get ahead of this, we'll be fighting a war on multiple fronts, against the authorities and against these new players."

Gero nodded slowly, his smirk fading as he considered Alexandre's words. "You're right," he conceded. "But we have one advantage they don't, experience. We've been in this business for years. We know how to play the long game. These new players will burn out quickly or get caught if we let them alone. But you're right that we need to start reasserting ourselves. And that means having merchandise ready when the demand picks up again."

Alexandre set his glass down on the table, leaning forward slightly. "That's exactly what I've been thinking. We need to rebuild our inventory, get the merchandise in place before the market heats up. We may not be able to run large auctions yet, but thanks to the dark web, we're already rebuilding a new clientele base. Smaller transactions, more discreet, and they're more profitable. We need to keep that momentum going."

Gero tapped his fingers thoughtfully on the armrest of his seat. "The dark web has been a lifeline," he agreed. "We've managed to move some of our current merchandise in small numbers, enough to keep the cash flow steady. But we need to be careful. We can't afford another mistake like that auction. The authorities are watching more closely now, and the last thing we need is to attract their attention."

"Agreed," Alexandre said with a nod. "But we won't let caution paralyze us. We have contacts in key ports, people we trust. They can help us start moving larger shipments discreetly, rebuilding our stock without drawing too much attention. We'll start small, but we'll scale up quickly once we're confident the market has stabilized."

Gero's eyes narrowed as he considered the plan. "We'll need to focus on quality," he said after a moment. "The street kids we target need to be carefully selected for health and looks. No one who will be missed, no one who will raise alarms if they disappear. We can't afford any heat."

Alexandre's smile was thin, almost predatory. "That's the beauty of it, Gero. The kids we take are invisible. They're already lost in the system, written off as beggars and delinquents. No one cares about them, and that's why they're perfect for what we need. We're doing the world a favor by getting them off the streets."

Gero chuckled darkly, a sound devoid of any real humor. "You've always had a way of justifying our work, Alexandre. But you're right. These kids won't be missed, and our clients have been getting restless. They'll pay well for fresh merchandise."

Alexandre nodded, his gray eyes gleaming with dollar signs. "Exactly. We're building a strong base on the dark web, creating a network of buyers who are willing to pay top dollar for the right product. We just need to make sure we're ready when the demand spikes."

Gero leaned forward, his gaze intense. "What about the new players? How do we handle them?"

"Carefully," Alexandre replied. "We don't want to provoke them into acting rashly. We'll let them think they're making progress, let them handle the low-end transactions that keep the authorities occupied. Meanwhile, we'll focus on the high-end clientele, the ones who are discreet, who understand the need for caution. As we re-establish our dominance, the new players will either fall in line, burn out, or be taken out. Either way it happens, we'll come out on top."

Gero's smirk returned, his eyes glinting with a mixture of amusement and approval. "I like it. We keep our profile low while we rebuild, let the others take the risks. And when the time is right, we strike. Genius."

"Precisely," Alexandre agreed, his voice cold and calculated. "We'll control the market again, and we won't make the same mistakes Gabriel made. We will stay away from the limelight."

The two men sat in silence for a moment, the only sound the soft hum of the jet's engines. Alexandre reached for his whiskey again, taking a slow sip as he considered their next moves. Gero, meanwhile, reopened his laptop, pulling up files and spreadsheets that detailed their current operations.

"We need to start moving on this immediately," Alexandre said after a moment, his voice decisive. "Contact our people at the ports, tell them to start preparing for larger shipments. Have our scouts begin identifying new merchandise. We'll need to vet them carefully before they're brought in."

"I'll handle it," Gero replied, already typing out messages to their contacts. "I'll have a list of contacts ready for you by the time we land."

Alexandre nodded, satisfied. "Good. We're done waiting, Gero. It's time to take back what's ours."

Gero glanced up, meeting Alexandre's gaze with a determined look of his own. "Consider it done."

The conversation shifted then, moving away from the logistics of their trafficking operation to more mundane business matters. They discussed shipments of oil and automobiles, the expansion of their legitimate businesses, and the various deals they had in the pipeline. But even as they talked, both men's minds remained focused on the darker side of their empire.

The botched auction in the States been a setback for the industry as a whole, but it was not a defeat. Alexandre and Gero were survivors, predators in a world that rewarded ruthlessness and cunning. They had built their empire from the ground up, and they would not let it fall so easily. The months of waiting, of careful rebuilding, were almost over. Soon, their network would be stronger than ever, and the new players in the market would learn the hard way that there was no room for anyone else at the top.

As the jet began its descent, the lights of the city below twinkling like stars, Alexandre leaned back in his seat, a satisfied smile playing on his lips. The future was clear to him now, the path forward illuminated by the plans they had set in motion. There was work to be done, and they were ready.

Gero closed his laptop, a similar expression of satisfaction on his face. "We'll be back in business soon," he said, almost to himself.

Alexandre nodded, his eyes glinting with a mixture of ambition and coldness. "And when we are, the market will be ours again. All of it."

The jet touched down smoothly, and the two men stood, straightening their jackets as they prepared to disembark. Outside, the world awaited them, a world that, soon, would bow to their power.

As they stepped off the plane, the crisp night air greeted them, a reminder that they were back on solid ground, both literally and figuratively. With a final glance at each other, Alexandre and Gero walked toward the waiting car, their steps in perfect sync, their minds already calculating the next move in the game they were determined to win.

The dark world was theirs to control, and they would stop at nothing to reclaim their throne.

CHAPTER 4

Kendrick "Kit" Thorne was born into the unforgiving streets of San Francisco, where survival was a daily battle. His early years were a blur of hunger, cold nights, and the constant threat of violence. Abandoned by his drugged-up parents when he was just a child, Kit learned quickly that the world was indifferent to his existence. But even in the darkest corners of the city, he found a glimmer of hope. With the help of beat cop, an elderly couple took him into their home and under their wings. They were kind but firm, teaching Kit the value of self-worth and the importance of knowledge. They drilled into him the belief that his circumstances did not define him, that he was capable of more than just surviving, he could thrive.

At 6'5" and 240 pounds by the time he reached his fifteenth birthday, Kit was a force on the street. His blonde hair, often kept short and slightly tousled, giving him a rugged yet polished appearance. Striking blue eyes, with a piercing intensity captivated and intimidated people he met in his daily street life.

Kit was a commanding presence, his tall, muscular frame exuding strength and power. His chiseled features, sharp jawline, high cheekbones, and a strong brow, made him stand out in any crowd. His uncommon, good looks were magnetic, but there was an edge to him, a sense of controlled danger that kept people at arm's length. The combination of his physicality and the sharpness in his gaze hinted at a man who has seen and done things that would break most others, and yet, he survived.

The couple's guidance was the lifeline Kit needed. He saw the fate of so many other street kids around him, lost to drugs, gangs, or worse, and vowed that he would not become another statistic. At 17, he earned his GED.

Through sheer will and hard work, Kit secured scholarships that allowed him to pursue an education in corporate business. He immersed himself in the world of takeovers, mergers, and strategic expansions, learning everything he could about how to build and sustain a successful enterprise. His education was not just about financial success, it was about acquiring the tools he needed to effect real change in the world.

Kit possessed an unyielding strength of will, a trait that had driven him from the streets to the heights of corporate success. He became relentless in pursuing his goals, especially later when it came to rescuing those who could not defend themselves.

By his late 20s, Kit had gained enough experience to buy a small business, which he quickly grew into a global corporation. His rise in the business world was meteoric, fueled by his relentless drive and a strategic mind honed on the streets.

Kit was a genius when it came to business strategy. He knew how to read the market, identify opportunities, and execute plans that outmaneuvered his competition. His corporate empire was built on skill in the boardroom. But Kit's ambitions were not just about accumulating wealth. Deep down, he was still that kid on the streets, and he had never forgotten those he had left behind.

His ultimate dream was to create safe havens for the homeless, places where they could find shelter, comfort, and dignity, free from the dangers of the streets. However, this proved to be a Herculean task. Most cities saw the homeless as a problem to be swept under the rug, not as people in need of help. Kit was undeterred, he had faced worse odds before.

Despite the darkness that sometimes clouded his past, Kit was a natural leader. His charisma drew people to him, and his team followed him not just out of loyalty but because they believed in his vision.

Kit's mind was always several steps ahead of whatever he had planned. He was a master at planning and executing complex operations, whether in the boardroom or on the streets. Kit was not afraid to make hard decisions, especially when lives were on the line. His experiences had taught him that sometimes, the end justify the means, and he can be cold and calculating when the situation demands it.

Beneath his hardened exterior, Kit had a deep empathy for the vulnerable, particularly street kids. He saw himself in them and felt a profound responsibility to protect them from the dangers he once faced.

Kit carried his past like a shroud. The memories of the friends he lost on the streets, the elderly couple who died before they could see his success, and the countless kids he couldn't save haunted him. These ghosts drove him but also left him with a sense of guilt and a fear that no matter how much he did, it would never be enough.

While Kit was driven by a desire to help others, his methods were sometimes ruthless. He has no qualms about using violence or manipulation if it meant protecting those he cared about. There was a part of him that enjoyed the power he wielded, and he sometimes struggled to keep that side of himself in check.

Kit's time on the streets taught him how to fight dirty and win. Over the years, he honed those skills, training in various martial arts and weapons. He was a formidable opponent, capable of taking down enemies with both brute force and tactical precision or simple cunning communication with them.

Kit's driving force was his desire to protect the vulnerable, particularly street kids who remind him of his younger self. He was determined to provide them with the opportunities he fought so hard to create for himself. Beyond that, Kit was driven by a need to prove that his life has meaning, that he could rise above his past and make a lasting impact on the world.

His ultimate goal was to establish a safe havens for the homeless in various cities across the US, places where they could rebuild their lives without fear. However, this goal was constantly challenged by the harsh realities of the world, forcing Kit to make difficult compromises and work within the current social system. He was also focused on dismantling human trafficking rings, particularly those that targeted street kids. These missions had become deeply personal for him, and he would stop at nothing to bring the criminals to justice.

Kit's team was composed of individuals who, like him, had faced hardship and come out stronger on the other side. He handpicked each member not just for their skills but for their shared commitment to the cause. While Kit was a demanding leader, expecting nothing short of excellence, he was also fiercely protective of his team. He viewed them as his family, the only real connection he had in a world that often felt cold and empty.

Now in his late 40s, Kit was at the height of his power, both in the business world and in his fight against human trafficking. His corporate empire continued to expand, providing him with the resources and influence needed to support his more covert operations. He learned of the trafficking auction in New York and was determined to infiltrate and take it down when the news hit that it had been a covert operation and had put a huge dent in the trafficking industry. He didn't see it making much difference in the number of street kids that were once again going missing and put investigating the organization on his list of things to do.

Despite his success, Kit was not at peace. The ghosts of his past, the lives he couldn't save, and the fear that he was becoming too much like the predators he hunted all weighed heavily on him. As he continued his mission, Kit knew he was walking a fine line between hero and monster, and he constantly grappled with the question of whether he could truly save others without losing himself in the process.

After a particularly grueling day of corporate meetings, he sat down with his rescue team for a relaxing dinner of grilled steaks and baked potatoes, courtesy of Miguel and Calista. The conversation was filled with laughter about the antics of everyone's day and just general jovial talk.

He loved living in West Virginia, vastly different from California and contrary to western belief, the people were not hicks and very welcoming. He had found and purchased a vineyard and winery, set up a base of operation in one of the barn he had built for his rescue operations, creating not only the perfect working environment for his rescue operation headquarters, but a family environment for his team, most of who had no family but the team. ThesSecond story of the barn was filled with insuite bedrooms, chef's kitchen, and living area, while the lower floor housed their tech room, equipment and vehicles.

The sun had dipped below the trees, casting the vineyard in a warm, golden glow. The air was filled with the scent of fresh-cut grass and the sweet tang of ripening grapes. The expansive veranda of Kit's estate overlooked rows of meticulously maintained grapevines that stretched out as far as the eye could see. It was a scene of tranquility, a place that had always provided a sense of peace and refuge from the stormy world beyond.

Tonight, the place was full of laughter, peace, and the smell of good food.

Kit stood at the head of the long wooden table that dominated the veranda, a broad grin on his face as he expertly wielded a carving knife, slicing into the thick, juicy steaks that had just come off the grill. The savory aroma filled the air, mingling with the laughter and chatter of his team. The group gathered around the table was a study in contrasts, each member bringing their own unique flavor to the mix, much like the rich variety of wines produced from the vineyard's grapes.

"Perfectly cooked, if I do say so myself," Miguel said with a grin, eyeing the steak as Kit handed him a plate. The towering enforcer's eyes gleamed with a mischievous twinkle, the promise of violence momentarily eclipsed by the simple pleasure of a good meal.

"Only the best for you, big guy. Thanks for manning the grill." Kit replied, his voice warm and jovial. He moved on to the next plate, dishing out generous portions of the meal.

Sofia sat nearby, her laughter ringing out like a melody as she playfully elbowed Miguel. "You'll have to do extra workouts to burn this off, M&M. Don't want you slowing down on us."

Miguel chuckled, taking a large bite of steak. "Please, Mama, I'm built for this. Besides, I'm already planning on running the perimeter in the morning. Gotta keep these muscles in top shape."

Across the table, Zara raised her glass in a toast. "To Miguel's culinary skills! If he ever decides to quit protecting the world, he's got a future as a chef."

The group laughed, and Miguel gave a mock bow. "You're too kind, Poly. But I think I'll stick to what I know best, grilling steaks and keeping you all out of trouble."

As the team settled into their meal, the conversation flowed easily, punctuated by the clinking of silverware and the occasional burst of laughter. It was a rare moment of togetherness, a chance to relax and enjoy each other's company in the safety of Kit's vineyard. But even as they indulged in the simple pleasures of good food and wine, a hidden thought remained at the edges of their consciousness.

It was Jane who finally broke the jovial mood, her voice cutting through the laughter like a scalpel through flesh. "I'm worried, Kit," she said, her tone somber. "The reports we've been getting... they're not just isolated incidents anymore. It's groups of kids. Mostly street kids."

The table fell silent, all eyes turning to Jane. Kit's smile faded, replaced by the seriousness that his team had come to know well. He set down his glass and leaned forward slightly, his striking blue eyes focused intently on Jane.

"Groups? Shit." Kit said quietly. "How fast is count growing?"

Jane pulled out her phone. "We're hearing about five to ten daily. These kids go missing without a trace. And it's not just the usual disappearances, these kids are vanishing completely, no sign of them anywhere."

Zara nodded in agreement, her brow furrowed in concern. "It's happening all over. We're seeing reports from Europe, South America, Asia... it's turned global. This isn't just some local gang running a trafficking ring. It feels more coordinated, more organized."

"Could be the kingpins that weren't caught in that New York sting," Miguel suggested, his tone darkening as the conversation shifted. "We know some of them slipped through the cracks during that sting. They're smart, connected, and they've had time to regroup."

Kit nodded, his mind already working through the possibilities. "That's what I'm afraid of. If they've reorganized and are expanding their operations, this could be the start of something new and big. Something we can't afford to ignore."

Sofia, usually the comforting presence in the group, looked unusually grim. "The thing is, we're not even sure what they're doing with these kids. No bodies, no nothing. It's like they've been swallowed by the earth. It's terrifying."

Jane leaned forward, her eyes filled with worry. "We need more information. We need to find out who's behind this, how they're doing it, and where these kids are being taken. We can't let them keep slipping through our fingers."

Kit glanced around the table, taking in the concerned expressions of his team. The jovial atmosphere had disappeared, replaced by deep concern. He could sense that the lives of countless children hung in the balance.

"I'm thinking we might need help," Zara suggested, breaking the silence. "especially if this is world-wide. The organization in New York, they did good work on that sting. Maybe we should reach out to them, see if they've heard anything. They might have leads we don't."

Kit considered this for a moment, his fingers drumming lightly on the table. He didn't like relying on outside help, his team was the best at what they did, and he trusted them implicitly. But something about this was different. If the scale of the problem was this large, this widespread, if the missing kingpins were involved, they'd need every resource available to stop them. The other organization might have information on the ones they didn't capture.

"Okay," Kit finally said, his voice resolute. "we'll contact them. See if they've noticed or heard anything we haven't. We might need to work together if we want to put a stop to this."

Miguel's hands clenched into fists, his expression dark. "And when we find them, we make sure they can't do this again... ever."

Sofia reached out and placed a hand on Miguel's arm, her touch gentle but firm. "We will. But we need to be smart about this. As much as we want, we can't just charge in guns blazing, we have to find these kids first, make sure they're safe and out of harm's way."

Kit nodded, thanking Sofia for the balance she brought to the group. "You're right. We need to be strategic. We find out who's behind this, we locate their operations, and then we go after them.

No mistakes. We save those kids, and we dismantle their network piece by piece."

Sofia, her voice soft but determined, added, "And we don't stop until we've found every last one of them."

The team nodded in agreement, the seriousness of their mission filling their hearts with sadness. The camaraderie that had defined the evening was still there, but it was quieted now by the knowledge of what lay ahead. The stakes had never been higher, and failure would not be an option.

Kit stood up from the table, his presence commanded the attention of each of his team members as he looked into their eyes. "We've faced challenges before, and we've come out on top every time. This will be no different. We'll figure out who's behind this, and we'll stop them." His words were met with solemn nods and murmurs of agreement.

Kit turned and gazed out over the vineyard, the peaceful rows of grapevines bathed in the soft light of the moon. This place had become a refuge for him, a sanctuary where he could escape the darkness of the world. But now, even here, the shadows were encroaching. The vineyard was a symbol of what he fought for, peace, safety, a life free from fear. But it was also a reminder of how fragile those things were, how easily they could be taken away.

"We start first thing tomorrow," Kit said, turning back to his team. "Zara, I want you to reach out to your contacts and see if you can get us a line to the New York task force. Miguel, Jane, start compiling everything we know about the missing kids. Cross-reference with the information from New York if they have any. Calista, we're going to need to mobilize our networks. Get the word out to our people in the field, let them know what we're looking for. Find me a contact for someone with that organization."

"Got it," Calista replied, already pulling out her phone to start sending messages.

The team split, each member heading off to prepare for the work ahead. The vineyard, once filled with laughter and light, now felt eerily quiet.

.Kit remained on the veranda, his thoughts busy as he watched his team go. He knew the road ahead would be long and difficult, but he knew they were up to the task. They had to be. Too many lives depended on it.

He took a deep breath, trying to shake off the unease that had settled over him. The night was still, the vineyard peaceful, but Kit couldn't shake the feeling that something was coming, something dark and dangerous that would test them all in ways they hadn't yet imagined.

He had faced darkness before, and he had come out stronger every time. This would be no different. He would fight for those who couldn't fight for themselves, just as he always had.

The stars twinkled overhead, a reminder that even in the darkest of times, there was still light to be found. Kit clung to that thought as he turned and headed inside, his mind already working through the steps they would take to find the missing children and bring them home.

The night was quiet, but Kit knew it was the calm before the storm. And when the storm came, he and his team would be ready to face it head-on.

CHAPTER 5

The heavy bass of the music thudded against the walls of Pop's Gentleman's Club, a rhythmic pulse that seeped into every corner of the dimly lit establishment. Neon lights flickered along the bar, casting a soft glow over the patrons who lounged at their tables, their eyes following the dancers who moved with seductive and practiced ease on the stages. Perfume curled lazily through the air, blending with the scent of whiskey, creating an atmosphere that was equal parts erotic and fun.

Charlie Donovan, known to the strip club scene as Diamond Frost, sat in her usual spot, a small, private corner booth near the back of the club, where she could observe the goings-on without being easily noticed. She could use the observation booth in the office to view the club, but it felt like an invasion of privacy, she only used it there if trouble was brewing.

Charlie was dressed in a sleek black dress, her temporarily platinum blonde hair cascading over her shoulders in soft waves. Her hazel green eyes, sharp and calculating, scanned the room as she sipped her drink, her mind working through the logistics of the night's business.

Pop's had now become more than just a strip club, she used it as her cover for the operations she ran behind the scenes. She could disappear as Diamond when she needed. Tonight, despite the usual hustle of the club, there was an unease in the air that she couldn't quite place. Something felt off, like a storm brewing, just waiting to blow.

As if on cue, her phone buzzed on the table, the screen lighting up with an unfamiliar number. Charlie's eyes narrowed as she reached for it, her mind immediately on high alert. She rarely received calls from unknown numbers, and when she did, it was rarely good news.

Charlie hesitated for a moment before answering, her voice calm and steady as she spoke. "This is Diamond. Please identify yourself before I hang up."

There was a brief pause on the other end, a hesitation that told me the caller was weighing their words carefully. Charlie started to disconnect.

"Charlie Donovan?" came the voice, soft but firm. "Or should I call you, Diamond Frost?"

Charlie's grip tightened on the phone, her knuckles turning white. The use of both names in the same breath set off alarm bells in her mind. Whoever this was, they knew more than they should.

"Depends on who's asking," she replied, her tone sharp, "and how you got this number."

"Name's Calista," the voice continued. "Calista LeBlanc. I don't mean to alarm you, but I've been trying to track you down for a couple of days. I need to ask you about the trafficking sting that went down in New York State. I think we might have a situation and be able to help each other if you know about it too."

Charlie leaned back in her seat, her mind racing. This was not the conversation she had expected to have tonight, and definitely not in her club. "The sting in New York?" She repeated, her voice carefully neutral and low. "And why would you think I'd know anything about that?"

There was a pause, and when Calista spoke again, there was a note of respect in her voice. "Because I saw you on the news," she said bluntly. "You were the one who spoke to the reporters afterward. I recognized you, your face, your voice. I did some digging, found the connection between you and Diamond Frost. It wasn't easy, but... well, here we are."

Her heart skipped a beat. Charlie had known it was only a matter of time before someone connected the dots, but she hadn't expected it to happen so soon. She glanced around the club, making sure no one was paying too much attention to her, then turned toward the wall behind her.

"And what exactly do you want, Ms. LeBlanc?" she asked, her voice dropping to a whisper. "What makes you think I'm the one you need to talk to?"

"Because," Calista replied, her voice steady, "you're one of the few people who's actually doing something about this trafficking issue. You and your team, whoever they are, you're making waves. I'm in the business of helping people too, and I think we're on the same side. But I need information, and you're the only one who might have it."

She sighed, running a hand through her hair. She hated being put on the spot like this, especially by someone she didn't know. But there was something in Calista's voice, an honesty that made me pause. Charlie could tell this woman wasn't bluffing. She had obviously done her homework, and it appeared she wasn't going to be easily brushed off.

"How did you find me?" she asked, her tone more curious now than accusatory. "What made you think I'd be willing to talk?"

"I told you, I saw you on the news," Calista said. "You stood out, and not just because you were speaking for the Feds. You had a look in your eyes, I've seen it before. I knew you were connected, and once I started digging, it wasn't long before I found Diamond Frost as an owner of several clubs, but then the paperwork associated with them had Charlie Donovan as signatory on the paperwork. Also, your name came up in certain circles that work with trafficking victims. It wasn't hard to figure out the rest."

She felt a chill run down her spine. Calista was clearly more resourceful than she had anticipated. "So, you know who I am, what I do," she spoke slowly, "what makes you think I'm going to share anything with you?"

"Because we're after the same thing," Calista replied. "We've discovered a new racket taking street kids. It appears to be well organized and it involves kids from around the world. The sting in New York was big, but we think there are still some big players out there, some that didn't get caught, dangerous ones. I have a little information, but I need more. I'm will to bet your organization has been contacted too."

Her eyes narrowed. She didn't like being cornered, but there was a certain logic to what Calista was saying. Still, she wasn't about to give away everything without knowing more about this mysterious woman. "Why should I trust you?" Charlie asked.

There was a moment of silence on the other end, and then Calista spoke again, her voice filled with a hint of vulnerability. "Because I'm not asking for trust," she replied. "I'm asking for a chance. If I'm wrong, you can cut me off, and you'll never hear from me again. But if I'm right... we could make a real difference."

Charlie stared at the table, her mind racing. This was a risk, no doubt about it. But she had always been a gambler, and there was something about Calista that told her this might be a gamble worth taking.

"Okay," she finally answered, her voice firm. "I'm not saying I'm going to help you, but I'll put you in touch with someone who might. Her name's Aria. If she thinks you're legit, we can talk more. But don't think for a second that I'm letting my guard down and doling out information."

"Understood," Calista said, her tone respectful. "Thank you, Ms. Donovan. I appreciate the chance."

Charlie ended the call, her mind already shifting gears. She needed to talk to Aria immediately. If this Calista was as good as she seemed, this could be a valuable connection. But if it was a trap...

She pushed the thought aside, not allowing herself to dwell on the possibility of betrayal. Aria had taught her to be cautious but also to recognize when an opportunity presented itself. This was one of those times.

She quickly dialed Aria's number, her fingers moving deftly over the screen. After a few rings, Aria's voice came through, calm and steady as always. "Charlie, what's up?"

"We've got a problem," Charlie spoke without preamble. "I just got a call from a woman named Calista LeBlanc. Says she's been tracking some new trafficking networks. She connected me to Diamond Frost. Says she wants to help, and she's looking for information."

There was a pause on the other end, and she could almost see Aria's mind working, processing the information. "She found you?" Aria asked, a note of concern in her voice. "That's not good."

"No, it's not," she agreed. "She seems legit. She knew a lot, and she wasn't overly pushy about it. I think she might be worth talking to, but I need you to vet her first. See what you think."

Aria was silent for a moment, then she spoke again. "Sure thing. I'll wait for her call, see what she knows. If she's on the level, we might be able to use her. But if there's even a hint of trouble, we cut her loose, she disappears."

"Perfect," Charlie replied, relief flooding her voice. "Thanks, Aria. I didn't want to make the call without looping you in first."

"You did the right thing," Aria replied. "I'll handle it from here. I'll call you back as soon as I have something."

"Thanks," she said again, her shoulders relaxing slightly. "Be careful, okay? We don't know who else might be listening."

"Always," Aria assured her. "Talk soon."

Charlie hung up the phone, her thoughts racing as she leaned back in her booth. The music in the club had faded into the background, the hum of conversation and clinking glasses a distant noise. She stared at the wall, her mind turning over the possibilities.

Calista LeBlanc could be a wild card, someone who could either be an asset or a liability. She could be connected to an organization, good or bad. Charlie had learned long ago not to trust easily, but she also knew that in this line of work, sometimes you had to take risks. The trafficking networks were vast, and they couldn't dismantle them alone. If Calista had information that could help them...

She shook her head, forcing herself to focus. Aria would handle it for now. She trusted Aria with her life, and if there was something off about Calista, Aria would find it.

For now, all Charlie could do was wait. The uneasy feeling that had been gnawing at her earlier was back, stronger than before. She had always known that her double life would catch up with her eventually, but she hadn't expected it to happen like this.

In the shadows of Pop's Gentlemen's Club, Charlie sat in silence, waiting for the next move in a game that could quickly become dangerous. With new traffickers out there, the stakes were going to shoot up again, and one wrong move could unravel everything they had built.

But if there was one thing she was good at, it was surviving. And she had no intention of letting anyone bring her down. She had come this far, gone through too much, and came out stronger for what she had survived to let some new person on the scene take it all away.

CHAPTER 6

Charlie leaned back against the plush cushions of her sofa, her gaze fixed on the view outside her apartment window. The Atlanta skyline was a sea of twinkling lights, the city alive with pulsing energy, even at this early hour, that seemed to fuel her every move. But that energy felt distant, muted by the concerns swirling in her mind.

Charlie's apartment was a sanctuary, a quiet corner compared to the gritty world she often worked in. The modern, minimalist décor exuded a sense of calm, something she desperately needed after the call I'd had with Calista. The sleek lines of the furniture, the cool tones of the walls, and the soft glow of the ambient lighting were all carefully curated to create a space where she could think clearly, where the challenges of her dual life could momentarily be set aside. But tonight, no amount of careful design could quell the unease that gnawed at her.

The sound of her phone vibrating on the coffee table snapped her out of her thoughts. She reached for it, her pulse quickening when she saw Aria's name flash on the screen. Without hesitation, she swiped to answer, the device automatically switching to video mode.

Aria's face filled the screen, her expression serious, yet there was a hint of something else, curiosity, perhaps? The light from her computer screen cast soft shadows across her features, making her dark eyes appear even more intense.

"Figured you were probably still awake." Aria grinned. "Weight of the world and all that."

"Hey," Charlie greeted her, trying to keep her tone neutral, though she knew Aria would see through it. "What did you find?"

Aria didn't waste time with pleasantries. "I dug into Calista LeBlanc, like you asked. And you're not going to believe what I found."

She leaned forward, her intrigue piqued. "Tell me."

Aria glanced away from the screen for a moment, clearly organizing her thoughts before she spoke.

"So, Calista is legit, more than legit, actually. She's connected to an organization that operates off the grid. The kind of thing you don't hear about unless you're deeply embedded in certain circles like ours. And get this, it's led by none other than Kendrick Thorne."

The name hit her like a cold gust of wind. Charlie sat back, her mind reeling. "Kendrick Thorne? The Kendrick Thorne? The billionaire?"

Aria nodded, her lips pressing into a thin line. "The same. He's known for his corporate empire, his charity work, all the usual billionaire stuff. But the big secret is that he's been running this underground network focused on rescuing homeless kids. The very kids who are being targeted by these new trafficking rings."

Charlie's thoughts raced, her mind flashing through the numerous news segments she'd seen about Kit Thorne over the years. He was always in the media, whether it was for his latest corporate acquisition or some philanthropic endeavor. But there had never been a hint of anything like this.

"I always thought he was just another rich guy playing the hero card," she said, her voice cracking with disbelief. "But this... this is something else."

Aria's expression softened slightly. "Yeah, I know. I was surprised too. But I found a post, hidden on several social media sites. It was buried deep, but once I found it, everything clicked. Kit's been orchestrating these rescue missions all over the world.

And from what I can tell, they're good at what they do. Which brings me to the reason Calista reached out in the first place."

Charlie nodded, the pieces starting to fall into place. "The missing street kids."

"Exactly," Aria confirmed. "Calista told me that Kit's been tracking an unusual spike in disappearances, similar to what we've been hearing about. She said they've been hearing new rumors, but nothing concrete. The kids are vanishing without a trace, just like the ones we've been trying to track down. Kit's team has done a few rescues, but they're worried it's just the tip of the iceberg."

She felt a chill run down her spine. The thought of more kids being taken, of them falling into the hands of traffickers, made her blood boil. But there was something else, too. A growing realization that maybe, just maybe, they were dealing with something much bigger than they'd anticipated, even after the huge dent they made with their sting.

"And they want to meet with us," she said, more of a statement than a question.

Aria nodded. "Kit's team thinks that if we pool our resources, we might be able to get ahead of this. Find out who's behind it, where the kids are being taken, and shut it down. But they're wary; Kit doesn't usually collaborate with outsiders, so this is a big deal for him."

Charlie drummed her fingers on the armrest, her mind racing through the possibilities. "What do you think, Aria? Can we trust them?"

Aria paused, her gaze steady. "I did my homework, Charlie. Everything checks out. Kit's clean, as far as his public persona goes, and his team... they're good. Calista is the real deal, smart, capable. I don't know about the other members of his team. I didn't find anything on the dark web about who is trafficking kids, but that doesn't mean it's not happening. It just means it's well hidden. And if Kit's reaching out, it means he's concerned. I think this is worth pursuing."

Charlie mulled it over, her instincts telling her that Aria was right. This wasn't just about them anymore, it was about something much larger, something that required more than just their team. But still, there was that lingering wariness, that instinctual need to protect her own.

"If we do this meeting," she said slowly, "we need to make sure it's on our terms. Neutral ground, somewhere safe."

Aria nodded. "Agreed. I suggested we meet in two days. How about Atlanta? It's close, it's familiar, and it gives us enough time to prepare."

She thought about it for a moment, then nodded. "Atlanta works. I can arrange a secure location, somewhere off the radar. I'll need to make sure everything's in place."

"Good," Aria said, a hint of relief in her voice. "I'll get in touch with Calista and set it up. I'll let you know the details once it's confirmed."

Charlie sighed, running a hand through her hair. "This is bigger than I thought, isn't it?"

Aria's expression turned somber. "I think so, Charlie. If Kit's involved, if he's reaching out to us... then yeah, it's big. We need to be ready for anything."

Charlie's gaze drifted to the window, the city lights twinkling like distant stars. For a moment she allowed myself to feel the weight of it all, the responsibility, the uncertainty, the fear that they might be in over their heads. But then she shook it off, forcing herself to focus. She had been through worse, and she had come out the other side. This was just another challenge, another battle to be fought.

"All right," she spoke, her voice steady. "Let's do this. But Aria, I want you to keep digging. I want to know everything there is to know about Kit, Calista, and their team. If we're going to work with them, I need to be sure we're not walking into a trap."

Aria nodded, her eyes sharp. "You got it. I'll start pulling everything I can find. We'll be prepared when we meet."

She felt a sense of calm settle over her. The next two days would be crucial, and she needed to be at the top of her game. There was no room for doubt, no space for hesitation. The lives of countless children depended on it.

"Thanks, Aria," she said, her voice softening slightly. "I know this won't be easy, but I trust you. Maybe Doc can get his people to find something too. He's got some amazing connections."

Aria smiled, a rare, genuine smile that softened her features. "You're right there. I'll fill him in. We've got this, Charlie. We'll make this work."

As the call ended, the screen went dark, leaving her alone in her quiet apartment. Charlie stood up, pacing the room as she tried to make sense of it all. Kit Thorne, she had never imagined that someone like him would be involved in something so dangerous, so off the grid. But then again, she knew better than most that appearances could be deceiving.

Charlie walked over to the window, her reflection merging with the cityscape beyond. The world outside seemed so calm, so ordinary, but she knew better. Beneath the surface, there were shadows... dark, insidious forces that preyed on the most vulnerable.

And now, it seemed, those shadows were moving again.

She took a deep breath, steeling herself for what was to come. There was no turning back now. In two days' time, she would meet with Kit Thorne, with his team, and together, they would face whatever was lurking in the darkness.

First, she needed to prepare. There were arrangements to be made, contingencies to be planned. Charlie had always been a careful strategist, and she wasn't about to let her guard down now. Not when so much was at stake.

As she turned away from the window, she felt a familiar sense of purpose rise within her. She had fought battles before, and had won. This would be no different. Kit Thorne might be a wildcard, but Charlie was confident in her ability to handle whatever came their way.

With a final glance at the city, she headed to her bedroom to begin planning. The meeting in Atlanta would be a turning point, she could feel it in her bones. And she was ready.

Whatever happened next, she would be prepared. This was a turning point.

CHAPTER 7

The night sky over Washington, DC was a blanket of darkness, pierced only by the distant glow of the city lights. The shipping lot, an industrial sprawl of metal containers stacked like giant Legos, was eerily quiet. The hum of the nearby highway was a faint backdrop to the tension that hung in the air like the thick fog that was rolling in. Kit crouched behind a stack of crates, his heart beating in a steady rhythm as he scanned the area through his night vision goggles.

"Everyone in position?" Kit whispered, his earpiece picking up his barely audible voice. The distress call had come in two days earlier, the team set up the extraction plan, but nothing ever truly went according to plan. Heavily armed men guarded the lot, mercenaries by the look of them, and there was no margin for error. They had to be quiet, efficient, and invisible.

"Techie ready," Calista's voice came through, calm and steady. Kit could hear the faint click of keys as she hacked into the security system, her fingers moving like lightning. "I'm in the network. Cameras are looping. We're good to go."

"M&M, copy that," Miguel replied, his voice a whispered growl. Kit could picture him, massive and imposing, already moving into position to take down the first guard. Miguel was built for this kind of work, and despite his intimidating size, he could move with surprising stealth.

"Bones in position." Jane's voice followed, laced with the clinical calm of someone who had seen too much and learned how to compartmentalize it. "Ready on your mark."

Kit took a deep breath, steadying himself. This wasn't their first mission, but each one carried its own set of risks. Tonight's objective was particularly sensitive, twenty children, all under the age of fifteen, supposedly crammed into a container on this lot. If even one of the guards got spooked, it could all go to hell in an instant.

"Move in," Kit ordered, his voice firm. He watched as his team responded, shadows in the night, barely visible as they melted into the darkness.

Miguel was the first to reach his target, a guard stationed near the perimeter fence. The man was oblivious, too focused on the cigarette he was lighting to notice the hulking figure creeping up behind him. With a swift, precise movement, Miguel clamped a hand over the guard's mouth, his other arm wrapping around the man's neck. There was a brief struggle, a muffled grunt, and then the guard went limp. Miguel lowered him to the ground silently, then keyed his mic. "One down."

Kit nodded to himself, satisfied. Miguel was a pro, and that was one less obstacle in their way. He moved forward, keeping low to the ground, his eyes scanning for any signs of movement. Ahead, he could see another guard patrolling near the row of containers where the kids were supposed to be held.

"Techie, what's the status on those cameras?" Kit whispered, his voice barely more than a breath.

"Cameras are looping, drone is scanning," Calista confirmed, her voice steady. "You're clear to move forward, Kit. I've got eyes on the entire lot."

Kit adjusted his grip on his silenced pistol, then moved swiftly toward the second guard. The man was alert, his head on a swivel as he scanned the lot, but he never saw Kit coming. Kit closed the distance in a heartbeat, his movements fluid and precise. He grabbed the guard from behind, pressing the muzzle of his pistol to the man's temple as he whispered in his ear. "Don't make a sound."

The guard tensed, his body going rigid, but before he could react, Kit pulled the trigger. The silenced shot was barely a whisper in the night, and the guard crumpled to the ground, lifeless. Kit stepped over the body, his eyes already moving to the next target.

"Two down," Kit reported.

"Bones, you're up," Kit said, giving the go-ahead for the next phase.

Jane moved with the precision of a surgeon, her steps silent as she approached the third guard. He was standing near a container, his attention fixed on something in the distance. Jane didn't give him a chance to notice her. She slipped behind him, pressing a scalpel-thin blade to his throat in one swift motion. The man gurgled softly as his life drained away, and Jane lowered him to the ground, her face expressionless.

"Three down," Jane's voice came through, cold and focused. "Area clear."

"Nice work," Kit acknowledged, moving forward with renewed urgency. They were getting closer to the container, closer to the children who desperately needed their help.

As Kit approached the container, he could see the dim glow of a flashlight flickering inside. There were still guards positioned around it, three of them, armed with automatic rifles. This was going to be the toughest part.

"Techie, can you give us a distraction?" Kit asked, his voice calm despite the tension in the air.

"On it," Calista replied. There was a brief pause, followed by a sudden explosion of static over the guard's radios. They froze, startled, their attention momentarily diverted.

That was all the time Kit needed.

He moved in, quick and silent, taking aim at the first guard. The silenced shot dropped the man instantly, and before the others could react, Miguel and Jane were on them. Miguel tackled the second guard, his massive frame overpowering the man in seconds, while Jane fired a single shot at the third guard, dropping him where he stood.

The lot fell silent once more, the only sound the faint hum of the container's refrigeration unit.

"M&M, you good?" Kit asked, his eyes scanning the area for any signs of reinforcements.

Miguel grunted, pulling himself off the unconscious guard. "All clear here, but let's move. I don't like being out in the open like this."

"Agreed," Kit said, approaching the container. He could hear faint whimpers coming from inside, and his heart clenched. The children were scared and probably cold, but the team needed to be careful, there was no telling what condition the kids were in.

"Bones, you're up," Kit said, stepping back to allow Jane to examine the container.

Jane moved forward, her hands steady as she reached for the container's latch. She paused for a moment, taking a deep breath, before carefully opening the door. The smell hit them first, a foul stench of sweat, urine, and fear. It was almost overwhelming, but Jane didn't flinch. She pushed the door open, revealing the interior.

The sight that met their eyes was worse than anything they had imagined.

Twenty children, all under the age of fifteen, huddled together in the cramped, dimly lit space. Their faces were gaunt, their eyes hollow with fear and exhaustion. Some were barely conscious, their bodies emaciated and dehydrated from days, maybe even weeks, of captivity.

Jane's breath caught in her throat. "Dear God," she whispered, quickly moving inside to assess their condition. "They're in bad shape. Severely dehydrated and malnourished. We need reinforcements. I can't handle this alone. I have several with labored breathing."

Kit's heart sank at the sight. These were just children, innocent lives caught up in a nightmare they could never have imagined. But there was no time to dwell on the horror. They needed to act, and they needed to act fast.

"Calista, get on the line with your Aria person," Kit ordered, his voice tight with urgency. "Tell her we need medical backup. Bones is saying this is more than we can handle on our own."

"On it," Calista responded immediately, her voice steady despite the grim situation.

As Jane, Sofia, and Zara moved from child to child, doing what they could to calm them, Kit and Miguel began to carefully extract the somewhat healthier children from the container, one by one. Some were too weak to move, their limbs like lead, and it took every ounce of restraint for Kit to keep his emotions in check. He had seen a lot in his years, but this... this was almost too much. It looked as if these children had been intentionally starved or forgotten. But then, why the guards?

Zara, with tears streaming down her face, spoke quietly. "These children are Guatemalan. None speak English. One of the oldest ones said they came straight from their country to here. They've been in this container for more than a month."

Kit was stunned. They had been snatched from the streets they knew and hauled like cattle to be used doing God knows what. Anger radiated off him and he struggled to keep calm in front of these pour souls.

Miguel winced as he crouched down to lift one of the smaller children, a sharp pain shooting through his calf. He glanced down, seeing the dark stain spreading across his pant leg. He had taken a bullet during the skirmish, but in the heat of the moment, he hadn't even noticed.

"Dammit," Miguel muttered, gritting his teeth against the pain.

Kit noticed the injury immediately, his eyes narrowing. "You're hit."

"Just a scratch," Miguel grunted, but Kit wasn't buying it.

"Bones, Miguel needs help," Kit called over to Jane, who was busy tending to one of the older kids.

Jane glanced at Miguel's leg, her expression hardening. "Sit down. Now," she ordered, her tone leaving no room for argument.

Miguel complied, though reluctantly, as Jane quickly assessed the wound. "It's a through-and-through," she said, her voice brisk. "You'll be fine, but I need to get this cleaned up before you start losing too much blood and to keep it from getting infected."

As Jane worked on Miguel, Calista's voice came through the earpiece again. "Aria's on it. She's contacting someone named Doc, he's got some medic friends in DC. They'll be here ASAP."

"Good," Kit replied, his tone clipped. "We'll hold the fort until they arrive."

The minutes dragged on, each one feeling like an eternity as they waited for the reinforcements to arrive. Kit's mind raced, trying to calculate their next move. They couldn't stay here, once the mercenaries didn't respond to check-ins, this place would be crawling with reinforcements. But moving twenty critically ill children through the city without attracting attention was a logistical nightmare.

Finally, the sound of vehicles approaching broke the tense silence. Kit tensed, but a moment later, he saw the familiar markings of old emergency vehicles pulling into the lot. Relief flooded him as a team of medics, older men and women, this Doc person's friends, piled out, their expressions grim as they assessed the situation.

"Thank God," Jane breathed, giving directions of who needed what, allowing the medics to do the majority of the work.

Kit watched as the medics moved efficiently, setting up IVs, administering fluids, and checking vitals with the practiced precision of professionals. It wasn't long before the children were being carefully loaded onto stretchers and into the waiting vehicles.

"We're taking them to a private facility," one of the medics explained to Kit as they worked. "It's secure, and we've got everything we need to stabilize them. They won't be going into the system."

Kit nodded, his mind still racing. "We need this area cleared out before whoever's behind this realizes what happened and reinforcements arrive."

"Go," the medic said, his voice firm. "We've got it from here. You'll only draw more attention if you stick around."

Kit didn't need to be told twice. He turned to his team, his expression hardening. "We're out of here. Move, now."

Miguel, his leg hastily bandaged, pushed himself to his feet with a wince. "I'm good to go."

"Bones, Techie, let's move," Kit ordered, already heading for the exit.

The team moved swiftly through the shadows, retracing their steps back to the extraction point. They didn't speak, the severity of what they had just witnessed weighed heavily on them all.

As they reached the perimeter fence, Kit paused, glancing back at the shipping lot. The children were safe, but for how long? The people who had orchestrated this were still out there, and if they had their way, this wouldn't be the last time children were used as pawns in their twisted game.

"We need to stop this," Kit said quietly, his voice filled with steely resolve. "This can't keep happening."

"We will," Calista replied, her voice equally determined. "But first, we've got a meeting in Atlanta."

Kit nodded, his mind already shifting to the next phase. The meeting with Charlie, Aria, and their team was more important than ever. If they were going to take down the network behind these disappearances, they needed to be united, prepared for anything.

"Let's go," Kit said, leading the way into the night. There was no time to waste.

CHAPTER 8

The morning air was crisp and cool, carrying the scent of pine and the earthy freshness of the forest surrounding the lodge. The lake, still as glass, reflected the towering trees and the cloud-dappled sky, creating a serene backdrop for what was sure to be a tense meeting. Kit Thorne stood at the edge of the wooden dock, his striking blue eyes scanning the horizon as he waited for the others to arrive. Despite the peaceful setting, his mind was anything but calm. This meeting would be crucial, and the stakes had never been higher.

Behind him, his team was assembling, each member quietly assessing the location and the situation. Calista was the first to speak, her gaze fixed on the lodge in the distance. "Nice place," she murmured, her voice carrying just enough edge to betray her wariness. "But something tells me we're not here for the scenery."

Miguel stood beside her, his massive frame almost blocking out the sunlight. He crossed his arms over his chest, the recent injury to his calf barely slowing him down. "No, we're not," he rumbled, his voice low. "But it's a hell of a lot better than some of the dumps we've been in."

Jane adjusted the strap of her medical bag, her eyes sweeping the area with clinical precision. "Let's just hope we don't need this," she said, patting the bag. "But considering the circumstances, I'd rather be prepared."

Kit nodded, appreciating his team's readiness. They were all here, Calista, Miguel, Jane, Sofia, Zara, each of them bringing their unique skills and experience to the table, on alert until they knew what they were facing. They had faced countless challenges together, and now they were about to face another, one that required not just their strength but also their ability to trust others.

"Let's go inside," Kit said, his tone measured. "Time to meet our new allies."

The lodge itself was a rustic, sprawling building made of weathered wood and stone, blending seamlessly into the natural surroundings. The large, wraparound porch offered a view of the lake, and the windows were wide, allowing sunlight to flood the interior. It was the kind of place that might have been used for family vacations, filled with laughter and warmth. But today, it was a meeting ground for two teams that had only recently crossed paths, united by a common enemy.

As Kit and his team approached the entrance, I swung open door, revealing my Charlie Donovan self. I stood in the doorway, my height commanding but not overtly intimidating. My platinum blonde hair had been washed out to reveal my auburn locks, pulled back in a sleek ponytail, and my piercing green eyes met Kit's with a mixture of curiosity and caution.

"Kit Thorne," I greeted, stepping aside to let them in. "Welcome. We've been expecting you."

"You must be Charlie Donovan," Kit replied, his voice steady as he crossed the threshold. "You look different with brown hair."

I smiled. "Auburn, please. One and only photo you'll see of me like that. Thanks for arranging this. It's good to meet you."

Kit appreciated my direct approach. "Apologies. Agreed. My team's ready."

As we stepped into the lodge's main room, the atmosphere shifted slightly, the air immediately filled with anticipation. My team was already seated, their eyes turning to the newcomers with a mixture of curiosity and wariness. The room was spacious, with a large stone fireplace at one end and several comfortable chairs arranged in a semi-circle. The walls were adorned with old photographs and hunting trophies, giving the space a rustic, lived-in feel.

Kit took a moment to assess the people in front of him. He had reviewed the files Calista had shared on each of them, knew their faces, but this was the first time his team was seeing them in person.

Aria, my right hand, was seated near the fireplace, her expression calm but alert. Kit had spoken to her over the phone once, and he knew she was someone not to be underestimated. Her sharp mind and strategic thinking showed in her face, and Kit could see the intelligence in her eyes as she sized up his team.

Beside her was China, the designer from LA. A short but striking woman with long, dark hair and an aura of quiet intensity. Her reputation as a skilled profiler preceded her, and Kit could sense the controlled power in her movements. She was someone who didn't waste words, but her presence alone spoke volumes.

Marley, a reporter stationed in LA as well, sported a nerdy appearance but radiated a fierce energy, leaning against the wall, his arms crossed over his chest. Kit knew he was the researcher of the group and someone who could hold his own in any fight. Marley's eyes flashed with curiosity as he glanced at Miguel, clearly sizing him up.

Izzy and Rafe sat together, their easy camaraderie evident in the way they leaned toward each other. Izzy was a tech and business expert, someone who could probably rival Calista in her skills, and Rafe was the team's medical expert. He was also our stealth expert, capable of moving through the shadows without making a sound. Kit recognized the bond that came from working together through thick and thin.

Then there was the old man, Doc, our male version of Aria with connections around the world, and Emily, a former children's nurse who now specialized in undercover work as well as helping children recover from abuse. They were the backbone of my team, providing support in ways that were crucial to the success of our operations.

Finally, Kit's gaze settled on Kimmie, the newest addition to Charlie's team. She was a teacher, skilled in calming children, with an old soul, haunted look in her eyes, and Kit could see the uncertainty in her, someone who had been through hell and who was still learning but had the drive to join the battle.

"This is my team," I said, gesturing to the group. "Aria, China, Marley, Izzy, Rafe, Doc, Emily, and Kimmie. We've been through a lot together, and we want to see what you've got to offer. Manny and Vicky got called out and will try to make it at a later date. They are the law enforcement officers that taught me trust and helped get me certified as an agent as well."

Kit nodded, showing surprise about me being law, and appreciating the introductions. "And this is mine," he replied. "Calista, our tech expert. Miguel, our muscle, Jane, our doctor, Sofia, social worker, and Zara, linguist. We've been in the trenches together for a while now, and we appreciate this meeting."

The two teams eyed each other, the initial tension slowly giving way to mutual respect. They were all here for the same reason after all, to stop the trafficking rings that were popping up and preying on the most vulnerable, innocents that had no one to watch over them.

"We've got a lot to discuss," I said, taking a seat near the fireplace. "But first, let's get something straight. We don't play games, and we don't waste time. If we're going to work together, we need to be completely honest with each other."

Kit took a seat opposite me, his expression serious. "Agreed. This isn't about egos or who's in charge. It's about saving lives."

Aria leaned forward, her gaze steady. "We've been tracking these disappearances for a while now, and we've got some intel that might help. But we need to know what you've seen, what you've learned."

Calista spoke up, her voice calm but with an undercurrent of urgency. "We've been working on this for months. The kids we've rescued... it's been brutal. They're malnourished, dehydrated, some of them barely clinging to life. And they're not just being taken locally, it's global. We've got intel from Europe, Asia, South America... it's a coordinated effort, and it's bigger than anything we've dealt with before. It's someone that doesn't care about the condition of the kids, they just want something to sell."

Miguel nodded in agreement. "We just pulled twenty kids out of a shipping container in DC yesterday. All under fifteen. They were guarded like a shipment of weapons, heavily armed, highly organized. This isn't just some local gang. This is a well-oiled machine."

My expression darkened, I felt my jaw tightening. "We've seen the same thing. Kids disappearing off the streets, no trace, no leads. And when we do find them... it's like you said, they're in bad shape. Whoever's behind this isn't just trafficking, they're treating these kids like cattle ready for slaughter."

Marley's voice cut through the room, sharp and fierce. "We need to shut this down. But to do that, we need to know who's running the show. We've got leads, but nothing solid. I've investigated as deep as I can and it's like these people are ghosts."

Jane spoke up, her voice filled with concern. "We've treated these kids, but we can't keep up with the numbers. And the trauma... it's beyond anything we've ever seen. We need more resources, more medical support, and we need it now. We're having to put the kids into the system and if they get better, they'll just hit the streets again."

Doc nodded in agreement. "We're stretched thin as it is. Our house is full. We can patch them up, and find them temporary living, but these kids need long-term care, psychological support, and a permanent place to live. And that's just the ones we've found. God knows how many more are out there."

I glanced at Aria, who gave a slight nod before speaking. "We've been digging into the dark web, trying to find where these kids are being sold, who's buying. But it's like chasing shadows. They're using encrypted channels, coded messages, it's almost impossible to track."

"Almost," Calista echoed, her mind already working on solving the problem. "If we can pool our resources, we might be able to crack some of those codes, find a pattern. But it's going to take time."

"And time is something we don't have much of," Kit added. "Every day, more kids are taken. We need to act fast, and we can't be reckless. We have to be methodical about this."

China, who had been silent until now, finally spoke, her voice low but firm. "We've got the firepower, and we've got some intel. What we need is a plan, a coordinated effort to connect the dots. We need people on the streets asking questions, being part of the unseen. We need to take their middlemen down systematically, cut off their supply lines, dismantle their network from the outside in."

Rafe nodded in agreement, his voice thoughtful. "And we need to hit them where it hurts, financially. Take away their resources. By doing that, we take away their money. If we can track the money from their buyers, if might lead us to the people at the top. The ones pulling the strings."

Calista, who had been furiously typing on her laptop, looked up with a determined expression. "I'm already on it. We need to find out who's doing the snatching and then who they are selling the kids to. If I have names, I'll find them and destroy them."

I leaned back in my chair, my eyes sweeping over both teams. "So, we've got the skills, the people, the determination. Now we just need to put it all together. We've got to get one step ahead of them, anticipate their moves."

Kit met my gaze. "I say we work together, share intel, and coordinate our efforts. We will be stronger as a united front. Create a network that is unbreakable and unbeatable. I'll have Calista work with Aria about connecting your equipment and ours to be able to work together. Everyone on a level playing field. But we need to be careful, one wrong move, and these people will disappear back into the shadows."

Aria stood up, her expression stern. "We start now. Calista and I will work for the next two days getting everyone connected. Before we go our separate ways, we'll all be hand in hand with each other. We'll divide up the tasks, intel gathering, financial tracking, preparing for the next rescue operation. We've got two teams, and we'll need every resource at our disposal if it's as big as we believe."

The room was silent for a moment, the gravity of the situation settling over everyone present. There was no denying the enormity of the task ahead, but there was also no doubt that they were the best chance these kids had.

Kit stood up, his voice firm as he addressed both teams. "We've all seen what these monsters are capable of. We know what's at stake. But together, we can stop them. We can bring these kids home."

I nodded, my eyes dancing with determination. "And we will. You and I need to get more homes established. You said you were fighting local agencies? We don't need anything from them but permits." She smiled broadly. "Looks like we're going to need the space. I'll show you how it's done. You game?"

Kit nodded affirmatively. "Let's do it."

Our teams, once strangers, were now united by a common cause and stood together, ready to face whatever came next. The lodge, with its peaceful surroundings, seemed almost too tranquil for the storm that was about to be unleashed. But we would be prepared.

CHAPTER 9

- "Vanishing Shadows: Surge in Missing Street Children Alarms Global Authorities"

The Guardian - London, UK

- "Silent Epidemic: Street Kids Disappearing Across Europe in Unprecedented Numbers"

Le Monde - Paris, France

- "Lost and Forgotten: Alarming Spike in Disappearances of Homeless Youth Across North America"

The New York Times - New York, USA

- "Gone Without a Trace: South American Cities Grapple with Mysterious Surge in Missing Children"

El País - Bogotá, Colombia

- "Ghosts of the Streets: Asia's Disappearing Youth Spark Fears of Widespread Trafficking"

The Straits Times - Singapore

- "Global Crisis: Missing Street Children Numbers Skyrocket, Authorities Fear Coordinated Effort"

The Sydney Morning Herald - Sydney, Australia

- "Dark Days: Homeless Youth Vanish in Record Numbers Across Africa's Urban Centers"

Daily Nation - Nairobi, Kenya

- "Unseen and Unheard: The Growing Crisis of Disappearing Street Children in the Middle East"

Al Jazeera - Doha, Qatar

- "A Generation Lost: Europe's Cities Confront the Mystery of Missing Street Kids"

Der Spiegel - Berlin, Germany

- "Shadows in the Night: Brazil's Disappearing Street Children Raise Trafficking Concerns"

Folha de S.Paulo - São Paulo, Brazil

- "Vanished Voices: Rising Number of Missing Street Children Leaves Asia on Edge"

The Japan Times - Tokyo, Japan

- "Disappearing Act: Alarming Trend of Missing Street Youths Spreads Across North America"

CBC News - Toronto, Canada

- "Silent Cries: Global Surge in Missing Street Children Stokes Trafficking Fears"

The Times of India - New Delhi, India

- "Where Have They Gone? Europe's Homeless Children Disappearing at an Alarming Rate"
- *BBC News - London, UK*
- "No Safe Place: Disappearance of Street Children Sparks International Outcry"

RT News - Moscow, Russia

Two months later, both teams had accomplished little in discovering who the operatives were that were snatching homeless children off the streets. With frustration they watched headlines from across the globe, searching for any tidbit that might show them who the culprits might be.

Statistics showed no assistance from law enforcement in protecting the many souls that were still on the streets. It was as if these unseen children were just that, unseen. Kit was beside himself, knowing that it would require more work for his team in tracking the kids and eliminating the threat to them.

As he sat with Jack, they talked about many things, including Charlie and her team that were spread out across the States. How were they managing to rescue the ones they did and where were they placing them?

The late afternoon sun bathed the Virginia countryside in a warm, golden light, casting long shadows across the rolling hills and lush greenery surrounding Kit's estate. The quiet of the early evening was broken only by the occasional rustle of leaves and the distant hum of cicadas. Kit sat back in his chair on the wide veranda, his gaze fixed on the horizon where the sky met the trees in a soft blur of color. The serenity of the scene contrasted sharply with the storm of thoughts churning in his mind.

Beside him, Jack, nursed a glass of bourbon, his weathered face thoughtful as he scanned the headlines on his tablet. The two men had spent countless hours in this very spot since Kit had bought it, discussing everything from business strategies to rescue operations. But lately, their conversations had been dominated by one grim topic, the alarming rise in missing street children.

"Another one," Jack muttered, his deep voice frustrated as he handed the tablet to Kit. The headline glared back at them in bold letters: **"Vanishing Shadows: Surge in Missing Street Children Alarms Global Authorities."** Below it, the article detailed the growing crisis, with reports of disappearances from cities all over the world.

Kit's jaw tightened as he read, his mind flashing back to the recent missions his team had undertaken. They had rescued dozens of kids from traffickers, but it wasn't enough. The scale of the problem was staggering, and for every child they saved, countless others remained in the clutches of predators.

"This is becoming the main topic of conversation for us," Kit said, his voice low. "Every day, it's more of the same. More kids gone, more lives destroyed. And we haven't even scratched the surface."

Jack nodded, his expression grim. "It's bad, Kit. Worse than I've ever seen. And it's not just here. Europe, Asia, South America, they're all seeing the same thing, a major uptick in kids disappearing. It's like these traffickers are coordinating, moving faster than we can keep up."

Kit leaned forward, resting his elbows on his knees as he stared out at the landscape. The tranquility of his home seemed worlds away from the horrors they were dealing with, the headlines kept it all too close.

"What I don't get," Kit began, "is how these kids are vanishing without a trace. We've got eyes and ears in so many places, but they're still slipping through. It's like they're being swallowed by the earth."

Jack took a slow sip of his bourbon, considering his words carefully before he spoke. "You know, Kit, I've been thinking about Charlie and her team. They've been handling rescues in different areas, scattered across the country, and they seem to be making some headway."

Kit glanced at Jack, intrigued. "Yeah, I've been wondering about that too. They're a small team, but they're getting results. And I've been thinking about where they're housing these kids after the rescues. Charlie never said much about it, but she must have some kind of system in place. She said she would take care of things there."

Jack nodded thoughtfully. "From what I've gathered, they've got safe houses set up in various locations, all off the grid. Calista says she's got some kind of trust that goes around buying houses, supposed to fix up and sell or rent. Charlie's been smart about it, keeping things decentralized, so if one location is compromised, the others stay safe."

"That makes sense," Kit mused, his mind turning over the possibilities. "But that takes resources. More than just a few people can manage on their own. She must have contacts, maybe even more allies than she's letting on."

Jack chuckled, a wry smile tugging at the corners of his mouth. "Charlie seems to be good at playing her cards close to the chest. But she's resourceful, her team is resourceful, and looks like they know how to get things done. I wouldn't be surprised if she's got a larger network than we realize, of people helping her."

Kit leaned back in his chair, rubbing a hand across his face. "You know, I've been thinking about something she mentioned a while back. She offered to help me set up shelters, places where homeless people and runaway kids could find safety and a shot at a better life."

Jack raised an eyebrow, his interest piqued. "And you didn't take her up on it?"

Kit shrugged, a faint smile playing on his lips. "You know me, Jack. I don't like asking for help unless I have to. I've always prided myself on being able to handle things on my own, and I've built this operation from the ground up with that mindset."

"But?" Jack prompted, sensing there was more to Kit's hesitation.

"But," Kit sighed, his gaze drifting back to the horizon, "the way things are going now... the situation demands it and going to the locals doesn't seem to be getting the job done. They don't want 'trash' as they put it, in their neighborhoods. These kids are disappearing faster than we can save them. We're fighting a war, and it feels like we're losing ground every day. Maybe it's time I admit that we can't do this alone."

Jack nodded, his expression serious. "There's no shame in accepting help, Kit. You've built something incredible here, but even the strongest walls can be made stronger with the right support. Charlie's offer might be just what we need to turn the tide."

Kit was silent for a long moment, weighing his options. He knew trusted Charlie, she had proven herself to be a capable leader and a fierce protector of those who couldn't protect themselves. But the idea of relying on someone else's resources, of merging his vision with another's, wasn't an easy pill to swallow.

Finally, Kit nodded, his decision made. "You're right, Jack. Things have changed, and we need to adapt. I'll contact Charlie in the morning and discuss what she offered. If we can set up shelters, safe houses, get kids off the streets... maybe we can start turning this around."

Jack smiled, a rare expression of approval on his weathered face. "Good. You're making the right call, Kit. This isn't just about saving a few kids, it's about creating a system that can keep them safe long-term. I think if anyone can help you do that, it's Charlie and her team."

Kit leaned back in his chair, the weight of the decision lifting slightly as he considered the possibilities. "We'll need to plan carefully," he said, his mind already shifting into strategic mode. "We can't just throw something together and hope it works. We need to find the right locations, secure the funding, and make sure these places are staffed with people we can trust."

"And you will," Jack assured him. "You've got the resources, the connections, and now, you've got the right partners. Charlie's team knows what they're doing, and with their help, we can start building something that'll make a real difference. Let her use your money since she obviously has something that works."

Kit nodded. "We'll start small, maybe a couple of shelters in key cities. Places where the need is greatest. And then we'll expand, bit by bit, until we've got a network that covers the entire country."

Jack grinned, raising his glass in a toast. "I'm pretty sure she's a step or two ahead of you on that but... To new beginnings, then. And to kicking these bastards where it hurts."

Kit chuckled, clinking his glass against Jack's. "To new beginnings," he echoed, taking a sip of his drink. The bourbon burned warmly in his throat, a reminder that even in the darkest times, there was always a glimmer of hope.

As the sun dipped lower in the sky, casting the landscape in a soft, golden light, Kit allowed himself a moment of quiet reflection. The road ahead was going to be difficult, but he had never shied away from a challenge. With Charlie's help, he knew they could build something powerful, something that would outlast the current crisis and provide a lasting refuge for those who needed it most.

"Do you ever think about how far we've come, Jack?" Kit asked, his voice contemplative. "From those days on the streets, just trying to survive?"

Jack's gaze softened, and he nodded slowly. "I think about it all the time, Kit. And I'm damn proud of what you've built. You've turned your pain into something that's helped a lot of people. Sadly, there's always more to do. Always another fight to be won."

Kit smiled, a mixture of pride and determination in his expression. "Yeah. And I'm not done yet. Not by a long shot."

They sat in comfortable silence for a while, the sun slowly setting behind the hills, painting the sky in shades of pink and orange. The peace of the evening was a contrast to the chaos that awaited them in the days and weeks ahead. Kit found comfort in the knowledge that he wasn't alone in this fight. With Jack and the team by his side, and soon with Charlie's team working in tandem with his own, he felt the change in the air, something good was coming.

As the last rays of sunlight dipped below the horizon, Kit stood up, stretching his legs as he turned to Jack. "I'm going to get some rest. Tomorrow's going to be a long day."

Jack nodded, finishing his drink before standing as well. "I'll be right behind you. And Kit... I'm glad you're making this call. It's the right move."

Kit smiled, clapping Jack on the shoulder. "Thanks, Pops. For everything."

With that, they headed inside, the warmth of the lodge greeting them as they stepped through the door. The world outside might be filled with darkness and uncertainty, but Kit knew that as long as they kept fighting, there was still hope.

Tomorrow, he would call Charlie. And together, they would take the next step in a battle that was far from over.

CHAPTER 10

The lodge on the outskirts of Atlanta had become a familiar meeting ground for Kit and Charlie's teams. The last time they had gathered here had been to lay the groundwork for their alliance, a tentative collaboration born out of necessity. Now, as Kit stepped onto the wide, wooden porch, he felt peace, tempered with curiosity. This meeting was about building something that would last, safehouses across the country, a network that would protect the most vulnerable and give them a chance at a better life.

The sun was just beginning to dip below the horizon, casting the lodge in a warm, golden light. Kit took a deep breath of the crisp evening air, appreciating the tranquility of the setting. It was hard to reconcile this peaceful scene with the dark, dangerous world they were working to dismantle. But the work had to be done, and tonight was a critical step in that process.

Inside the lodge, the atmosphere was one of quiet determination. Charlie's team had already assembled around the large wooden table that dominated the center of the room. The walls, adorned with old photographs and hunting trophies, seemed to close in slightly as the conversation shifted from pleasantries to the serious business at hand.

Charlie, still learning to be a strong and calm leader, greeted Kit with a nod. "Glad you could make it, Kit. We've got a lot to cover."

Kit returned the nod, noting that Charlie was still one to just dive right in and took a seat opposite her. His team, Calista, Miguel, and Jane followed suit, each of them finding a spot around the table. Zara and Sofia were present but sat behind Kit to watch. The dynamic between the two teams had shifted since their last meeting, there was a new respect, a shared purpose that had grown from their recent collaboration.

"So," Charlie began, her voice steady, "we've all seen how bad things are getting out there. The headlines, the disappearances... it's escalating, and we need to do more than just reactive rescues. We need to build something that can protect these kids long-term. Safehouses, spread across the country, in every major city."

Kit nodded, his mind already turning over the logistics. "I've been thinking about this since your offer at our first meeting. We need to be strategic, finding the right locations, getting the necessary permits, making sure these places are safe and secure."

Aria, seated beside Charlie, leaned forward slightly. "That's why we're rehabbing old buildings. It's quicker, more cost-effective, and it keeps things under the radar. We can move in quietly, do the necessary renovations, and have these places up and running in no time. Building rehabs are the craze right now, so who would look at someone new coming onto the scene. The cities would rather someone else use their money than the city spend theirs on razing them."

Kit blinked, surprised. He had been envisioning new constructions, something grand and flashy, but what Aria was suggesting made far more sense. "Rehabbing old buildings..." he repeated, his tone thoughtful. "That could work. It would certainly speed things up, and you're right, it wouldn't draw as much attention."

"And we're talking about buildings that are already in areas where they're needed most," Marley chimed in, his voice brimming with energy. "Old schools, abandoned warehouses, even some old apartment complexes that've been sitting empty for years. We get the right people in there, and we can make them livable again."

Doc, Charlie's ranch manager, and Aria's sidekick in most matters, who had been quietly listening, now spoke up. "I've got connections, retired military contractors, electricians, plumbers. They're good people, and they've got experience with this kind of work. If we can get the equipment and materials to them, they could have these buildings up and running within two months. Maybe even less, depending on the condition of the place."

Kit was impressed. He had considered himself well-versed in the art of logistics, but the way Charlie's team was breaking down the process, it was clear they had a deep understanding of the darker side of the world, the streets. They knew how to navigate it, how to turn it to their advantage, and most importantly, how to protect those who had been forgotten by society.

"Two months," Kit mused aloud, considering the possibilities. "That's fast. If we could get even a handful of these safehouses operational in that time, it could make a real difference."

Aria nodded, her eyes gleaming with knowledge. "I've already started compiling a list of potential locations. There are plenty of old buildings in relatively good shape sitting empty in the cities we're targeting. We just need to secure them and get the work started."

"And funding?" Kit asked, looking around the table. "We'll need a steady stream of it to make sure this doesn't collapse before it even starts."

Charlie met his gaze evenly. "I have a foundation we can use temporarily. But if we are to be united, we need to set up something legitimate that can funnel money into the project without drawing too much attention to us personally. I know you've got the resources, Kit, and we can leverage them without putting your name on the front page."

Kit nodded, appreciating her pragmatism. "I've got contacts who can help with that. We'll need to be discreet, but if we do this right, we can stay under the radar and still get the funding we need. Hell, if it comes down to it, I'll just funnel my own money into it."

Miguel leaned back in his chair, his usual stoic expression giving way to a hint of approval. "I think this is the right move,

Kit. Better safe than sorry. You're in the news enough with being a billionaire, this would let the bad guys know you're on to them."

Jane, ever the practical voice of reason, added, "And we need to think about staffing these places. We can't do it all ourselves. We'll need people who can manage the day-to-day operations, nursing staff, people that are good with kids, people we trust."

"Already thought of that," China said, speaking for the first time. Her voice was low, but it carried a world of experience. "We've got a network of people who've been working with us since we brought down the first cartel. Social workers, counselors, former law enforcement. They've been doing this work under the radar and they're good at it. We can bring them in to run these places. They're older, retired, but ready to back a good cause."

Kit was impressed by how thorough Charlie's team was. They had thought of everything, from the logistics of rehabbing buildings to the operational aspects of running the safehouses. The more he listened, the more he realized just how valuable this partnership was going to be.

"And security?" Kit asked, his mind always on the safety of those they were trying to protect. "These places will be targets. We need to make sure they're secure, that no one can get to these kids once they're inside."

Rafe's voice crackled through the speaker of Aria's phone before anyone could answer. "We've got that covered, Kit," he said, his tone confident. "Izzy and I've been working on a security protocol, cameras, alarm systems, safe rooms. We'll make sure these places are fortresses. No one's getting in unless we want them to. Besides, all the people working there are retired military or law enforcement. I'd put them against my favorite young cop any day."

Izzy's voice joined Rafe's, her tone as sharp as ever. "And I'll find some people who can monitor everything remotely. We'll have eyes on all the safehouses 24/7. If anything goes down, we'll know about it before they do."

Aria looked at her phone with a smile, then glanced up at Kit. "Sorry, they couldn't make it in person, but they're still with us."

Calista chimed in on that note. "I've got a company that will donate the electronics we need to set this all up. If whoever heads up your security and IT can meet with me, we'll get schematics of the buildings and find the best places to station surveillance cameras."

"I'll get something set up soon," Aria replied. "There's a whole network of IT we've got access to."

Kit smiled, shaking his head slightly. "Good work, all of you. Let's make sure these places are as secure as we can get them."

Rafe's voice came back, the slight hint of amusement in it. "You got it, sir. We'll have the initial set of plans ready for you to review by the end of the week."

"Perfect," Kit replied, feeling the pieces fall into place. This was starting to look like something real, something that could actually change the game.

The discussion continued into the evening, as the two teams began hunting for listings of empty buildings in major cities across the U.S. Calista's fingers flew over her laptop keyboard as she pulled up real estate databases, scanning for properties that fit their criteria. Aria was doing the same, her eyes focused on the screen in front of her.

"There's an old school building in Detroit that's been abandoned for years," Calista said, pointing to the listing on her screen. "It's got the space we need, and it's in a part of the city where we could really make an impact. The underground plumbing is good, the foundation is sturdy. Aesthetics and windows and double checking the foundation."

Aria nodded, jotting down the details. "And there's a warehouse in Los Angeles that could be converted into a shelter. It's got good bones, and it's in an area where there's a lot of need."

Charlie leaned back in her chair, satisfied with the progress they were making. "This is good," she said, her voice filled with pride. "We're not just talking about it anymore, we're making it happen. Centers for the forgotten. Good job guys."

Kit couldn't help but feel a sense of pride as he looked around the room. They were doing something that mattered, something that would make a real difference in the lives of these kids. And they were doing it as a team.

But even as the conversation continued, Kit's mind drifted back to something Jack had said during their last conversation. The world was getting darker, and the challenges were growing more complex, but with the right allies, the right strategy, they could push back against the darkness rolling in.

As the night deepened, Kit made a silent promise to himself. They would build these safehouses, they would protect these kids, and they would fight back against the darkness that threatened to consume them.

And they wouldn't stop until the job was done.

Finally, after hours of discussion, Kit stood up, stretching his legs as he addressed the group. "We've made a lot of progress tonight. Let's keep this momentum going. We'll finalize the locations, start securing the permits, and get the rehab work started. And once these places are up and running, we'll start moving kids in."

Charlie nodded, her eyes meeting Kit's. "And we'll have someone from our teams there every step of the way. Aria knows what we need and probably has a person or persons who will be willing to take on the job."

Aria assured them she did and would fill them in on what was wanted and needed.

The teams began to gather their things, the energy in the room still buzzing with the excitement of what they had accomplished in a few short hours. As Kit and his team moved to the stairs and the floor where their rooms were located.

"Charlie," Kit said, his voice low as he caught her attention before they left. "Thank you. For everything. I don't think I realized just how much we needed this partnership until tonight."

Charlie smiled, a rare, genuine smile that softened her usual steely demeanor. "It's good to work together, Kit. And I have a feeling we're just getting started."

Kit nodded, knowing she was right. This was just the beginning. The real work was about to start, and with Charlie and her team by his side, Kit felt ready to face whatever challenges lay ahead.

As Kit walked out on the veranda outside his room and into the cool night air, Kit glanced up at the stars, feeling a new and stronger sense of purpose. The road ahead was going to be rough and long, but he felt they were on the right path. And for the first time in a long time, Kit felt hopeful.

Tomorrow, they would start turning their plans into reality. And with every step, they would get closer to making the world a safer place for those who needed it most... the lost.

CHAPTER 11

The night air in Montreal was cool, crisp, and laced with the scent of pine from the surrounding forests. There was a deep heated tension simmering beneath the surface as Alexandre DuBois and Gero Meyer made their way through the crowded club. The two men, ever the picture of sophistication, moved with the ease of predators in their element, their tailored suits and polished demeanor marking them as men of power and influence. People stepped aside as they passed.

They were in Canada under the guise of legitimate business, meeting with potential clients who were interested in their import/export services. To the outside world, Alexandre and Gero were successful businessmen, their company known for its efficiency and discretion in moving goods across the globe. But those who knew them well understood that their true wealth came from far darker dealings, specifically, the trafficking of human lives.

The club was loud, filled with the pulsating beat of music and the low hum of conversation. Beautiful women and men drifted through the crowd, offering drinks and whispered promises to those who could afford the luxury. Alexandre and Gero made their way to a private booth at the back of the club, where a group of well-dressed men awaited their arrival.

The evening began with the usual pleasantries, drinks, small talk, and the exchange of business cards. The potential clients were keen to impress, eager to align themselves with Alexandre and Gero's indelible reputation. As the night wore on, the conversation began to shift, taking on a more cautious, measured tone.

One of the men, a tall, thin figure with a sharp gaze, leaned in closer to Alexandre, his voice barely audible over the music. "Mr. DuBois, I understand your company offers a wide range of shipping services. I was wondering if you could accommodate a... special request."

Alexandre's eyes flickered with interest, though his expression remained impassive. "We handle many types of cargo," he replied smoothly. "But we're always interested in new opportunities. What did you have in mind?"

The man smiled, his lips curling in a way that hinted at something darker beneath the surface. "I've heard that you and Mr. Meyer are particularly skilled at moving goods that require a certain level of discretion. Perhaps goods that might not be... entirely legal in other parts of the world?"

Gero, seated beside Alexandre, glanced at the man with a practiced smile. "We do pride ourselves on our ability to deliver, regardless of the challenges. But such services come with certain risks and are costly. We would need to know more about what you're asking."

The man hesitated, his eyes darting around the club as if to ensure they weren't being overheard. "Let's just say that I have a shipment that needs to be moved out of the country, quickly and quietly. It's live cargo, and it's of... considerable value."

There it was. The unspoken truth finally laid bare, though still cloaked in a veil of ambiguity. Alexandre exchanged a brief glance with Gero, both men silently weighing the potential risks and rewards of the proposition.

Alexandre leaned forward, his voice dropping to a near-whisper. "Moving such... delicate cargo is no small task. We would need to verify the value of the shipment before committing our resources. It wouldn't do to get involved in something that might not be worth the effort."

The man nodded, clearly expecting this response. "Of course. I anticipated as much. I can arrange for you to inspect the merchandise. It's currently being held at a secure location outside of the city, an old farmhouse about an hour's drive from here. If you're interested, I can provide the address."

Gero gave a slight nod, his mind already calculating the logistics. "We're interested. But understand that this is a time-sensitive matter. We'll need to see the merchandise tonight, and if everything checks out, we can arrange for transportation within the next twenty-four hours."

The man smiled, clearly pleased. "I'll have the address sent to you immediately. And don't worry, gentlemen, you'll find the compensation to be more than satisfactory."

The conversation shifted back to lighter topics, but Alexandre and Gero were no longer interested. Their minds were already focused on the potential payout and the steps needed to secure the cargo. The club, with its noise and frivolity, faded into the background as they silently prepared for the task ahead.

Half an hour later, they were in the back of a black SUV, their two bodyguards seated up front. The address had been sent to them via encrypted message, and they were now on their way to the farmhouse. The drive was mostly silent, the only sound the low hum of the engine and the occasional murmur from the driver as he communicated with the security detail.

As they left the city behind, the landscape gradually shifted from urban sprawl to open fields and dense forest. The road grew narrower, winding through the trees until it finally opened up into a gravel path that led to the farmhouse.

The building itself was a dilapidated structure, long abandoned and covered in a thick layer of dust and grime. It was the kind of place that would have gone unnoticed by anyone passing by, a perfect location for hiding something, or someone, that you didn't want found.

The SUV pulled to a stop in front of the farmhouse, and Alexandre and Gero stepped out, followed closely by their bodyguards. The air was still, almost unnaturally quiet, as if the very night was holding its breath.

"Stay alert," Alexandre muttered to their guards as they approached the front door. "Something doesn't feel right."

Gero's hand instinctively moving to the small pistol holstered at his side. They had both learned long ago that caution was the key to survival in their line of work.

The door creaked open under the weight of Gero's hand, revealing the dark interior of the farmhouse. The faint smell of decay wafted out, mingling with the scent of damp earth. The bodyguards entered first, their flashlights cutting through the darkness as they moved to secure the area.

It didn't take long to find the first body.

One of the guards gestured to the ground, where a man lay crumpled in a pool of blood, his throat slashed. His lifeless eyes stared up at the ceiling, frozen in an expression of shock.

"Damn it," Gero hissed, his eyes narrowing. "Looks like we're not the first ones here."

They moved deeper into the farmhouse, their footsteps echoing in the silence. More bodies were found, each one a guard who had been stationed at the farmhouse to protect the cargo. But the cargo itself, the children they were supposed to be moving, were nowhere to be seen.

And then they heard it, a faint rustling sound coming from one of the back rooms. Alexandre motioned for silence, and they crept toward the noise, their weapons drawn and ready.

Inside the room, they found the source of the noise.

A man was crouched beside a hidden trapdoor, trying to pry it open with a crowbar. His clothes were disheveled, his face streaked with dirt and sweat. He hadn't noticed them yet, he was too focused on his task.

"Who the hell are you?" Gero barked, his voice low and menacing.

The man froze, his head snapping up to meet their gazes. There was a moment of stunned silence, and then he sprang to his feet, his hand reaching for a gun at his side.

But the bodyguards were faster.

In a flash, they were on him, wrestling the gun from his hand and pinning him to the ground. The man struggled, but it was a losing battle, he was no match for the brute strength of the trained guards.

"Let him up," Alexandre ordered, stepping closer as the guards hauled the man to his feet. "We need to know what he's doing here."

The man was breathing heavily, his eyes wild with a mixture of fear and defiance. "You don't need to know anything," he spat, blood dripping from a split lip. "I'm trying to save them."

Alexandre's eyes narrowed. "Save who? The kids? Where are they?"

The man didn't answer, his eyes darting to the trapdoor he had been trying to open.

Gero followed his gaze, then nodded to one of the guards. The guard bent down, using the crowbar to pry the door open, revealing a small, dark cellar below.

There were no children inside.

Gero frowned, looking back at the man. "Where are they?" he demanded, his patience wearing thin.

"I don't know," the man admitted, his voice hoarse. "They were here. I saw them... but when I got back with the van, they were gone."

Alexandre exchanged a glance with Gero. This wasn't making sense. If the kids were gone, who had taken them? And why leave the guards behind, dead but not moved?

Before they could question the man further, the unmistakable sound of sirens filled the air, distant but rapidly approaching.

"Cops," Gero muttered, his expression darkening. "I think this was a setup. We need to get out of here. Now."

Alexandre nodded, but his eyes remained fixed on the man, who was now struggling against the guards holding him.

"Who are you?" Alexandre asked, his tone icy. "Why were you here alone?"

The man's defiant gaze met his own, and for a moment, there was only silence. Then, in a voice filled with both pain and strength, the man answered, "Guess."

The gunshot sliced through the air exploding as it exited the side of the man's head. Leaving him lay, Alexandre, Gero, and the bodyguards quickly left and found a spot to hide until the police cars passed. Silently, the SUV eased in the opposite direction they had come until the driver felt it was safe to turn the lights on. They had to find an alternate route back to Montreal, where they located the man who connected with them. He did not make it out of the party alive.

Alexandre and Gero left Montreal for Denmark, the closest place they could get to quickly. Gero let it be known within their organization what had happened and ordered his people to find out who was responsible for the setup. He also ordered them exterminated like the bugs they were. His final request was to find the missing merchandise and confiscate it.

CHAPTER 12

The air in the lodge was filled with the aroma of coffee and the quiet murmur of conversation. Kit and his team were gathered around the large wooden table that had become their makeshift command center until the renovations had been complete on the permanent one downstairs, the soft glow of the lamp casting long shadows across the room. They had been working late into the evening, hashing out the final details for their next series of safehouses. The mood was focused, determined, as everyone worked to finalize plans and review logistics.

Both teams had decided to purchase the lodge and turn it into their command center, always having at least one member of each team on hand. Three weeks after their last meeting they came together to finalize some paperwork for the foundation and funds, making sure to leave no stone unturned to conceal the identity of the people behind the foundation.

Charlie was unusually quiet. She sat at the far end of the table, her eyes focused on the screen of her phone. Kit noticed her distracted demeanor and the way she occasionally glanced at the device, as if waiting for something. He decided to give her space, knowing that when she was ready, she would share whatever was on her mind.

Just as Kit was about to suggest a break, Charlie's phone buzzed on the table, the vibration startling everyone into silence. Charlie glanced at the screen, her expression tightening. The name displayed there was enough to make her stomach drop, Mr. Holloway, her accountant and the grandfather of her fiancé, Chase.

Charlie picked up the phone, her voice steady as she answered, "Mr. Holloway?"

There was a long pause, and Kit could tell from her expression that something was very wrong. Her usually composed demeanor began to crack as she listened to whatever Mr. Holloway was telling her on the other end of the line. The team, sensing the shift in the room's atmosphere, fell silent, their eyes now on Charlie.

"What happened?" Charlie asked, her voice barely above a whisper. Her hand gripped the edge of the table so tightly that her knuckles turned white.

Kit exchanged a worried glance with Calista, who had stopped typing mid-sentence. The tension in the room was high, each team member waiting in uneasy silence.

"No…" Charlie's voice cracked, and she suddenly stood up from the table, walking to the far side of the room as if trying to escape the news. She pressed her free hand to her forehead, her breath coming in short, ragged gasps.

"Chase…" she managed to say, her voice cracking. "Where… where is he now?"

Kit's heart sank. He knew Chase was someone important to Charlie, her fiancé, the person she trusted above all others. And now, whatever news Mr. Holloway had delivered, it was tearing her apart.

The conversation on Charlie's end became disjointed, her words broken up by sharp breaths as she fought to keep herself composed. Kit wanted to go to her, to offer some sort of comfort, but he knew this was a moment she needed to process on her own.

Finally, Charlie's voice, small and broken, said, "I'm so sorry, Mr. Holloway. I… I can't believe this." She listened for a few more moments, then her voice hitched audibly at whatever Mr. Holloway had just said.

"Find the SOBs and destroy them." Was the last thing Mr. Holloway spoke before disconnecting.

The line went dead, and Charlie slowly lowered the phone from her ear. She stood there for a moment, as if in a daze, before she finally turned around to face the room. Her face was pale, her eyes wide and hollow with shock. The confident, unshakeable leader Kit had come to know so well was gone, replaced by someone lost in a sea of grief.

Aria stood up, taking a hesitant step toward her. "Charlie... what happened?"

She swallowed hard, her voice trembling as she spoke. "Chase... Chase is dead. He was investigating a lead on his own, something about a group of homeless kids in Montreal. The information wasn't verified, and he didn't want to put anyone else at risk, so he went by himself."

She paused, her eyes filling with tears that she refused to let fall. "He found an abandoned farm outside Montreal. The authorities think he discovered something, or someone, but before he could report back, they... they executed him. A single bullet to the head."

The room fell deathly silent. Kit felt a cold chill wash over him, the gravity of the situation sinking in. Charlie's fiancé, a man she clearly loved and trusted, had been murdered while trying to protect the very people they were all fighting for.

Miguel's face hardened, his jaw clenched in anger. Calista looked down, her hands trembling slightly as she tried to process what she had just heard. Jane put a hand over her mouth, her eyes filled with sympathy and sorrow for the loss Charlie was enduring. They had not met Chase yet, but Charlie had spoken of him often and lovingly.

Aria walked over to Charlie, her voice gentle, and placed her arms around her. "Charlie, I'm so sorry. I can't imagine what you're going through right now, but I want you to know that we'll find the bastards that did this. Whatever you need, whatever you want to do, we're here."

Charlie nodded, and across the room, Kit could see that she was barely holding herself together. "Mr. Holloway... he's devastated," she said, her voice barely audible. "He told me... he told me to find the people responsible and destroy them."

The words hung in the air, the request heavy with grief and anger. Kit knew that there was no way Charlie could focus on anything else until she had fulfilled that promise. And he understood why, if it were him, he would want nothing more than to hunt down the monsters who had taken the person he loved and make them pay.

"We will," Kit said, his voice steely with resolve. "We'll find them, Charlie. And we'll make sure they can never do this to anyone else."

Aria stood back, "It's someone with power. Only trained bodyguards execute people, and only when they are ordered to. Whatever Chase discovered, we now have to discover. When we do, we'll blast them all to hell."

Charlie looked up, her eyes red rimmed. "I believe it's connected to the trafficking ring we are trying to find. We need to find out every piece of information we can about that day and night. We find out who was at that house, we find the people who are stealing the street kids. I won't stop until they are caught. Chase..." she choked, "Chase was everything to me. He was my partner, my rock. And now he's gone, because of those bastards."

Kit walked over and placed a comforting hand on her shoulder. "We'll start by finding out everything we can about that farm. If they were holding kids there, then someone must have seen something. We'll track down every lead, follow every trail, until we find out who's responsible."

Charlie nodded, her breath coming in shuddering waves as she fought to keep her emotions in check. "Thank you," she whispered, the words barely audible. "I... I need a moment."

Kit watched as she walked out onto the porch, her footsteps heavy and slow. The teams remained silent, each of them grappling with their own thoughts and emotions. This wasn't just another mission, now, this had become personal, and Kit and Aria, heck the whole team, knew that it had just become the most important fight of Charlie's life.

When Charlie returned after a few minutes, her face was still pale, but there was a fire in her eyes that hadn't been there before. She was still grieving, but now that grief had transformed into something more, a raging desire for justice, or perhaps revenge.

"Let's get to work," she said, her voice stronger now. "We need to find out who was at that farm, who was running the operation, and who the buyers were. I want to know everything about them, every detail, every name. I want to know who owns that property and I want them thoroughly vetted."

Calista nodded, already pulling up maps and information on her laptop. "I'll start by looking at satellite images of the area around Montreal. We can pinpoint the exact location of the farm and start working from there. I'll also check satellite photos of the last 72 hours, we might end up with images of people and vehicles."

Miguel cracked his knuckles, a grim look on his face. "And once we find them, we make sure they pay for what they've done. No one gets away with this." Kit new that Miguel's justice ticker just hit high, and he would become unstoppable when the murderers were found.

Kimmie spoke up, her voice calm, her eyes filled with empathy. "And Charlie, my sister, when you're ready... I'm here. I know this is beyond difficult, and I'm not letting you go through it alone."

Charlie gave her a grateful nod. "Thank you, Kimmie, you'll end up being my shoulder, but right now, I need to focus. I need to find these people and end this."

Kit sat back down at the table, his mind racing with possibilities and strategies. He hadn't seen Charlie in action before, but from what he was witnessing now, she was relentless, methodical, and fiercely protective of those she cared about. But this was different. This was personal in a way that Kit hadn't seen in anyone he worked with before, and it only made him more determined to help her succeed.

"Let's start gathering intel," Kit said, directing the team. "We'll reach out to our contacts in Canada, see if they've heard anything about this farm. Check on any upper crust parties that might have been going on. We'll also look into any recent disappearances in Montreal, if kids are being snatched, let's pray someone noticed something."

Charlie took a deep breath, steeling herself for what lay ahead. "And once we have what we need... we take them down. Every last one of them. There will be no prisoners."

The room fell into a focused silence as everyone began their tasks, the energy in the room shifting from shock and sorrow to determination and action. Charlie's pain was still fresh, her loss still raw, but now it had a purpose, a direction. Sadly, at the cost of a loved. She knew they would find the people responsible and make sure justice was served.

Deep down, Charlie also knew that justice might not be enough. Chase had been taken from her in the most brutal way possible, and the void he left behind could never be filled. The only thing she could do now was to ensure that no one else would have to experience the same pain she was feeling.

As the night wore on, the team worked tirelessly, piecing together clues and following leads. Charlie remained focused, her mind sharp despite the turmoil in her heart. She couldn't afford to falter, not now, not when she was so close to finding the answers she needed.

And as the hours passed, one thing became increasingly clear, this wasn't just about one small operation, one farm, or even one life, this was about stopping an evil that had taken root in the world, an evil that preyed on the most vulnerable and innocent, an evil that appeared to be growing.

And Charlie was determined to be the one to uproot it, no matter the cost.

When dawn finally broke, casting a soft light over the lodge and the surrounding forest, the team had made progress, small steps, but steps in the right direction. The information they had gathered pointed to a larger network, a web of connections that spread far beyond Montreal.

Charlie looked at the faces around the table, Kit, Aria, Kimmie, Doc, Calista, Miguel, Jane, all of them ready to do whatever it took to help her in this fight. She felt a wave of gratitude, mixed with the cold, hard resolve that had kept her going through the night.

"We're going to get them," Kit said, his voice firm. "Our teams will do this together as a united front. We'll get justice for Chase."

Charlie nodded, her voice steady as she replied, "Yes."

And with that, they set their plans into motion, knowing that the path ahead would be difficult, dangerous, and filled with challenges. That was enough to give them the strength to face whatever came next. Time for a little trip across the border.

CHAPTER 13

The private jet descended smoothly through the clouds, revealing the sprawling landscape of Quebec below. Kit, Zara, and Sofia sat quietly in the luxurious cabin, each lost in their own thoughts as they prepared for the task ahead. Their mission to Montreal wasn't just a routine investigation, it had become personal, and they all felt the weight of it.

Kit, the wealthy benefactor and the public face of this operation, had chosen Zara and Sofia for this mission for a reason. Zara's linguistic skills and ability to blend in with various cultures made her an invaluable asset, while Sofia's background as a former street kid turned social worker gave her the empathy and insight needed to work in the darker corners of the city if needed. Together, they would discover what had happened at the abandoned farm.

As the jet touched down on the tarmac, Kit glanced at Zara, who was reviewing a map of the area. "Remember, we're here to play a role. The more convincing we are, the more likely we are to get the information we need."

Zara nodded, her expression focused. "We've got this, Kit. Just keep the realtor busy, and Sofia and I will do the rest."

Sofia offered a reassuring smile, though her eyes betrayed the tension she felt. "We'll find something, Kit. There's always a clue somewhere."

The jet taxied to a stop, and within minutes, they were disembarking, stepping into the crisp Montreal air. A black SUV awaited them on the tarmac, the driver holding a sign with Kit's name on it. They quickly loaded their bags into the vehicle and set off toward the outskirts of the city.

The drive to the farmhouse was uneventful, the urban landscape gradually giving way to rolling fields and dense woods.

The realtor, a cheerful woman named Isabelle, had been more than accommodating when Kit had arranged the visit, eager to show off the property to someone of his stature. To her, this was a potential sale, a chance to impress a wealthy client.

But for Kit, Zara, and Sofia, this was a clue finding tour. First, evidence of children being housed here, second, who was the ghost involved.

The SUV finally turned onto a gravel road, leading them to the abandoned farmhouse. The building was exactly as it had been described, old, weathered, and seemingly untouched by time. It sat in a clearing surrounded by trees, the perfect location for something, or someone, that wanted to remain hidden.

As they pulled up to the house, Kit was the first to step out, greeting Isabelle with his trademark charm. "Thank you for meeting us, Isabelle. From what I've seen driving up, this place has a lot of potential, don't you think?"

Isabelle beamed, clearly flattered by the attention. "Oh, absolutely, Mr. Thorne. It's a bit run-down, but with some work, it could be a wonderful retreat. Perfect for the kind of project you're planning."

Kit nodded thoughtfully, his gaze drifting over the property. "Yes, I can see that. But I'd like to know more about the land, the history of the area. Maybe you can walk me through it?"

"Of course!" Isabelle chirped, eager to please. "Let's start with the land. It's quite extensive, as you can see. Over there, we have…"

Kit listened intently, asking question after question, his tone polite but insistent. He wanted to keep Isabelle occupied for as long as possible, giving Zara and Sofia the time they needed to investigate the house thoroughly, so he discussed his plans to establish some type of farm or maybe a vineyard like what he had in Virginia. Isabelle just chatted away with possibilities.

Inside the farmhouse, Zara and Sofia wasted no time. The air was stale, heavy with the scent of decay and abandonment. Dust motes floated in the beams of sunlight that filtered through the dirty windows, casting an eerie glow on the faded wallpaper and cracked floorboards.

"We need to be thorough," Zara whispered, her voice barely above a breath. "There could be anything here."

Sofia nodded, already moving through the first room, her keen eyes scanning every corner, every crevice. She checked under the floorboards, behind old furniture, even inside the walls where the plaster had crumbled away. But so far, there was nothing, no sign of recent activity, no indication that the house had been used for anything other than sheltering dust and cobwebs. It appeared as no one had been here for a long time. Both women wondered how that had been managed.

Zara moved to the kitchen, her steps careful as she avoided the more unstable sections of the floor. The room was as dilapidated as the rest of the house, with broken cabinets and a rusted stove that looked like it hadn't been touched in decades. But there was something about the room that made her pause, a faint scuff mark on the floor, almost invisible beneath the grime.

She crouched down, examining the mark more closely. It wasn't much, but it was something, a sign that someone had been here recently, moving through the house with enough haste to leave a trace.

"Sofia," Zara called quietly, motioning for her to come over.

Sofia joined her, peering down at the scuff mark. "You think someone was here?"

Zara nodded. "Looks like it. But if they were moving fast, it might mean they didn't want to be here long. Let's keep looking."

They continued their search, moving from room to room, checking every possible hiding place. Then, in one of the back rooms, Sofia found it, a trapdoor, partially obscured by a moldy rug. She pulled the rug aside, revealing the wooden hatch beneath.

"Zara, over here," Sofia whispered urgently.

Zara joined her, and together they lifted the trapdoor, revealing a dark, narrow staircase that led down into the cellar below. The air that wafted up was cold and damp, carrying with it the unmistakable scent of earth and rot... and unwashed bodies.

"Let's go," Zara said, her voice steady.

They descended the stairs, their footsteps echoing in the confined space. The cellar was small and cramped, with low ceilings and dirt walls that made it feel more like a tomb than a storage space. There were a few old crates and barrels, but nothing that looked out of place, at least, not at first glance.

Sofia moved to the far wall, running her hand along the dirt, feeling for any signs of disturbance. Zara did the same on the opposite side, her fingers tracing the contours of the walls, searching for any hidden compartments or concealed doors.

But there was nothing, no fresh marks, no signs that the cellar had been used recently.

"It doesn't look like anyone's been down here for a while," Sofia said, her voice tinged with frustration. "But the smell."

Zara frowned, her mind racing. "Maybe, but that scuff mark upstairs... someone was definitely here. They could have cleared out quickly, but this cellar... it feels like it was used for something. Maybe to hide people, maybe to store something. We just don't know."

Sofia sighed, a mixture of disappointment and determination in her eyes. "Let's head back up. We'll take another look around the house, just to be sure."

They ascended the stairs, closing the trapdoor behind them and replacing the rug. As they made their way back through the house,

Zara couldn't shake the feeling that they were missing something important.

Meanwhile, outside, Kit had kept Isabelle engaged, asking about the history of the farmhouse, the surrounding land, and any potential hazards that might come with the property. He had already determined that the realtor knew little beyond what was on the listing, but he kept her talking anyway, ensuring that Zara and Sofia had enough time to conduct their search.

As he walked around the property with Isabelle, something caught Kit's eye, a small patch of black paint on a tree near the road. It was subtle, easily missed, but something about it stood out to him.

"Isabelle, what's that over there?" Kit asked, pointing to the tree.

Isabelle followed his gaze, her brow furrowing in confusion. "I'm not sure. I didn't notice it before. It's probably just some kids messing around, or maybe someone marking the property line."

Kit nodded, but he wasn't convinced. "Would you mind if I took a closer look?"

"Of course not," Isabelle replied, clearly eager to accommodate him.

Kit approached the tree, examining the black paint more closely. It wasn't a simple mark, it was a small square of paint stuck in the bark. He reached out, running his fingers over the paint, feeling its texture. It was fresh, some type of chip or something.

"This hasn't been here long," Kit murmured to himself, his mind racing with possibilities.

He carefully pulled out the small chip of the paint, placing it in a plastic bag he had brought with him. It wasn't much, but it was something that might lead them to whoever had been here before.

As he turned back to the house, Zara and Sofia emerged from the front door, their expressions a mix of frustration and determination.

"Anything?" Kit asked as he rejoined them.

"We found a trapdoor leading to a cellar," Zara reported. "But there's no sign that it's been used recently. Just some old crates and barrels, nothing suspicious. But we did find a scuff mark in the kitchen, like someone was moving quickly."

"And this," Kit added, holding up the bag with the paint sample. "I found it on a tree near the road. It's fresh, probably left in the last few days."

Zara and Sofia exchanged a glance, both understanding the significance of the find.

"There was a smell of unwashed bodies lingering. That would be one of the first to go if the house has stood empty for any length of time. As for the chip, it's not much," Sofia admitted, "but it's something. Whoever was here might have clipped the tree trying to get away quickly."

Kit nodded, his mind already turning to their next steps. "We'll have Aria or Calista analyze the paint, see if it matches anything in their databases. And I'll contact the local constable to see if they've had any reports of unusual activity in the area."

Just as Kit finished speaking, a police cruiser pulled up to the farmhouse, its lights off. A middle-aged constable stepped out, his expression wary as he approached the group.

"Good day. Hello, Isabelle" the constable greeted them in a thick Quebecois accent. "I'm Constable Dupuis. I was told there were potential buyers interested in this property?"

Kit extended his hand, offering a polite smile. "Yes, that's correct. We're just having a look around, considering our options."

Dupuis nodded, though his eyes were sharp as they swept over the three of them. "This place has been abandoned for years. Strange that people would be interested in it now."

Kit kept his smile in place, though he could sense the constable's suspicion. He noted the word, people. "We're considering it for a charitable project. A place to house underprivileged children. I understand it's in rough shape, but we've dealt with worse."

The constable's expression softened slightly at that, but he still seemed cautious. "There was an incident here not long ago. A man was found outside dead, shot in the head. Don't think he ever made it in the house. It's an open investigation, so I can't share many details, but... I'd advise you to be careful walking around out here. Hunters have been known to mistake people for wildlife."

Kit's heart skipped a beat at the mention of the shooting, and what sounded like a subtle threat, but he kept his voice calm. "Thank you for the warning, Constable. We'll take it into consideration."

Dupuis nodded, tipping his hat slightly before returning to his cruiser. As the constable drove away, Kit turned to Zara and Sofia, his expression grim.

"We need to move quickly," Kit said, his voice low. "There's more going on here than we thought. I'll have Calista look into the constable's computer system, see if she can find out more about that investigation."

Zara and Sofia nodded in agreement, their minds whirling with the information.

"We didn't find much here," Sofia said, "but we're not done yet. We'll find out what happened, Kit. We have to, for Charlie and those kids."

With that, they returned to the SUV, ready to head to Montreal. They had more questions than answers, but they knew they were on the right track. As they drove away from the farmhouse, Kit couldn't shake the feeling that they were getting closer to something that could finally give them the breakthrough they needed. Something was being hidden, the question was... what?

He was determined to see it through to the end, no matter what it took.

CHAPTER 14

Montreal buzzed with the hum of city life as Kit, Zara, Sofia traveled through its bustling streets. The cold winter air was sharp, biting at their faces as they made their way to one of the most exclusive areas of the city. The mission was clear, dig deeper into the night of the incident at the abandoned farmhouse, particularly to see if there had been any elitist gatherings where high-profile corporate figures might have convened. There are usually activities hidden in the background at these events.

Kit, ever the strategist, had his mind fixed on the objective. They had spent the previous evening poring over the information that Calista had sent from Virginia. She had uncovered details of a lavish party held the night Chase Holloway was killed, a gathering of some of the most influential corporate magnates from around the world. The guest list was exclusive, the details of the event tightly guarded, but Calista had managed to break through those barriers and obtain a list of attendees.

As they walked through Old Montreal, Zara kept a vigilant eye on their surroundings. She had a knack for reading people and situations, and today was no different. Sofia, too, was focused, though her thoughts drifted to the pain Charlie was enduring. She knew how close Charlie had been to Chase and how much his death had affected her. This mission wasn't just business, it had become personal.

"According to Calista's list, two of the attendees live here in Montreal," Kit said, breaking the silence as they approached a sleek, modern building. "One is an automobile purchaser, known for dealing in the rarest and most exclusive cars. The other is a shipping magnate. We'll start with the car dealer, he might be easier to engage in conversation."

Sofia nodded. "If he was at that party, he might have seen or heard something. It's a long shot, but we need to check every lead."

Zara adjusted the scarf around her neck, her eyes scanning the building they were about to enter. "Kit, remember, you're here as a wealthy businessman with a sudden interest in luxury cars. Keep it casual, let him do most of the talking."

Kit gave a small smile, his mind already shifting into the role he needed to play. "Don't worry. I've got this."

They entered the building, the lobby an opulent display of wealth and power. The receptionist, a sharp-looking woman with a poised demeanor, greeted them as they approached.

"Good afternoon," Kit said with a charming smile. "I'm here to see Mr. André Beaulieu. I believe he's expecting me."

The receptionist's eyes flicked to her computer screen as she confirmed the appointment. "Yes, Mr. Thorne. Mr. Beaulieu is expecting you. Please follow me."

Kit followed her through the lobby and into an elevator, Zara and Sofia staying behind to blend into the surroundings and maintain their cover. The elevator ascended smoothly, stopping at the top floor. The doors opened to reveal a spacious, tastefully decorated office. A tall man with graying hair and a tailored suit stood waiting.

"Mr. Thorne, welcome," André Beaulieu greeted Kit, extending a hand. "It's a pleasure to meet you."

Kit shook his hand firmly, his smile never wavering. "Thank you, Mr. Beaulieu. I appreciate you taking the time to meet with me on such short notice."

Beaulieu gestured for Kit to follow him to a seating area by the large windows that overlooked the city. "Please, call me André. And I must admit, I was intrigued by your sudden interest in our unique automobiles. We don't often get new clients with such enthusiasm."

Kit chuckled, playing the part. "Oh, it wasn't sudden. I've always had an eye for fine things, André. Recently, I've become fascinated with the world of luxury cars. I am in Montreal on business but taking time to see the sights with my assistants. I've been told you're the man to talk to if I'm looking for something truly special."

André's eyes gleamed with pride as he nodded. "Indeed. I have access to some of the most exclusive and rarest vehicles in the world. So tell me, Mr. Thorne, what exactly are you looking for?"

Kit paused for a moment, his earpiece crackling to life as Miguel's voice came through, providing him with the necessary details. "I'm looking for something unique, something that speaks to exclusivity. I've heard about a vintage Aston Martin that might be available. Perhaps you could tell me more about it?"

André's expression lit up, and Kit could see he was pleased with the direction of the conversation. "Ah, the Aston Martin. A beautiful piece of engineering, a true collector's item. But such treasures don't come cheaply or easily, Mr. Thorne. It requires connections, the right kind of influence."

Kit leaned forward, feigning interest. "That's precisely why I'm here, André. I'm willing to pay whatever it takes, but I'm also interested in the process, how one acquires such rare items."

André smiled, clearly enjoying the attention. "It's not just about money, Mr. Thorne. It's about knowing the right people, attending the right events, and being in the right place at the right time."

Kit's heart quickened slightly. He knew this was his opportunity to steer the conversation toward the party that Calista had uncovered. "Speaking of events," Kit said, casually leaning back in his chair, "I recently heard about a gathering of some of the most influential people in the world. I imagine you must have been there. It sounded like the kind of place where deals are made, and connections are built."

André's eyes flickered with recognition, but his expression remained neutral. "Ah, you must be referring to the soirée a few weeks ago. Yes, I was there. Quite an exclusive affair. Only the most influential attending."

Kit kept his tone light, though he could feel intense interest building inside of himself. "I can only imagine the kind of deals that were discussed that night. Did anything particularly interesting come up?"

André hesitated for a moment, his gaze narrowing slightly as he studied Kit. "It was a gathering of like-minded individuals, Mr. Thorne. Discussions were held, but nothing I would consider out of the ordinary. Of course, in our world, what's considered ordinary might be quite different from the norm."

Kit nodded, picking up on the subtle hint. "I understand. It must be fascinating to be part of such a select group, where the ordinary is anything but."

André's lips curved into a faint smile. "Indeed. But you didn't come here to talk about parties, Mr. Thorne. You came for cars, did you not?"

Kit's earpiece buzzed with Miguel's voice again, urging him to stay on track. "Of course, of course," Kit said smoothly. "But you know how it is, business and pleasure often intertwine. I'm just trying to get a sense of the landscape, the people, the connections."

André relaxed slightly, seemingly satisfied with Kit's explanation. "Well, Mr. Thorne, if you're truly interested in starting your collection, I might have just the vehicle for you. It's not the Aston Martin, but something even more exclusive. I can arrange a private viewing if you'd like."

Kit's mind raced. He hadn't come here to buy a car, but if this gave him an opportunity to learn more about André's connections and potentially link him to the incident at the farmhouse, it was worth pursuing. "I'd be very interested in that, André. When can we arrange it?"

"Tomorrow evening," André replied. "I'll have my assistant contact you with the details. And who knows, maybe you'll meet a few of my other clients, people who share your taste in exclusivity."

Kit smiled, though inside he was already planning his next move. "I look forward to it."

The meeting wrapped up quickly after that, with André promising to send the details of the private viewing by the end of the day. Kit thanked him again and made his way back to the lobby, where Zara and Sofia were waiting.

"How'd it go?" Zara asked as they stepped outside into the cold.

"Good," Kit replied, his mind still buzzing with the information he'd learned. "He confirmed he was at the party, but he didn't give much away. He did mention that tomorrow night he's hosting a private viewing of some exclusive cars. It might be an opportunity to meet others who were there."

Sofia frowned slightly. "It's a start, but we need more. If we can get inside his circle, we might find out who else was at the party and what they know about the farmhouse."

"Agreed," Kit said, his breath visible in the cold air. "We're running out of time, though. The trail is getting colder, and we still don't have solid leads on who was involved in Chase's death or if there were children there."

Zara's expression softened slightly as she looked at Kit. "Well, someone was there that needed a bath, several someones from the stench." She sighed. "We'll find them, Kit. It's just a matter of time. But we need to be careful. If they suspect anything, they could disappear or even us. I'm not ready to leave this world yet."

Kit nodded, appreciating her words. "Let's regroup back at the hotel. I'll contact Calista and Aria and update them on what we've found. We'll need Calista and her to dig deeper into André's connections."

As they made their way back to the SUV, Kit couldn't shake the feeling that they were on the right track to discovering the secret of the abandoned, maybe even one step closer to uncovering the secrets hidden behind the opulent façade André Beaulieu. With every step forward, the danger increased. He knew they were walking a fine line, one misstep away from disaster.

Back at the hotel, Kit immediately called Calista, relaying everything he'd learned during the meeting with André. Calista connected in Aria who was methodical and efficient, taking detailed notes and asking all the right questions.

"We'll start digging into André's connections," Aria said over the phone. Her voice was steady, but Kit could hear the underlying tension. "Calista has already started working on pulling up his financials, property records, and any communications that might link him to other individuals on that guest list. If he's involved in anything shady, we'll find it."

"Good," Kit replied, glancing at Zara and Sofia, who were quietly discussing their next steps. "We need to be ready for tomorrow night. I'll go to this private viewing and see what I can find out. But if things go sideways, I want to make sure we're prepared."

"Understood," Aria said. "I'll have Calista on standby, monitoring everything in real-time. We'll be in your ear the whole time, guiding you through it. Just remember, Kit, this guy could be dangerous, and more than likely, he's not the only one and he's not the guy running the show even though he appears to be. Keep your guard up."

"I will," Kit assured her. "Thanks, Calista, thanks, Aria."

After ending the call, Kit turned to Zara and Sofia, who had been listening intently. "Aria and Calista are digging into André's connections. We need to be ready for anything tomorrow night. This private viewing could be our best chance to get closer to the truth or getting us 'lost' in the wilderness."

Zara nodded, her face thoughtful. "I'll do some research on the other attendees. If we can identify anyone who might be connected to the farmhouse incident, we'll have leverage. We need to go in there knowing as much as possible."

"And I'll keep an eye on the local news," Sofia added. "If there's anything going on that could affect the situation, we need to know. The last thing we want is to walk into a trap."

Kit appreciated their thoroughness. He knew this mission was about more than just uncovering the truth, it was about avenging Chase and preventing further atrocities to the missing kids. The stakes were high, and there was no room for error.

The next day passed in a blur of preparation. Zara spent hours poring over the guest list and researching the backgrounds of anyone who might have connections to André or the farmhouse. Sofia monitored local news and social media for any signs of unrest or unusual activity in the area. Kit reviewed his role for the evening, going over every possible scenario in his mind.

By the time evening fell, the tension in the hotel room was high. Kit stood in front of the mirror, adjusting the collar of his tailored suit. He looked every bit the part of a wealthy businessman with a penchant for luxury, a role he was used to, but hated. Tonight, the stakes felt different. He could feel the weight of their actions causing tension in his neck and shoulders.

"Remember," Zara said, her tone serious as she handed Kit a minute earpiece. "You're not just there to buy a car. You're there to gather intel, to see who's involved and what they know. Stay calm, stay focused, and if anything feels off, get out of there."

Kit nodded, slipping the earpiece into place. "I'll be careful. You two stay close to the hotel. If anything happens, we'll regroup here." He chose to attend alone, one for the safety of Zara and Sofia, two, it might lead to quicker connections with the entertainment if he was there as a bachelor. Sometimes the help will talk not realizing what they are saying.

"Yes, boss," Sofia saluted and chuckled. "Just trying to calm you. Don't want you to explode before the party gets started. Good luck, Kit. We'll be in your ear every step of the way."

Kit gave them both a reassuring smile, though inside, his mind was already racing through the possibilities of what the night might bring. He left the hotel and made his way to the address André had provided for the private viewing.

The venue was a large, modern estate on the outskirts of Montreal, surrounded by high walls and guarded gates. As Kit arrived, he noticed the expensive cars lined up in the driveway, an indication of the wealth and exclusivity of the event. He handed the valet his keys, noting the security presence as he made his way inside.

The interior of the estate was opulent, with high ceilings, marble floors, and walls adorned with expensive looking art. The guests were dressed in designer clothing, their conversations a murmur of business deals, investments, and the latest trends in luxury.

Kit was immediately approached by André, who greeted him warmly. "Mr. Thorne! I'm glad you could make it." He snapped his fingers, and a server appeared. Kit took a glass. "Let me show you the cars we have on display tonight. I think you'll find them quite impressive."

Kit followed André through the estate, making polite conversation as they passed through rooms filled with rare and expensive vehicles. It was clear that André took pride in his collection, his voice animated as he described the history and uniqueness of each car.

But Kit's mind was focused on more than just the cars. As they moved through the crowd, he subtly scanned the room, noting the faces and interactions of the other guests. Many of them were familiar from the guest list Calista had provided, powerful men and women who operated in the boardrooms of the corporate world.

Miguel's voice crackled in Kit's ear, guiding him through the conversation. "Ask about the car's provenance, Kit. He might let something slip."

Kit nodded slightly, turning to André as they approached a sleek, black Aston Martin. "This is an incredible piece, André. Where did you find it?"

André smiled, clearly pleased with Kit's interest. "This one has quite the story, actually. It was part of a private collection in Europe, hidden away for decades. I acquired it through a contact at one of the more exclusive auctions. It wasn't easy, but for a car like this, it's worth the effort."

Kit listened carefully, picking up on the details. "I imagine you've had to make some interesting connections in your line of work. It must be fascinating to meet people from all over the world."

André chuckled, nodding in agreement. "Indeed, Mr. Thorne. It's a world of its own, where connections are everything. You'd be surprised at the lengths people will go to secure something unique, whether it's a car, a piece of art, or... other interests."

Kit's interest piqued. "Other interests? I'm intrigued."

André gave a knowing smile but didn't elaborate. "Let's just say that the world of luxury is full of unusual surprises. But tonight, we're here to appreciate these fine automobiles."

Kit nodded, playing along. He could tell that André was hinting at something deeper, something that connected to the darker aspects of the world of the exceptionally wealthy.

As the evening wore on, Kit continued to engage with the guests, each conversation a careful dance of questions and observations. He learned that many of the attendees had been at the party the night of Chase's death, though none were willing to discuss it in detail. The atmosphere was one of caution, as if everyone knew there was more beneath the surface but were unwilling to expose it.

Finally, as the event began to wind down, Kit found himself alone with André once more. "Thank you for inviting me tonight, André. It's been an enlightening experience."

André smiled, his demeanor relaxed. "The pleasure was mine, Mr. Thorne. I'm glad you enjoyed yourself. I hope Delilah wasn't too much of a bother."

Kit smiled, "She was a perfect companion. Quiet and unassuming. Thank you for sharing her with me."

Kit then hesitated for a moment and decided to take a final shot. "Before I go, André, I have to ask, how do you manage to keep everything so... discreet? Escorts, vintage wine that is very difficult to attain? In your line of work, I imagine there are risks involved."

André's expression didn't change, but there was a subtle shift in his eyes, something colder, more calculating. "Discretion is key in any business, Mr. Thorne. And it's something I take very seriously. But as long as you have the right people on your side, there's nothing to worry about."

Kit nodded, sensing the conversation had reached its limit. "Of course. I appreciate the insight, André. I look forward to working with you."

With that, Kit took his leave, making his way back to the car. As he drove back to the hotel, he replayed the evening's events in his mind, analyzing every word, every interaction. He had learned much, but there was still so much hidden beneath the surface.

When Kit returned to the hotel, Zara and Sofia were waiting for him in the suite. He recounted the evening in detail, sharing everything he had observed, and the subtle hints André had dropped.

"We're getting closer," Zara said thoughtfully. "André knows more than he's letting on. We just need to find the right leverage."

"And we will," Kit replied, his resolve firm. "We're not giving up until we find out who was responsible for Chase's death. We are done here at present, don't want to overstay our welcome. Andre will contact me soon, of that I'm sure. He wants to sell a car."

As the night deepened, the trio talked about what their next moves might be. They knew they were getting closer to the truth with every step, now they just had to find out what was being hidden.

CHAPTER 15

The private jet touched down gently on the familiar tarmac of Virginia, the wheels skimming the runway with barely a jolt. Kit leaned back in his seat, letting out a breath he hadn't realized he'd been holding. The return flight from Montreal had been quiet, each of them lost in their own thoughts. The investigation at the farmhouse had yielded frustratingly little, but the encounter with André Beaulieu had left them with a just enough information that they felt like they were closer to unraveling some of the mystery. The constable's error gave them hope there was information Calista or Aria could find in reports.

As they disembarked and made their way to the waiting SUV, Kit's mind was already turning over the possibilities. André Beaulieu, the charming, well-connected automobile dealer, had been a fascinating character, one who clearly knew something more than he was letting on. Kit couldn't shake the feeling that their encounter had been more than just a brush with high society, it had been a glimpse into the shadowy world they were trying to penetrate. It seemed to Kit that Andre might be the front man and potential recruiter for whoever was funding him.

The drive to Kit's vineyard was short, and by the time they arrived, the sun was setting, casting the rolling hills in a golden glow. The sprawling estate, usually a place of peace and tranquility, now felt like a fortress preparing for a siege. Kit's mind was restless, eager to dive into whatever information Calista and Aria had managed to dig up on André.

As they walked into the main house, the air was filled with the scent of freshly brewed coffee and something sweet baking in the oven, a small comfort that had a calming effect on all three of them. Calista was waiting for them in the living room, her laptop open and several documents spread out on the coffee table.

"Welcome back," she greeted them, her tone professional but relieved. "Aria sent her information, and I've got something you'll want to see."

Kit nodded and replied with a snarky remark. "Good to see you too, Calista. We're fine." She made a face, he smiled. "What do you have for us?"

Calista motioned for them to sit, her fingers tapping rapidly on the keyboard as she brought up the dossier Aria had compiled. The screen filled with images, documents, and various reports, each one adding another layer to the picture being painted.

"André Beaulieu," Calista began, her tone measured as she zoomed through the data. "Born in Quebec, raised in a wealthy family with strong ties to the automotive industry. He's made a name for himself as one of the most successful and discreet dealers of luxury and rare automobiles in the world. His client list reads like a who's who of the global elite, CEOs, royalty, high-ranking officials. Mommy and Daddy would not fund his business after his first failure, but he's getting money from someone and keeping his doors open,"

Kit leaned forward, his interest piqued. "Sounds like the perfect cover for someone who wants to operate in the shadows."

Calista nodded. "Exactly. But it gets more interesting. After the New York trafficking sting, Beaulieu disappeared for about two months. No public appearances, no business dealings, nothing. Then, suddenly, he reappeared in Montreal, where he's been ever since."

Sofia, who had been listening intently, frowned slightly. "Two months... That's enough time to lay low, reassess, and move operations somewhere less conspicuous."

"Precisely," Calista agreed. "During my research, I found that several of the individuals arrested in the trafficking ring in New York sting were also clients of Beaulieu. There's no direct evidence linking him to the trafficking itself, but the connections are there, too many to ignore."

Kit exchanged a glance with Zara, who had remained silent but watchful. "What kind of connections?"

Calista pulled up a series of documents, highlighting specific names. "Take a look at these transaction records. They're all encrypted, but I managed to decrypt a few. Payments made from shell companies linked to known traffickers, large sums, too large for just car purchases. And they're all routed through accounts that Beaulieu had access to. These two names keep popping up Alexandre Dubois and Gero Meyer. Both inherited small corporations, but they have since become extremely wealthy in the import/export business."

Kit's eyes narrowed as he absorbed the information. "So, we're looking at a guy who deals in more than just cars. He's facilitating transactions, possibly laundering money, and using his business as a front. And those two could be transporting automobiles but add trafficked victims and the income increases dramatically."

"That's what it looks like," Calista confirmed. "And there's more. Some of the properties he owns in Canada and Europe have been flagged in reports of suspicious activity, high turnover of occupants, increased security measures, but no official record of tenants."

"Safehouses," Zara said quietly, her voice laced with certainty. "He's providing stash houses for traffickers and their operations."

Kit's pulse quickened. This was the break they'd been searching for, a possible link that could tie together the loose ends they'd been chasing. André Beaulieu wasn't just a high-end car dealer, he was a key player in the nearly invisible trafficking network that had been eluding them.

"What about the farmhouse?" Kit asked, his mind racing. "Was there anything connecting him to that?"

Calista shook her head. "Nothing concrete, but I did find a few references to properties he's been trying to offload recently. The farmhouse could have been one of them, but it's hard to say without more data. The trail's gone cold there, at least for now."

Kit leaned back in his chair, his thoughts a whirlwind of possibilities and strategies. André Beaulieu had slipped under their radar, his legitimate business dealings masking his involvement in something far more sinister. But now that they had a lead, Kit knew they had to follow it and act quickly and decisively.

"We've got him," Kit said, his voice laced with determination. "Or at least, we've got a piece of him. If he's as involved as we think, he'll have his fingers in a lot of pies, trafficking, money laundering, maybe even more. We need to follow the money, track his movements, and see where it leads."

Sofia nodded in agreement. "We need to be careful. If he senses we're onto him, he could shut everything down and disappear again."

"That's why we need to move fast," Kit replied. "But we also need to be smart. We can't tip our hand too early."

Zara, who had been quiet until now, spoke up, her voice thoughtful. "André's the type who thrives on connections. He's built a network of wealthy and powerful people who trust him to be discreet. If we can disrupt that trust, make him feel the pressure, he might slip up."

Kit nodded, his mind already formulating a plan. "Agreed. We'll start by tracking his finances more closely. Calista, I want you to dig deeper into those accounts, find out where the money's coming from and where it's going. Get Aria to see if she can find any links between his properties and known trafficking routes. We'll need to look into his clients, especially those who were involved in the New York sting. See if there are any organizations still operating, they might be the key to connecting the dots."

Calista, Sofia, and Zara all nodded, their expressions filled with determination. This was what they had been waiting for, a real lead, a chance to catch the bad guys.

Kit took a deep breath, letting the enormity of the situation settle over him. They were close to discovering the web that was ensnaring so many innocent lives. He knew that the closer they got, the more dangerous the game would become.

André Beaulieu was a man who operated in the shadows, who used his wealth and influence to hide his true activities. But now, Kit and his team had a spotlight on him, and they were determined to expose everything he was hiding or covering.

"We need to be prepared for anything," Kit said, his voice firm. "André's not just going to sit back and let us take him down. He's going to fight, and he's going to use everything he has to protect himself. Unfortunately, we don't know who his bosses are yet. That could get someone hurt."

"We'll make sure to be ready," Calista replied. "This isn't the first time we've gone up against someone like him, but it might be the last time he goes up against someone like us."

Kit allowed himself a small smile, the fire of determination burning bright in his chest. "Let's get to work," Kit said, standing up and looking around at his team. "Let Aria know what info we have, she's good at finding things others cannot. We've got a trafficking ring to dismantle." He paused, then asked, "How is Charlie holding up?"

Calista answered, "As well as can be expected. I don't think she's in denial or mourning for that matter, sounds like she's pissed as hell and out for blood. Aria says she's become a jet setter and travels back and forth between NYC and Atlanta working her clubs."

This caught Kit off guard for a moment. He realized that people dealt with tragedy in different ways, but something niggled in his brain that Charlie might be doing more. He would have to figure out how to catch her and keep her out of the trouble he knew she was looking for.

"Book me a flight to Atlanta. I've got some business to take care of. Keep me posted on anything you find. We need to get to them before Charlie does."

The team dispersed, each of them diving into their respective tasks with renewed energy. Kit watched them go, feeling a sense of pride and confidence in the people he had surrounded himself with. They were the best, and together with Charlie's team, he felt they were going to fifure things out quickly.

As Kit turned to leave the room, his phone buzzed with a new message. He glanced at the screen and saw a text from an unknown number.

"You're playing a dangerous game, Thorne. Walk away while you still can."

Kit's jaw tightened as he read the message, his mind racing with possibilities. It was a warning, one he hadn't expected, but that didn't make it any less chilling.

But Kit wasn't one to back down. He deleted the message, pocketed his phone, and walked out of the room, his resolve stronger than ever.

Whoever sent the message had made a mistake by threatening him. Now, it was only a matter of time before Kit and his team found them and brought them to their knees. That is if Charlie didn't find them first. He knew that's what she was doing. Alone and without help.

The game had just begun, and Kit Thorne was ready to play.

——

The evening sun cast long shadows across the rolling hills of Kit Thorne's vineyard, the golden light reflecting off the rows of grapevines that stretched out like green waves toward the horizon. The serenity of the setting stood in complete contrast to the fire that had been simmering for the past few days. Kit and Jack once again sat on the wide front porch of Kit's sprawling estate, the sound of distant birdsong mingling with the gentle rustle of leaves in the evening breeze.

Kit swirled the amber liquid in his glass, his gaze fixed on the landscape before him but his mind miles away, back in Montreal and on Charlie. The investigation had yielded frustratingly little, and that failure hung heavily on his shoulders. His team was inside the house, some researching, others trying to relax after days of intense focus. But Kit found no solace in the calm of the vineyard, no peace in the beauty of the setting sun. His thoughts were a maelstrom of frustration, anger, and something darker, something he wasn't ready to voice just yet.

Jack sat beside him, his posture relaxed but his eyes sharp, watching Kit closely. The two men had shared countless moments like this over the years, moments of quiet reflection and hard conversations. But tonight, there was a different energy between them, something more charged, more urgent.

"I can see it's eating at you," Jack said finally, breaking the silence. His voice was deep and gravelly, carrying the weight of years and hard-won wisdom. "You're thinking about Montreal and Charlie, aren't you?"

Kit took a long sip of his whiskey, letting the burn of the alcohol ground him for a moment. "Yeah," he admitted, his voice low. "We went there hoping to find something, anything, that could give us a real lead. But all we came away with was more questions. The kids are still disappearing, and we're no closer to stopping it. We at least have acknowledgement that this Chase guy was killed. The lie behind why is now the big question."

Jack nodded slowly, understanding the frustration that gnawed at Kit. "We've been here before, Kit. Dead ends, false leads, it's part of the job. But I know that look in your eye. You've got something on your mind, something you're not saying."

Kit was silent for a long moment, staring into the distance as if the answer he sought might be hidden somewhere in the rolling hills. When he finally spoke, his voice was filled with a bitterness he rarely let show. "We didn't find what we were looking for, Jack. But what we did find… it's not enough. Not nearly enough. A scrap. And meanwhile, kids are still being taken, still being lost to the darkness. Every minute that passes, another one could be gone. We're running out of time. And Charlie's up to something. We haven't known these people that long, but by the look in her eyes when she accepted that her man had been killed, she's going to do something unexpected and rash. I'm going to see her."

Jack watched him, his expression unreadable. "So, what are you thinking?"

Kit leaned back in his chair, his gaze dropping to the glass in his hand. He swirled the whiskey again, the amber liquid catching the last rays of sunlight. He knew what he had to say, but the words were heavy, and they stuck in his throat. Finally, he forced them out. "After I figure this Charlie thing out, I'm going to have to go dark."

The statement hung in the air between them, heavy with implications.

Jack didn't respond immediately. He took a sip of his own whiskey, considering Kit's words carefully. Going dark wasn't something to be taken lightly. It meant disappearing from the grid, cutting ties with the safety nets, and operating entirely in the shadows. It was dangerous, isolating, and it often meant crossing lines that could never be uncrossed.

"You know what that means," Jack said finally, his voice quiet but firm. "Once you go down that road, there's no coming back. Not really. You're talking about walking into the lion's den with nothing but your wits and your fists."

Kit nodded, the tension in his shoulders visibly easing now that he had spoken the words aloud. "I know. But I don't see another way, Jack. We've been hitting brick walls, and every second we waste, more kids are being taken. Whoever's behind this... they're good. They're too good. And if we keep playing by the rules, we're going to lose. I can't let that happen."

Jack sighed, leaning back in his chair as he gazed out over the vineyard. He had known Kit long enough to understand his determination, his need to protect the vulnerable at any cost. He felt that Charlie was vulnerable. But this was different. Kit was contemplating something that could change him, something that could take him to a place he might not return from.

"You're talking about going off the radar, Kit," Jack said, his tone more somber now. "No backup, no safety net. Just you against them. You've got a team here, people who have your back. Don't shut them out."

"I'm not shutting them out," Kit replied, frustration creeping into his voice. "But there are some things they can't be involved in, things I don't want them involved in. If I go dark, it's on me. It has to be that way."

Jack studied Kit for a long moment, his friend's words not setting well with him. "And what about Charlie? You know she's not going to just sit by while you disappear into the shadows. She's got skin in this game too. If she figures out what you've done, she'll probably be right behind you. She's pretty wealthy in her own rights."

Kit's expression tightened at the mention of Charlie. He would have to tell her what he was planning, and he knew she wouldn't take it well. But this was something he needed to do, something he felt compelled to handle on his own. "I'll tell her if it feels right to do so," Kit said quietly. "But this isn't about her. You know that and I think she will too. It's about the kids, Jack. It's about stopping the people who are doing this. And if I have to go to some dark places to get it done, then that's what I'll do."

Jack shook his head slowly, his heart heavy with the knowledge of what Kit was about to undertake. "You're a good man, Kit. But you're also human. And going dark... it can change you. It can make you do things you never thought you were capable of. Are you ready for that?"

Kit met Jack's gaze, his eyes hard and unyielding. "I don't have a choice. I've made my decision."

Jack could see that there was no talking Kit out of it. The man had a look in his eyes that Jack had seen only a few times before, a cold, steely resolve that bordered on obsession. It was the look of someone who was willing to sacrifice everything, including his own soul, to achieve his goal.

"Then you know I'll back you, whatever happens," Jack said, his voice steady despite the turmoil he felt in his gut. "But you need to be careful, Kit. The darkness has a way of swallowing you whole. Don't lose yourself in it."

Kit nodded, grateful for Jack's support, even if it came with a warning. "I won't. But I need to do this, Jack. For the kids. For this Chase person. For everyone who's counting on us."

Jack raised his glass, a solemn toast to the difficult road ahead. "Then here's to the fight, my friend. May you find the light, even in the darkest places."

Kit clinked his glass against Jack's, the sound echoing in the stillness of the evening. He took a long drink, the whiskey burning its way down his throat, solidifying his plan. The decision was made, the path set. There was no turning back now.

As the sun dipped below the horizon, casting the vineyard in shadows, Kit felt the pressure of what lay ahead smothering him. He was about to step into a world where the rules didn't apply, where survival meant being willing to do whatever it took. And as much as it unsettled him, he knew it was the only way to end the nightmare that had taken so many innocent lives.

The night would be long, the road treacherous, but Kit was ready. He would go dark, delve into the shadows, and face the monsters lurking there. Because if he didn't, who would?

Jack finished his drink, setting the empty glass down on the table beside him. "Whatever you need, Kit, I'm here. Just don't try to carry the whole world on your shoulders. If it gets to be too much, call me. I'll get you out."

Kit offered a faint smile, though it didn't reach his eyes. "I'll try not to. And I will. But I can't make any promises."

Jack nodded, understanding the burden that Kit was about to take on. He knew that his friend would walk through fire if it meant saving even one child. But he also knew that the fire could leave scars that might never heal.

The two men sat in silence for a while longer, the cool night air wrapping around them. There was nothing more to say, no words that could ease the tension or lighten the load. Kit's mind was already in the shadows, plotting his next move, preparing for the battles to come.

Finally, Kit stood, the decision now firmly rooted in his heart. "I'm going to get some rest," he said, though he knew sleep would be elusive. "Tomorrow, I'll start making the arrangements. No one outside of me and you are to know about this. I'll handle it all."

Jack remained seated, watching as Kit turned to leave. "Goodnight, Kit. And remember, no matter how dark it gets, there's always a way back to the light."

Kit paused at the door, his back to Jack. "I'll keep that in mind."

With that, Kit stepped inside, leaving Jack alone on the porch. The vineyard, usually a place of peace and solace, now felt heavy with the darkness that Kit was about to embrace.

As the stars began to twinkle in the night sky, Jack closed his eyes, offering a silent prayer for his friend. The journey ahead was going to be heart wrenching for everyone involved, thinking their boss and friend had turned. He hoped they all knew Kit better.

CHAPTER 16

The private jet hummed softly as it cut through the night sky, heading from New York to Atlanta. Charlie Donovan sat in one of the plush leather seats, staring out at the dark clouds beyond the window. She had made the purchase soon after the sting was done at her ranch, needing to be able to come and go when she wanted instead of being at the mercy of booking a flight. The steady rhythm of travel had become her only solace since Chase's death. Flying between her clubs in New York and Atlanta was the only way she could manage to keep going, to keep her mind occupied and her heart from breaking into pieces she couldn't put back together.

Chase's death had left a void inside her, a deep ache that nothing seemed to soothe. Her first true love and now he was gone. She had thrown herself into her work with a relentless drive, promising the elder Mr. Holloway that she would find the killers and bring them to justice. But despite all her efforts, the search had yielded nothing. Every lead had dried up, every potential clue had turned to dust in her hands.

The constable in Montreal, the one who had shared information with Kit, was withholding something, she was sure of it. But no matter how hard she pushed, no one had been able to uncover what it was. It hadn't been in the incident report Aria had downloaded, and the frustration of hitting yet another wall was wearing on Charlie's patience.

As the plane descended toward Atlanta, Charlie leaned back in her seat, closing her eyes and rubbing her temples. She could feel exhaustion from her head to her toes, the stress of the past few weeks catching up with her. But there was no time for rest. She had promised Mr. Holloway that she would find those responsible for Chase's death, and she intended to keep that promise.

The plane touched down smoothly, and within minutes, Charlie was in the back of a black sedan, heading toward Pop's Gentleman's Club. It was late by most people's standards, but clubs were just ramping up. The city lights blurred past her as the driver navigated the familiar streets. Pop's had always been a place of refuge for her, a place where she could take control, assert her power, and remind herself that she was still in charge, still capable of making things happen.

But tonight, as she dropped off in front of the club, the usual sense of empowerment was shaded with something darker, a frustration that chewed at her insides, making her restless. She stepped out of the car, her stilettos clicking against the pavement, and made her way toward the entrance.

As she approached, something in the shadows caught her eye. A huge figure stood just beyond the glow of the streetlights, partially hidden in the darkness. A rush of fear shot through her, a primal instinct she hadn't felt in a long time. Her hand went instinctively to the small knife she always carried in her bag, but then the figure stepped forward, and relief washed over her.

"Kit," she breathed, her voice filled with surprise and something close to gratitude.

Kit stepped out of the shadows, his tall, muscular frame unmistakable even in the dim light. He offered her a small, reassuring smile, though his eyes were filled with concern. "Charlie."

She relaxed slightly, though her heart was still pounding. "What are you doing here?"

"I was in the area," Kit replied, his tone casual. "Thought I'd check in on you."

Charlie studied him for a moment, her mind racing with the implications of his presence. Kit was the last person she had expected to see tonight, but somehow, his appearance didn't feel like a coincidence. She knew Kit was not that type of person. He was here on a mission.

Instead of heading into Pop's, Charlie gestured toward a small café around the corner. "Let's grab a coffee."

Kit nodded, falling into step beside her as they made their way to the café. The place was quiet, a cozy spot with dim lighting and only a few patrons scattered at the tables. Charlie chose a corner booth where she could keep an eye on the door and the street outside, an old habit she never quite broke after Gabriel had her abducted, even when she thought she was in relatively safe surroundings.

They ordered their drinks, black coffee for Kit, a cappuccino for Charlie, and settled into the booth. For a moment, neither of them spoke, the silence between them filled with unspoken thoughts and lingering questions.

Kit broke the silence first, his voice gentle but probing. "How are you holding up?"

Charlie took a sip of her cappuccino, the warmth of the drink doing little to ease the cold knot in her stomach. "I'm managing," she replied, her tone carefully controlled. She wasn't ready to open up about the turmoil wreaking havoc inside her, not even to Kit.

Kit nodded, understanding her need for distance but unwilling to let the conversation slip into superficialities. "I've been keeping tabs on the situation in Montreal. We're still looking into that constable. I'm convinced he knows more than he's letting on."

Charlie sighed, setting her cup down. "I know. But every time I think we're getting close, something blocks us. It's like chasing shadows."

There was a moment of silence, then Kit leaned back in his seat, shifting the conversation away from the melancholy that hung between them. "So, what's going on with the clubs? You've been expanding, right?"

Charlie was grateful for the change in topic, even if it was just a temporary reprieve. "Yeah, I've been pushing hard. We're turning Pop's into the premier club in the city, and I've got plans for the others too. Burlesque, strip clubs, they're not just entertainment. They're an art form. I want to make them top-notch, something people talk about for years."

Kit smiled, sensing the passion in her voice. "I've got no doubt you'll make that happen. You seem to have a way of turning things to gold from what I've been told."

Charlie couldn't help but return the smile, a hint of sadness showing. "It's the only thing that makes sense right now. The only thing I can control."

Kit took a sip of his coffee, his eyes never leaving hers. "You know, you don't have to do this alone. You've got people who care about you, people who want to help."

Charlie's smile faded, replaced by a look of weariness. "I know. But this... what happened to Chase... I need to see it through. I promised Mr. Holloway, and I promised myself. I have to find who did this. It was an effing execution."

Kit nodded, understanding the depth of her desire. "It was. And you will. But don't lose yourself in the process, Charlie. Don't let this take everything from you."

She looked away, her gaze drifting to the street outside. "It already has," she whispered, her voice barely audible. "We hadn't known each other long, but there was something between us that just clicked. I'm not saying we were soul mates, but some days, it sure felt like it. We never got to go the distance."

Kit reached across the table, gently placing his hand over hers. "Believe me when I say I understand. I lost mine when I was much younger, and it tore my heart in two. I think I just stopped looking at that point. Let's make sure it doesn't take any more from you."

Charlie looked back at him, her eyes filled with a mixture of gratitude and sorrow. She hadn't realized how much she needed someone to say that, how much she needed someone to remind her that she wasn't alone in this fight.

For a while, they sat in comfortable silence, the moroseness of the conversation lifting slightly as they sipped their drinks. The café was warm, a small haven of normalcy in the middle of the chaos of their lives.

Finally, Kit spoke again, steering the conversation toward a lighter topic. "I've been working on a few corporate takeovers recently. Some defunct companies that still have potential. Rebranding them, giving them a new lease on life. It's been... interesting."

Charlie arched an eyebrow, intrigued. "I've heard you've always had a knack for that. Turning something broken into something valuable."

Kit chuckled, a rare sound that softened the tension between them. "It's all about seeing the potential, the possibilities. Just like with your clubs. You take something raw, something people overlook, and you turn it into a masterpiece."

Charlie smiled, a genuine one this time, and the heaviness in her chest eased just a little. "Maybe we're more alike than we think."

"Maybe," Kit agreed, his voice warm with understanding. "We've both got our battles, our ways of dealing with the world. But it's good to know we've got each other's backs."

Charlie nodded, the connection between them stronger than it had been in a long time. "Yeah, it is."

They spent the next hour talking about their businesses, the new safehouses, their plans for the future. The conversation was light, easy, a welcome distraction from the troubles of the world suffocating them both. Charlie found herself laughing at one of

Kit's stories, a sound she hadn't heard from herself in what felt like an eternity.

As the night wore on, the café began to empty out, leaving just a few stragglers at the tables. Charlie glanced at the clock on the wall, realizing how late it had gotten.

"I should probably get back," she said, though she didn't really want to leave the comfort of their conversation.

Kit nodded, understanding. "Me too. But I'm glad we did this. It was... good."

"Yeah," Charlie agreed, standing up and grabbing her coat. "It was."

They walked out of the café together, the cool night air sending shivers through their warm bodies.. The streets were quiet, the city settling into the late hours.

Kit walked her back to Pop's, and as they reached it, he turned to her, his expression serious once more. "Charlie, if you ever need anything at all, you know you can call me, right?"

Charlie nodded, feeling the sincerity in his words. "I know, Kit. And... thank you. For everything."

He smiled, a small, reassuring smile that made her feel just a little bit stronger. "Anytime." He paused. "Hey, I'll be in town for a while, let's have dinner somewhere."

Charlie agreed and told him about her favorite barbecue place, giving him the address and promising to meet him for dinner the next day before she came to the club. He smiled at her acceptance.

With that, they said their goodbyes, and Charlie watched as Kit walked to his car, the night swallowing him up as he disappeared into the shadows.

As she entered Pop's, Charlie felt revived. She would find Chase's killers. She would fulfill her promise to Mr. Holloway. And when the time came, she would make sure that those responsible would pay.

But for now, she allowed herself to focus on the present, on the small victories, and on the connection she had felt with Kit. The fight was far from over, but tonight, for the first time in a long time, Charlie felt like she might just be able to win. The catfight she could hear from the dressing room assured her that life had returned to normal... well, almost normal.

CHAPTER 17

The expensive gold toned SUV pulled up in front of a warehouse on the outskirts of Montreal. The building blended in with the other industrial structures that dotted the area, but to those in the know, it was far from ordinary. This was where André Beaulieu conducted his less-than-legitimate business dealings, a place where secrets were kept, and deals were made away from prying eyes.

As the SUV came to a stop, the driver stepped out and opened the back door. Alexandre and Gero emerged, their imposing figures immediately commanding attention. Both men were, as usual, dressed in impeccably tailored suits that did little to soften their ruthless demeanors. Behind them, their bodyguards, a pair of hulking men with cold, steely eyes, stood watchful and ready.

The warehouse doors opened to reveal André Beaulieu, standing nervously just inside. He was a man known for his connections, for the ability to procure anything for anyone, but in the presence of Alexandre and Gero, André felt a shiver of fear. He knew what these men were capable of, knew the price of failure when dealing with them.

"André," Alexandre greeted him with a cold smile that didn't reach his eyes. "It's been a while."

"Too long," Gero added, his voice smooth but with an edge that suggested impatience.

André swallowed hard, stepping back to allow them to enter. "Gentlemen, welcome back to Montreal. I trust your journey was uneventful?"

"Let's not waste time with pleasantries," Alexandre said, brushing past him. "We have business to discuss."

André nodded quickly, leading them deeper into the warehouse. The interior was a maze of crates and containers, all meticulously organized but giving off the impression of controlled chaos. They reached a small office at the back, where André gestured for the men to sit. Alexandre and Gero took their seats, their bodyguards standing just outside the door, ever vigilant.

André moved behind his desk, trying to steady his nerves. He knew this meeting was crucial, that his life could very well depend on what happened in the next few minutes.

"You wanted to discuss the import/export business first?" André began, his voice calm despite the tension in the room.

Alexandre waved a hand dismissively. "We'll get to that. First, we want to know about the farmhouse."

Gero's eyes narrowed as he leaned forward slightly, his presence radiating menace. "We lost a lot of money on that little fiasco, André. The kids vanished, the guards were killed, and no one seems to know what the hell happened. We're here to get answers."

André felt his stomach twist, but he forced himself to remain composed. "I understand your frustration, and I assure you, I've been working to resolve the situation. The kids were taken by a small-time trafficker, someone trying to make a name for himself by cutting into our business. He thought he could move in on our territory without repercussions."

"And?" Alexandre prompted, his tone icy.

"And he's been dealt with," André continued, his voice steadier now. "Efficiently. He won't be causing any more problems. The kids were recovered, and they're currently being prepped for shipment. Everything is back on track."

Gero exchanged a glance with Alexandre, both men considering André's words. They were used to dealing with men who would say anything to save their own skin, but they also knew that André had been reliable in the past. Still, trust was not a commodity they gave easily.

"You're sure?" Gero asked, his voice low and dangerous. "Because if we find out you're lying…"

"I'm not lying," André interjected quickly. "I've handled everything. The constable in the area was paid off, the incident report was altered to remove any mention of the... unpleasantness. As far as anyone knows, it was a hunting accident gone wrong. No one is looking for the kids, and no one is the wiser."

Alexandre leaned back in his chair, his gaze piercing. "And the merchandise?"

"The merchandise will be ready for transport by the end of the week," André replied, trying to project confidence. "I've taken every precaution to ensure there won't be any more issues."

Gero nodded slowly, though his expression remained skeptical. "And what about the new clients you mentioned?"

This was the part André had been dreading, the part where he had to tread carefully. He had information, yes, but how he presented it could determine whether he walked out of this meeting alive.

"I've come across someone who might be of interest," André said carefully. "A man by the name of Kendrick Thorne. He's wealthy, well-connected, and has recently been asking questions, discreetly, of course, about certain... opportunities in our line of work."

"Kendrick Thorne?" Alexandre repeated, frowning. "The corporate mogul?"

"The very same," André confirmed, sliding a file across the desk toward them. "I've done my homework, vetted him thoroughly, and from what I've gathered, he's clean. No connections to law enforcement, no red flags. Just a man looking to expand his business endeavors."

Gero picked up the file, flipping through the contents. Inside were reports, background checks, and photographs, all meticulously compiled by André's network of informants. "And what makes you think he's legitimate? That he's not just some plant looking to bring us down?"

André held his breath for a moment before answering. "I've had him watched closely. He's careful, but not overly so. He's made inquiries through intermediaries, never directly, but he's shown a clear interest in our operations. From what I can tell, he's looking for a way in, a way to diversify his portfolio, so to speak."

Alexandre took the file from Gero, scanning the information with a practiced eye. "If he's as interested as you say, we should meet him. Face to face."

André nodded, though inside, he was far from calm. "I can arrange that. I'll set up a meeting where you can feel him out, see if he's worth bringing into the fold."

"And if he's not?" Gero asked, his tone leaving no doubt as to what he was implying.

"If he's not," André said, choosing his words carefully, "then we'll deal with him accordingly."

Alexandre and Gero exchanged another glance, a silent conversation passing between them. Finally, Alexandre set the file down and looked directly at André.

"Set up the meeting," he said, his voice flat. "Soon. We're ready to get back to business, and we don't have time for games. Better yet, set up one of your famous car shows, invited the prime list only. We'll be able to ascertain if he is worthy by listening to his conversations. Make sure the place is wired from the inside out."

André nodded, relief flooding through him even as the tension remained. "I'll make the arrangements. You'll hear from me within the next few days."

Gero leaned back, his eyes still locked on André. "André, you've always been a valuable asset to us. Don't make us regret trusting you."

"I won't," André assured them, though he knew the truth was more complicated than that. "I know what's at stake."

The room fell into silence, the gist of the conversation hanging in the air. Finally, Alexandre stood, signaling that the meeting was over. Gero followed suit, and together they left the office, their bodyguards falling into step behind them.

As the warehouse doors closed behind them, André let out a shaky breath realizing he'd make the cut once again. His hands trembled slightly as he reached for the glass of water on his desk, gulping it down in a desperate attempt to steady himself.

He had survived the meeting, but only just. Alexandre and Gero were dangerous men who wouldn't hesitate to eliminate anyone who posed a threat to their operations. André knew he had played his cards right this time, but the game was far from over.

He had bought himself some time, but now he had to deliver. The meeting with Kendrick Thorne had to happen, and it had to go smoothly. Any misstep, any sign of weakness, and it could all come crashing down.

André sat back in his chair, the adrenaline still pumping through his veins. He had come close to the edge tonight, but he had managed to pull himself back. Now, he had to focus on the next move, getting Kit to another car auction, making sure everything was in place.

He couldn't afford to fail. Not when the stakes were this high.

As he picked up the phone to make the necessary calls, André couldn't shake the feeling that he was walking a tightrope, one misstep away from a deadly fall. But he had been in this business long enough to know that fear was part of the job. It was what kept him sharp, what kept him alive.

André dialed a number, his mind already working through the logistics of what needed to happen next. He had upped the anty by suggesting a new member for their circle.

His call was answered by Liesle, his assistant, and he issued the orders. His next call was to his car person, fill the showroom with the most exclusive cars he could find, in one week's time.

CHAPTER 18

The sun had long set over the vineyard, leaving Kit's Virginia estate bathed in the cool, tranquil darkness of the night. Inside the spacious study, Kit sat at his desk, his face illuminated by the soft glow of the laptop screen before him. Across the room, Jack leaned against a bookshelf, his arms crossed as he waited for the call to begin.

The tension Kit felt was causing his head to ache, a reflection of the seriousness of the discussion that was about to take place. Kit had been working non-stop, piecing together information about the shadowy trafficking ring that had been eluding them for far too long. Hopefully tonight, they were finally going to bring all the pieces together, to see if they could connect the dots and take a step closer to bringing these monsters down.

The screen flickered to life, and Aria's face appeared, her expression focused and intense. Charlie's image soon followed, her eyes sharp and focused. Kit glanced at Jack, who gave a subtle nod, signaling that they were ready.

"Good evening, everyone," Kit began, his voice steady. "Thank you for making the time. I know we've all been working tirelessly on this incident, and I feel we're getting closer to something big. Aria, you've been digging deep, why don't you start by filling us in on what you've found?"

Aria nodded, her gaze serious as she began to speak. "We've been tracking the movements and activities of several key individuals who we believe are at the top of this trafficking network. Alexandre DuBois and Gero Meyer are the primary suspects, they're well-known importer/exporters with a long history of shady dealings, mostly working abroad. Recently, however, they've been making moves into the US and Canada, likely to expand their operations."

Charlie leaned forward slightly, her face illuminated by the dim light of her own screen as Aria continued. "André Beaulieu is another piece of the puzzle. He's heavily involved in the exotic and exclusive car business, and on the surface, his connection to Alexandre and Gero seems to be through exporting these cars to foreign countries. But I believe there's more to it than that."

Kit's eyes narrowed as he absorbed the information. "Anything else, Aria?"

Aria hesitated for just a moment, her eyes flickering with something unreadable before she continued. "Kit, your dossier, the one available to the public, was uploaded by Andre just before a meeting took place between him, Alexandre, and Gero. I wasn't able to pinpoint the exact location of their meeting beforehand, so I couldn't intercept any communications. But the timing of the dossier upload and the meeting is too close to be a coincidence."

Kit's face showed a flash of amazement. "You got all of that? Aria, Charlie is right, you're a force. That's more than we've been able to gather in weeks."

Aria offered a small, modest smile. "I had some help, but yes, we've been able to piece together a lot. The problem is, we still don't know exactly what was discussed in that meeting. They're very careful, using secure channels that even I have trouble accessing. Whatever they talked about, it's something they're keeping under tight wraps."

Charlie's voice cut through the conversation, sharp and probing. "Kit, what are you planning to do about this meeting? If they're talking about you, you need to be prepared for whatever comes next."

Kit felt their gazes on him, particularly Charlie's, who was studying him with a mix of concern and suspicion. He knew they could sense that he was holding something back, that he had a plan he wasn't sharing. But he wasn't ready to divulge anything, not yet.

Before he could respond, Aria's voice broke through his thoughts. "Kit, I know you've got something in mind, but I have to strongly recommend that you don't go at this alone. Despite your... formidable size and skills, you should still have a bodyguard. Someone who can watch your back, especially if things go sideways. And with whatever you're contemplating, they usually do."

Kit's initial reaction was to dismiss the idea, he didn't need a babysitter, and he certainly didn't want to put anyone else in danger. But there was something in Aria's tone, a quiet insistence that made him pause.

"And who would you suggest?" Kit asked, though he already had a feeling he knew the answer.

"Miguel," Aria said without hesitation. "He's tough, experienced, and he knows how to handle himself in dangerous situations. Plus, he's the right size and he's already part of your team, someone you trust."

Kit sighed, realizing that she was right. He couldn't afford to take unnecessary risks, not with everything that was at stake. "Fine. I'll ask Miguel. But he stays in the background, as a bodyguard I hired, I don't want anyone knowing I've got backup and that he's connected to me."

Aria nodded, satisfied with his response. "Good. And what about you, Charlie?"

Kit glanced at Charlie, who raised an eyebrow in curiosity. "What about me?" she asked, a hint of amusement in her voice.

"If I'm going to have a bodyguard, so should you," Kit said, his tone serious. "You're flitting around asking questions, it's going to make you just as much a target in this as I am."

Charlie smirked, a spark of mischief in her eyes. "Don't worry about me, Kit. I've got Grunt from Pop's. He's more than capable of handling any trouble that comes my way."

Kit felt a flicker of relief, though he still wasn't entirely comfortable with the idea of Charlie being in danger. He knew better than to argue with her, he had been told that Charlie was more than capable of taking care of herself, and she had made it clear that she didn't need anyone's protection.

Aria's gaze lingered on Kit, and he could tell she was holding something back, something she wasn't saying outright. He'd known been told that Aria had this look when she was onto something, and the way she was looking at him now made him uneasy.

"What is it, Aria?" Kit asked, his tone sharper than he intended.

Aria hesitated, then spoke carefully. "Kit, I know you're planning something, and I know you don't want anyone else involved. But whatever it is, just remember that you have people that will back you up if needed. You don't have to keep secrets here."

Kit felt a pang of guilt at her words, but he pushed it down. He wasn't ready to share his plans, not yet. He knew that Aria was right, he couldn't do this alone, and he would need her help, along with the rest of the team, to see it through, but that was later, right now was his time.

"I appreciate that, Aria," Kit said, softening his tone. "And I'll keep that in mind. But for now, let's focus on what we know. Alexandre and Gero are moving into the US and Canada, expanding their operations. André is the link between them, using his car business as a cover. We need to figure out how to meet with these men, how to get close enough to take them down."

The group fell into a thoughtful silence, each of them considering the implications of what they had learned. Kit's mind was racing, trying to piece together a plan that would allow him to meet with Alexandre and Gero without tipping them off. He knew it wouldn't be easy, but it was a risk he was willing to take.

Finally, Aria broke the silence. "I've been looking into potential locations where they might hold meetings, places that aren't heavily monitored or secure. I'll keep digging and see if I can find anything that might give us an edge."

Charlie nodded, her expression thoughtful. "André seems to be the key here. He's the one connecting the dots between us and them. If we can figure out what he's planning, we might be able to get our foot in the door."

Kit agreed, though his mind was still spinning with unanswered questions. How was he going to meet with these men without compromising everything they discovered? What was Aria holding back, and why did he have the feeling that she knew more about his plans than she was letting on?

The call continued for a few more minutes, the group discussing possible strategies and contingencies. As they wrapped up the conversation, Kit couldn't shake the feeling that they were missing something, that there was a piece of the puzzle still out of reach.

As the call ended and the screen went dark, Kit leaned back in his chair, his mind churning with thoughts. He had always been a man who thrived in the shadows, who knew how to navigate the dangerous waters of the underworld. But this time, he couldn't figure out the game, and the risks were growing greater than what he had ever faced.

His phone chirped, pulling him from his thoughts. Kit glanced down at the screen and saw a new text message from an unknown number.

"It's André. I would like to speak to you when you are available."

Kit's jaw tightened as he read the message, his mind racing. André was reaching out, likely to arrange the very meeting Kit had been contemplating. This was the moment he had been waiting for, the chance to confront the men responsible for so much suffering.

But as he stared at the message, Kit couldn't help but feel a sense of unease. He was about to step into a world of darkness and danger, one where the line between right and wrong was blurred beyond recognition. And this time, he wasn't sure he would come out the other side the same man.

CHAPTER 19

The plan had been formulating in Charlie's mind for weeks, ever since she learned that Chase had been killed. She made a promise to his grandfather and decided to take matters into her own hands, to do whatever it took to bring down the men responsible for the trafficking ring that had stolen so many innocent lives and murdered Chase. Charlie had her own motivations for going it alone, ones that she kept close to her chest.

Chase's death had left a gaping wound in her heart, a wound that no amount of work or distraction was healing. She had promised Mr. Holloway that she would find those responsible and bring them to justice, and that promise had become her sole focus. But as the days turned into weeks, and the leads grew cold, Charlie realized that if she was going to keep that promise, she would need to do more than just follow the breadcrumbs found by Kit and her teams. She would take matters into her own hands.

And so, she made a decision, one that she hadn't shared with anyone, not even Aria. She would go dark, infiltrate André Beaulieu's world of exotic cars, and uncover the truth for herself. But to do that, she needed a new persona, one that could seamlessly blend into the world of the ultra-wealthy without raising suspicion.

Gone was the guise of Diamond Frost, the persona she used in the club scene, a name that commanded respect and fear in equal measure. This time, she would be Charlotte O'Donovan, an expensive horse breeder and racer, looking to expand her business into the exotic car market. It was a role that would require more than just a change of personality, it would require a complete transformation. To her knowledge, the paperwork from a previous sting had not been destroyed, so she could use that for her cover story.

The first step was to build the persona, and that meant shopping. But not just any shopping, she needed to immerse herself in the world of the wealthy, to dress and act the part of someone who belonged in the exclusive circles that André frequented. She started in Atlanta, hitting the high-end boutiques and designer stores that catered to the rich and famous. She purchased clothes that cost more than most people's cars, outfits that screamed wealth and status. Tailored suits, custom-made dresses, designer shoes, and handbags that could buy a small house. Every detail was meticulously planned, from the jewelry she wore to the scent of the perfume she chose.

Charlie despised spending the money his way, she had always been practical, even in her role as Diamond Frost, choosing to invest her earnings in her clubs and her team rather than frivolous luxuries. But this was different. This was a role, a character she was creating, and every penny spent was an investment in her plan.

The next step was New York. She traveled to the city under the guise of a business trip, but her true purpose was to further refine her new persona. In New York, she visited the most exclusive boutiques, where the wealthy shopped without a second thought. She purchased more clothes, accessories, and even commissioned a custom-made riding outfit from a renowned designer. Each purchase was carefully considered, each piece chosen to enhance the image she was crafting.

Charlotte visited the best restaurants, went to horse stables to view the top horses and hob nob with their owners. Getting her name in the fold, so to speak. Luckily, people had heard of the ranch, and also heard that Mrs. Donovan had passed. Charlie quickly corrected and stated O'Donovan, wanting people to believe they had mistaken the name. Association was everything.

By the end of the week, Charlotte O'Donovan was ready. She was polished, sophisticated, and dripping with wealth, everything

André Beaulieu would expect from a client interested in the world of exotic cars. But more than that, she was a woman with a reputation, someone who could hold her own in the circles of power and influence. A horse breeder and racer with an eye for fine automobiles, looking to diversify her portfolio.

Day four saw Charlie traveling to Montreal. She arrived under the radar, avoiding the usual luxury hotels and choosing instead to stay at a discreet, high-end bed and breakfast that catered to clients who valued their privacy. She needed to keep a low profile, to avoid drawing attention to herself until she was ready to make her move.

Montreal was a city of contrasts, a place where old-world charm met modern sophistication. It was the perfect setting for someone like Charlotte O'Donovan, a city that thrived on wealth and exclusivity. Charlie spent the first day settling in, visiting a few local stables under the pretense of checking out potential new racing prospects. She made a show of being interested, asking the right questions, making connections, but her mind was already on the next step, finding a way into André's world.

The following day, she began visiting car showcases, the kind that only offered high-end exotic cars. These were not the kind of events advertised in the papers or online, attendance was by invitation only, and the guest lists were tightly controlled. But Charlie had prepared for this, using her connections and the persona of Charlotte O'Donovan to gain access.

The first showcase was held in a luxurious private estate on the outskirts of Montreal, a place that oozed wealth and privilege. Charlie arrived in a sleek black car, stepping out with the confidence of someone who belonged in such a setting. The estate was a marvel, with manicured gardens, a sprawling mansion, and a collection of the most expensive cars money could buy displayed like works of art.

She spent the first hour mingling with the other guests, carefully observing the dynamics of the room. It didn't take long to notice the undercurrents, the subtle exchanges between those who were there to do more than just admire the cars. Deals were being made, alliances formed, all under the guise of casual conversation. But there was no mention of this André person.

Her third day in, she attended another showcase, this one in the heart of the city. The event was smaller, more intimate, and Charlie felt she was getting closer to her goal. The cars on display were breathtaking, rare models, custom-built machines designed for the elite. But Charlie wasn't interested in the cars. She was watching the people, listening to the conversations, waiting for her moment.

And then it happened. As she was examining a particularly striking Aston Martin, a man approached her, a man she recognized from the photographs Aria had shown her.

André Beaulieu.

Jackpot.

"Impressive, isn't it?" André said smoothly, his eyes appraising both the car and Charlie with equal interest.

Charlie turned to him, her expression one of casual interest. "Indeed. It's a beautiful machine. I've always had a passion for horses, but I'm starting to think there's room in my stable for something with a bit more horsepower."

André smiled, clearly intrigued. "Charlotte Donovan, if I'm not mistaken?"

"O'Donovan," Charlie offered a polite smile, extending her well-manicured hand. "You have me at a disadvantage, Mr...?"

"Beaulieu," André replied, shaking her hand with a firm grip. "André Beaulieu. I've heard of your reputation in the horse racing world. It's not often we see someone with your background taking an interest in cars."

He had done his homework. Thank goodness Aria's teaching her how to create online profiles worked. While she was involved in the horse world, it wasn't as extensive as her new profile indicated. She threw a silent thank you to Aria.

"I'm always looking for new opportunities," Charlie said, her tone light. "Diversifying my investments, expanding my horizons. And I've found that the world of exotic cars is quite... exciting."

André's eyes gleamed with interest. "You're in the right place, then. These cars are more than just vehicles, they're investments, pieces of art, and for those who know how to appreciate them, they can be quite profitable."

"That's what I'm hoping," Charlie replied, her voice smooth as silk. "I've been in Montreal for a few days now, visiting various showcases, trying to get a feel for the market. But I have to admit, I'm looking for someone who can guide me through it, someone who knows the ins and outs of the business."

André's smile widened, and Charlie knew she had him hooked. "I'd be happy to help you, Ms. O'Donovan. Perhaps we could arrange a private showing? I have a collection that I think you'd find most interesting."

Charlie's heart raced, but she kept her expression composed. "I'd like that, Mr. Beaulieu. Let's arrange something soon."

"Of course," André said, his tone warm and inviting. "I'll have my assistant reach out to you with the details. In the meantime, enjoy the showcase. And if you see anything that catches your eye, don't hesitate to let me know." He paused. "I believe I have something happening that might interest you. Would you care to attend a special private showing I'm holding this weekend?"

"I would be delighted," Charlie replied, her smile never wavering. "Thank you, Mr. Beaulieu. I look forward to your show."

André nodded, giving her one last appraising look before moving on to the next guest. As he walked away, Charlie allowed herself a moment of satisfaction. She had done it. She had infiltrated André's world, and now she had an opening, a way to get closer to the truth.

But she knew she had to be careful. André was potentially dangerous, and she was walking a tightrope... alone. One wrong move, one slip, and everything could come crashing down. But this was what she had spent the last few years training for, what she had spent the last few weeks preparing for. She would play the role of Charlotte O'Donovan to perfection, and she would uncover the truth, no matter what it took.

As she left the showcase, her mind was already racing with plans, with ideas for how to walk through the next steps. She had a meeting with André, a chance to get inside his world, to see the connections that linked him to Alexandre and Gero.

For now, she had to play the part and continue the charade of the wealthy horse breeder dipping her toes into the world of exotic cars. She would charm, she would deceive, and she would uncover the darkness that she was sure lurked beneath the surface of André's world.

And when it was all over, she would make them pay for what they had done to Chase, and to all the others who had suffered at their hands.

Charlie O'Donovan, Diamond Frost, Charlotte O'Donovan, it didn't matter which name she used. What mattered was the mission, the goal, and she would see it through to the end.

As she returned to her hotel that night, she felt a sense of power that fueled her every move. The game was on, and she was ready to play. André Beaulieu had no idea what was coming.

CHAPTER 20

Aria had made a trip to the lodge near Atlanta to see how Calista worked. The tension in command center was high. The digital screens lining the walls of the command center flickered with live feeds, maps, and data streams, all working in sync to paint a detailed picture of the streets near Andre's business and home in Montreal. Aria sat at the head of the operation, her fingers deftly tapping on her keyboard as she directed the flow of information. Next to her, Calista was immersed in her own screen, eyes narrowed in concentration as she pulled up intel and coordinated with Aria.

It had all started with a tip. a whisper that a major trafficking sale was about to take place in Montreal. Both Aria and Calista had received the same tip through different channels, and after a brief, tense discussion, they agreed to send their people to verify the information. Neither could afford to ignore it, the stakes were high that it was children again.

Less than twelve hours later, their suspicions were confirmed. The photos that arrived in Aria's inbox showed an old warehouse on the outskirts of Montreal, its exterior giving no hint of the horrors contained within. But hidden in the bowels of the warehouse, over forty souls were caged like animals, waiting to be sold off to the highest bidder. The thermal images were grainy, taken from a distance, but they were clear enough to reveal the desperation etched on the faces of the captives.

Aria's jaw tightened as she studied the photos. The tip had been solid, and now it was up to them to act. "Calista, what's the address?"

Calista's fingers flew over the keyboard, and within moments, the coordinates were pulled up and displayed on the main screen. "Got it. Sending the coordinates to all team members now."

Aria nodded, her mind already working through the logistics of what needed to happen next. "We need to move fast. If this sale goes through, those people could disappear forever."

But as she sent out the call to mobilize her team, a new problem arose, neither Kit nor Charlie was responding. Neither were Miguel and Grunt. Aria tried Kit's line again, her frustration mounting as it went straight to voicemail. She attempted to reach Charlie, but it was the same story, no response.

"Damn it," Aria muttered under her breath. She turned to Calista, who had been monitoring their communications. "Anything?"

Calista shook her head, her expression mirroring Aria's concern. "Nothing. They've gone dark. No pings on their phones, no signals, nothing."

Aria's mind raced, trying to piece together what could have happened. Those four were seasoned enough to know not to go dark, they wouldn't just vanish without a reason. But with no way to contact them, she had to assume they were on their own, wherever they were.

"We can't wait for them," Aria said finally, her voice firm. "We have to act now. Get in touch with local law enforcement and other agencies. We need to coordinate a plan of action that prioritizes the safety of the victims and the capture of everyone involved in this sale."

Calista nodded and immediately set to work, sending out encrypted messages to the Montreal police and the specialized task forces that dealt with human trafficking. Aria watched her work, her thoughts divided between the upcoming operation and the gnawing worry about Kit and Charlie.

As the plan came together, totally impressed with Calista's work, Aria outlined the details, making sure every aspect was covered. The raid would be swift and precise, with multiple teams converging on the warehouse from different angles. The primary goal was to secure the safety of the victims. While the initial teams would secure the traffickers, and any buyers present at the sale, secondary would care for the victims, making sure none needed medical care.

"Keep the area around the warehouse under constant surveillance," Aria instructed. "I want eyes on every possible escape route. If anyone tries to slip away, we need to be ready."

"Yes, ma'am," one of the operatives responded, his voice crisp and professional.

Despite the meticulous planning, Aria couldn't shake the feeling of unease. Kit and Charlie's disappearance at such a crucial moment was more than just a coincidence, it had to be connected to what was happening in Montreal. But without more information, all she could do was move forward with the operation and hope they would resurface soon.

Little did Aria and Calista know, Kit and Charlie were, in fact, very close by, closer than anyone could have anticipated.

——

At that very moment, Kit and Charlie were mingling with the wealthy elite at an exclusive exotic car showcase hosted by André Beaulieu. The event was a glittering affair, held in a luxurious venue adorned with chandeliers and velvet ropes. The air buzzed with the low hum of conversations, the clinking of champagne glasses, and the occasional roar of an engine being revved for show.

Gleaming under the soft spotlights were the finest examples of automotive engineering, sleek, powerful machines that spoke of wealth and status. But for Kit Thorne, the luxury around him barely registered. His mind was preoccupied with the unexpected turn of events.

André Beaulieu had just introduced him to two men he knew were far more dangerous than their polished exteriors suggested, Alexandre DuBois and Gero Meyer, the very men he had been working so hard to discover. Import moguls that he believed were behind the shadow trafficking ring haunting the world.

Kit, dressed in an impeccably tailored suit, exuded confidence as he roamed the room, his sharp blue eyes taking in every detail.

Charlotte O'Donovan, the persona Charlie had so meticulously crafted, was equally in her element, her every movement a calculated blend of sophistication and allure.

The two of them moved through the crowd, carefully observing, listening, and making the right connections never spotting each other. Despite the opulence around them, both Kit and Charlie were keenly aware of the potential danger that lurked beneath the surface.

As André led him further into the showroom, preparing to showcase a new line of exclusive cars, Kit's attention was suddenly pulled in a different direction. Out of the corner of his eye, he caught sight of a familiar figure, a woman with an air of confidence and elegance, dressed in a tailored suit that spoke of wealth and power. She was standing with her back to him, engaged in conversation with another guest, but Kit recognized her immediately.

Charlie. What the hell is she doing here?

Kit's stomach tightened as he realized the woman was doing exactly as he was... going dark. Charlie Donovan, here, at the same event, clearly playing a part just as he was. This was a complication neither of them had anticipated, and one that could blow their covers if they weren't careful.

Before he could gather his thoughts, André's voice cut through the murmur of the crowd. "Ah, I see you've already noticed one of our esteemed guests," André said, turning toward Charlie. "Mr.

Thorne, allow me to introduce you to Ms. Charlotte O'Donovan, a renowned horse breeder and racer who is looking to expand her interests into the automotive world."

Charlie turned to face them, her eyes widening ever so slightly as she locked eyes with Kit. For a brief moment, surprise flickered in her gaze, quickly replaced by a cool, composed expression. Kit was equally taken aback, though he masked it well, his face betraying nothing as he approached her.

"André, thank you for the introduction," Charlie said smoothly, offering Kit a polite smile. "Mr. Thorne, it's a pleasure to meet you."

Kit inclined his head, slipping into the role he had been playing all evening. "Ms. O'Donovan, the pleasure is mine. I've heard a great deal about your successes in the racing world."

They shook hands, their grips firm, but beneath the veneer of civility, their eyes locked in a silent exchange. It was a look that promised trouble, a look that said they had a lot to discuss once they were out of sight of prying eyes.

André, oblivious to the tension between them, smiled warmly. "It seems we have quite the gathering of influential people tonight. I'm sure you'll both find plenty to discuss."

Kit forced a smile, though his mind was racing. He had to find a way to talk to Charlie, to figure out why she was here and how they were going to work this situation without blowing their covers.

"Indeed," Kit said, keeping his tone light. "Ms. O'Donovan, I'd be interested to hear more about your ventures."

Charlie's smile was tight, the underlying tension between them almost visible. "And I yours, Mr. Thorne. Perhaps we could find a moment later to discuss it?"

"Of course," Kit replied, knowing they were both thinking the same thing, how to get out of this without attracting suspicion.

André, sensing the beginning of a business connection, nodded approvingly. "Excellent. In the meantime, please enjoy the rest of the showcase. We have some truly remarkable vehicles on display tonight."

Kit and Charlie exchanged another brief look, one that spoke volumes. They were in deep, and now they had to tread carefully, ensuring that neither André nor the dangerous men he associated with saw through their charade.

As André moved on to greet other guests, Kit and Charlie found themselves standing side by side, their gazes locked on the cars before them but their thoughts far from the luxury around them.

"What the hell, Charlie?" Kit muttered under his breath, keeping his expression neutral.

"Later," Charlie replied, her voice just as low. "For now, just play the part. This place is probably bugged to the hilt."

Kit nodded, though his jaw was tight with frustration. They had both stepped into a game far more dangerous than they had anticipated, and now they were going to have to play it together, whether they liked it or not.

As they continued to move through the showroom, making small talk with other guests and pretending to be nothing more than two businesspeople with mutual interests, the tension between them never eased. Every glance, every word was loaded with unspoken challenges and unvoiced fears.

By the time the event began to wind down, Kit and Charlie had managed to maintain their covers, but the promise of a reckoning hung between them like a storm cloud.

As they made their way to the exit, Kit shot one last look at Charlie. "Meet me outside. We're not done here."

Charlie's eyes flashed with a mixture of annoyance and agreement. "Don't keep me waiting." She could tell he was not a happy camper.

With that, they separated, each heading in different directions, but both knowing that the conversation they were about to have was going to be anything but pleasant.

The night wasn't over yet, and the real danger was only just beginning.

Kit had just finished a conversation with a potential buyer when he felt his phone vibrate in his pocket. He discreetly checked the screen but found no new messages or calls. A quick glance at Charlie confirmed that she had felt it too, an odd sensation, as if something was off, but neither could pinpoint what it was.

As the evening wore on, the atmosphere in the room began to shift. Kit noticed André Beaulieu speaking in hushed tones with a man who looked distinctly uneasy. Moments later, André's eyes flickered in their direction, and Kit felt the hairs on the back of his neck stand up. Something was happening.

Charlie caught Kit's eye, her expression betraying a flicker of concern. She had seen the same exchange, and her instincts were telling her that whatever was going on, it involved them.

It wasn't long before André approached them, his usual polished demeanor slightly strained. "Mr. Thorne, Ms. O'Donovan," he greeted them with a smile that didn't quite reach his eyes. "I hope you're enjoying the showcase?"

"Very much so," Kit replied smoothly, though his senses were on high alert. "You have an impressive collection here."

"I'm glad to hear it," André said, his tone still overly pleasant. "In fact, I was hoping you might be interested in something a bit more exclusive. There's a private showing happening shortly, a chance to see some vehicles that aren't on the market yet. I think you'd find it quite interesting."

Kit exchanged a brief glance with Charlie, both of them understanding the subtext. This wasn't just a car showing, it was something more, something that could be dangerous. Neither could see their bodyguards, Miguel and Grunt. Something was definitely wrong.

"Sounds intriguing," Charlie replied with a smile that matched André's. "We'd love to see what you have to offer."

"Excellent," André said, clearly pleased with their response. "If you'll follow me, we'll head to the viewing."

Kit and Charlie fell into step behind André, their minds racing as they tried to anticipate what was about to happen. As they moved through the corridors of the venue, Kit noticed the shift in the atmosphere, security was tighter, and the staff seemed more on edge. Whatever this private viewing was, it was clearly not just about cars.

They were led to a secluded wing of the building, where the décor became more utilitarian, the luxury giving way to something far more functional. André paused in front of a large door, turning to face them.

"Before we go in," André said, his tone taking on a more serious edge, "I should mention that this showing is by invitation only. The guests you're about to meet are... particular about their privacy, so I ask that you respect that."

"Of course," Kit said, his voice calm despite the growing unease in his chest.

André nodded and opened the door, gesturing for them to enter. As they stepped inside, Kit's eyes quickly scanned the room, taking in every detail. The room was dimly lit, with only a few spotlights illuminating the two cars on display. But it wasn't the cars that caught his attention, it was the men standing between them.

Alexandre DuBois and Gero Meyer were waiting for them, their expressions cold and calculating. Kit felt a jolt of recognition, realizing that these were the men Aria had warned them about, the possible kingpins of the trafficking ring they had been chasing.

Charlie, too, recognized the danger immediately. She kept her composure, but inside, she was already calculating the risks, planning her next move.

André stepped forward, breaking the tense silence. "Mr. Thorne, Ms. Donovan, allow me to introduce Alexandre DuBois and Gero Meyer. They're very interested in meeting you."

Kit's mind raced as he tried to assess the situation. This wasn't just a car showing, it was an inquisition, a test to see if they could be trusted, or if they were a threat.

Before Kit could respond, the door behind them clicked shut, a lock could be heard, the sound ominously final. They were trapped, and the real game was about to begin.

——

Meanwhile, back at the command center, Aria and Calista were finalizing the details of the raid on the warehouse. The team was in position, ready to move at a moment's notice. But Aria's mind was still on Kit and Charlie, the unknown gnawing at her as she replayed their last conversation in her head.

The rescue mission was about to begin, and there was no turning back. Aria could only hope that Kit and Charlie were safe, wherever they were.

Just as she was about to give the final order to proceed, a message came through on one of the secure channels.

"We've got a problem."

Aria's heart sank as she read the words. There was no time to dwell on it now, the mission had to go on. But whatever was happening, she knew that it was about to get a lot more complicated.

As the team moved into action, Aria couldn't shake the feeling that something was about to go very, very wrong.

——

Kit's phone vibrated in his pocket, but he couldn't reach it, not with the eyes of Alexandre and Gero locked on him.

Charlie's purse was making odd noises, she just smiled and ignored it as Andre stepped closer to her.

CHAPTER 21

The message had appeared on Aria's screen like an ominous whisper in the storm of data streaming through her command center.

"We've got a problem."

The sender: Grunt, Charlie's bodyguard.

Aria's pulse quickened as she processed the potential implications. Grunt was not one to send out a distress signal lightly, and if he was saying there was a problem, it meant something had gone very wrong. But there was no time to dwell on it, she had a mission to run, and the rescue operation was about to commence.

"Begin the operation," Aria ordered, her voice steady despite the turmoil inside her. The command center came alive with activity as Aria and Calista confirmed the go-ahead and the operatives began moving in on the warehouse in Montreal. Aria watched the live feeds from the drones hovering above the site, the tension in the room thickening as the team converged on the target.

But in the back of her mind, Aria couldn't shake the worry gnawing at her. Kit and Charlie had gone dark, and now Grunt was signaling trouble. She needed to stay focused, to keep her team on track, but the unease was like a shadow she couldn't outrun.

——

Meanwhile, inside the luxurious venue where Kit and Charlie had been playing their respective roles, the atmosphere had shifted from one of opulent indulgence to something far more sinister. The two of them stood side by side, maintaining their carefully crafted personas as they faced Alexandre and Gero, who had subtly surrounded them with a small army of bodyguards.

Kit's instincts were on high alert. The subtle shift in the room's energy, the glint of suspicion in Alexandre's eyes, and the tightening of Gero's expression all pointed to one thing, they were about to be tested, perhaps even exposed.

"Mr. Thorne, Ms. O'Donovan," Alexandre began, his tone deceptively polite, "I must admit, we're curious about your interest in our little gathering. It's not often we have newcomers so eager to invest in such... exclusive automobiles."

Kit remained calm, his expression unreadable as he responded. "I've always had an interest in high-end investments, particularly those that offer a significant return. Exotic cars are just one of many avenues I'm exploring."

Charlie chimed in, her voice smooth and unflappable. "As for me, I'm always looking for ways to diversify my portfolio. Cars, like horses, are a form of art, one that can be both beautiful and profitable."

Gero stepped closer, his gaze sharp as he studied them. "And your bodyguards? It's unusual for investors to bring such heavy security to a car show."

Charlie's eyes narrowed slightly, a flash of irritation crossing her features. "What wealthy individual doesn't have security in this day and age? My bodyguard is there to ensure my safety, just as I'm sure yours are here for the same reason." She looked around the room at the huge men standing there.

Kit nodded in agreement. "Precisely. In our world, security is a necessity, not a luxury."

The tension was strong as Alexandre and Gero exchanged a glance, clearly weighing their next move. Kit's muscles tensed, ready for whatever might come next. He could sense that the situation was teetering on the edge of violence, and he knew that both he and Charlie were in real danger.

Just as things seemed ready to escalate, André Beaulieu suddenly appeared, his face flushed with barely concealed excitement. He stepped between the two groups, addressing Alexandre and Gero with a hurried whisper that Kit and Charlie couldn't quite hear.

"They've been caught," André said, his tone urgent and laced with panic.

Kit's eyes flicked to Charlie, their expressions carefully neutral, but inside, their minds were racing. Caught? What was going on?

Gero's expression darkened as he listened to André, while Alexandre remained impassive, nodding slightly as he absorbed the news. Whatever had happened, it was clear that it was bad news for the two men, and possibly even for Kit and Charlie.

After a moment of hushed conversation, Alexandre turned back to Kit and Charlie, his demeanor shifting once more to one of cool professionalism. "It seems something has come up that requires our immediate attention. However, I would very much like to continue our conversation. Would the two of you care to join us for dinner at one of my favorite restaurants in Montreal?"

Kit and Charlie exchanged a brief glance, both of them playing their parts to perfection. Charlie allowed a flash of irritation to show on her face, while Kit raised an eyebrow, giving the impression of being mildly offended by the earlier line of questioning.

"I must say," Charlie began, her tone clipped, "I find it rather off-putting to be questioned in such a manner, then invited to dinner. I came here under the impression that this was a professional gathering."

Kit nodded in agreement, his voice cold. "If this is how you treat potential investors, I'm beginning to wonder if this was a mistake."

Alexandre held up a hand, a placating smile on his face. "Please, allow me to apologize. We meant no offense, and I assure you, all will be explained over dinner. It would be an honor to have you both join us."

Charlie hesitated for a moment, then gave a curt nod. "Very well. But I expect a more civil conversation."

"Of course," Gero added smoothly, his smile not quite reaching his eyes. "We look forward to it."

With that, the tension in the room eased, if only slightly. Alexandre and Gero gestured for them to follow, and Kit and Charlie were escorted toward the front entrance of the venue. As they walked, Kit's mind raced, trying to piece together what had just happened. The mention of someone being "caught" had set off alarm bells in his head, but without more information, he could only speculate.

They reached the front doors, where the cool night air greeted them. Waiting just outside, looking anxious and alert, were Miguel and Grunt, their eyes immediately locking onto Kit and Charlie as they approached, each surprised to see the other side of their team.

Grunt stepped forward, his expression a mixture of relief and frustration. "Boss," he said quietly to Charlie, "we got an issue."

Charlie shot him a look that told him now was not the time. "Later," she said firmly, maintaining her calm exterior.

Miguel, ever the professional, simply nodded at Kit, his eyes scanning the area for any potential threats. "Everything okay?"

"For now," Kit replied, his voice low. "But stay close. This isn't over."

Alexandre and Gero exchanged a few more words with André before turning back to Kit and Charlie. "Shall we?" Alexandre asked, his tone courteous but with an undercurrent of something darker.

Kit and Charlie both gave polite nods, slipping seamlessly back into their roles. "Lead the way," Kit said, his voice steady.

As they were escorted to a waiting limousine, Kit's mind was racing with questions. What had gone wrong? Who had been caught? And more importantly, what were Alexandre and Gero planning next?

They climbed into the limousine, the door closing with a soft click behind them. As the vehicle pulled away from the venue, Kit and Charlie found themselves seated opposite Alexandre and Gero, with André sitting next to Gero, looking increasingly nervous. Grunt and Miguel followed in their respective automobiles.

The atmosphere inside the limousine was heavy with unspoken tension. Kit and Charlie kept their expressions neutral, playing the part of slightly offended investors who had reluctantly agreed to continue the evening elsewhere. But beneath the surface, both of them were on high alert, ready for whatever might come next.

As the limousine wound its way through the streets of Montreal, Kit's phone vibrated in his pocket again, but he couldn't risk checking it, not with Alexandre and Gero watching them so closely. He would have to wait until the right moment and hope that whatever message was waiting for him could provide some clarity of what the hell was happening.

For now, all they could do was play their parts and hope that the evening didn't end in disaster.

As the city lights flickered past the windows, Kit couldn't shake the feeling that they were being drawn deeper into a trap, one they might not be able to escape.

——

The operation's room was buzzing with the frenetic energy of a successful operation, but Aria couldn't shake the gnawing worry that had been festering in the back of her mind. She had just finished giving the order to begin the raid on the Montreal warehouse when Grunt's cryptic message had popped up on her screen.

She hadn't had time to respond then, the operation needing her full attention. But now that the rescue was underway and everything seemed to be going according to plan, she finally typed out a quick response.

"**What's happening and where are you?**"

Aria's fingers drummed against the edge of the desk as she waited for the reply, her eyes flicking between the various screens displaying live feeds from the operation. Moments later, Grunt's response came through.

"I can't say. Charlie has disappeared."

Aria's heart skipped a beat. "**Disappeared?**" She quickly typed back.

"**Disappeared how? What do you mean, you can't say? Where was she last?**"

But before Grunt could respond, another operative called out to Aria, drawing her attention back to the operation. The rescue was in full swing, and the stakes were high. She couldn't afford to be distracted now, not when lives were hanging in the balance.

With a frustrated sigh, she pocketed her phone and refocused on the task at hand. The images from the warehouse were grim, over forty victims, all of them frightened and malnourished, but alive. The team was moving swiftly, securing the perimeter and taking down anyone who resisted. It was a well-executed operation, but Aria's mind kept drifting back to Grunt's message and the unsettling news about Charlie.

Minutes felt like hours as the operation progressed, but finally, the confirmation came through her earpiece.

"Operation successful. All victims accounted for, and we've got 70 mid-level buyers and two mid-level traffickers in custody. No sign of higher-ups."

Aria allowed herself a brief moment of relief. It wasn't the full victory they had hoped for, those at the top of the trafficking ring had not appeared at the sale, but it was still a significant blow to the operation. Forty lives saved, and more of the network dismantled. It was a victory, but one with a bitter aftertaste.

As the team on the ground began moving the rescued victims to a secure location, Aria's thoughts snapped back to Charlie. She grabbed her phone, quickly buzzing Charlie's number, hoping against hope that she'd pick up. The line rang and rang, but there was no answer. She tried again, and again, but still nothing.

"Damn it, Charlie, where are you?" she muttered under her breath, the fear building in her chest. Kit was still out of reach too, and the silence from both of them was driving her crazy.

By the time the last of the victims had been safely transported to a secure location, Aria's worry had morphed into a potent mix of anger and fear. She checked her phone again, her heart skipping a beat when she saw a new message from Grunt.

"Charlie has resurfaced."

Aria's breath caught in her throat, but as she read and reread the message, frustration bubbled up within her. That was all Grunt had said, no details, no explanation, just that Charlie had resurfaced. It wasn't enough.

She quickly typed out a response.

"Where is she? What happened?"

But before she could send it, she received another update from the field team. The final tally, forty rescued, seventy buyers and two traffickers in custody. It was a solid outcome, but it wasn't the one they had been hoping for. The operation had been a success, but not the complete takedown they'd needed.

"Good work, everyone," Aria said through gritted teeth, trying to keep her focus on the positives. But as soon as she disconnected the call, she felt the wave of anxiety wash over her again.

Charlie had resurfaced, but what about Kit? What were they involved in that had caused them to drop off the radar? And why the hell weren't they answering their phones?

Aria's phone buzzed again, but it wasn't Kit or Charlie, it was Calista who had left the room, her tone as sharp as a knife. "Still no word from Kit or Charlie?"

"No," Aria replied, her voice tight with frustration. "Grunt said Charlie resurfaced, but nothing else. Kit's still dark."

"Damn it," Calista spat, echoing Aria's feelings exactly. "What the hell are they doing? They were supposed to be on standby, not going rogue!"

Aria could hear the tension in Calista's voice, a mirror of her own. "Whatever they're doing, they're on their own, and they're not giving us anything to work with. I don't like this, Calista. Not one bit."

"Neither do I," Calista agreed. "I don't know about Charlie, but this isn't like him. Something's up, and when we find them, they're going to have a lot to answer for."

Aria nodded, though Calista couldn't see her. "Agreed. But right now, we need to figure out where the hell they are and what's going on. Keep trying to reach them. I don't care what it takes, we need answers."

"I'm on it," Calista replied, her voice a determined growl. "They won't stay hidden for long."

Aria ended the call, her mind racing as she stared at the darkened screens around her. The rescue operation had been a victory, but it was overshadowed by the gnawing uncertainty of Kit and Charlie's disappearance. Whatever they were involved in,

Aria had the sinking feeling that it was far more dangerous than anything they'd anticipated.

There was going to be a reckoning, that much was certain. And when Aria and Calista finally got ahold of Kit and Charlie, there would be no escaping the consequences of their actions.

But for now, all Aria could do was wait, and hope that they would surface before it was too late.

CHAPTER 22

The limousine glided smoothly through the streets of Montreal, its tinted windows offering a distorted view of the city lights flickering by. Inside, the atmosphere was deceptively calm, a thin veneer of civility masking the tension simmering beneath the surface. Kit and Charlie sat side by side, their expressions carefully controlled as they played their roles to perfection, two wealthy investors, slightly ruffled by earlier events, but still intrigued by the potential of new business ventures.

Opposite them sat Alexandre and Gero, the men Kit and Charlie thought to be the shadowy figures at the helm of a global trafficking ring. With them was André, the lynchpin who had brought them all together, though whether he was fully aware of what he'd done remained to be seen.

Alexandre was the first to speak, his voice smooth and practiced, like a seasoned diplomat easing tensions. "Mr. Thorne, Ms. O'Donovan, I want to extend my sincerest apologies for the... unusual approach we took earlier. It was not our intention to offend you, but rather to ensure that all parties involved are on the same page. We value discretion above all else in our dealings."

Kit leaned back slightly, his expression cool. "I can appreciate the need for caution, Mr. DuBois. However, I must admit, it's not every day that I'm questioned like a common criminal. I trust we won't have a repeat of this misunderstanding."

Charlie nodded in agreement, her gaze sharp. "It was an uncomfortable situation, to say the least. I don't often find myself in rooms where my motives are questioned so directly."

Gero, ever the diplomat, smiled slightly, spreading his hands in a gesture of conciliation. "We understand, and we're prepared to make amends. You have our word that such an approach will not happen again. We're men of business, just as you are, and we value our relationships with potential partners."

Kit and Charlie exchanged a glance, appearing mollified, though the tension in their postures suggested they weren't entirely convinced. That was exactly the impression they wanted to give, interested, but cautious and a little peeved.

"Very well," Kit said finally, his tone measured. "Let's consider the matter settled. I'm still interested in what you have to offer."

"Good," Alexandre replied, his smile widening. "I think you'll find we have much to discuss over dinner. I assure you, the remainder of tonight will be far more enjoyable."

As the limousine pulled up in front of an upscale restaurant, Kit and Charlie took a moment to admire the elegant façade, a masterpiece of old-world charm and modern luxury. It was a place where deals were made over fine wine and gourmet cuisine, the kind of establishment that catered to the elite and powerful.

They were escorted inside, where a private dining room awaited them. The room was decorated in rich, dark woods, with soft lighting casting a warm glow over the table set with the finest china and crystal. A waiter appeared instantly, offering a selection of rare vintages as they settled into their seats.

The conversation began as expected, with the usual pleasantries exchanged as they sampled the wine and admired the menu. The first course arrived, a delicate arrangement of foie gras and truffle, paired with a crisp white wine. Kit and Charlie played their parts well, engaging in light conversation about their supposed interest in the exotic car market.

"You'll find our inventory quite impressive," Gero said as they discussed potential investments. "We deal in the rarest models, vehicles that are more than just cars, they're statements of power and status."

"I've always believed that cars, like any fine art, are investments worth making," Kit replied, his voice casual as he sipped his wine. "I've already instructed my legal team to prepare the necessary documents. You'll have proof of funds within the next day."

Charlie nodded, her tone businesslike. "The same goes for me. I'm eager to see what opportunities lie ahead."

Alexandre smiled, clearly pleased with their enthusiasm. "I'm confident you'll find our offerings more than satisfactory. And, of course, once the paperwork is in order, we'll move forward with the transaction."

The dinner continued, the courses growing more elaborate with each passing moment. As they moved on to a rich main course of wagyu beef and lobster, Kit subtly steered the conversation toward broader topics, hinting at his interest in other forms of investment.

"I've always found that diversifying one's portfolio is the key to long-term success," Kit said thoughtfully, cutting into his steak. "Exotic cars are just one avenue. I'm always looking for new ventures, particularly those that might be... less conventional."

Alexandre and Gero exchanged a brief look, their interest clearly piqued. But it was Charlie who delivered the first real probe, her voice smooth as silk.

"Indeed, the world of commodities is vast, and often, the most lucrative opportunities lie in markets that aren't always visible to the public eye," Charlie remarked, her tone almost offhanded. "Certain goods, for example, can serve multiple purposes, depending on who's doing the buying."

For a split second, there was a flicker of something dangerous in Alexandre's eyes, an acknowledgment of the underlying meaning in her words. But his response was as polished as ever.

"You're absolutely right, Ms. O'Donovan," Alexandre said, his voice measured. "But those conversations are best saved for a later date, perhaps after we've completed our initial business. I'm sure we'll have much more to discuss once we've established a foundation of trust."

Kit and Charlie both understood the subtext perfectly. Alexandre had just confirmed that there were indeed other, darker investments to be made, but only once they'd proven themselves with the car deals. They now knew they had found the top bosses of the shadow traffickers, they just needed the proof.

But patience was key. They couldn't push too hard or too fast, not without risking exposure. For now, they would have to play along, bide their time, and wait for the right moment to strike. Alexandre looked coiled and ready to spring at any moment.

"Of course," Kit replied smoothly, offering a smile that was equal parts charm and calculation. "We look forward to continuing our discussions."

Charlie nodded in agreement, her own smile carrying a similar edge. "We're both eager to see where this partnership leads."

As the dinner progressed, the conversation drifted back to safer topics, luxury goods, investments, and the benefits of high-end networking. Kit and Charlie played their roles to perfection, even discussing investing in high dollar breeding horses, buying and breaking down defunct corporations, appearing every bit the wealthy investors they were pretending to be, while keeping their true objectives hidden beneath layers of civility.

Dessert was served, an artful display of chocolate mousse and raspberry coulis, paired with an exquisite vintage port. The atmosphere in the room had relaxed considerably, the earlier tension giving way to a sense of camaraderie, albeit a superficial one.

As they finished their meal, Alexandre leaned back in his chair, a satisfied smile on his face. "This has been a most enjoyable evening. I believe we have the makings of a very profitable partnership."

"I'm inclined to agree," Kit said, raising his glass in a toast. "To future endeavors."

"To future endeavors," Charlie echoed, her gaze steady as she clinked glasses with the others.

The evening ended on a cordial note, with promises of further meetings and assurances that the paperwork would be forthcoming. Kit and Charlie played their parts to the very end, their smiles never wavering as they parted ways with Alexandre, Gero, and André outside the restaurant.

As they stepped out into the cool night air, they were met by Miguel and Grunt, both of whom were visibly relieved to see them. Kit and Charlie exchanged a brief glance, the tension between them masked by their calm exteriors.

"We'll talk later," Kit said quietly to Charlie as she stepped into their private vehicle.

"Definitely," Charlie replied, her tone equally subdued.

As the cars pulled away, taking them back to their respective hotels, Kit couldn't shake the feeling that they were on the brink of something huge that could finally bring down the trafficking ring they had been unable to find. But the game was far from over, and they would need every ounce of cunning and patience to see it through.

They had found the top bosses, but now they needed the evidence to take them down. And for that, they would have to wait, watch, and be ready to strike when the moment was right.

For now, they had bought themselves time. It was a game of craps like no other.

——

The night air was crisp as Kit Thorne stepped out of the limousine, his thoughts swirling with the events of the evening. Dinner with Alexandre, Gero, and André had gone as well as could be expected, but Kit's mind was still racing. They were playing a dangerous game, and the stakes had never been higher. What gnawed at him now wasn't just the risk they had taken, but the fact that Charlie had managed to slip away before he could confront her.

He had seen the signs, Charlie's quick glances at her phone, the way she had subtly edged toward the car door. But he'd been distracted, caught in a conversation with Miguel about the rescue that had taken place earlier right there in Montreal. By the time he realized what she was doing, she was already gone.

"Miguel," Kit muttered as they walked toward the hotel entrance, his voice low and tense. "Did you see where Charlie went?"

Miguel, ever the reliable second-in-command, had noticed. He pulled out his phone, the faint glow of the screen illuminating his features as he tapped a few keys. "She's staying at a bed and breakfast on the outskirts of the city. I managed to track her phone before she went off the grid."

Kit's lips curled into a grim smile. "Good work. Let's go."

Miguel raised an eyebrow. "Now? It's late, and she might be on high alert. I'm sure Aria has been trying to reach her about this raid as well."

Kit shook his head, his mind already made up. "Then we'll secure rooms there tonight. I don't want her slipping away again. We'll confront her in the morning."

Miguel nodded, recognizing the determination in Kit's tone. "I'll make the arrangements."

As they climbed back into the car, Kit's mind churned with frustration and questions. Charlie had been pushing boundaries all night, testing him in ways that left him both intrigued and infuriated. Whether they want it or not, they were now in this together, but her independent streak was beginning to cause more problems than it solved.

By the time they arrived at the bed and breakfast, Miguel had already secured rooms for them. The place was quaint and quiet, not like the high-brow hotel they'd just left behind. Kit checked in under an alias, his thoughts still on the upcoming confrontation. Miguel, as always, was a silent but steady presence at his side, keeping watch for any sign of trouble.

Once inside their small suite, Kit tossed his suit jacket onto a chair and loosened his tie, but sleep was the furthest thing from his mind. He needed answers, and he knew Charlie had them. Tomorrow, there would be no more games.

The morning arrived far too quickly, the pale light of dawn filtering through the curtains as Kit dressed in a fresh shirt and slacks. There was a quiet intensity in the air, a sense of anticipation that settled over him. Miguel met him in the hallway, both men sharing a brief nod before heading to the dining area.

The bed and breakfast's dining room was a small, cozy space with a few tables set with fresh flowers and white linens. The smell of coffee and freshly baked pastries filled the air, but Kit barely noticed. His focus was on the door, waiting for Charlie to appear.

It didn't take long.

Charlie walked into the room, her expression confident and composed, until she saw Kit and Miguel seated at a table near the window. She froze mid-step, her eyes widening in shock. It was a rare moment of unguarded emotion from her, and Kit took a small, grim satisfaction in catching her off guard.

Recovering quickly, Charlie's face hardened into a mask of indifference as she crossed the room. Grunt, her ever-loyal bodyguard, was right behind her, his massive frame blocking out the light from the doorway as he entered.

"Well, this is a surprise," Charlie said coolly as she approached their table. But the slight edge in her voice betrayed her irritation. "I didn't expect to see you here."

Kit leaned back in his chair, his gaze penetrating. "I could say the same, Charlie. Care to join us?"

Charlie glanced at Miguel, who smiled and gave her a small nod of acknowledgment, then at Kit. After a moment's hesitation, she pulled out a chair and sat down, Grunt taking the seat next to her. The tension at the table was heavy, the air thick with the unspoken challenge between them.

Breakfast was served with extreme politeness, the waitstaff oblivious to the simmering battle as they placed plates of eggs, bacon, and fresh fruit on the table. Kit waited until the waiter left before speaking, his voice low and measured.

"You disappeared last night, Charlie. Care to explain why?"

Charlie's fork paused halfway to her mouth, her expression carefully controlled. "I didn't realize I needed your permission to come and go as I please, Kit. I'm not one of your employees."

Kit's eyes narrowed. "You're right. But we're now partners in this, and partners don't just vanish without a word."

Charlie set her fork down with deliberate calmness, her eyes meeting his with a mixture of defiance and frustration. "And what exactly were you planning to do, corner me after dinner and demand answers? I wasn't, and am not, in the mood for a confrontation, Kit."

Miguel and Grunt exchanged uncomfortable glances, clearly wishing they were anywhere else but at that table. The strain between Kit and Charlie was unmistakable, and the conversation felt like a powder keg ready to explode.

Kit's voice was icy as he responded, his words measured. "You're right, this is a confrontation. You've been pushing boundaries, making decisions without consulting the rest of us, and it's putting the entire operation at risk."

Charlie's eyes flashed with anger, but she kept her tone even. "I've been doing what I need to do to get the job done. We don't have time to play it safe, Kit. If we want to bring these bastards down, we need to take risks."

"Risks?" Kit's voice sharpened. "Or reckless gambles? You're out for revenge. You're not the only one in this game, Charlie. We're a team, and that means making decisions together."

Charlie leaned forward, her voice a dangerous whisper. "If I waited for consensus every time I needed to make a move, we'd still be sitting in that damn restaurant, sipping wine and pretending we're just rich investors. I'm doing what needs to be done."

"And where exactly does disappearing without a word fit into that plan?" Kit shot back, his frustration evident. "You're not invincible, Charlie. You could have been caught, or worse."

Charlie's jaw tightened, the tension between them ratcheting up another notch. "I know how to handle myself, Kit. I've been through worse. I don't need you or anyone else holding my hand. And might I mention, you have disappeared as well. Yes, I talked with Aria."

Miguel cleared his throat, trying to cut through the rising storm. "Look, we all want the same thing here. Maybe we just need to find a better way to communicate, without stepping on each other's toes."

Grunt nodded in agreement, his deep voice rumbling like distant thunder. "Yeah, I get that you both want to win this thing, but we're stronger together. Let's not forget that. We thought you had been kidnapped, that's why we contacted Aria." He tinged a little pink. "Well, I did."

Charlie glared at Grunt, then back at Kit, her expression softening just a fraction. "I'm not trying to undermine you, Kit.

But I'm not going to sit back and wait either. We needed a way to find them. I did that. You appear to have done the same thing. We need to keep moving forward, and that means sometimes acting on instinct."

Kit held her gaze, the tension between them still simmering, but now tempered with a grudging respect. "I get that, Charlie. But we can't afford to be divided, especially not now. We're so close, and one wrong move could blow this entire operation. If these guys are who I think they are, they don't play. Obey or disappear."

A brief silence settled over the table as the two of them stared each other down, neither willing to back down, but both recognizing the truth in the other's words.

Finally, Charlie exhaled slowly, picking up her fork again. "All right, Kit. I hear you. But you need to trust that I'm in this with you, and I'll trust that we're on the same page. I'm not backing out now."

Kit nodded, the anger in his eyes dimming slightly. "Fair enough. But no more disappearing acts. We stick together from here on out."

Charlie gave a small, almost imperceptible nod. "Deal."

Miguel and Grunt, feeling that the worst of the storm had passed, relaxed slightly, though they were still on edge, as if waiting for another flare-up.

As breakfast continued, the conversation shifted to safer topics, plans for the day, logistical concerns, and updates on the rescue that Aria had been sending. But the underlying issue remained, a reminder that the stakes were higher than ever, and that trust was a fragile, precious commodity.

By the time the meal ended, Kit and Charlie had reached a tenuous truce, but both knew that the path ahead would be filled with challenges. They would need to rely on each other more than ever if they were to succeed, but the cracks in their partnership were still there, waiting to be mended, or exploited.

As they rose from the table, Kit caught Charlie's eye, a silent message passing between them. They weren't finished yet, there was still much to discuss, and even more to resolve.

"Let's get to work," Kit said quietly, as they headed for the door.

Charlie nodded, her expression unreadable. "Agreed. There's no time to waste."

As they left the bed and breakfast, the sun had risen fully. The city was waking up, unaware of the high-stakes game being played in its midst. And for Kit and Charlie, the game was just beginning. Time to play a card or two.

CHAPTER 23

Kit and Charlie's team members that could make it to the lodge at the request of Aria did so. She noted that her LA team could not leave their jobs and would schedule a video conference for those who could not be physically present later. Doc and Emily stayed at Charlie's ranch along with Kimmie, as they were working with some distressed young children that had been brought in. The small raids were leading to having more bodies than room, but they would turn no one away.

The office was bathed in the soft, ambient light of late afternoon as Calista and Aria sat at their desks, fingers flying over their keyboards. Calista, her screen was a maze of data streams, encrypted files, and a series of notifications that kept pinging with each new bit of intel she uncovered. It was a familiar rhythm, one that usually brought her a sense of control and order. But today, her mind was spinning with a mixture of frustration and concern.

She had been tracking Kit and Charlie's movements as closely as she could, though not in the traditional sense. Physically, both had gone dark, but there were other ways to keep tabs on them. Calista had been monitoring their digital footprints, and what she had found wasn't sitting well with her.

"They're up to something," she muttered, her brow furrowing as she reviewed the latest logs. Kit and Charlie had both contacted their attorneys, moved some assets, and were living high on the hog, moves that set off all kinds of alarms in Calista's mind. They hadn't reached out to their teams, and that alone was troubling.

Their thoughts were interrupted by the shrill ring of the phone on Aria's desk. Aria glanced at the caller ID and saw it was Devlin, Charlie's lawyers. Her pulse quickened as she picked up the receiver.

"Devlin," she said curtly, already bracing herself for whatever news he was about to drop.

"Aria," Devlin's voice came through, calm but with an undercurrent of urgency. "I thought you should know, Charlie's been in contact with me. She's making some moves that I think you need to be aware of. She's investing a significant amount of capital into a business deal with a man named André Beaulieu. She was... less than forthcoming about the details, but it's clear she's involved in something big."

Aria's mind raced. "I figured as much. And Kit?"

"Nothing directly from Kit, but he's got his own people," Devlin replied. "If Charlie's in on something, you can bet Kit's not far behind. I think they started whatever separately, but for whatever reason are now together."

Aria's jaw clenched. "Thanks, Devlin. Keep me posted if you hear anything else."

There was a slight pause, "You coming home soon?"

Aria smiled, warmed by the husky tone of his voice. "As soon as I can figure out what that girl is up to."

"Good. Miss you." And hung up.

As she hung up, her mind already working through the information Calista had discovered. Charlie's movements were becoming clearer, and if she was making a substantial investment through André, it wasn't just about cars. No, there was something deeper at play, something that likely involved the very men they were trying to bring down, Alexandre DuBois and Gero Meyer.

Calista's thoughts were interrupted again, this time by the slamming of hands-on top of a desk. Aria was not happy.

Calista sighed, knowing exactly what was coming. She stopped looking at her screen and focused on Aria after she typed something in, pulling up more data on Kit and Charlie's recent activities.

Aria began talking, her tone sharp with irritation. "Calista, what the hell is going on? Kit and Charlie have gone dark, and now I'm hearing they're making major financial moves without looping us in. What are they doing? Charlie's been in touch with her lawyer."

Calista didn't waste time with pleasantries. "She's investing heavily into André Beaulieu's business. I don't have all the details, but from what I've gathered, this isn't just about cars. Kit's likely doing the same, though I haven't been able to confirm it yet. His wealth manager won't confirm either way. Whatever they're up to, they're keeping it close to the chest."

Aria's frustration was visible. "Damn it! They should have come to us first. We're supposed to be a team, but they're acting like this is a solo mission. This isn't just reckless, it's dangerous."

"I agree," Calista said, trying to keep her tone steady despite her own rising concerns. "But looks like they're in deep now. We need to figure out how to support them without blowing their cover. They're not just walking into a lion's den, they're volunteering to be the bait."

Aria was silent for a moment, the weight of the situation sinking in. Finally, she spoke, her voice softer but no less determined. "Keep tracking them. If they make any more moves, I want to know immediately. And if you get the chance, remind them that they're not invincible."

"Will do," Calista replied, turning back to her computer.

She leaned back in her chair, staring at the screens in front of her. Kit and Charlie were playing a dangerous game, one that could end very badly if they weren't careful. She just hoped they knew what they were doing.

——

In Montreal, Kit and Charlie were standing in the lavish showroom of André, the man who had become their gateway into the world of Alexandre and Gero. The day had been a whirlwind of meetings and formalities, all culminating in this moment, securing their investments and solidifying their cover.

The atmosphere in the showroom was one of understated luxury, with soft lighting and polished floors that reflected the gleaming cars on display. Kit and Charlie had just finalized their investments, each of them transferring a substantial amount of money into André's business accounts. The numbers were staggering, but necessary if they wanted to keep up the charade.

André, for his part, was practically glowing. He stood across from them, his smile wide and eager, as though he were the cat that had just caught the canary. "Mr. Thorne, Ms. O'Donovan, I must say, your investments are most welcome. I assure you, you won't be disappointed."

Kit offered a polite smile, though his mind was focused on the task at hand. "We're still deciding on which cars to purchase. There's quite a selection here, and we want to make sure we choose wisely."

Charlie nodded in agreement, her own smile charming but distant. "Indeed. We've been impressed by your inventory, André. But such decisions take time."

André's eyes gleamed as he stepped forward, gesturing for them to follow him. "Of course, of course. In the meantime, I'd like to offer you something as a token of Mr. DuBois' and Mr. Meyer's apologies for the treatment you received last night. Please, come with me."

Kit and Charlie exchanged a brief, cautious glance before following André deeper into the showroom. He led them to a secluded corner, where two nearly identical Aston Martins sat side by side, their sleek bodies shimmering under the overhead lights.

"These," André said with a flourish, "are for you. Consider them our way of making amends."

Kit and Charlie were momentarily stunned. The cars were works of art, each one a shone with luxury and power. They could practically see the drool forming at the corners of André's mouth as he handed them each a set of keys. He must have been paid well for these.

Charlie recovered first, her voice smooth as she accepted the keys. "André, this is incredibly generous. Thank you."

Kit nodded, slipping the keys into his pocket. "Yes, thank you. We appreciate the gesture."

André beamed, clearly pleased with himself. But before they could say more, his phone buzzed in his pocket. He pulled it out, reading the message with a frown that quickly turned into a look of concern.

"Is something wrong?" Kit asked, his tone casual despite the unease curling in his gut.

André hesitated for a fraction of a second before shaking his head. "No, nothing to worry about. But if you'll excuse me for just a moment, I need to make a quick call."

Kit and Charlie exchanged another look, both of them sensing that something was amiss. André stepped away, his voice low as he spoke into the phone. They couldn't make out what he was saying, but the fear in the air was unmistakable.

When André returned, his expression was carefully neutral, but there was a tightness around his eyes that hadn't been there before. "I apologize for the interruption," he said smoothly. "There is something I'd like to discuss with you both in my office."

Kit's instincts were screaming at him that something was wrong, do not follow, but he kept his expression calm. "Lead the way," he said, gesturing for André to go ahead.

They followed him to his office, a lavishly decorated room with leather furniture and expensive artwork on the walls. Once inside, André walked behind his desk, opening a drawer and pulling out two small, ornate boxes. He handed one to Kit and the other to Charlie.

"These," he said with a smile that didn't reach his eyes, "are invitations to a very exclusive gala this evening. Black tie, of course. I think you'll find it to be quite an interesting event, one that may even involve your next newest investments."

Charlie's heart sank as she opened the box, revealing a golden invitation inside. The hidden meaning was clear as day, and a chill ran down her spine. She knew exactly what kind of gala this was, an upscale auction, the kind that dealt in more than just luxury goods.

Kit's expression remained carefully neutral, but she could see his jaw tense up. He had an idea.

"Thank you, André," Kit said, his voice steady. "I will do my best to be free to attend."

Charlie took a calming breath, "Of course, I will be happy to attend. I believe my schedule is free for the evening. Thank you."

André's smile widened, and for a moment, Charlie could almost see the predator lurking beneath the surface. "I'm sure you'll find it most enlightening. I look forward to seeing you both there."

Kit and Charlie exchanged one last glance before leaving the office, their minds racing with the implications of what they had just learned. The moment they were outside and away from prying eyes, Charlie's frustration bubbled to the surface.

"Damn it, Kit," she muttered under her breath, her voice laced with tension. "We're walking into a nightmare. Alone."

Kit's jaw tightened as he responded, his voice low. "I know. But we don't have a choice. We both knew what we were doing when we came here."

"The question is, do you think you can keep it together? You've never been to one of these. They are an atrocity. You won't like it." Charlie spoke, her tone sharper than she intended. "If you lose it in there, we're done."

Kit shot her a hard look. "I'll be fine, Charlie. Just focus on getting what we need."

Charlie sighed, her frustration giving way to resignation. "Fine. Let's just get this effing over with."

They reached their new cars, the Aston Martins gleaming in the afternoon sun, but neither of them took any pleasure in their luxurious gifts. They both knew what awaited them that evening, and it was far from the glamorous world of high-end investments.

As they drove away, Charlie's mind was already working on a plan, a way to get through the night without blowing their cover. But no matter how she looked at it, there was no easy way out.

They were walking into the lion's den, and all they could do was hope they would make it out alive.

CHAPTER 24

The evening arrived with a noticeable feeling of tension and anticipation, and as Charlie Donovan prepared herself, she knew that tonight, more than ever, every detail mattered. The persona she had carefully crafted, Charlotte O'Donovan, the wealthy, enigmatic horse breeder and investor, had to be flawless. And tonight, she needed to dazzle, to capture the attention of the elite and dangerous individuals she was about to mingle with, without giving away her true intentions and pray that no one was there from the New York operation.

She stood before the full-length mirror in her suite, studying her reflection with a critical eye. Her dark auburn hair, which usually framed her face in a cascade of rich waves, had been transformed. Now, it was a brilliant shade of platinum blonde, a change she had made specifically for this persona. The color was striking against her fair skin, lending her an air of sophistication and mystery. Her hair was swept into an elegant updo, soft tendrils framing her face, and secured with diamond-encrusted pins that glittered in the light.

The gown she had chosen for the evening was nothing short of breathtaking. It was a creation fit for royalty, crafted from luxurious black satin that hugged her figure in all the right places before flaring out slightly at the hips in a subtle, yet dramatic, mermaid silhouette. The neckline was daring but tasteful, a deep V that showcased her décolletage without crossing into vulgarity, while the back plunged low, leaving much of her back exposed, the smooth expanse of skin interrupted only by the delicate straps crisscrossing over her shoulder blades.

The fabric shimmered as she moved, catching the light with every step. The gown was adorned with intricate beadwork along the bodice, tiny black diamonds that added a subtle sparkle, drawing the eye to her hourglass figure. Her waist was cinched with a matching black satin belt, and the skirt flowed gracefully to the floor, ending in a slight train that trailed behind her, adding to the gown's regal elegance.

Her jewelry was understated yet luxurious, dangling diamond earrings that caught the light with every turn of her head, and a matching diamond bracelet that encircled her wrist like a glittering cuff. Around her neck, she wore a simple pendant, a single, flawless emerald set in platinum, resting just above the swell of her cleavage. The choice of emerald was deliberate, an echo of the persona she had created, a woman of wealth and power, with an eye for the rare and exquisite.

Her makeup was expertly applied, accentuating her striking features. Smoky eyeshadow in shades of charcoal and silver made her green eyes stand out even more, while her lips were painted a deep, bold red, contrasting her pale skin and blonde hair. The overall effect was one of captivating beauty, a woman who commanded attention the moment she entered a room.

As she slipped on her black satin stilettos, adding inches to her height, Charlie took a deep breath, steadying herself. The reflection staring back at her was every inch the role she needed to play tonight, elegant, powerful, and untouchable. But beneath the surface, her heart pounded with the knowledge of what lay ahead and the certainty they were walking into something dark and unknown.

She was ready.

In another part of the exclusive bed and breakfast, Kit was also preparing for the evening's event, his thoughts focused on the delicate balance he would need to strike tonight. The man staring back at him in the mirror was a far cry from the street-smart kid who had clawed his way out of the depths of San Francisco's rough neighborhoods. Now, he was the epitome of sophistication and power, a man who looked like he belonged in the world of the ultra-wealthy, because in many ways, he did.

His tuxedo was a masterpiece of tailoring, custom-made to fit his tall, muscular frame perfectly. The jacket was a deep, inky black, the fabric smooth and matte, with peak lapels that added a sharp edge to his silhouette. The shoulders were broad and structured, giving him an imposing presence, while the jacket nipped in slightly at the waist before tapering down to rest just above his hips. The trousers were slim, with a sharp crease running down the front, ending just above his polished black leather shoes.

Beneath the jacket, he wore a crisp white dress shirt, the collar stiff and clean, with black mother-of-pearl buttons that added a touch of understated luxury. His bow tie was perfectly tied, a black satin that matched the lapels of his jacket, and a black silk cummerbund encircled his waist, completing the classic look.

Kit's blonde hair, which usually had a slightly tousled, carefree look, was neatly combed back, the natural waves tamed but still hinting at their presence. His striking blue eyes, always intense, seemed even more so tonight, as if the weight of the evening had sharpened his focus. There was a ruggedness to his features that the tuxedo couldn't entirely hide, a reminder of the man he was beneath the polished exterior.

He looked every bit the part of a powerful, wealthy businessman, a man who could command a room with a single glance, whose presence alone demanded respect. But Kit knew that tonight, he would need more than just appearances. He would need to keep his emotions in check, especially if the night went in the direction he feared it might.

With a final adjustment of his cufflinks, Kit was ready. He slipped his phone into the inner pocket of his jacket, taking one last look in the mirror before heading out. Tonight, he and Charlie would need to be at the top of their game.

Miguel and Grunt, Kit and Charlie's loyal bodyguards, were waiting in the lobby, their usually casual appearances transformed into something far more formal. Both men had been required to don tuxedos for the evening, a sight that was as unusual as it was striking.

Miguel, with his powerful, muscular frame, filled out the tuxedo with ease. The jacket strained slightly across his broad shoulders, emphasizing the strength that lay beneath the fabric. His hair was slicked back, and the slight shadow of stubble on his jawline added a rugged edge to the otherwise polished look. He looked every bit the part of a high-class bodyguard, elegant but undeniably dangerous, a man who could easily blend into the background while being ready to spring into action at a moment's notice.

Grunt, towering and imposing as ever, was a formidable presence in his tuxedo. The black fabric seemed to absorb the light, making him appear even larger and more intimidating. His hands, thick and calloused, looked almost out of place against the pristine white cuffs of his dress shirt. But despite the formal attire, there was no mistaking the barely contained power in his movements, the way his eyes constantly scanned the room for threats.

Both men were more accustomed to jeans and tactical gear than black tie events, but tonight, they looked the part. And yet, there was an air of unease about them, a sense that they were out of their element, even as they moved with the quiet efficiency of seasoned professionals.

When Kit and Charlie descended the grand staircase of the B&B lobby, Miguel and Grunt were there to meet them, their expressions a mix of awe and concern. Kit, stunning in his tuxedo, exuded an air of confidence and control, while Charlie, with her platinum blonde hair and exquisite gown, was a vision of elegance and power.

For a moment, all four of them stood in silence, the gravity of the evening hanging over them like a shroud. Then Kit gave a slight nod, signaling that it was time to go.

Miguel and Grunt fell into step behind them, the perfect picture of high-class security, but both men couldn't shake the feeling that tonight was going to be anything but ordinary.

As they stepped out into the waiting limousine, the night air crisp and cool, Charlie cast a glance at Kit, her expression unreadable. "Ready for this?" she asked, her voice low.

Kit met her gaze, his blue eyes steady. "As ready as I'll ever be. Just remember, no matter what happens, we stick to the plan. We're just investors."

"Well then, I think there's some things I need to explain to you gentlemen."

They looked at her, causing a knot of fear to build in her chest and her mouth to go dry.

As the limousine pulled away from the curb, heading toward the gala, she couldn't shake the feeling that they were walking into something far darker than they had anticipated.

But there was no turning back now. The game was in motion, and all they could do was play their parts, and hope they made it through the night unscathed.

——

The limousine moved smoothly through the streets of Montreal, the city lights casting a soft glow through the tinted windows. Inside, the atmosphere was heavy with unbridled tension, a heavy silence settling over the group as they made their way to the gala. Charlie sat across from Kit, her expression a mask of composure, though the anxiety gnawing at her was barely contained. Miguel and Grunt sat on either side of Kit, their eyes focused, jaws clenched, and every muscle in their bodies taut with the anticipation of what lay ahead.

Charlie knew that the calm before the storm was the most crucial moment, and she needed to prepare them for what they were about to face. She took a deep breath, her gaze shifting between the three men, and began to speak, her voice steady but laced with a seriousness that commanded their attention. She had the driver close the partition and clicked a device in her purse that would disable any bugs placed in the limo.

"Listen up," Charlie spoke, her tone leaving no room for argument. "Tonight is going to be unlike anything you've ever experienced, and you need to be ready, mentally, emotionally, and physically. This isn't just another high-stakes business deal. What we're walking into is a nightmare. And you have to be prepared for that."

Kit's eyes locked onto hers, his expression unreadable, but she could see the anger simmering beneath the surface. Miguel and Grunt exchanged a quick glance, their usual confidence slightly shaken by the gravity in Charlie's voice.

"Go on," Kit told her, his voice calm but with a sharp edge. He wasn't a man who liked surprises, and Charlie could sense his need for information. This was definitely going to be a surprise.

Charlie nodded. "The gala we're attending tonight isn't just about showcasing luxury items." She paused. "Well, it is, but not the kind you're thinking of. It's an auction. And the merchandise? It's human beings. Specifically, children. We're about to walk into a room full of some of the most depraved people on this planet, people who view human lives as commodities, as things to be bought and sold."

She let that sink in, watching as the words took hold. Kit's expression darkened, his fists clenching in his lap. Miguel's jaw tightened, a muscle jumping under his skin, and Grunt's eyes narrowed, his hands flexing as if he needed something to grip to keep his control.

"Before we go any further," Charlie continued, "you need to understand one thing, you cannot react. I know it's going to be difficult. Hell, it's going to be damn near impossible. But if we lose our cool, if we give ourselves away, we'll blow our cover, and we'll lose any chance of rescuing these kids."

The tension in the limo was almost suffocating now, a noticeable force that seemed to take the air out the limo. Charlie felt it too, but she had to stay focused. They had to stay focused.

"Charlie, how the hell do you expect us to stay calm?" Miguel's voice was low and tight, barely controlled. "You're telling us we're about to walk into a room where kids are being sold like cattle, and we're supposed to just... what? Smile and nod?"

Charlie's eyes softened slightly as she looked at Miguel, understanding the turmoil he was feeling. "I know how it sounds, Miguel. I know it's going to tear you apart. But you have to remember why we're there. We're there to gather information, to identify these kids, and to make sure they're rescued. If you lose control, if any of us lose control, we risk everything."

Kit leaned forward slightly, his voice cold and measured. "What's the plan, Charlie? How do we ensure these kids get out?"

Charlie met his gaze, her own eyes reflecting the weight of the responsibility she felt. "I've been in contact with Aria and Doc." Kit winced. "We have a plan in place. Aria sent me a contact who provided me with tiny tracking chips. I'll be placing them on each victim as I inspect the merchandise. Once we have those chips in place, Aria's team will be able to track them, and Doc has connections here in Montreal who will assist in the rescue. By the end of tomorrow, those kids will be out of harm's way."

The men were silent for a moment, processing the information. Kit's expression was thoughtful, calculating. He was always looking for angles, for the best way to approach a situation, and Charlie could see him working through the logistics in his mind.

"You're going to be inspecting them?" Kit asked, his voice carefully controlled. "How are you going to get close enough without raising suspicion?"

Charlie's lips twitched in a dry, humorless smile. "As Charlotte O'Donovan, the wealthy horse breeder and investor, I'm someone who deals in high-value commodities. They'll expect me to inspect the merchandise, to assess its worth before making a bid. It's the perfect cover. I accidentally let it slip that I've done this before. Oops." Charlie gave a surprised look, trying to ease the tension.

"And what about us?" Grunt's deep voice rumbled from beside her, his gaze intense. "What are we supposed to do while you're inspecting these kids?"

"You're my security," Charlie said, looking at Grunt and then at Miguel. "You're there to keep me safe and to make sure nothing goes wrong. But you're also there to watch, to observe, and to remember everything you see. We need to gather as much intel as possible, faces, names, anything that can help us take these bastards down. I had the top button on each of your shirts replaced with a video and audio device. Aria and Calista will be monitoring and taking down information. It does not help us however, we are still on our own."

The tension in the limousine was almost unbearable now, the reality of what they were about to face settling in, causing heart rates to accelerate. Charlie could see the anger in their eyes, the barely contained fury at the thought of what they were about to witness. It mirrored her own feelings, but she knew she had to keep them focused.

"Look," she said, her voice softening slightly, "I know what I'm asking of you is damn near impossible. I know that every instinct in your bodies is going to be screaming at you to take these people down the moment you see what's happening. But we have to play the long game. We can't save these kids or future kids if we don't get the information we need. So, whatever you see, whatever you hear, you have to stay calm. Stay detached. Remember, this is business. We're there to make a deal, nothing more."

Kit's eyes met hers, his expression hard as steel. "You'd better be right about the plan. If anything goes wrong…"

"I am. It won't," Charlie cut him off, her voice firm. "I won't let it. We're going to get through this, and we're going to save those kids. But we have to do it right."

The limousine fell into a heavy silence, the only sound the soft hum of the engine as they continued toward the gala. Each of them was lost in their own thoughts, preparing for the horrors they knew they were about to face. The weight of the night pressed down on them, but there was also a grim determination in the air.

After a few minutes, Charlie broke the silence, her tone dry but laced with a warning. "So, boys, remember, this is business. Stay detached, calm, cool, and collected, no matter what you see, hear, or feel. We can't afford to slip up, not now."

Miguel and Grunt both nodded, though the tension in their bodies hadn't lessened. Kit's expression was as unreadable as ever, but Charlie knew him well enough to see the storm brewing behind his eyes.

As they neared their destination, Charlie took one last deep breath, steeling herself for what was to come. Tonight would test them all in ways they had never been tested before, but if they stayed focused, if they stayed in control, they would get through it.

And then, when the time was right, they would take these monsters down.

The limousine pulled up in front of the grand building where the gala was being held, its imposing structure made one feel safe and secure, which contradicted what was about to take place within its walls. The driver opened the door, and Charlie stepped out first, her gown flowing elegantly around her as she exited the vehicle. Kit followed, his expression one of calm authority, with Miguel and Grunt bringing up the rear, their eyes scanning the surroundings for any sign of danger.

As they approached the entrance, the night air was filled with the sound of soft music and the low hum of conversation from the other guests arriving. The grandeur of the event masked the evil lurking beneath the surface, but Charlie knew that this was the calm before the storm.

She glanced at Kit, who gave her a slight nod, a silent acknowledgment that they were in this together. They had to be. There was no room for error. Charlie became Diamond Frost. Cold, calm, ready to deal with the big boys. With one final, steadying breath, Charlie led them into the lion's den.

CHAPTER 25

Charlie's heart was heavy with guilt as she finally dialed Aria's number. The familiar beep echoed in her ear as the call connected. She had been dreading this conversation, knowing full well what awaited her on the other end of the line. When Aria picked up, her voice was sharp and immediate, cutting through the silence like a knife.

"Charlie, what the hell are you doing?"

Charlie winced but said nothing, allowing Aria to continue uninterrupted. She had expected this, knew it was coming, and in truth, she knew Aria had every right to be furious.

"You go dark, you don't tell anyone where you are, you don't communicate, and now I find out you've been making deals and setting up God knows what without even a heads-up? Are you out of your mind, Charlie? Do you have any idea how reckless this is? How dangerous?"

The words came out in a torrent, each one hitting Charlie with the weight of Aria's anger and concern. Charlie remained silent, letting Aria vent. She needed this, needed to get it all out, and Charlie owed her that much.

"I trusted you," Aria continued, her voice trembling slightly, the anger giving way to something deeper, something more painful. "I trusted you to keep us in the loop, to work with us, not to go off on your own like some kind of lone wolf. This isn't like before, Charlie. These guys aren't about being noticed and praised. They're about hiding in the shadows, stealing the light. What we're doing is about all of us, about the people we're trying to save. You don't get to make decisions like this on your own!"

The silence that followed was deafening. Charlie could hear Aria's heavy breathing on the other end, the weight of her words settling between them like a bomb about to explode.

Finally, Aria spoke again, her voice softer but no less intense. "Well?"

Charlie took a deep breath, her throat tight. "You're right, Aria. I'm sorry. But now's not the time to hash this out. I need your help."

Aria's silence was telling, but she didn't interrupt. Charlie pressed on, knowing she needed to get to the point before Aria could ask more questions.

"I'm going to need chips, forty of them, small enough to implant by touch. And I need four small audio and video devices that can be worn discreetly. I don't have time to explain everything right now, but I need these things as soon as possible."

Aria's voice was cold, the anger still simmering beneath the surface. "And why, exactly, should I trust you to do this on your own, Charlie? After what you've just done, how do I know you're not just going to run off and leave us all in the dark again?"

Charlie sighed, her frustration mounting. "Aria, I get it. I really do. But right now, I'm asking you to trust me one more time. This is bigger than just us. It's about saving kids, and I can't do that without your help."

The line was silent for a moment, and Charlie could almost hear the wheels turning in Aria's mind. Finally, Aria spoke, her tone resigned but firm. "The person's already on their way to meet you. I'll text you the location."

Relief flooded through Charlie, but she knew better than to let it show. "Thank you, Aria. I know I've put you in a tough spot, and I'll make it right. But for now, I need to trust me and prepare. We're headed to a gala tonight, and it's going to be... difficult."

Aria's voice softened, but there was still a hard edge to it. "Charlie, you need to be careful. Whatever it is you're doing, remember, you're not invincible. Don't think for a second that you can do this without us."

"I know," Charlie replied quietly. "I'll be in touch soon. Just... keep the channels open."

Without waiting for a response, Charlie ended the call, the conversation settling heavily in her mind. Aria was right, of course. She had been reckless, maybe even selfish, in how she had handled things. But there was no time to dwell on that now.

The text from Aria came through almost immediately, giving Charlie the location where she would meet the contact. She took one last deep breath before heading out, her mind already shifting to the next task at hand.

——

The meet-up location was an unassuming café on a quiet street, the kind of place that wouldn't draw too much attention. Charlie entered the café and spotted a man sitting alone in a corner booth, a cup of coffee in front of him. He looked up as she approached, his eyes sharp and assessing.

"You're Charlie Donovan," he said, more a statement than a question.

Charlie nodded, sliding into the seat across from him. "And you have what I need?"

The man reached into a small leather bag at his side and pulled out a slim case. He opened it, revealing a series of tiny chips and four small devices that looked like buttons. "These are the chips," he explained, sliding the case toward her. "They're activated by touch and will emit a signal that can be tracked by your team. The other devices are audio and video recorders. I disguised them as buttons, so you can attach them to your clothes without drawing attention."

Charlie inspected the items carefully, nodding in approval. "And the necklace?"

The man reached into the bag again and pulled out an exact replica of the necklace she was wearing, a simple pendant with a small emerald set in silver. "It's identical to the one you have on, but with the recording device built in."

"Good," Charlie said, slipping the new necklace into her bag. " can't even see a difference. Impressive."

The man leaned back in his seat, his expression unreadable. "This is risky, you know. If they catch on…"

"They won't," Charlie interrupted, her voice firm. "I've done this before."

He didn't push the issue, simply nodding in agreement. "Good luck, then."

Charlie stood, her bag slung over her shoulder. "Thanks. I'll need it."

As she walked out of the café, her mind was already racing ahead to the gala. She knew what she was about to face, the depravity, the horror, the darkness that would envelop the room as soon as the auction began. She had seen it all before, back when she was working with Trent as Diamond Frost, the cold, calculating businesswoman who could walk through hell and not flinch.

And that's who she would have to be tonight. Charlotte Donovan was no longer enough to shield her from what was to come. She needed the steel and the ice that came with being Diamond Frost. It was the only way she could survive this night.

——

Back at the hotel, Charlie returned to her suite. The room was dimly lit, the only sound the soft hum of the city outside. She pulled out the case with the chips and the devices, laying them out on the table in front of her.

She knew what she had to do. Each chip had to be implanted by a simple touch, on the arm, the shoulder, the back, wherever she could make it seem natural. The video and audio devices were ready to be swapped out with the buttons on the men's shirts, the tiny recording devices so discreet that even the most observant eye wouldn't notice them. She quickly broke into their rooms and swapped the buttons as instructed.

As she methodically went through the preparations, her mind drifted back to the many auctions she had attended as Diamond Frost. The cold detachment, the practiced indifference, the way she had to shut off her emotions to survive the horrors she witnessed. She had thought she left that part of her behind when the auction rescue was done at her ranch, but tonight, she would need Diamond more than ever.

Charlie paused, staring at her reflection in the mirror. The platinum blonde hair, the flawless makeup, the gown that clung to her like a second skin, all of it was part of the persona, part of the armor she was putting on to face the night. But it was the look in her eyes that caught her attention, the same icy resolve that had carried her through those dark days as Diamond Frost.

She had thought that part of her was gone, buried deep beneath the woman she had become. But as she looked at herself now, she realized that Diamond Frost had never really left. She had just been waiting for the right moment to re-emerge.

And tonight, that moment had come.

With a steady hand, Charlie swapped out the necklace, the cold metal of the new pendant resting against her skin. The chips were carefully tucked into a hidden pocket in her gown, ready to be used at the right moment.

As she finished her preparations, Charlie took one last look in the mirror. The woman staring back at her was calm, cold, and ready for whatever the night would bring.

"It's only business," she whispered to herself, a mantra she had repeated countless times before.

And with that, Diamond Frost was back.

The drive to the gala was quiet, the air in the limousine heavy with unspoken tension. Kit, Miguel, and Grunt sat across from Charlie, their expressions unreadable but their eyes sharp with focus. They had no idea what was waiting for them inside, but Charlie did. And as much as she warned them, tried to prepare them for the horrors they were about to witness, she knew that nothing she could say would truly prepare them.

She could only hope that Diamond Frost's cold and haughty return would be enough to get them all through the night.

As the limousine pulled up in front of the grand venue, Charlie took a deep breath, steeling herself for what was to come. The doors opened, and the cold night air rushed in, a sharp contrast to the warmth inside the car.

Charlie stepped out first, her stilettos clicking on the pavement as she straightened her gown and adjusted the pendant around her neck. Kit followed, his expression one of calm determination, with Miguel and Grunt bringing up the rear, their eyes scanning the surroundings for any sign of trouble.

They were ready, so was she. Diamond Frost was back for an encore, and tonight, she would do whatever it took to save those kids, even if it meant walking through hell one more time.

CHAPTER 26

The mansion loomed large against the darkened sky, its grandeur almost intimidating as Kit, Charlie, and their bodyguards, Miguel and Grunt, made their way up the marble steps to the entrance. The opulence was evident even before they stepped inside, the sheer size of the estate, the intricate details on the carved wooden doors, and the soft glow of chandeliers visible through the windows all spoke of immense wealth and power.

As they entered the mansion, they were immediately struck by the sheer extravagance of the interior. The foyer opened up into a massive ballroom, where glittering crystal chandeliers hung from the high ceiling, casting a warm, golden light over the room. The walls were adorned with priceless art, and every surface seemed to gleam with polished gold or marble. The room was filled with people, all dressed in the finest designer clothes, their laughter and conversation creating a soft hum that filled the air.

Andre Beaulieu was there to greet them the moment they entered, his smile wide and oozing with charm. He moved toward them with an air of confidence that bordered on arrogance, his gaze flicking between Kit and Charlie with undisguised interest.

"Mr. Thorne, Ms. O'Donovan," Andre greeted them, his voice smooth as silk. "I'm so glad you could make it. And I see you've brought your, ah, associates with you." He glanced at Miguel and Grunt, acknowledging them with a nod, though the faintest hint of condescension lingered in his tone.

Miguel and Grunt responded with curt nods, their expressions impassive. They were here to do a job, nothing more.

Andre's smile widened as he turned back to Kit and Charlie. "You two make quite the pair. I dare say you'd make a rather cute couple."

Charlie's eyes narrowed slightly, her response cold and immediate. "I highly doubt that will happen."

Andre laughed, the sound rich and unforced, as if he truly found the idea amusing. "Well, we'll see. The night is young, after all." He gestured around the room with a flourish. "Please, feel free to mingle. We're still waiting on a few guests, but in the meantime, enjoy yourselves."

Charlie's gaze swept across the room, noting the opulence in every corner, the wealth on display not just in the decor, but in the people themselves. Everyone here was dressed to the nines, dripping in jewels, their conversations laced with subtle boasts of their fortunes and connections. There was no sign that this was anything but a gathering of the fabulously wealthy, a party to celebrate success and excess. But Charlie knew better, and the knowledge made her stomach churn.

Kit gave Andre a polite smile, his eyes cold and calculating. "I don't like cold fish." Charlie glared at him. "Thank you for the invite, Andre. Think I'll mingle."

With that, they parted ways, Kit heading toward one side of the room while Charlie made her way to the other, Miguel and Grunt shadowing them at a discreet distance. The air was thick with the scent of expensive perfume and cologne, mingling with the aroma of gourmet hors d'oeuvres being offered by waiters moving through the crowd with silver trays. The sound of laughter and clinking glasses echoed in the grand space, but beneath it all, there was an undercurrent of something darker, something that set Charlie's nerves on edge.

As she moved through the room, Charlie made sure to keep her posture relaxed, her expression one of mild interest, while her eyes took in every detail. She knew Aria and Calista were watching through the hidden cameras embedded in her necklace and the buttons on the men's shirts, capturing images of the guests for later identification. She made it a point to engage in small talk with a few of the attendees, drawing out conversations that would allow the cameras to get a good look at their faces.

One man, an older gentleman with a neatly trimmed beard and an expensive-looking cane, caught her eye as he discussed his latest acquisitions with a group of admirers. His tone was casual, almost bored, as he spoke about his investments, but Charlie could hear the subtext, the way he spoke about "merchandise" and "lots" with a certain detachment that made her skin crawl.

"Of course, the trick is to find the right balance," the man was saying, his voice smooth and cultured. "You don't want too much of the same type, you know? It's all about variety, something for every taste. That's what keeps the buyers interested."

Charlie forced a smile, her heart pounding in her chest as she listened. "And have you had much success with that strategy?"

The man glanced at her, his eyes gleaming with a mix of pride and condescension. "Oh, indeed. It's all about knowing your clientele, my dear. You can't just throw anything at them and expect it to sell. You need to understand what they're looking for, what will catch their eye."

"And what about you?" another woman in the group asked Charlie, her tone curious. "What brings you here tonight?"

Charlie took a sip of her champagne, her smile never wavering. "I'm here to explore new opportunities. I'm always looking for something... unique."

The man nodded approvingly, clearly pleased by her answer. "A woman after my own heart. Well, I'm sure you'll find tonight's offerings to your liking."

Charlie nodded, her smile tight as she moved on, the conversation leaving a bitter taste in her mouth. She could feel the rage simmering just beneath the surface, threatening to break through her carefully crafted facade. But she couldn't afford to lose control, not here, not now. "Breathe," she told herself. "It's just a job." She knew it wasn't.

As she continued to circulate, she caught sight of Grunt across the room, his massive frame tense and his expression dark. She knew what he was feeling, she could almost see the anger radiating off him in waves. Making her way over to him, she paused briefly by his side, leaning in as if to share a quiet word with an employee.

"Grunt," she whispered, her voice low and steady, "I need you to keep it together, friend. Pretend you're with me on a buying trip for the club. It'll help."

Grunt's jaw clenched, but he gave a slight nod, his eyes still scanning the room. "It's hard, Charlie. These people..."

"I know," she said, her tone gentle but firm. "But we have to play the long game. Remember why we're here. Stay focused. Stay calm. Breathe."

Grunt exhaled slowly, some of the tension leaving his body, though not enough to fully ease her worry. "I'm trying, but..."

"We'll make it through," Charlie reassured him. "Just a little longer. You've got this."

As she moved away, Charlie caught Kit's eye from across the room. He was engaged in a conversation with a pair of men who exuded the same casual cruelty she had seen in the older gentleman. Their expressions were cool, their laughter easy, but Charlie could see the darkness lurking beneath the surface, the way their eyes gleamed with barely concealed malice. Kit was playing his part well, nodding along as they spoke, his demeanor one of interest and attentiveness. But she could see the tightness in his shoulders, the way his hands rested too still at his sides, as if he were holding himself back.

Charlie felt a surge of anxiety. Kit had been through his share of dangerous situations, but this was different. This wasn't just business, it was a moral abyss, a place where the line between right and wrong was not just blurred but obliterated. She knew how difficult it would be for him to stay detached, especially when the reality of what they were dealing with became more apparent.

She just hoped they could make it through the night without incident.

The minutes ticked by with agonizing slowness as the room continued to fill with guests, all of them exuding the kind of wealth and power that came from living on the edge of morality. The excitement in the air was heavy, and Charlie could feel it in every glance, every murmured conversation. The opulence around them was a veneer, a gilded mask hiding the rot beneath.

Finally, she saw Andre move toward the center of the room, a glass of champagne in hand, his face alight with a smile that didn't reach his eyes. He clinked his glass with a silver spoon, the sound ringing out above the din of conversation, and the room gradually quieted as all eyes turned to him.

Andre stepped up on a small, elevated platform that had been discreetly placed next to him, a gleaming smile on his face as he raised his hands to command the attention of the guests. The low hum of conversation gradually quieted as all eyes turned toward him, the anticipation in the room thickening with each passing second.

"Ladies and gentlemen," Andre began, his voice smooth and confident, carrying easily across the grand room. "The moment you've all been waiting for has arrived. It is with great pleasure that I announce the commencement of tonight's exclusive auction."

He paused for a moment, letting his words sink in, his gaze sweeping across the assembled guests who were now hanging on his every word.

"As many of you know, this evening is not just about luxury and opulence, though, of course, that is always a part of what we do. Tonight, we are offering something truly extraordinary. The merchandise you are about to witness is of the highest quality, carefully selected to meet the most discerning of tastes."

Andre's smile widened, a glint of something darker flickering in his eyes. "In a few moments, the merchandise will be displayed for your examination. You will have thirty minutes to inspect what is on offer, to assess the value, and to make note of what might pique your interest. Please, take your time. This is an opportunity to acquire something truly unique, and I trust you will find it to your liking."

He gestured toward the back of the room, where a set of double doors were slowly opening, revealing the dimly lit space beyond. "Our staff will be on hand to assist you, should you have any questions. And remember, discretion is paramount. We are all here for one reason, to ensure that tonight's transactions are both lucrative and private."

Andre's tone grew a touch more serious as he continued, his voice lowering just enough to be conspiratory. "I must remind you that what transpires here tonight remains within these walls. Our shared interest in maintaining confidentiality ensures that we can continue to conduct business of this nature in the future."

His smile returned, bright and inviting, as he concluded, "So, without further ado, I invite you to enter the display area and take a closer look at the offerings. The auction will begin shortly after the examination period. I wish you all the best of luck in securing what you desire."

With a final, sweeping gesture, Andre stepped down from the platform, signaling the beginning of the examination period. The guests began to move toward the open doors, their expressions eager, their movements calculated as they prepared to assess the merchandise.

The guests responded with polite applause, and Charlie could feel the undercurrent of excitement running through the room.

This was what they had been waiting for, the real reason these monsters were here.

Charlie's heart sank as she looked around the room. This was it, the moment they had been preparing for. Soon, the auction would begin, and they would be face-to-face with the true horror of what these people were capable of. She only hoped they could get through it without anyone losing their composure.

As she made her way back toward Kit, she couldn't help but notice the tension in the air had grown even stronger. The casual conversations had taken on a sharper edge, the smiles a little too wide, the laughter a little too forced. Everyone was waiting for the main event, and the anticipation was almost unbearable.

When she reached Kit, he was finishing his conversation with the two men, his expression carefully controlled. As soon as they were alone, she leaned in, her voice barely above a whisper.

"It's starting soon," she said, her tone urgent but calm. "Are you going to be able to handle this?"

Kit nodded, his eyes meeting hers with a mix of rage and resolve. "I will handle things just fine. How's Grunt?"

"Barely holding it together," Charlie admitted, her voice heavy with concern. "But he'll make it."

Kit's jaw tightened, and she could see the same anger simmering just beneath the surface. "Let's hope so."

Charlie forced a small, tight smile. "Remember, Kit, this is just business. Stay detached, stay calm."

"I know," he replied, his voice hard. "But that doesn't make it any easier."

"No, it doesn't," Charlie agreed. "Let's get through it."

As they prepared for what was to come, Charlie couldn't shake the feeling of dread that had settled in her chest. The night was only just beginning, and the worst was yet to come. All they could do now was brace themselves for the horrors ahead and hope that they could get out with their humanity intact.

The room was dimly lit, the air thick with a mixture of expensive perfume and the unmistakable stench of depravity. As Charlie and Kit stepped into the display area, Miguel and Grunt close behind, the murmur of low voices and the shuffling of feet were the only sounds that accompanied the gruesome spectacle before them.

She heard Miguel whisper, "What the f-ing hell!"

Lining the walls were a series of large gilded birdcages, each containing a child in some form of macabre old world style dress, their eyes wide with fear, their small bodies trembling. The harsh reality of what was happening was inescapable, and Charlie could feel the anger rolling off Kit, Miguel, and Grunt in waves.

Charlie's heart pounded in her chest as she scanned the room, trying to keep her expression cold and detached. She had to be Diamond Frost tonight, not Charlotte O'Donovan, not Charlie, just a cold, calculating businesswoman who saw nothing more than potential assets in front of her.

But as she turned to glance at Kit, she saw the barely controlled rage in his eyes, his fists clenched so tightly at his sides that his knuckles were white. Miguel and Grunt were no better, their faces were set in hard, grim lines, their eyes flashing with fury. It was clear that they were struggling to maintain control, and Charlie knew that if they didn't rein in their emotions, everything would explode into chaos.

She stepped closer to them, her voice a low, icy whisper as she glared coldly at each of them in turn. "Control yourselves," she hissed, her tone sharp and unforgiving. "If you can't, I'll create a scene and have you removed. Do you understand?"

Kit's eyes flicked to hers, the fury simmering just beneath the surface, but he gave a slight nod. Miguel and Grunt followed suit, their expressions still tense but slightly more controlled.

"Good," Charlie muttered, her voice still edged with frost. "Now, follow my lead."

She turned her attention back to the room, forcing herself to walk with a calm, measured stride as she approached the first cage. The child inside, a boy no older than eight, looked up at her with wide, tear-filled eyes. Charlie's heart twisted painfully in her chest, but she kept her expression neutral, her hand reaching out to touch the boy's cheek in what appeared to be a casual inspection.

"Not the first time at one of these, is it?" came a smooth, oily voice from beside her.

Charlie didn't have to turn to know who it was, Andre had slid up beside her, his presence unwelcome. She allowed herself a small, tight smile as she let her hand linger on the boy's cheek for a moment longer, secretly slipping one of the tiny tracking chips just inside his ear.

"No," Charlie replied, her tone cool and detached. "This isn't my first child auction. But I must say, I'm impressed with the selection."

Andre chuckled, clearly pleased with her response. "I knew you were a woman of taste. Anything catching your eye?"

Charlie glanced around the room, allowing her gaze to sweep over the other cages, each one containing a child more pitiful than the last. "I like to view the merchandise," she said, her voice smooth as silk. "But I have little use for them personally. My lifestyle is far too busy to be burdened with a child."

She allowed a hint of something darker to creep into her voice as she continued, "That said, I'm always willing to make an investment. Perhaps I'll find something that would make a suitable gift for a friend."

Andre's smile widened, his eyes gleaming with satisfaction. "I have no doubt you'll find something to your liking. Take your time, my dear. The auction won't start for another few minutes."

Charlie nodded, already moving on to the next cage, where a little girl with blonde curls huddled in the corner, her eyes filled with terror. As she knelt to inspect the girl, she could feel Kit's gaze burning into her back, his disgust radiating off him. But she didn't let it distract her. She reached out, brushing a strand of hair behind the girl's ear as she pretended to examine her.

"Beautiful," Charlie murmured, her voice almost too soft to hear. "But I'm not sure she's quite what I'm looking for."

She slipped the chip into place, her touch light and practiced, before standing and moving on to the next child. This one was a boy, perhaps ten years old, with dark hair and a defiant look in his eyes. Charlie met his gaze briefly, seeing the spark of fight still left in him, before she turned her attention to his physical condition.

"He's a little older than I prefer," she said aloud, knowing Andre was still watching her closely. "But there's a certain... potential here."

The boy flinched as she reached out to touch his shoulder, and Charlie had to fight the urge to pull back, to comfort him, to do anything but what she was doing. But she forced herself to remain cold, calculating, as she slipped the chip just inside the boy's collar.

"Potential indeed," Andre remarked, his tone approving. "I think you have an eye for this sort of thing, Ms. Donovan."

Charlie gave a noncommittal hum in response as she straightened and moved on to the next child. Each one she touched was another child marked for rescue, another life she hoped would be saved by the end tomorrow. But with each touch, she could feel the tension in the room growing, the barely contained rage of the men with her becoming harder and harder to ignore.

By the time she reached the last cage, Charlie could sense that Kit, Miguel, and Grunt were hanging on by a thread. The child inside this final cage was a girl, no more than six years old, with wide brown eyes and tangled hair. She looked up at Charlie with a mixture of fear and hope, as if sensing that this woman in front of her might be different from the others.

Charlie knelt down, reaching out to stroke the girl's hair, her voice low and soothing as she said, "There, there. Let's see what we have here."

She slipped the last chip into place, her fingers trembling slightly as she did so. The girl's small hand reached up to touch Charlie's, and for a brief moment, Charlie's cold facade cracked. She squeezed the girl's hand gently before pulling away, forcing herself to stand and regain her composure.

"Lovely," she said, turning to Andre with a smile that didn't reach her eyes. "But I think I've seen enough for now."

Andre beamed at her, clearly pleased with her performance. "Of course, my dear. I think you'll find the auction quite... exhilerating."

Charlie nodded, glancing back at Kit, Miguel, and Grunt, who had been watching her every move with a mixture of horror and anger. She could see the strain in their eyes, the way their muscles were coiled, ready to spring at any moment. They looked like they could go berserk at any second, and she knew she had to get them out of this room before something snapped.

"Shall we?" she said, her voice calm but with an underlying urgency that she hoped they would understand.

Kit nodded, his expression stony as he followed her out of the display area. Miguel and Grunt were right behind them, their steps heavy with barely restrained fury. Charlie led them down the hall toward the auction room, the sound of their footsteps echoing in the silence.

As they reached the doors of the auction room, Charlie paused, turning to face them. "Remember what I said," she whispered, her voice low and intense. "Stay calm. Stay detached. We're almost through this."

Kit's jaw clenched, but he gave a curt nod. Miguel and Grunt did the same, though she could see the strain in every line of their bodies. They were wound so tight, a mosquito bite could set them off.

Andre stood before the doors to the auction room, again on his pedestal, waiting for the last person to pay attention to him. He cleared his throat dramatically.

"Ladies and gentlemen," Andre called out, drawing everyone's attention once again. "I trust you've had ample time to examine the merchandise and make your selections."

There was a ripple of murmured agreement, a quiet buzz of excitement running through the crowd.

"Tonight, we offer more than just an opportunity to invest," Andre continued, his voice taking on a grander, almost theatrical tone. "We offer the chance to secure the finest, the rarest, the most exquisite acquisitions imaginable. What you have just seen is but a glimpse into the world of exclusive opportunity that awaits you within these walls."

"Shit," Charlie whispered, "they have more inside"

Kit tensed even more and was extremely close to coming undone, Charlie just touched his hand to calm him. It worked.

Andre stepped aside, extending an arm toward the grand doors behind him, which were now slowly swinging open, revealing the opulent theater beyond. "And now, it is my great pleasure to invite you to enter the theater for the main event. The auction is about to begin, and I assure you, it will be a night to remember."

Andre's smile grew even more pronounced, a gleam of excitement in his eyes as he delivered the final words. "Best of luck to all who enter. May the most discerning among you emerge victorious, and may your investments bring you great satisfaction."

With that, Andre gestured for the guests to proceed into the theater, where the real business of the evening would take place. The guests began to move forward, their anticipation causing their eyes to light up with the thrill of what was to come.

Taking a deep breath, Charlie walked through the doors and led them inside the auction room. The space was grand, with rows of plush seats arranged around small table and the stage where the auction would soon take place. There were five covered cages placed behind the auctioneer's podium. The guests were already filing in, their expressions eager and anticipatory, oblivious to the turmoil raging inside Charlie and her companions.

They found their seats near the front, and as they sat down, Charlie could feel what they were about to witness settling heavily on her shoulders. She glanced at Kit, who was staring straight ahead, his eyes cold and unreadable. Miguel and Grunt were stationed on a wall close to their table, their faces grim.

The auctioneer, a tall man with a booming voice and an air of authority, stepped up to the podium on the stage, signaling the beginning of the auction. The room fell silent, all eyes focused on the stage as the first cage was illuminated and the 'prize' inside revealed.

Charlie held her breath, praying that they would all make it through the night without losing control, without giving themselves away. It was a delicate balance, one that could tip at any moment.

The auctioneer's voice rang out, sharp and clear, as he began the bidding. "Ladies and gentlemen, our first lot for the evening..."

Charlie's heart pounded in her chest, the first cage held a child of no more than three or four years old. Dear God. As the bidding war began, the numbers climbing higher and higher as the guests competed for the "merchandise" on display. She forced herself to remain calm, to maintain her cold, detached demeanor, even as her mind screamed in horror at what was happening.

Kit's hands clenched into fists, his knuckles white, but he remained silent, his eyes fixed on the stage. Miguel and Grunt were barely holding it together, their breathing heavy, their expressions dark with rage.

As the auction continued, Charlie could feel the rage from the men growing. Each cage revealed a child that was barely out of toddler stage. Scared, garishly dressed, and apparently drugged as they made no sound. She knew they were one misstep away from disaster. They had to see this through, no matter the cost.

The auctioneer's voice droned on, and through it all, Charlie remained still, cold, and calculated, Diamond Frost, in all her icy glory, determined to survive the night.

The last of the children were brought out, and Charlie's heart sank further as she saw the fear in their eyes, the despair that clung to them making them appear even smaller. She knew she couldn't let it show. She couldn't let herself break.

The auction would soon come to an end, but the real battle was just beginning. She had to keep Kit, Miguel, and Grunt from going rogue and attempting a rescue. She slipped out to the restroom, where she texted Aria that she had better have a team to get the children tonight and there were five that were not tagged. Kit was not going to leave this place until he knew the kids were safe. Charlie got no reply.

CHAPTER 27

Charlie stepped out of the ladies' room and found her immediate challenge was keeping Kit, Miguel, and Grunt from blowing their cover before the rescue could be executed. As she made her way back to the table, she noticed the way Miguel and Grunt were eyeing the room where the children were being taken, their faces grim and their bodies taut with barely restrained fury.

They were on the edge, ready to explode, and Charlie knew that if they acted on their instincts now, people would be hurt, possibly the children, and everything would be lost. She needed to think quickly, to create a diversion that would keep them from doing something reckless.

Just as she was wracking her brain for a solution, she noticed a waiter passing by with a tray of champagne. The glint of the glasses caught her eye, and in that split second, an idea formed. It was risky, but it was the only option she had.

Charlie waited until the waiter was just within reach, then with precise timing, she "accidentally" tripped, stumbling into him. The tray tipped precariously, and in a split second, champagne flutes toppled over, their contents cascading down the front of her dress.

The cold, sticky liquid soaked through the fabric, and Charlie immediately launched into a performance worthy of the finest theater.

"Oh, you imbecile!" she shouted, her voice laced with outrage as she coughed and sputtered, wiping futilely at the wet mess on her gown. "Look what you've done! This dress is ruined! I'm tall enough, you couldn't have missed me!"

The waiter paled, he had no clue what had just happened, his eyes wide with horror as he stammered apologies, clearly terrified at the scene she was causing. Around them, heads turned, guests murmuring as they watched the commotion unfold. The attention was exactly what Charlie needed. No one saw Charlie slip five hundred dollars in his pocket.

Miguel and Grunt, who had been on the verge of making a move toward the room with the children, froze in place, their attention diverted by Charlie's outburst. Kit, ever quick on the uptake, realized immediately what she was doing and stepped in to support her performance.

"Grunt," Charlie snapped, still playing the part of the outraged heiress, "get me out of this wretched place at once! I've had enough of this disaster!"

Grunt, clearly struggling to suppress his emotions, nodded stiffly and moved to her side. Kit, stepping into his role seamlessly, offered her a look of concern. "Ms. O'Donovan, let me offer you the use of my limo," he said smoothly, motioning for Miguel to follow. "It's the least I can do after this... unfortunate incident. I think the young man tripped over my foot."

Charlie huffed, tossing her hair back with an air of indignation as she continued to dab at her dress with a napkin. "Fine, but only because I refuse to stay here a moment longer."

As they made their way toward the exit, Charlie's eyes met Andre's, who had been drawn by the commotion. He approached them quickly, his face a mask of concern.

"Ms. O'Donovan, please accept my deepest apologies," Andre said, his voice dripping with sincerity as he tried to placate her. "I assure you, this is not how we conduct business. Allow me to personally escort you home..."

"Absolutely not," Charlie cut him off sharply, glaring down at him with all the hauteur and height she could muster. In her stilettos, she had a good two inches on him, and she used that to her advantage, standing tall and looking down her nose at him. "I would rather eat dirt."

Andre blinked, clearly taken aback by her intensity. "Ms. O'Donovan, I..."

"Don't you dare," she interrupted again, her voice cold as ice. "I came to Montreal with high expectations of making a significant investment, and instead, I've been treated horribly. I even invested in your business after that horrible treatment the other night, but after this... disaster, I have serious reservations about continuing any further."

Andre's face paled slightly, the realization that he was about to lose a significant investor dawning on him. "Ms. O'Donovan, please, if there's anything I can do..."

"There isn't," Charlie snapped, her eyes flashing with anger. "Just leave me be, Andre. I'll contact you if I decide to do further business, but don't expect to hear from me anytime soon."

Kit, playing his part perfectly, looked appropriately embarrassed by the entire situation. "I'll see that Ms. O'Donovan gets home safely, Andre," he said, his tone apologetic. "We'll be in touch to discuss further investments once things have settled."

Andre, clearly desperate to salvage the situation, nodded hastily. "Of course, of course. My deepest apologies once again. I hope we can make this right."

Charlie didn't bother to respond, simply turning on her heel and striding toward the entrance with Grunt by her side. Kit and Miguel followed closely behind, their expressions carefully neutral as they left the grand auction room behind.

Once outside, the cool night air hit them, a huge contrast to the stifling atmosphere inside. Kit's limo was already waiting, and the driver quickly opened the door for them. Charlie slid into the backseat first, followed by Grunt, Kit, and Miguel telling the driver to piss off and find another limo.

As soon as the doors shut and they were driving off, Charlie dropped the act completely. She stopped wiping at her dress and let out a long, exhausted breath, her eyes closing for a moment as the tension began to drain from her body.

"That was Oscar-worthy, don't you think?" she said finally, a small, tired smile tugging at her lips as she looked at the two men in back with her and Migel in the rear-view mirror.

For a moment, there was silence, and then... laughter. It started with Kit, a low chuckle that quickly grew into a full, hearty laugh. Miguel and Grunt followed suit, their laughter a mix of relief and amusement as the stress of the evening began to ease.

Charlie's smile widened, the sound of their laughter helping to lift the weight off her shoulders. "I can't believe that actually worked," she admitted, shaking her head in disbelief.

"Neither can I," Kit replied, still chuckling as he leaned back in his seat. "It was brilliant. You really had Andre running scared. Wonder what Alexandre and Gero thought."

"I'm sure it was hilarious to them." Charlie stated. "However, if they think we are in this together, things could get sticky. I mean, we practically showed up at the same time, now we're seen around town together. Let's hope it's just a matter of pheromones between the two of us."

"God help me." Kit chuckled. "What a way to start a sting. You were pretty over the top."

"I just did what I had to," Charlie said, shrugging as she started wiping the sticky champagne from her arms and face. "We needed a distraction, and that waiter was in the right place at the right time."

"Just remind me never to get on your bad side," Miguel joked, his eyes twinkling with amusement. "That was some Grade-A acting."

Grunt, who had been the most tense of the group, finally allowed himself to relax, a small smile breaking through his usually stoic expression. "You saved us in there," he said simply, his voice gruff but sincere. "I was about two seconds away from doing something really stupid."

Charlie reached over and gave his arm a reassuring squeeze. "You did great, Grunt. We all did. But now we have to get out of here before things go south."

They pulled up to the bed and breakfast, and as soon as they were inside, the mood shifted from relieved to businesslike. Charlie was already thinking ahead, her mind moving at a million miles an hour.

"I'm not staying here another night," she announced as they entered the house. "I've already contacted my pilot. We'll be leaving Montreal within the hour."

Kit nodded, his expression serious. "I'll have my team make the necessary arrangements. We'll be leaving right behind you."

Charlie disappeared into her room to quickly change out of the champagne-soaked dress. She slipped into something more comfortable, a pair of fitted pants and a black sweater, before returning to the main area where Kit, Miguel, and Grunt were waiting.

Once they were packed and ready, they headed back to the limo that had remained on standby. They would text the company that the limo was at the airport. The drive to the airport was swift and uneventful, the mood in the car subdued once more. There was still a lot of tension, but it was mixed with a sense of relief that they had made it through the night without any major incidents.

At the airport, Charlie's private jet was already prepped for takeoff, the crew moving with efficient precision as they loaded her luggage. Charlie turned to Kit, Miguel, as they stood by the plane, the cool night air ruffling their hair.

"Thank you," she said sincerely, looking at each of them in turn. "I couldn't have done this without you."

Kit gave her a small, approving smile. "You did good, Charlie. You held us together."

Charlie nodded, feeling a pang of something close to guilt. "I just hope Aria got my message and those kids get saved tonight. She's mad and not talking to me."

"They will," Kit replied confidently. "And we'll see you at the lodge soon."

Charlie smiled faintly, appreciating his optimism. "I'll see you back in the States, then."

Miguel gave her a small salute, while Grunt helped her up the steps.

"Take care, Charlie," Miguel said gruffly. The lady had impressed him tonight. He now deemed her family.

"You too," she replied before turning to board her plane.

Once inside, she settled into the plush seat, Grunt a little further behind, exhaustion finally catching up with her. As the plane taxied down the runway, she let her thoughts drift, a mixture of relief and dread swirling in her mind.

Tonight had been a success, but there were still so many pieces in play, so many unknowns. Where in the hell were Alexandre and Gero? She knew they were there, Andre said they would be. Well, she had done her part for now. She knew she would have to make contact with Andre tomorrow to keep suspicion of her having anything to with the missing kids, if Aria got them tonight. She needed focus off her and Kit. She texted him that he needed to do the same as her in making contact.

As the plane lifted into the night sky, Charlie closed her eyes, letting the gentle hum of the engines lull her into a light sleep. Tomorrow would bring new challenges, but tonight, she could finally allow herself to rest.

CHAPTER 28

The lodge in Atlanta was beautiful as ever, its outward charm and tranquility contrasting the hostility filling the air inside. Charlie and Kit sat at the large, oval-shaped conference table, their expressions filled with guilt. Around them, their respective teams were gathered, both in person and connected via video conference. The screens displayed the faces of their team members who couldn't be there in person, their expressions ranging from concerned to downright angry.

On Charlie's side, the screen showed China, Kimmie, Charlie's best friend, Doc and Emily at the ranch, Izzy, Rafe and Marley in LA. Kit's side featured Jack, Jane, Sofia, and Zara. Also present were Devlin, Charlie's attorney, Manny, her friend and the Atlanta head detective and Vicky, her fellow FBI agent. Grunt and Miguel were there in person, standing behind Kit and Charlie, both of them wisely choosing to stay silent as they knew they were just as much in the hot seat as their bosses. Aria and Calista stood across from them, both shooting darts with their eyes at the foursome.

The atmosphere was charged, everyone waiting for the inevitable explosion of emotions. And it didn't take long for Aria, who was clearly leading the charge, to start.

"Are you two out of your goddamn minds?" Aria's voice was sharp and scathing, her anger evident even through the screen. People cringed. "You went dark! You didn't inform anyone! Do you have any idea how reckless and dangerous that was?"

Charlie winced, feeling the full brunt of Aria's fury. She knew it was coming, but that didn't make it any easier to bear. Kit, sitting beside her, maintained a stoic expression, though the tension in his posture betrayed his tension. He wasn't used to someone berating him, especially someone he barely knew.

"We're supposed to be a team," Aria continued, her voice rising. "We're supposed to be in this together. But instead, you both decide to go off on your own little mission, dragging Grunt and Miguel along for the ride, without so much as a heads-up to the rest of us. Do you have any idea what could have happened? What almost happened?"

Calista, Kit's tech wizard, jumped in, her tone no less heated. "I was monitoring everything, trying to figure out why the hell I couldn't get a read on either of you. You know how close we were to thinking something had gone wrong? We almost blew the whole operation because we didn't know what the hell you were doing!"

Jack, Kit's oldest friend and mentor, was next. His voice was stern, carrying the weight of years of experience. "You're both better than this. You know how important it is to keep your team in the loop. Going dark like that? It's a rookie mistake, and you're no rookies."

Kimmie, who rarely got angry, had her arms crossed, her brow furrowed with frustration. "Charlie, you of all people know better. We've been through enough together to know that keeping secrets like this only puts everyone in more danger. You should have told us." Her anger flared through the screen, causing Charlie to wince again.

Marley, always the calm one, spoke up with a measured tone, but there was a distinct edge to his words. "We've worked hard to build this trust, this unity. Going dark breaks that trust, and it makes us question whether or not we're really working as a team."

Even Sofia, the gentle soul of Kit's team, voiced her disappointment. "We're here to support each other, to help each other through these dangerous situations. But we can't do that if we don't know what's going on."

The barrage of reprimands continued, each team member voicing their concerns, their frustrations, and their anger. Devlin, always the calm and collected attorney, added his piece with a legal edge. "You both know how precarious our position is. If something had gone wrong, the fallout would have been catastrophic, not just legally, but for the lives we're trying to save."

Manny and Vicky, representing the law enforcement side of things, emphasized the danger of operating without a clear plan shared with the whole team. "You're putting lives at risk," Vicky said bluntly. "Not just your own, but the lives of the people we're trying to protect. We need to be able to coordinate our efforts, and that means communication."

By the time everyone had spoken, the room was heavy with concern and of their collective disappointment and anger. Charlie and Kit sat in silence, taking it all in, knowing that every word was justified.

Finally, Aria spoke again, her tone slightly softer but no less firm. "Moving forward, there will be no more of this going dark. We maintain contact every chance we get, and we don't make unilateral decisions that could endanger the entire operation. Is that understood?"

Charlie and Kit exchanged a glance, the guilt and regret evident in their eyes. Charlie was the first to speak, her voice low and sincere. "You're right. All of you. We were reckless, and we made a huge mistake. The opportunity was there and I took it without thinking. We should have kept you in the loop, and I'm sorry. I promise it won't happen again."

Kit nodded in agreement, his tone equally contrite. "We acted on impulse, and a little bit of rage, and that was wrong. We let our emotions get the better of us, and it could have cost us everything. We're sorry, and we'll make sure it doesn't happen again."

Kit and Charlie had taken each other's reasoning in connecting with the Montreal organization and made it their own in their apologies. They looked at each other knowingly, silently agreeing they had made a mistake.

Aria looked at them both, her expression softening slightly. "Good. Because we can't afford any more mistakes like that. If they start really looking into your profiles, it's going to cause a lot of problems. That's why you have us, and you both need to remember that."

There was a moment of silence, the tension slowly beginning to disappear as the sincerity of Kit and Charlie's apologies settled in. Finally, Doc, ever the jokester, broke the tension with a grin.

"Apology accepted. But you two owe us big time. I'm thinking a nice dinner, maybe some top-shelf whiskey, and definitely no more surprises."

Rafe chimed in with a laugh. "Yeah, and maybe next time, let's just stick to the plan, huh? My young heart can't take another stunt like that."

The good-natured kidding continued for a few moments, the atmosphere gradually shifting from anger to camaraderie. The teams knew that, despite the mistakes, they were stronger together, and that bond couldn't be easily broken.

As the video conference began to wind down, Aria pulled up her notes on the rescue operation, her expression turning serious once more. "Now, on to more pressing matters. The children we rescued are safe and being taken care of. We managed to make it look like one of the serving staff leaked information about the auction, so none of the people attending will suspect anything. We were careful to rescue the kids as they were being transported out, so there's no direct connection to any of the attendees."

"That's good news," Charlie said, relief washing over her. "And what about Alexandre and Gero?"

Aria's expression darkened slightly. "Unfortunately, they've both gone back to their home countries, and we couldn't find any concrete evidence that they attended the gala. They're covering their tracks well, which means they're going to be even harder to pin down moving forward."

Kit frowned, his mind already working on the next steps. "We'll need to be even more careful then. They're smart, and they'll be on high alert after this. We can't afford to make any more mistakes."

Calista nodded in agreement. "I'll keep digging, see if I can find any traces of their activities. But for now, we need to regroup and figure out our next move."

Charlie coughed, "I've got a next move."

Everyone shot her a suspicious look.

"I left the gala under... shall we say difficult circumstances. I threatened to pull my investment money out. I could contact Andre apologizing for my outburst and request another meeting." She wanted to giggle at the acting she'd done that night. "Only problem is, I'm not going back to Canada. I want this done on our turf."

Aria looked at Charlie questioningly. "And?"

"I'm going to invite them to a high dollar auction."

The video monitor and the room erupted. "What!"

Charlie sighed, the thought of what she was about to suggest making her stomach sour. "We've bought ourselves some time, but we're far from being in the clear. We need a way to keep them interested and make sure they don't slip away."

Doc, ever the voice of reason, spoke up with a tight, strained tone, knowing what was coming. "I don't think your idea is a good one. We need to stay focused, use our sources to locate these men and surveil them. We can't let our emotions, no matter how deserved they are, drive us to make decisions that could jeopardize everything we've worked for."

The teams nodded in agreement, the seriousness of the situation settling in once more. Despite the earlier tension, they knew they had to move forward as one, working together to take down the trafficking ring that was causing so much pain and suffering.

"It's the only way I know how to keep them interested." Charlie responded. "If we could find their dark web site, none of this would be necessary, but since we haven't any evidence yet, we've got to hook them with something dynamic, expensive, and as illegal as hell."

Chatter filled the room as Charlie filled them in on her idea. Kit, ever the businessman watched quietly before expressing his thoughts.

"She's right, you know." The room went silent. "It was clear they run the show. Somehow, we need to get Andre out of the picture, and they will have to choice but to run things themselves or shut it down. With the money involved, they won't shut it down. Then we can lure them by offering a venue for them to use for one of their galas."

Discussion raved on for another hour, and soon, everyone was convinced that it was the best way to keep their people safe, build a relationship with Alexandre and Gero, and as Charlie so eloquently stated, "Destroy the sons of bitches."

As the final goodbyes were said and the video conference disconnected, the lodge fell into a quiet stillness. The weight of the change of mission ahead hung heavily in the air, but there was also an expectancy of what was to come lingering.

Aria, ever the planner, sat with Charlie, Kit, going over the details of the rescue and the cover story they had created. "We've done everything we can to make it look like an internal leak," she explained. "We're keeping tabs on the children, and they're being taken care of by trusted people. So far, everything points to us being in the clear, but we'll need to stay vigilant."

Charlie nodded, grateful for Aria's meticulous attention to detail. "Thank you, Aria. I don't know what we'd do without you."

Aria gave her a small smile, the earlier anger gone, replaced by the deep bond of friendship and trust they shared. "Just doing my job, Charlie. But you two need to be careful. Alexandre and Gero are dangerous, and they won't go down without a fight."

Kit, who had been silent thinking about all of his conversations with the two men, finally spoke up. "I know how to get to them. It's deals they want. High-end merchandise for their business. I can make that happen. But you have to trust me." Aria glared at him. Calista snorted. "I'm going to offer them a deal they can't refuse because Charlie is going to pull out for now."

It was Charlie's turn to glare.

"Just for now." Kit repeated. "I want them to be focused, and trying to schmooze two of us is not allowing them to. With them focused on me, we'll be able to find the lair where they are holding children. Trust me on this."

Aria nodded in agreement. "You're right. I don't know how, but I'm trusting you not to screw things up. Let's get Charlie on her call and ready to disgrace a group of men."

With the meeting concluded, Aria gathered her notes and left for her room, leaving Charlie, Kit, Grunt, and Miguel alone in the quiet of the room. The tension from earlier had finally dissipated, replaced by a feeling of camaraderie.

Charlie looked at Kit, a small smile tugging at her lips. "Well, that could have gone worse."

Kit chuckled softly, shaking his head. "Could have gone better too. But we survived, and that's what matters."

Grunt, always the man of few words, simply nodded in agreement. "I tell ya, I was puckered there for bit."

Miguel, trying to be the optimist, added with a grin, "And next time, let's try to avoid any more Oscar-worthy performances, huh?"

Charlie laughed, the sound light and genuine for the first time in what felt like ages. "Deal."

As they settled into the quiet of the lodge, the four people sipped their drinks and enjoyed the quiet. They knew things were going to get a little crazy and wanted as much down time as possible. Kit asked about the dark world of trafficking and Charlie explained it in detail so all three men would be prepared for next time. And sadly, there would be more next times. This battle was far from over, but they were going to be ready for whatever came next.

CHAPTER 29

Charlie leaned back in her chair, a sly smile playing on her lips as she dialed Andre's number. The lodge in Atlanta was quiet, the afternoon light filtering through the curtains, casting soft shadows across the room. Kit sat across from her, his expression calm but focused. They both knew this call was crucial to setting their plan in motion, and Charlie was more than ready to play her part.

The phone rang twice before Andre's smooth, polished voice came through the line. "Ms. O'Donovan, to what do I owe the pleasure?"

Charlie didn't waste any time. She immediately launched into her well-rehearsed tirade, her voice laced with annoyance and disdain. "Andre, let's cut the pleasantries. I'm still fuming over the fiasco at that so-called gala. I can't believe I wasted my time and money on such a half-classed event. You assured me it would be worth my while, and instead, I ended up with a ruined dress and a wasted evening."

Andre hesitated for a moment, clearly caught off guard by her abruptness. "Ms. O'Donovan, I deeply apologize for..."

"Apologies won't fix this," Charlie interrupted, her tone sharp. "I expected professionalism, Andre. I expected something... more. What I got was a far cry from what was promised. If it weren't for that lovely Aston Martin, I would be demanding a full refund. As it stands, I'm keeping the car as compensation for the disaster I endured."

"Of course," Andre said quickly, trying to placate her. "The Aston Martin is yours, with our compliments. I assure you, this isn't the experience we intended to provide, and I will personally see to it that..."

"I'm not interested in your assurances," Charlie cut him off again, her voice dripping with impatience. "What I am interested in is whether my investment will actually make any money. I'm beginning to have serious doubts about your ability to deliver on your promises, Andre."

She paused, letting her words hang in the air for a moment before continuing, her tone taking on a more calculated edge. "And just so you're aware, there are other events taking place in the U.S. that are far more professional. Cleaner, healthier merchandise, and a much more organized operation. I'll be attending those instead of wasting my time with any more of your half-baked ventures."

There was a brief silence on the other end of the line, and Charlie could almost hear Andre's mind racing as he tried to salvage the situation. "Ms. O'Donovan, I assure you…"

"I don't want your assurances, Andre," Charlie snapped, cutting him off for the third time. "I want results. I want my investment to pay off. If it does, maybe I'll consider doing business with you again in the future. But don't hold your breath."

With that, Charlie hung up, the satisfaction of setting the bait coursing through her veins. She turned to Kit, her smile widening. "Well, that should get him worried. Your turn."

Kit nodded, already pulling out his phone. "Let's see if we can push him over the edge."

He waited a calculated twenty minutes before dialing Andre's number, giving the man just enough time to stew in his unease. When Andre picked up, his voice was tense, lacking the smooth confidence it usually held.

"Mr. Thorne, I wasn't expecting to hear from you so soon."

Kit's voice was the epitome of calm and professionalism as he responded. "Andre, I wanted to apologize for not returning to the gala in time to complete the evening. When I arrived back at the location, it was dark, and there was no sign of activity, so I returned to my hotel. I hope I didn't miss anything important."

"Oh, no, no," Andre stammered, clearly flustered. "The evening wrapped up sooner than expected. Nothing you need to worry about."

Kit nodded as if he believed every word. "Good to hear. However, I do have a more pressing matter to discuss. I need to speak with either Alexandre or Gero about shipping some private stock merchandise. Would you be able to arrange for one of them to contact me?"

Andre's hesitation was palpable. "I could certainly pass along the message, Mr. Thorne, but... might I ask what sort of merchandise you're referring to? Perhaps I could assist you myself."

Kit's voice took on a slight edge, the kind that made it clear he was not a man to be trifled with. "I would prefer to discuss the details with someone who has the authority to make decisions, Andre. I'm not in the habit of dealing with middlemen when it comes to matters of importance."

Andre swallowed audibly. "Of course, Mr. Thorne. I'll make sure one of them contacts you as soon as possible."

Kit gave a curt nod, though Andre couldn't see it. "Thank you. I'll be waiting."

He ended the call, setting his phone down on the table with a quiet finality. "That should do it. If he wasn't already on edge, he certainly is now."

Charlie laughed softly, her eyes gleaming with satisfaction. "You could practically hear the sweat dripping down his face. Now let's see what he does next."

—

Andre sat in his office, the phone still clutched in his hand, his mind reeling from the two conversations he'd just had. He had barely recovered from Charlie's tirade when Kit had called, and now he felt like the walls were closing in on him. The situation was spiraling out of control, and he didn't know how to stop it.

In the span of two weeks, his carefully curated world had been turned upside down. He had gained two new clients, both of whom now seemed more trouble than they were worth. The gala, which was supposed to solidify his standing among the elite, had gone sour in every conceivable way. And now, to top it all off, the merchandise from the gala. the children, had gone missing without a trace.

Andre felt a cold sweat break out across his forehead. Alexandre and Gero were not men to be trifled with. They had entrusted him with a significant part of their operation, and he had failed spectacularly. The thought of their reaction to this latest debacle made his stomach churn.

He couldn't afford to wait. With trembling hands, Andre picked up the phone again and dialed Alexandre's private number. The call was answered on the third ring, and Alexandre's voice, cold and devoid of any warmth, came through the line.

"Andre. What is it?"

Andre swallowed hard, forcing himself to speak. "We have a problem, Alexandre. A couple of problems, actually."

There was a pause, the silence heavy with expectation. "Continue."

Andre took a deep breath, steeling himself. "First, the gala... it didn't go as planned. I don't know how long you stayed after the debacle with Ms. O'Donovan, but our clientele departed rather quickly after that. The merchandise disappeared after the clientele left, and we have no leads on where it might be. It's as if they vanished into thin air."

Another pause, longer this time, and when Alexandre spoke again, his voice was dangerously quiet. "And you're just telling me this now?"

"I... I wanted to try to resolve it before bringing it to your attention," Andre stammered, his voice betraying his fear. "But I've hit a dead end. There's more. The new clients, Ms. Donovan and Mr. Thorne... they're both causing... complications."

"What kind of complications?" Alexandre's voice was low, each word enunciated with chilling precision.

"Ms. Donovan is furious about the gala. She's hinted that she might take her business elsewhere, to competitors in the U.S. She's questioning the professionalism of our operations, and she's made it clear that she's not satisfied."

"And Mr. Thorne?" Alexandre prompted, his tone indicating that Andre was quickly running out of chances.

"Mr. Thorne requested to speak with you or Gero directly about shipping some private stock merchandise. He was very insistent that he deal only with someone in charge, not a middleman. He wouldn't give me any details."

The silence that followed was deafening, and Andre could feel his heart pounding in his chest, waiting for the axe to fall. Finally, Alexandre spoke again, his voice as cold as ice.

"You've made a mess of this, Andre. Gero and I will deal with you later. For now, send me Mr. Thorne's contact information. I want to know exactly what he's up to so I will handle this myself."

"Yes, Alexandre. Right away," Andre replied, his voice shaking with barely concealed fear.

The call ended abruptly, leaving Andre staring at the phone, his hands trembling. He knew he was in deep trouble. Alexandre and Gero were not forgiving men, and he had failed them in the worst possible way. If he didn't turn things around quickly, his life could very well be on the line.

Desperation clawed at him as he began making the necessary arrangements. He would set up the meeting with Kit, but he knew that wouldn't be enough to save him. He needed to find a way to recover the missing merchandise, to salvage what little credibility he had left.

As he sat there, the walls of his office closing in on him, Andre couldn't shake the feeling that his world was crumbling around him, and there was nothing he could do to stop it.

——

Back at the lodge, Charlie and Kit exchanged satisfied glances as they sat in the quiet of the room. They knew that they had successfully planted the seeds of doubt and fear in Andre's mind. Now, it was just a matter of time before those seeds grew into full-blown panic.

Charlie leaned back in her chair, a sly smile playing on her lips. "I'd say that went rather well."

Kit nodded, his expression one of quiet confidence. "We've got him by the short and curlies. Now we just need to keep the pressure on and see what shakes loose."

Charlie chuckled softly. "Poor Andre. He has no idea what's about to hit him."

Kit's smile was more of a grim acknowledgment than amusement. "Let's just hope he's scared enough to make mistakes. That's when we'll strike."

Charlie nodded, her mind already racing with the possibilities. "He's desperate. Desperate people do stupid things."

"And when he does," Kit said, his voice resolute, "round two begins."

As the two of them sat in the lodge, plotting their next move, they knew they were on the verge of something big. The pieces were starting to fall into place, and soon, they hoped to have the upper hand in this dangerous game they were playing.

They also knew that the stakes were higher than ever. One wrong move could bring everything crashing down. For now, they were in control, and that was all they needed to keep pushing forward.

The bait had been set, and now it was only a matter of time before Andre made his next move. When he did, Kit, Charlie, and their teams would be ready.

CHAPTER 30

Kit had returned to Virginia and now sat in his study, the flickering glow of the fire casting long shadows across the room. The ambiance was calm as Kit prepared for what could be one of the most critical conversations he'd ever had. The thought of what he was about to suggest made him feel contemptable, but he knew that the outcome of the conversation hinged on his ability to pull off this deception.

Across from him, Calista was perched on the edge of the leather armchair, her laptop balanced on her knees, her fingers flying over the keys as she monitored the encrypted communication channels. Her expression was focused, her sharp mind already running simulations of every possible outcome.

"Are you ready for this?" Calista asked without looking up, her voice calm but carrying a hint of concern.

Kit nodded, his gaze fixed on the phone in front of him. "I don't have a choice. We need to keep up appearances if we're going to bring these bastards down."

Calista's fingers paused on the keyboard, and she looked up, her eyes meeting Kit's. "Just remember, he's going to dig deep. Make sure everything checks out. Aria's got the backstory covered, but you need to sell it."

Kit gave her a tight smile. "I know. I'll handle it."

Just then, the phone rang, the sound slicing through the quiet of the room like a blade. Kit took a steadying breath and picked up the receiver, his voice cool and collected as he answered.

"This is Kit Thorne."

"Mr. Thorne," came the smooth, accented voice of Alexandre DuBois. "Thank you for taking my call."

Kit leaned back in his chair, his demeanor that of a man completely in control. "Of course, Mr. DuBois. I appreciate you getting back to me so quickly."

"I understand you have some... private stock merchandise you're looking to move," Alexandre said, his tone casual but with an undercurrent of curiosity. "I'm interested in hearing more about this."

Kit allowed a small smile to touch his lips, even though Alexandre couldn't see it. "Indeed, I do. It's a collection of exotic cars, specially modified, as well as some rare wines. The cars are high-end, unique in their modifications, things that make them stand out from the usual fare. As for the wines, they're from a personal collection I've been working on for years."

There was a pause on the other end of the line, and Kit could almost hear the gears turning in Alexandre's mind. "Exotic cars and rare wines," Alexandre repeated thoughtfully. "That's quite a combination."

Kit chuckled lightly, making sure to keep his tone casual. "Wine is a passion of mine, you could say. The cars I came into recently. But as much as I enjoy them, I'm looking to offload this particular stock. It's time to make room for new acquisitions."

Alexandre's voice took on a more businesslike tone. "I see. And you're looking to ship these items discreetly, I assume?"

"Discretion is paramount," Kit confirmed. "I don't want any complications or unwanted taxes. The last thing I need is for this to attract unwanted attention."

"Of course," Alexandre agreed. "I understand perfectly. We can discuss the logistics in detail when I arrive in the States. I'd like to inspect the merchandise personally before we proceed."

Kit nodded, though Alexandre couldn't see him. "That's fine. I'm confident you'll find everything to your liking."

There was another brief pause before Alexandre's tone shifted slightly, becoming more conversational. "I must say, Mr. Thorne, it's rare to find someone with such... eclectic tastes. By the way, have you had any contact with Ms. O'Donovan since the night of the gala?"

Kit allowed a slight frown to creep into his voice. "Not since that night, no. I'll be honest, I wouldn't want to be in your shoes if she's still as upset as she was when we last spoke. She was absolutely livid about the whole situation."

Alexandre chuckled, though there was a hint of tension behind the sound. "Yes, Ms. O'Donovan sounded to be quite... spirited. We will have to find a way to make it up to her."

Kit nodded to himself, sensing an opportunity. "You know, she let something slip during our examination of the stock that piqued my interest. She mentioned she's been involved in purchasing 'merchandise' for years, and it got me thinking... I wonder if she has resources here in the States. I might be interested in exploring that avenue of income as well. Do you happen to know how I could get in touch with her?"

The line went quiet for a moment, and Kit could almost feel Alexandre's mind working through the implications of what he'd just said. Finally, Alexandre responded, his tone measured. "Ms. O'Donovan seems to be a... complicated individual. But I'll see what I can do about finding her. In the meantime, I'll be arriving in the States in a few days. I'd like to view the property to be exported and discuss the logistics in person."

"Just one more observation, Mr. DuBois."

"Of course."

"You were not there the night of the gala, but you were there before. Was this your gala or was it Andre's? I want to make sure I'm dealing with the right people if I decide to seek other avenues of investing." Kit remembered to keep the whole deal about investing.

"I assure you, Mr. Thorne, the event was mine. Unfortunately, because I am a secretive person, very seldom do I attend in person. I was there, just... privately." Alexandre shared.

"I see." Kit acknowledged. "And it makes me happy that there are ways to not be seen at events like this." He decided to try to get more information. "It would be nice if there was some form of online presence, then a person wouldn't have to travel at all or if they travel as I do, still have the opportunity to view an event and make a purchase."

"Oh, but that is possible, Mr. Thorne. We have a wonderful site that displays our merchandise as it comes in. This builds interest as we prepare for each event, or we can sell the merchandise once it has been examined and confirmed sellable." Alexandre's voice sounded very proud of this accomplishment.

"Well, that is good to hear." He left the question out.

Alexandre cleared his throat. "Look for ShadowExchange."

Calista did a happy dance, and her fingers set the keyboard on fire.

"Thank you for sharing that information." Kit spoke as sincerely as he could. "I will be looking into it."

Kit's smile widened, knowing he'd hooked Alexandre. "I'll make the necessary arrangements for when you arrive. I look forward to meeting you in person again, Mr. DuBois."

"As do I, Mr. Thorne," Alexandre replied smoothly. "Until then."

With that, the call ended, and Kit set the phone down, his expression triumphant.

Calista, who had been listening in, leaned back in her chair, a satisfied grin on her face. "Well, big man, you better get your ducks in a row quickly. Alexandre's definitely intrigued, but he's not going to be easy to fool."

Kit nodded, already mentally planning the next steps. "I know. We need to make sure everything is airtight before he arrives. There can't be any loose ends."

Calista's grin faded slightly as she thought about the implications of Alexandre's upcoming visit. "He might also want to visit with Charlie. Things are certainly falling into place, but we need to be ready for anything."

Kit's expression grew serious. "Charlie can handle herself. She's already set the stage, and now it's up to us to keep this going. We need to make sure that by the time Alexandre arrives, everything looks exactly as it should."

Calista nodded, her mind already racing with the technical preparations she'd need to make. "I'll start working on the cover stories and background checks and get Aria to doublecheck. We need to make sure that everything holds up under scrutiny."

Kit stood up from his chair, his mind sharp and focused. "And I'll make sure the merchandise is ready for inspection. Aria's already found a government warehouse full of seized exotic cars and managed to procure them. We can use those as the bait. As for the wines, they're legitimate, and they'll help sell the story."

"Good," Calista said, closing her laptop and standing as well. "Let's get to work. We've got a lot to do before Alexandre arrives."

As they left the study, Kit couldn't help but feel a sense of satisfaction. The pieces were finally starting to fall into place, and with each step, they were getting closer to bringing down Alexandre, Gero, and their entire trafficking operation.

But he also knew that they were walking a dangerous line. One wrong move, one misstep, and everything could come crashing down around them. Kit was taking a huge risk but was now willing to see it through to the end.

The next few days would be crucial. They would need to move quickly, making sure every detail was perfect, every lie convincing, every piece of the puzzle fitting seamlessly together. Alexandre and Gero were powerful and dangerous, but Kit and his team were more than ready to take them on.

As Kit and Calista began the preparations, the clock was ticking. Alexandre would be arriving soon, and when he did, Kit intended to be ready. Billionaire mogul mode was turned on and ready to work.

Two hours later, Calista came to him with something he was not going to like.

CHAPTER 31

The humid night air clung to Kit's skin as he crouched behind a row of rusted shipping containers near the docks of Houston. The faint scent of saltwater mixed with the acrid tang of diesel fuel, created an almost unbreathable atmosphere. The faint sound of waves lapping against the nearby pier was almost drowned out by the distant hum of engines and the occasional shout from dockworkers wrapping up their shifts.

Kit signaled for them to hold their positions. The team was spread out around the perimeter of the warehouse, each member in their designated spot, ready to move at a moment's notice. Jack was perched on a nearby rooftop, his drones hovering silently above the target, feeding live footage to the team's comms.

"This place is crawling with them," Jack's voice crackled softly in Kit's earpiece. "Looks like they're prepping to move fast. I count four guards outside, two more inside. They're armed and twitchy. Something's spooked them."

Kit scanned the area through his binoculars, his sharp blue eyes narrowing as he watched the traffickers hastily moving between the warehouse and the docked freighter. The group of homeless teens they were here to rescue. some of whom had parents with them, were being herded like cattle, their hands bound, faces pale with fear.

"They're definitely spooked," Kit muttered under his breath. He turned to Miguel, who was crouched beside him, his muscular frame barely concealed by the shadows. "M&M, you ready?"

Miguel nodded, his dark eyes gleaming with a mix of determination and barely restrained anger. "Always ready, boss. Let's get those kids out of there."

"Techie, you've got the security feeds?" Kit asked, glancing over at Calista who was hunkered down with her laptop, her fingers flying across the keyboard as she hacked into the warehouse's camera system.

"Almost there," Calista murmured, her voice calm despite the tension. "Give me one more second... and... got it. Cameras are on a loop. They won't see us coming."

"Good work," Kit replied, his voice low and controlled. "Bones, Poly, you're on standby. If things go south, be ready to move in. Sofia, click twice when you're close."

Jane and Zara, the team's medic and linguist, were positioned closer to the building, ready to provide medical support and communicate with the captives once they were freed. Sofia was going to distract them by knocking on the door. Jane's eyes were steely, but there was a flicker of concern as she glanced at Kit. "Be careful in there, Kit. Don't do anything reckless."

Kit offered her a tight smile. "Reckless? That's Miguel's job."

Miguel grinned, his usual dark humor surfacing despite the situation. "Damn straight."

The banter helped ease the tension, but the seriousness of the situation quickly returned as they refocused on the task at hand.

"Let's move," Kit ordered, his voice firm.

The team moved silently and swiftly, sticking to the shadows as they approached the warehouse. The distant sound of a foghorn echoed across the docks, adding to the eerie ambiance of the night. Kit's senses were on high alert, every nerve in his body taut as they closed in on the building.

As they reached the side of the warehouse, Miguel positioned himself at the door, waiting for Sofia's signal. Kit glanced up at Jack's drone feed, which showed the guards still patrolling the perimeter, unaware of the team's presence.

"On my count," Kit whispered. "Three... two... one." They heard the knock and Sofia's click in their earpieces.

Miguel kicked the door wide open with a powerful thrust, the blast of sound of metal door thankfully muffled by the noise of the docks. The team surged inside, weapons drawn, moving with practiced precision. The interior of the warehouse was dimly lit, the flickering fluorescent lights casting long shadows across the concrete floor.

They were met with immediate resistance. One of the guards inside, clearly jumpy from whatever had spooked them earlier, opened fire the moment the door burst open. Bullets whizzed past Kit's head as he dove behind a stack of crates, returning fire with controlled bursts.

"M&M, cover me!" Kit shouted, his voice barely audible over the cacophony of gunfire.

Miguel responded instantly, his powerful frame absorbing the recoil of his rifle as he laid down suppressive fire, forcing the guards to take cover. Kit used the opportunity to move closer to the captives, who were huddled in the center of the warehouse, their eyes wide with terror.

Calista, who had slipped in behind them, was already working to disable the electronic locks on the cages. Her fingers flew over the keypad, and after a few tense moments, the door clicked open with a satisfying beep. Sofia was there to calm them as the team completed their tasks.

"Got 'em!" she called out, her voice tight with concentration.

But just as Kit began to move forward, a sharp pain exploded in his side. He stumbled, gasping as the world seemed to tilt around him. He looked down to see blood spreading across his shirt, a bullet wound just below his ribs, the bullet found the one spot that was exposed.

"Kit!" Jane's voice rang out in his earpiece, full of panic.

"I'm good," Kit gritted out, his vision blurring slightly as he pressed a hand to the wound. "Just a graze. Keep moving."

But the pain was intense, and he could feel his strength waning. Calista, who had also been hit, was slumped against the wall, clutching her shoulder where a bullet had torn through. She looked up at Kit, her expression a mixture of pain and apology.

"We've got to get these kids out of here," she said, her voice shaky.

Kit nodded, pushing through the pain. "Jack, what's the status outside?"

"Not good," Jack replied, his voice tense. "They've got reinforcements coming in from the docks. You need to get out, now."

"We're not leaving without those kids," Kit growled, his voice hardening.

Miguel, who had taken down the last of the guards inside, rushed over to help Kit. "Boss, you're hit bad. We need to get you and Calista out of here."

"Not yet," Kit insisted, his voice strained. "Get the kids first."

The group of children and parents, now freed from their bonds, were herded toward the door by Zara and Sofia, who were speaking to them in soothing tones, switching seamlessly between languages to calm their fears. Jane moved quickly to assess Kit's and Calista's injuries, her medical bag already open as she worked to stabilize them.

"Hold still, Kit," Jane ordered, her voice firm but gentle. "I need to stop the bleeding."

Kit winced as she applied pressure to the wound, but he kept his focus on the mission. "Miguel, get them out of here. I'll cover you."

Miguel hesitated, his loyalty to Kit warring with the need to follow orders. But a sharp look from Kit was all it took to make up his mind.

"Move, move, move. Let's go!" Miguel barked, ushering the captives toward the exit.

Just as they reached the door, the sound of engines revving outside signaled the arrival of the trafficker's backup. The door burst open, and more gunmen flooded into the warehouse, their weapons drawn.

"Down!" Kit shouted, firing at the advancing men even as the pain in his side threatened to overwhelm him.

Chaos erupted as gunfire filled the air, the crack of bullets deafening in the confined space. Miguel, ever the warrior, charged into the fray, taking down two of the gunmen brutally. But the odds were stacked against them, and it quickly became clear that they were outnumbered.

"Aria, we need backup!" Kit yelled into his comms, he had ordered Calista to contact Aria for help.

"I'm on it!" Aria's voice crackled back. "You idiot, why didn't you tell me you were doing this? Hold tight, I'm sending operatives to your location now!"

"We're out of time," Kit muttered, his vision swimming as he fought to stay conscious. He could feel his strength slipping away, the blood loss taking its toll. "Get them out, Miguel. Now."

Miguel nodded, his face set in grim determination as he continued to fire at the advancing traffickers. Calista, despite her injury, managed to take down another gunman with a well-aimed shot, but she was clearly struggling to stay upright.

"Go!" Kit ordered, his voice hoarse.

With no other choice, Miguel and Zara led the group of captives out of the warehouse, covering their retreat with suppressive fire. Jane stayed by Kit's side, her hands working quickly to stabilize him, even as the gunfire continued to erupt around them.

The last of the traffickers inside the warehouse went down with a final, desperate burst of gunfire several men that had just appeared. Kit could feel himself slipping into unconsciousness, his body growing weaker with each passing moment.

"Kit, stay with me!" Jane pleaded, her voice urgent as she applied pressure to his wound. "You can't pass out now!"

Kit was barely holding on. The world around him was fading, the sounds of battle growing distant as darkness encroached on his vision. His last conscious thought was of the children, praying that they would be safe.

When he finally succumbed to the darkness, it was with the knowledge that he had done everything he could.

——

Kit awoke to the soft hum of the jet engines, the familiar scent of leather and antiseptic filling his senses. His head was pounding, and every breath sent a sharp pain through his side, but he was alive. That much was clear. The world around him came into focus slowly, the soft glow of overhead lights revealing the interior of the private jet.

He tried to sit up, but a firm hand on his chest pushed him back down. "Easy there, Kit," a familiar voice said. It was Jane, her tone a mix of relief and sternness. "You're not going anywhere just yet."

Kit blinked up at her, his vision still a little blurry, but he could make out her worried expression. "Jane?" he rasped, his throat dry. "What happened?"

"You took a bullet, that's what happened," she replied, her hands moving with practiced precision as she checked his bandages. "And then you decided to play hero instead of letting me do my job."

Kit winced as the pain flared up again, but he forced a weak smile. "Can't help it. Occupational hazard."

Jane didn't look amused. "Well, your occupational hazard nearly got you killed. You lost a lot of blood, Kit. If we hadn't gotten you stabilized on the ground, you might not have made it."

Kit's smile faded as the memories of the warehouse came rushing back. The gunfire, the children, the traffickers... "The kids... did they make it?"

Jane nodded, her expression softening. "Yes, they're safe. Miguel and Zara got them out in time. They're on their way to a secure location now, thanks to Aria's people. They took out the last of the dark ops."

Relief flooded Kit, and he let out a slow breath. "Good. That's all that matters."

Jane finished her check and sat back in her seat, her eyes never leaving his. "You scared the hell out of us, Kit. You can't keep going into these things headfirst."

Kit closed his eyes, exhaustion weighing heavily on him. "I'm sorry, Jane. I was thinking about those kids at that auction. I just knew I had to get them out of there."

Jane's expression softened further as she reached out and gently touched his arm. "I get it, Kit. I've seen the brutality of trafficked victims. Just... try not to make it any harder than it has to be, okay?"

Kit nodded, though he couldn't quite manage the smile he wanted to give her. "Okay."

He let his eyes close again, the hum of the jet engines lulling him into a more relaxed state. But before he could drift off again, another voice cut through the haze.

"That was some stunt you pulled back there, bossman."

Kit opened his eyes to see Miguel standing at the foot of the bed, his arms crossed over his broad chest, a faint smirk on his face. His leg was wrapped in a bandage, but he looked otherwise unharmed.

"Miguel," Kit greeted him, his voice still rough. "Glad to see you're in one piece."

Miguel's smirk widened slightly. "Takes more than a bullet to take me down. You look like hell. I'm supposed to be the front man. Always."

"Feel like hell too," Kit admitted, trying to shift into a more comfortable position but wincing as the movement pulled at his injury. "I'll live and let you take lead another day."

"Damn right you will," Miguel said, his tone turning serious. "You're not allowed to check out on us, got it?"

"Got it," Kit replied, managing a weak grin.

Jane rolled her eyes, but there was a hint of a smile on her lips. "All right, you two lovebirds, that's enough macho talk for now. Kit needs to rest."

Kit didn't argue, the weight of everything catching up with him as his body demanded rest. But before he could settle back into sleep, another thought nagged at him. "Where's Calista? She got hit too."

Jane's expression turned more serious. "She's fine. It was a clean through-and-through, just like yours. She's resting in the back, probably tinkering with her gadgets to pass the time."

Kit sighed in relief, closing his eyes again. "Good. I was worried."

Jane gave his arm a reassuring squeeze. "We're all okay, Kit. You did good. Now get some rest."

This time, Kit didn't fight the pull of sleep. The exhaustion and pain were too much, and he let himself drift off, trusting that his team had everything under control.

——

When Kit woke again, the jet was no longer moving. The engines had been shut down, and the only sound was the quiet hum of the air conditioning. For a moment, he was disoriented, unsure of where he was, but then the memories came flooding back.

He was in his room in Virginia, the familiar scent of the vineyard drifting in through the open window. The soft light of dawn filtered through the curtains, casting a gentle glow across the room.

Kit tried to sit up, but the pain in his side prohibited that, and he had to bite back a groan. Before he could make another attempt, the door to his room opened, and Jane stepped inside, carrying a tray of medical supplies.

"You're awake," she said, her tone relieved as she set the tray down on the bedside table. "How are you feeling?"

"Like I got shot," Kit replied dryly, though there was a hint of humor in his voice. "But I'll live."

Jane smiled faintly as she began checking his bandages again. "That's what I like to hear. You're lucky, you know. If that bullet had hit you any lower, we wouldn't be having this conversation."

Kit nodded, his expression serious. "I know. Thanks, Jane."

She waved off his gratitude, her focus on her work. "Just doing my job."

Once she was satisfied that his bandages were secure, Jane sat back in her chair, her expression turning more serious. "You need to take it easy for a while, Kit. No more heroics, no anything for a few of days. You need to heal."

Kit didn't argue, knowing she was right. "I will. Promise." He looked concerned. "Shit. I've got to meet with Alexandre in a couple of days. What do you think?"

Jane touched the wound as saw Kit trying not to wince. "Yeah. Doctor's orders then. You're going to stay right here, be a couch potato, and do absolutely nothing."

"Not going to happen. I've got to get everything ready." He struggled to sit up.

"Kit, you've got a major wound. You lost way too much blood. You stand up now, you're going to hit the floor. Two days minimum to recoup. Then I might let you up. I will get Miguel if I have to." She threatened.

Exasperated, Kit relaxed back into bed. "48 hours, I'm up."

Jane seemed satisfied with that, and she gave him a small smile before standing up. "Good. Now get some more rest. You've got a long recovery ahead of you."

As she left the room, Kit leaned back against the pillows, staring up at the ceiling. He knew he was lucky to be alive, but there was still a lot of work to be done. The mission wasn't over, and there were still people out there who needed his help, and he had that friggin' meeting with Alexandre.

But for now, he would rest. He owed his team that much.

——

A few hours later, Kit was awakened by the sound of footsteps approaching his room. The door opened, and this time, it was Calista who entered, her shoulder bandaged but her expression bright.

"Hey, big guy," she greeted him with a grin. "How's the patient?"

"Still breathing," Kit replied, his voice stronger than before. "How about you? How's the shoulder?"

Calista shrugged, wincing slightly at the movement. "Nothing I can't handle. Besides, I've got a new project to keep me busy."

Kit raised an eyebrow. "Oh? What's that?"

Calista's grin widened as she pulled a small device from her pocket. "Remember those security feeds I hacked into at the warehouse? Well, I managed to pull some data before we left. I'm still going through it, but I think I've found something interesting."

Kit's interest was piqued. "What kind of something?"

Calista's expression turned more serious. "It's a lead. A possible location for the trafficker's next move. I need to dig deeper, but if I'm right, we might have a chance to take make a huge dent in their operation. Look at the containers, the logo. Does it look familiar?"

Kit's mind was already racing with possibilities, but he forced himself to slow down. "Damn. They're already in the States. Okay. Let's take it one step at a time, Calista. We've still got a lot of work to do, and I'm not exactly in top form right now."

Calista nodded, her grin returning. "No worries, boss. We'll handle it. You just focus on getting better. It only proves their container was docked here, nothing more. It's been seized, but I'm hoping because it's foreign, they'll release it and then to try to follow it and see where it ends up."

Kit smiled, feeling frustration and relief that he had such a capable team by his side. "Thanks, Calista." If they could stop this trafficking at ports in Houston, it would put an eye on traffickers using containers to ship their victims. It was a start.

She gave him a mock salute before heading for the door. "Anytime. And hey, don't forget to rest. I need you back in action sooner rather than later. We've got rich bad guys to capture."

As she left the room, Kit settled back into the pillows, feeling another nap coming on. The mission wasn't over, and he needed someone to keep an eye on Houston. As much as he didn't want to, he knew he was going to have to fully align himself and his team with Charlie and her team. They used the lodge together for the Canada mission, might as well make it the central operations location. He'd bring that up at their next meeting of the minds.

For now, he would rest. Too soon, they would be back in the fight, ready to take down the traffickers once and for all. After his nap, he would connect with Charlie and Aria.

CHAPTER 32

Alexandre was sitting in the opulent study of his Marseille mansion, the warmth of a crackling fire doing little to dispel the cold fury that gripped him as he stared at the innocuous message on his phone. The message was brief, the words carefully chosen to avoid suspicion, but the meaning behind them was clear.

The shipment had been seized.

His jaw clenched, his fingers tightening around the sleek device as he read the message again, the message causing more fury. The cargo, human lives that were meant to be auctioned off in France, was now in the hands of unknown operatives. The automobiles that served as the cover for this shipment would also be lost if he couldn't convince the authorities he was innocent, a significant blow to his meticulously crafted operation.

His entire body radiated fury as he rose from his leather chair, the usually pristine room suddenly feeling too small, too confining. The loss of the shipment was bad enough, but the implications were even worse. Someone had not only discovered his operation but had the audacity to strike at it with precision.

Whoever these operatives were, they were good, too good. Alexandre's mind raced as he considered the possibilities. There were very few people in the world capable of pulling off such a raid without alerting him beforehand. And now, the clock was ticking. Every moment that passed was a moment closer to the potential exposure of his entire network.

The thought made his blood run cold, but only for a moment. Alexandre DuBois was not a man to be easily cowed or deterred. No, this would only serve to steel his resolve. He would find out who was responsible, and when he did, he would take great pleasure in dismantling their lives piece by piece.

For now, however, there were more immediate matters to attend to.

He turned to the antique mahogany desk, opening a concealed drawer and withdrawing a small, encrypted satellite phone. This was not the kind of call one made over unsecured lines. He dialed a number that few in the world knew existed and waited for the call to connect.

"Gero," he said when the line clicked open, his voice a low, dangerous rumble.

"Alexandre," Gero Meyer's voice was smooth, calm, too calm. "I assume you've received the news."

"I have," Alexandre replied, the words like shards of ice. "Our shipment has been compromised. The cargo is lost at this point. I'm trying to convince the authorities that I had just leased space on the freighter."

There was a brief pause on the other end of the line, and Alexandre could almost hear Gero's mind calculating, assessing the situation. "That's... unfortunate. What do you intend to do?"

"I intend to clean house," Alexandre said, his voice hardening. "Initiate the protocol. Every single one of those incompetent fools who allowed this to happen will be eliminated, starting with Andre. I want them replaced with our more reliable assets."

Gero didn't hesitate. "Consider it done. Andre will be taken care of, along with the rest of the lower-tier personnel. I'll contact the replacements immediately. We can't afford any more mistakes."

Alexandre's lips curled into a cruel smile. "No, we cannot. Ensure that it is done swiftly and without complications. I want this operation back on track as soon as possible."

"Of course," Gero replied smoothly. "And what of your upcoming meeting in the States?"

"I will still be leaving for the States today," Alexandre said, his mind already shifting gears to the next phase of his plan. "I have a meeting with Kendrick Thorne in two days time. He has expressed interest in doing business with us, and I believe he may be a valuable asset."

"Kendrick Thorne," Gero mused. "The one from Virginia. I believe you might be right. He's made quite a name for himself in the corporate world. I'll have him investigated further."

"Yes," Alexandre said, his tone thoughtful. "There's something about him that intrigues me. I can't quite put my finger on it, but I will attempt to find out more during our meeting. If he proves to be as useful as I suspect, he may be worth bringing into the fold."

"And Ms. O'Donovan?" Gero asked, a hint of amusement in his voice. "I hear she was less than pleased with the way things turned out at the gala."

Alexandre's expression darkened. "Yes, she was quite vocal about her displeasure. But I have no intention of letting her slip away. She's too valuable, and I intend to woo her back into the fold as well. I believe she can be... persuaded."

Gero chuckled softly. "I have no doubt. Best of luck, Alexandre. I look forward to hearing how your meetings go."

"They will go as planned," Alexandre said with cold certainty. "And once I return, we will deal with whoever is responsible for this... disruption."

"Agreed," Gero said, his voice holding a hint of steel. "Safe travels, Alexandre."

The call ended with a soft click, and Alexandre set the phone down on the desk, his mind already working through the logistics of the upcoming meetings. There was much to do, and little time to do it. He would need to be at his best, sharp and focused, if he was to turn this setback into an opportunity.

He stood there for a moment longer, staring out the window at the sprawling city of Port of Marseille, his thoughts dark and calculating. Whoever these operatives were, they had made a grave mistake. They had taken something from him, and that could not go unpunished.

But for now, he had other matters to attend to. He turned from the window, striding purposefully out of the study and into the hallway, where his personal assistant was waiting with his travel itinerary.

"Sir," the assistant said, bowing slightly. "The jet is ready whenever you are."

"Good," Alexandre replied, not breaking stride as he headed for the exit. "We leave immediately."

As he descended the grand staircase and stepped into the sleek black car waiting for him, his mind was already on the meeting with Kendrick Thorne. There was something about Thorne that intrigued him, something that didn't quite add up. But he would soon find out what it was.

The car sped through the streets of Marseille, heading for the private airstrip where his jet awaited. Alexandre leaned back in the plush leather seat, his thoughts a whirl of plans and possibilities.

When he reached the States, he would meet with Thorne, and he would see for himself whether the man was truly as innocent as he appeared. And if Thorne was hiding something, Alexandre would find out. No one crossed him and got away with it.

The flight to the States was long, but Alexandre spent the time going over the details of the upcoming meeting, reviewing the background information on Thorne, and considering his approach. He had no intention of revealing too much, too soon. Thorne would have to prove himself, to show that he was worthy of being brought into the inner circle.

As the jet touched down on American soil, Alexandre felt like a lion on the prowl. He would reclaim control of the situation, restore order to his operations, and crush anyone who dared to stand in his way.

The car waiting for him at the airstrip was discreet, the driver efficient and silent as he drove the streets toward the luxurious hotel where Alexandre would be staying. Alexandre watched the city pass by through the tinted windows, his mind focused on the task ahead.

When he arrived at the hotel, his suite was ready, the staff attentive but unobtrusive as they ensured his comfort. But Alexandre had little interest in the luxuries around him. His thoughts were on Thorne, on O'Donovan, and on the people he would need to eliminate to set things right.

He made a quick call to his new operatives, confirming that the "housecleaning" was underway. Andre would be the first to go, his replacement was already enroute. Alexandre had no tolerance for failure, and Andre had failed spectacularly.

As he ended the call, a knock on the door signaled the arrival of room service. Alexandre allowed himself a small indulgence, a glass of his favorite vintage wine, as he reviewed his notes one last time.

Tomorrow, he would meet with Kendrick Thorne, and he would begin the process of determining whether Thorne was the asset he needed, or another obstacle to be removed.

And after that, he would deal with O'Donovan. She was too valuable to lose, her underground contacts were important, and Alexandre was confident that he could bring her back into the fold, one way or another.

But beneath it all, simmering like a dark undercurrent, was the knowledge that someone had dared to challenge him, to interfere with his plans. That someone had rescued the human cargo he had meticulously planned to auction, had taken what was his.

They would pay for that. Oh, they would pay dearly.

As Alexandre finished his wine and prepared for the meeting ahead, he allowed himself a moment of satisfaction. He was a man who thrived on power, on control, and he would not let anyone take that from him.

Whoever these operatives were, they had just made the biggest mistake of their lives.

And soon, they would realize it.

CHAPTER 33

The hum of fluorescent lights buzzed overhead as Vicky and Charlie stepped into the marble-floored lobby of the FBI headquarters in Washington, D.C. The chill in the air was more than just the crispness of the air conditioning, it was the cold atmosphere that greeted them as soon as they crossed the threshold. Both women, one seasoned in her respective field, one still learning, couldn't help but feel uncomfortable as they passed through security.

Charlie, ever observant, noted the lack of the usual bustling agents she recalled from TV shows in the halls. It was quieter than she remembered from her one and only visit. The tension was almost suffocating, as if the building itself was holding its breath.

Vicky, an FBI agent with a sharp mind and an even sharper wit, walked beside her, her eyes narrowing as they made their way deeper into the building. "You notice anything odd?" she murmured under her breath.

Charlie nodded slightly, her lips pressed into a thin line. "It's too quiet. Where the hell is everyone?"

The question lingered in the air as they continued down the corridor. They passed a few agents, most of whom either avoided eye contact or gave them cursory glances. But there were a couple who didn't bother to hide their scrutiny, their eyes following the two women with a mix of suspicion and curiosity.

"Something's definitely up," Vicky whispered, her tone laced with suspicion. "They're eyeballing us like we're the ones under investigation."

Charlie gave a slight smirk, but it didn't reach her eyes. "Wouldn't be the first time. But yeah, something's not right."

They were soon escorted by a stone-faced agent to the director's office, a room that exuded power and authority with its dark wood paneling, polished furniture, and the weight of countless decisions made within its walls. The director, a stern man in his late fifties with a reputation for being no-nonsense, sat behind his massive desk. His expression was unreadable as he watched them enter.

As soon as they took their seats, a large monitor on the wall flickered to life. The room was filled with the sound of distant gunfire and the chaos of a nighttime raid. The video showed a rescue mission unfolding in Houston, shadowy figures moving with deadly precision through a warehouse as bullets flew. The footage was grainy, and the faces of the operatives were obscured, but the intensity of the operation was clear.

When the video ended, the director leaned forward, his eyes narrowing as he regarded the two women. "What do you know about this?" he asked, his voice low and edged with suspicion.

Charlie and Vicky exchanged a brief glance. Both knew how to handle themselves in high-pressure situations, but this was different. They were on someone else's turf now, and the stakes were high.

"Nothing," Vicky answered first, her tone calm but firm. "We weren't aware of any trafficking action in Houston. This is the first we're seeing of it."

Charlie nodded in agreement. "My focus has been elsewhere. We've been dealing with other matters, mainly strippers and runaways. Houston wasn't on our radar."

The director's gaze shifted to Charlie, scrutinizing her with the intensity of a man who had spent decades reading people. "Ms. Donovan," he said slowly, "we're aware of your... involvement in various rescues of homeless individuals, especially runaways. Care to explain your role in these recent operations?"

Charlie met his gaze evenly, her expression impassive. "There's nothing to explain, Director. My business has always been about protecting the vulnerable, especially in the clubs I own. When it comes to runaways, we've handled cases as they came to us, but there hasn't been much need for rescue since the sting at the ranch. We've kept things quiet."

The director didn't look satisfied with her answer. He leaned back in his chair, his fingers steepling as he considered their responses. "You need to understand that this situation appears to involve some ultra-wealthy individuals from other countries. People with resources and influence that could complicate matters significantly. If you or your associates are involved, I strongly advise you to step back and let us handle it."

Vicky and Charlie exchanged another glance, the silent communication between them clear. They had no intention of stepping back if something nefarious was going on. But they weren't about to say that outright.

"We understand," Vicky said, her tone measured. "If any information comes our way, we'll make sure to share it with you."

"Good," the director said, though his tone suggested he wasn't entirely convinced. "This is a delicate situation. Tread carefully."

As they were dismissed and left the office, the tension followed them down the hall. The questions swirling in their minds only grew louder. When they were finally out of earshot, Vicky turned to Charlie, her voice low but laced with concern. "Something's definitely up. They wouldn't pull us in just to tell us to back off unless there's something big going down. And that raid in Houston, do you know anything about it?"

Charlie's mind was already racing, connecting the dots as they walked briskly toward the exit. "I don't, but I have a feeling we need to check in with Kit," she said. "If anyone knows what's really going on, it's him. My suspicion is it was him and his team. Aria sent out operatives just a few days ago to somewhere. That's all she told me."

Vicky nodded in agreement. "I'll reach out to him as well. Two of us working on him should garner some information. But first, let's get out of here. I don't like the vibe in this place."

They quickened their pace, the unease from their meeting with the director propelling them forward. As they stepped outside into the warm D.C. air, the contrast from the cold, tense atmosphere did little to ease the tension that had taken root inside them.

Vicky pulled out her phone as they made their way to the car. "I'll call Kit. If he's in on this, we need to know what's going on."

Charlie nodded, her expression still serious. "And if he's not, we need to figure out who the hell is."

They drove in silence, the weight of the situation settling in. Both women had seen more than their fair share of dark dealings and dangerous missions, but this felt different. It was as if they were on the edge of something much bigger, something with the potential to unravel everything they'd worked for.

Vicky tapped out a quick message to Kit, her fingers moving with practiced ease. She kept it vague, not wanting to tip off anyone who might be monitoring communications. **"Need to talk. Urgent. Call me."**

As they wound their way through the traffic, Charlie's mind kept replaying the footage from the Houston raid. The precision of the operatives, the intensity of the firefight, it didn't match with any of the usual agencies. And the fact that the director had shown it to them, implying some level of suspicion, made her even more uneasy.

"Kit's got to know something," Charlie muttered to herself, her fingers tapping against the armrest. "He's too deep in this world not to. It was too precise."

Vicky glanced over at her. "And if he doesn't? What then?"

Charlie's eyes narrowed as she looked out the window, watching the buildings blur past. "Then we figure it out ourselves.

I'm not sitting back while someone new plays a game this dangerous on our turf." She knew she sounded like a gang banger, but hell, they had worked hard to keep their organization a secret and this could blow the cover of any decent rescuer out there. "People aren't being careful enough."

Vicky nodded, her expression resolute. "Damn right. We've worked too hard to let some shadow operation screw everything up."

As they reached their hotel, Vicky's phone buzzed with a response from Kit. She glanced at it, her brow furrowing slightly. "He's calling."

Charlie parked the car, and they both sat in silence as Vicky answered the call. "Kit, it's Vicky. Charlie and I just had a meeting with the FBI director. Something's went down in Houston, and we need to know what you've heard if anything."

There was a brief pause on the other end before Kit's voice came through, calm but with an edge of concern. "Houston? I wasn't aware of anything happening there recently. What exactly did they tell you?"

Vicky relayed the details of the meeting, including the footage they were shown and the director's warning. "They seem to think we're involved, Kit. But we're in the dark on this one. If you know something, now's the time to share."

Kit was silent for a moment, long enough for Vicky and Charlie to exchange worried glances. Finally, he spoke, his tone more serious than before. "I haven't heard anything concrete, but there have been whispers. A lot of movement in the trafficking circles recently, and some of it's connected to Houston. It's possible someone's trying to make a move."

"Wait a minute, Kit," Charlie interjected, her patience wearing thin. "If there's something happening, we need to know. We can't afford to be blindsided. What aren't you telling us?"

Kit replied, his voice steady. "I'll dig deeper, see what I can find. But until then, keep your heads down. If the FBI's involved, this could get messy."

Vicky sighed, running a hand through her hair. "Messy's an understatement. We need to be ready for whatever's coming."

"I'll keep you in the loop," Kit promised. "But be careful. There are a lot of eyes on this right now, and not all of them are friendly."

The call ended, leaving both women sitting in the quiet of the car, wondering why Houston was becoming a big deal. There had been several successful rescues at those docks, this is the first one that was put on radar. Now they had more questions than answers, and the sense of unease was growing stronger.

Charlie broke the silence, her voice low and determined. "He's lying. If there is another organization out there rescuing, they got caught. We're not waiting around for someone else to screw things up. We dig, we find out what's really going on, and we take control of this situation."

Vicky nodded, her expression mirroring Charlie's resolve. "Agreed. If Aria was involved and sent out operatives, she would have told me, right?"

As they exited the car and made their way into the hotel, both women knew something was not right. They videoed Aria as soon as they were in their room.

"Ladies," Aria chirped cheerfully. "Whatever are you doing together? And where are you?"

Charlie new for certain that something was being kept from them. "Aria, what's going on with this Houston thing? We're in DC. The director just grilled us. Thankfully neither of us knew what the hell he was talking about."

Vicky chimed in. "And when I contact Kit, he appeared to be clueless as well. Now, someone is lying. I didn't make this trip for nothing, and answers need to be forthcoming yesterday."

"Did they go on a rescue without contacting anyone?" Charlie asked.

Aria paused, went and closed a door to the room she was in and walked to her desk before answering. "I promised Kit I wouldn't say anything but now were caught, and I don't want things to get worse."

Charlie felt chills run up and down her arms. "Aria, you are the one who made us swear not to leave anyone out of the loop. You climbed our butts as I recall. Now here you are doing exactly what we promised you we wouldn't do. Spill."

Aria had the good graces to look embarrassed. She took a deep breath and told the whole story of the rescue in Houston as she knew it, including Kit calling for backup. When she was done, she could see how pissed Charlie was.

"Charlie, there's something else as well." Aria looked contrite.

"And what might that be?" Charlie snarked out.

"Kit and Calista were shot."

Charlie felt herself blanch. "Shot! What the hell! Are they okay?"

"Yes. Both through-and-through. Calista in the shoulder and is fine. Kit's was a body shot. He lost a lot of blood but will recover."

Vicky didn't know this team well enough, so she just sat listening, but knew that gunshot wounds could be fatal, even through-and-throughs. "He's seen a doctor I assume?"

Aria replied, "Yes. Jane is an operative working with him. Very skilled surgeon so he's in good hands." Aria directed her next comment to Charlie. "I know it doesn't help, but I didn't know anything about this until he called asking for backup. Thankfully I have people in all major cities and was able to get them quickly. From the sounds of things, it was going downhill before my guys showed up."

Charlie felt the anger radiating off her and decided then and there that if both teams were going to work as a unit, per Aria's orders, it's time they did. She decided to drive to Kit's vineyard/headquarters and set things straight. She and Vicky chatted a bit more and Charlie promised a dinner when she got back to Atlanta where Vicky was still working undercover in the bar scene.

No one had seen this coming, and in the future, they would be better prepared. And if anyone, especially the FBI, thought they could take them down, they were in for a rude awakening.

CHAPTER 34

The tires crunched on the gravel driveway as Charlie's car rolled to a stop outside Kit's sprawling vineyard estate in Virginia. The early afternoon sun washed over the lush, rolling hills in a golden light, but the beauty of the scenery did little to ease her nerves. She had driven straight from Washington, DC, her mind racing the entire way, thinking about the delicate situation they were all tangled in. The meeting with the FBI had rattled her more than she'd let on, and now she was here to get some answers, and maybe to provide a few of her own.

She stepped out of the car, adjusting her sunglasses as she took in the peaceful surroundings. Kit's vineyard was a place of quiet luxury, the kind of place that exuded wealth without being ostentatious. It was a far cry from the hustle of DC, but there was an underlying sense of purpose here, a purpose that mirrored Kit's own character.

Charlie hadn't been here before and would have loved a golden tour, but there was an urgency she couldn't ignore so it would have to wait for another day. She made her way up to the main house, the large wooden door opening before she even had a chance to knock.

Zara greeted her with a warm smile. "Charlie, it's good to see you. Come in, come in."

"Thanks, Zara," Charlie replied, stepping into the cool, shaded interior of the house. "I hope I'm not intruding."

"Not at all," Zara assured her, leading her into a spacious living room that overlooked the vineyard. "We've actually been expecting you."

Charlie raised an eyebrow as she took a seat on one of the plush sofas. "Expecting me?"

Zara nodded. "Aria might have texted that you were on your way. Kit's resting right now, so you'll have to deal with us for a bit."

Charlie chuckled, though there was an edge to her laughter. "I can handle that. How's he doing?"

Zara's expression sobered. "He's recovering, but it was close, Charlie. Too close. Jane's been keeping a close eye on him, but you know Kit, he's already trying to get back on his feet."

"That sounds like him," Charlie muttered, shaking her head. "Stubborn as a mule."

Sofia entered the room, carrying a tray with glasses of iced tea. She set it down on the coffee table with a smile. "Charlie, it's good to see you again. How was the drive?"

"Long," Charlie admitted, accepting a glass. "But I had a lot to think about."

"I imagine so," Sofia replied, settling into a chair across from her. "How did things go in DC?"

Charlie took a sip of the tea, savoring the coolness. "Not great. The FBI's breathing down our necks, asking a lot of questions about that raid in Houston. Vicky and I literally knew nothing, but it's clear they suspect something."

Jack, who had been quietly observing the conversation, finally spoke up. "They're not the only ones asking questions. We've been getting a lot of unwanted attention since Houston, from many different groups. Kit's not going to be happy about the heat this is bringing. Somehow there was a camera that slipped through our system. That's how the FBI got involved."

"That's why I'm here," Charlie said, leaning forward slightly. "I need to know what the plan is, and I need to figure out how we're going to handle Alexandre DuBois."

Sofia and Zara exchanged glances, then Sofia nodded toward the hallway. "Jane's in the kitchen. She can give you a better rundown of Kit's condition."

Charlie stood and followed Sofia down the hall to the kitchen, where the scent of fresh herbs and garlic filled the air. Jane was at the counter, chopping vegetables with practiced precision of someone who knows how to handle a knife. She looked up as they entered, her sharp eyes immediately assessing Charlie.

"Charlie," Jane greeted her, setting down the knife. "You're just in time. I was about to check on Kit."

"Great. How's he really doing?" Charlie asked, leaning against the counter.

Jane wiped her hands on a towel, her expression turning serious. "He's stable. He's lucky it didn't hit anything vital, but he's lost a lot of blood. He needs a few more days to recover, but you know Kit. He's already trying to figure out how to get through the meeting with Alexandre without passing out."

"And none of us were informed of this meeting for some reason." Charlie felt her anger rising again. "I get that he's always been head honcho, but he could have at least just let us know he was having it."

Calista walked in, smiling, her arm in a sling. "Charlie, I heard what you said and totally agree, but Kit's been on his own so long, it's going to take a lot for him to want to join teams. He's not a trusting type of guy."

Charlie sighed. "I figured as much. That's why I'm here. I have an idea, but it's going to require some help from you all."

Jane's eyebrows rose. "Go on."

Charlie quickly outlined her plan, her voice steady as she explained how she would invite Alexandre to her ranch under the guise of patching things up after the debacle in Montreal. She would offer him a chance to meet in a more professional setting, with the promise of future business opportunities, provided he could keep things discreet.

"I'll make it clear that the meeting has to happen immediately because I'm supposedly scheduled for an overseas trip in a couple of days," Charlie said. "If he agrees, that'll give Kit the extra time he needs to recover, and we can buy ourselves some breathing room."

Jane considered the plan, her gaze thoughtful. "It could work. Kit will hate the idea, but he can't handle the meeting in his current state. This might be the best option we have."

Charlie glanced at Sofia and Zara, who both nodded their agreement. Jack, who had followed them into the kitchen, stroked his chin thoughtfully.

"It's risky, but it could work," Jack said finally. "If Alexandre agrees, it'll give us some time to get things set up for Kit's comfort while Alexandre is there."

Charlie nodded, a determined look on her face. "Then it's settled. I'll make the call."

Jane placed a hand on Charlie's arm. "Be careful about what you're stepping into, Charlie. Alexandre is dangerous, and if he even suspects you're playing him..."

Charlie smiled, though it didn't reach her eyes. "I know, Jane. I've been walking that line for a long time. But I'm not about to let him or anyone else harm anymore kids. If he thinks he's dealing with rich, twisted snobs, especially one that occasionally buys kids, we'll have a better chance of being in know with his trafficking plans."

She left the kitchen and made her way to the study, where she could make the call in private. Her cell phone felt heavy in her hand as she dialed Alexandre's number, her heart pounding as she waited for him to pick up.

After a few rings, Alexandre's smooth, cultured voice came through the line. "Ms. O'Donovan. To what do I owe the pleasure?"

Charlie didn't waste any time with pleasantries. "Alexandre, I wanted to talk to you about our last encounter. The gala in Montreal."

There was a brief pause, and Charlie could almost hear the wheels turning in his mind. "Yes, that was... unfortunate. I apologize for the inconvenience."

Charlie let out a soft, disdainful laugh. "Inconvenience? That's putting it lightly. But I'm willing to put that behind us, if you can assure me that any future dealings will be handled with more professionalism."

"Of course," Alexandre said smoothly. "I assure you, Ms. O'Donovan, that such a situation will not occur again. We've had a... change in the organization."

That sounded ominous to Charlie. "I'm glad to hear that," Charlie replied, her tone cool. "I'm at my ranch at the moment, and I'm scheduled to leave for an overseas trip in two days. I was thinking we could meet here tomorrow to discuss how we can move forward."

There was a moment of silence on the other end, and Charlie held her breath, waiting for his response.

"Tomorrow," Alexandre repeated, his tone thoughtful. "That could be arranged. I'll have my assistant make the necessary changes to my schedule."

"Good," Charlie replied, her voice firm. "I'll see you then."

They exchanged a few more words, and then the call ended. Charlie let out a breath she didn't realize she'd been holding and leaned back in the chair, closing her eyes for a moment to gather her thoughts.

She couldn't afford to show any weakness around Alexandre. This had to be perfect.

She returned to the living room, where the team was waiting. "It's done. Alexandre agreed to meet me at the ranch tomorrow."

"Good," Jack said, nodding approvingly. "That gives Kit extra time to heal."

"Now what about Kit?" Charlie asked, turning to Jane. "Do you think he'll be up for the meeting?"

Jane hesitated, then nodded slowly. "He should be, as long as he rests until then. But it's going to be tight."

Charlie let out a sigh of relief. "Then make sure he gets the rest he needs. No one tells him about this until it's over. As far as he knows, Alexandre has other business that delayed their meeting."

The others nodded in agreement, and they spent the next hour going over the details of the plan, refining it until there were no loose ends.

By the time they were finished, it was late afternoon, and the vineyard was bathed in the warm light of the setting sun. Charlie felt a sense of calm wash over her as she looked out at the beautiful landscape. It was a far cry from the dark, dangerous world she was about to reenter.

But this was the life she had chosen, and she wasn't about to back down now.

——

The next morning, Kit awoke in his bed, feeling slightly more rested but still in pain. He pushed through it as he always did, his mind already on the upcoming meeting with Alexandre. He had to be ready.

He was surprised, however, when Jane walked in with a tray of food and a stern look on her face.

"You're not getting out of that bed today," she informed him, setting the tray down on the nightstand.

"Jane, I have a meeting with Alexandre," Kit protested, attempting to sit up.

"And you'll be ready for it," Jane said firmly, pushing him back down. "But only if you rest. Doctor's orders. He called and rescheduled for two days from now."

"Really? And where was I?" Kit grumbled.

"Asleep, like you needed to be. I checked your calendar, it was open."

Kit grumbled some more but didn't argue. He knew better than to fight Jane when she was in full "Bones" mode. He glanced at the clock, noting the time. "Where's the team?"

"Handling things," Jane said vaguely, avoiding his gaze.

Kit narrowed his eyes. "What's going on?"

Jane busied herself with the tray, avoiding his question. "Nothing you need to worry about right now. Just focus on getting better."

Kit wasn't convinced, but he was too tired to argue. He lay back on the pillows, his mind already drifting as the pain medication Jane had slipped him earlier started to take effect.

As he slipped back into sleep, he couldn't shake the feeling that something was happening, something they weren't telling him.

——

Back at her ranch, Charlie was in full Charlotte O'Donovan mode, preparing for Alexandre's arrival. She had spent the night going over every detail, every possible outcome, and was determined to make this meeting go exactly as planned.

As she walked through the front of the ranch, inspecting the horses and the staff who would be present, she couldn't help but feel a thrill of anticipation. This was it. The next move in their dangerous game.

She was ready. The stage was set, and now all she had to do was play her part perfectly.

She glanced at her watch. Alexandre would be arriving soon. This was going to be an interesting two days.

CHAPTER 35

The sun was just beginning to dip below the horizon, casting a golden glow over the sprawling expanse of Charlie's ranch. As Alexandre DuBois stepped out of his sleek black car, he took a moment to survey the surroundings, noting the meticulous care that had been put into maintaining the ranch. Everything was pristine, polished, just like the woman he was here to see.

As he walked toward the main house, his phone vibrated in his pocket. A brief flash of annoyance crossed his features, he detested interruptions, especially when he was about to engage in delicate negotiations. But something told him this was an interruption he couldn't afford to ignore. He pulled out his phone and glanced at the screen.

The message was from one of his newest generals, a man who had served him faithfully for years that he placed in Andre's job after having Andre disposed of. One of the man's specialties was digging up information that most people would never think to look for. The subject line was simple, but it caught Alexandre's attention immediately: **"Interesting Developments."**

Alexandre tapped the screen, and a series of images and documents began to load. The first was a photograph taken in Atlanta a few months back, shortly after Chase Holloway's death. The image showed Kit Thorne, looking as composed and sharp as ever, sitting at an intimate dinner table with a woman who bore an uncanny resemblance to Charlotte O'Donovan. The only difference was her hair color, it was lighter, more of a blonde, almost a golden hue. But the resemblance was undeniable.

Alexandre's eyes narrowed as he studied the image. The woman in the photo was not quite the same as the Charlotte O'Donovan he had come to know, less polished and refined, and with an edge that he couldn't quite place. He scrolled down to the next piece of information, a series of dates and locations that traced the movements of both Kit Thorne and Charlie Donovan over the past several months.

Each piece of data aligned too perfectly to be a coincidence. The two had crossed paths far more often than he had realized and, before they met in Canada. Then came a final image, Charlotte, now with her auburn hair, standing in front of a group of reporters at this very ranch. The article accompanying the photo detailed a massive sting operation that had taken place here, leading to the arrest of several high-profile criminals involved in human trafficking. The date of the article corresponded with the time Kit Thorne had gone dark, supposedly for personal reasons.

Alexandre's breath hitched slightly as the pieces began to fall into place. Kit Thorne and Charlotte O'Donovan were not just casual acquaintances, they were connected in ways that could jeopardize everything he was working toward. The woman who had been so vehemently upset at the gala, who had demanded professionalism from him, was the same woman who had been involved in the very sting operation that had cost him millions. He was sure of it.

And now she had invited him here, to her home. Alexandre's mind raced as he processed the implications. This was no coincidence. Charlotte O'Donovan was playing a very dangerous game, and she had invited him to her ranch under the guise of making amends. But now, he saw her true intentions. She was trying to get closer to him, to dig deeper into his operations, all while playing the role of a sophisticated businesswoman.

His plans changed in an instant. He could no longer afford to treat this as a simple business meeting. Charlotte O'Donovan was a threat, one that needed to be neutralized before she could do any more damage.

Alexandre slipped his phone back into his pocket, a cold smile curving his lips. This evening was about to take a very different turn.

He straightened his jacket and walked toward the entrance of the house, where Aria, pretending to be a member of Charlie's staff greeted him with a polite bow. "Mr. DuBois, welcome. Ms. O'Donovan is expecting you."

"Thank you," Alexandre replied smoothly, masking the storm of emotions brewing beneath his calm exterior. "I'm looking forward to our conversation."

He was led through the tastefully decorated foyer and into a formal sitting room that overlooked the vast acres of the ranch. A small table was set with her finest china and crystal glasses for tea or a drink, a reflection of the elegant but unpretentious style that Charlotte O'Donovan was known for.

Charlie herself was standing by the large bay window, her back to him as she gazed out at the dusky landscape. Her now platinum hair caught the light, casting a warm glow around her. As he entered, she turned to face him, a tight but welcoming smile on her lips.

"Alexandre, I'm so glad you could make it," she said, crossing the room to greet him. She extended her hand, and he took it, noting the firmness of her grip.

"Thank you for inviting me, Ms. O'Donovan," Alexandre replied, his tone smooth, almost charming. But there was a new edge to his voice, one that Charlie couldn't miss.

"Please, Charlotte will be just fine." Charlie told him, still smiling.

Dinner was called and they made their way across the foyer into a very formal dining room. Alexandre helped Charlie with her chair and sat across from her at a smaller table situated in a corner. Charlie laughed about eating at the children's table, but since there were no children, she thought it would be more comfortable. Alexandre smiled and nodded.

They exchanged the usual pleasantries as they took their seats at the table. The staff began serving the first course, a light salad with fresh greens and a citrus vinaigrette. But even as they made small talk, discussing the beauty of the ranch and the quality of the wine from her vineyard, Alexandre's mind was racing with calculations.

He needed to play this carefully. Charlotte O'Donovan was smart, smarter than he had given her credit for. She had managed to hide her true identity from him since he had met her but while infiltrating his world. Now that he knew, he had the upper hand.

As the conversation turned to business, Alexandre decided to test the waters. "You know, Charlotte, I've been thinking a lot about that night in Montreal. It seems we both may have underestimated one another."

Charlie's eyes flickered with something, surprise, perhaps, or maybe curiosity, but her expression remained composed. "It was an unfortunate situation," she agreed, her tone measured. "But I'm glad we're moving past it. There's a lot of potential in our partnership, if we can find common ground."

"Indeed," Alexandre said, leaning back slightly in his chair. "But I've also been doing some digging. It's fascinating what one can uncover with the right resources."

Charlie tilted her head, a slight frown creasing her brow. "Is that so?"

"Yes," Alexandre continued, his voice casual, but with an underlying intensity. "For example, I came across some rather interesting information recently. It seems you have a talent for... surprise appearances."

Charlie's hand froze momentarily on her glass, but she quickly recovered, taking a sip of wine before responding. "I'm not sure what you mean, Alexandre."

Alexandre's smile didn't reach his eyes. "Oh, I think you do. But don't worry, I appreciate a woman who knows how to keep secrets. It makes business much more... interesting."

Charlie set her glass down slowly, her gaze steady as she met his eyes. "Are you implying something, Alexandre?"

"Not at all," he replied, his tone almost playful. "I'm simply acknowledging that we all have our roles to play. Yours is clearly more complex than I initially thought."

The atmosphere in the room had shifted, the air thick with unspoken tension. Charlie knew that Alexandre had discovered something, but what? How deep had his digging gone?

Before she could respond, Alexandre leaned forward slightly, his expression turning serious. "But enough games, Charlotte. Let's be honest with each other. We both know that tonight isn't just about making amends for what happened in Montreal. There's more at stake here, isn't there?"

Charlie's mind raced as she considered her next move. She couldn't afford to show weakness, not now. She had to keep the upper hand, or at least make him believe she still held it.

"Perhaps there is," she said slowly, her voice calm and controlled. "But that's why we're here, isn't it? To find out exactly where we stand."

Alexandre's smile returned, colder this time. "Exactly. And I think we're about to find out."

The rest of the dinner passed in a carefully orchestrated dance of words, both of them testing the boundaries, pushing just enough to see how the other would react. But as dessert was served, it became clear to Charlie that Alexandre was no longer content to play along. He wanted answers, and he was determined to get them.

As they finished their meal, Alexandre set down his fork and folded his hands on the table, his gaze locked onto Charlie's. "Charlotte, I appreciate your hospitality tonight, but I think it's time we cut to the chase. I want to know exactly where you stand in all of this."

Charlie arched an eyebrow, feigning ignorance. "I'm not sure I follow."

Alexandre's patience snapped, just slightly, as he leaned forward, his voice dropping to a near whisper. "Don't play coy with me. You know exactly what I'm talking about. The gala, the sting operation, the fact that you and Kit Thorne have been dancing around each other for months, maybe even longer. I want to know why."

Charlie's heart pounded in her chest, but she forced herself to remain calm, her mind scrambling for a way out of this. She needed to deflect, to buy herself time.

"I think you're reading too much into this, Alexandre," she said, her tone light but firm. "Yes, Kit and I have crossed paths before, but that's the nature of our business. We're in the same circles. But that doesn't mean there's some grand conspiracy."

Alexandre wasn't convinced. He pulled out his phone, tapping a few buttons before sliding it across the table to her. "Then explain this."

Charlie looked down at the screen, and her blood ran cold. It was the photo of her and Kit having dinner in Atlanta, the one taken just after Chase's death. She looked different enough in the photo, her hair color, her style, but it was unmistakably her.

She glanced back up at Alexandre, who was watching her with an intensity that bordered on predatory. "This was taken months ago. Long before the gala, long before any of this. I don't see how it's relevant."

"It's relevant because you lied to me," Alexandre said, his voice tight with barely contained anger. "You've been lying to me this entire time."

Charlie knew she had to tread carefully. "I've never lied to you, Alexandre. Maybe I haven't told you everything, but that's different. We all have our secrets."

"Secrets," Alexandre repeated, his expression hardening. "Well, here's one of mine. I don't trust you, Charlotte. Not anymore."

Charlie's heart raced as she realized just how precarious her position had become. She needed to turn this around, and fast.

"I'm sorry you feel that way," she said slowly, deliberately. "But if we're going to move forward, you need to understand something: I work in many different worlds, not just horses. Sometimes it calls for unusual characters to be played. But I thought we were here to discuss a partnership."

"Partnership?" Alexandre's voice dripped with sarcasm. "Is that what you want call this?"

Charlie forced herself to stay calm. "Yes, Alexandre. And if you can't see that, then maybe we're done here. I will be happy to spend my money elsewhere."

Alexandre stared at her for a long moment, his expression unreadable. Then, finally, he leaned back in his chair, a slow, calculating smile spreading across his face.

"We'll see, Charlotte. We'll see."

As they rose from the table and stepped out into the cool night air, Charlie knew that this was far from over. She had managed to buy herself a little more time, but Alexandre was a man who never forgot a slight, never forgave a betrayal.

And she had just become his next target.

She walked with Alexandre to the horse pavilion where they examined the Arabians she kept after the auction. Breeding them had turned out advantageous and she now had four mares and the original stallion. Alexandre was impressed and made an offer to buy one of the stallion colts. Charlie noted it in the stable book and told Alexandre someone would contact him about finalizing the paperwork.

Charlie offered Alexandre a room for the evening since they still had business to discuss, but he declined stating he would see her tomorrow and they would discuss some of the options he had. Charlie acknowledged this and stood on the steps as he entered his limo.

As they parted ways, Alexandre's mind was already working through the next steps. Charlotte O'Donovan, or whoever she really was, had made a grave mistake in underestimating him. And now, he would make sure she paid for it.

The game was on, and Alexandre DuBois was playing to win.

CHAPTER 36

Charlie stood on the front porch of her ranch, watching the taillights of Alexandre's car disappear into the darkness. She'd managed to keep her composure during the dinner, deflecting Alexandre's probing questions and maintaining her carefully constructed facade. But now that he was gone, the reality of her situation crashed down on her like a tidal wave.

She wasn't sure how long she stood there, gripping the railing so tightly that her knuckles turned white, before she finally turned and walked back into the house. The warmth of the interior did nothing to dispel the chill that had settled in her bones. She felt as though she was unraveling, the threads of her carefully woven life coming apart with each passing second.

The kitchen lights were still on, casting a soft glow over the polished countertops and the dark wooden cabinets. Doc and Aria were waiting for her, their expressions filled with concern. Doc, always the one to lighten the mood, tried to crack a smile when he saw her. But even he could see that something was deeply wrong.

Charlie didn't say a word as she walked into the kitchen, her mind a whirlwind of fear, doubt, and desperation. She could feel the panic clawing at the edges of her mind, threatening to pull her under. Everything she'd built, her clubs, her operations, her carefully managed personas, was teetering on the brink of collapse, and she had no idea how to stop it.

Doc watched her for a moment, his brow furrowed in concern, before he spoke up. "You know, Charlie, if you keep pacing like that, you're gonna wear a hole right through the floor. And as much as I enjoy a good construction project, I'm not sure I'm up for repairing a crater in your kitchen."

CHARLIE'S CHILDREN: GUARDIAN OF THE LOST 2 287

Charlie paused mid-step, her breath coming in shallow gasps as she looked at him. Normally, his jokes would have made her smile, maybe even laugh. But tonight, they barely registered.

Aria, ever the pragmatic one, moved to the counter and poured a generous amount of whiskey into a glass, then handed it to Charlie. "Here, sip this. It'll help."

Charlie took the glass with trembling hands, but instead of sipping, she downed the entire contents in one go. The burn of the alcohol seared down her throat, making her cough and sputter. The warmth spread through her chest, but it did little to calm the storm raging inside her.

"I'm screwed," she finally whispered, her voice cracking as she set the empty glass down on the counter. "Alexandre knows. He knows something's up, and I don't exactly what he knows, but he knows. It's only a matter of time before he finds out the whole truth."

Doc exchanged a worried glance with Aria, then stepped closer to Charlie, his voice gentle but firm. "Charlie, you need to calm down. Panicking won't do us any good. We need to think this through."

"Calm down?" Charlie repeated, her eyes wide with fear. "Doc, he's going to come back here tomorrow, and I have to somehow convince him that everything he's dug up is on the up and up. How am I supposed to do that?"

Aria, who had been quietly thinking while she observed the exchange, finally spoke up, her tone measured and calm. "We have to build a new narrative. One that explains everything he's found without leading him to the real truth."

Charlie looked at her, desperation in her eyes. "But how? What can we say that won't sound like a bunch of lies?"

Doc rubbed his chin thoughtfully, then snapped his fingers as an idea took hold. "Okay, listen to this. As far as anyone outside our teams knows, Charlotte O'Donovan is just a wealthy businesswoman with a taste for success. What if we build on that?"

Charlie frowned, not quite following. "What do you mean?"

Doc's eyes sparkled with the excitement of his own idea. "We say that you bought into some gentleman's clubs because they were lucrative business opportunities. But when you didn't like the way they were being run, you decided to take a more hands-on approach. You changed your appearance, hence the different hair colors, and ran the clubs yourself, to clean things up and make them more profitable. The ranch? That was just another investment, a way to diversify. You were planning to host events, maybe even expand into the high-end leisure market."

Charlie started to nod slowly as she began to understand. "So, the auburn hair was just part of the disguise. And I was here at the ranch when the raid happened, getting ready for a party. I didn't know anything about what was going on at the other end of the property because it has a private entrance."

Doc grinned, glad to see her following along. "Exactly. You were just the unlucky new owner who got caught up in the mess. You had no idea what was happening on the other side of the ranch, and you've been trying to distance yourself from it ever since."

Aria had been typing away on her laptop, her fingers flying across the keys. "I'm updating the public records now," she said, her voice calm and focused. "The sale of the property will be backdated to match Doc's story, and I'm planting some articles about your supposed frustration with the previous management of the clubs. When Alexandre looks deeper into it, everything will check out."

Charlie stared at them, a mix of hope and fear swirling in her chest. "You really think this will work?"

Doc's grin softened into a more reassuring smile. "Charlie, you're one of the best at playing the game. We just need to give you the right cards to play. This story makes sense, and it ties up the loose ends. You just have to sell it."

Aria glanced up from her laptop, her expression serious. "You'll need to make sure Kit and his team know all of this. Alexandre's going to grill him as well when he meets with him tomorrow. We will coach you through it, make sure it's airtight."

Charlie swallowed hard, the thought of what she had to do scaring the hell out of her. "I can do that. I've acted as someone else before."

Doc nodded approvingly. "That's the spirit. Just keep it simple, stick to the real story as much as possible, and don't give away anything you don't have to."

For the first time that evening, Charlie felt a flicker of hope. Maybe they could pull this off. Maybe she could keep Alexandre at bay long enough to figure out her next move. But just as she was starting to feel more confident, Doc's expression grew serious again.

"But, Charlie," he said, his voice dropping to a more somber tone, "you're going to have to tell Alexandre this whole story tomorrow when he comes. Face-to-face."

The calm that had been slowly building in her shattered, replaced by a fresh wave of anxiety. The thought of sitting across from Alexandre, looking him in the eye, and telling him this carefully crafted half lie made her stomach twist in knots. She could feel the panic rising again, threatening to drown her.

Deep down, she knew Doc was right. There was no other option. Alexandre would be back tomorrow, and if she wanted any chance of getting into his inner circle, she had to be ready.

"Okay," she said, her voice trembling slightly but filled with determination. "Let's practice."

The next several hours were spent going over every detail of the story, rehearsing it until it felt like second nature. Doc played the role of Alexandre, throwing out questions and doubts, while Aria provided feedback and adjusted the narrative as needed. They coached Charlie on her tone, her body language, and her responses, making sure that everything aligned with the persona they had created.

Charlie stumbled a few times, her nerves getting the better of her, but each time, Doc and Aria were there to steady her, to guide her back to the story. They went over it again and again, refining it until there were no gaps, no inconsistencies.

As the night wore on, exhaustion began to take its toll, but Charlie pushed through it. She couldn't afford to let her guard down, not now. They practiced until she could recite the story in her sleep, until every word felt natural, every detail ingrained in her mind.

Finally, as dawn was beginning to break, Doc leaned back in his chair, a satisfied smile on his face, and with a deep southern accent spoke, "I think you've got it, Ms. Charlotte. You're ready."

Charlie nodded, though her heart still pounded with anxiety. "I just hope he buys it."

"He will," Aria said firmly, closing her laptop and standing up. "We've covered everything and your online profile matches it. You've got this, Charlie. You're stronger than you think."

Charlie took a deep breath, trying to steady her nerves. She had to believe them. She had to trust that all the preparation, all the practice, would pay off.

"Thank you," she said quietly, her voice filled with genuine gratitude. "I don't know what I'd do without you guys."

Doc smiled warmly. "That's why we're here. I like picking up the fallen pieces, keeps me on my toes."

Aria nodded in agreement. "And remember, if anything goes wrong, improvise... quickly."

Charlie forced herself to smile, drawing strength from their words. She had come this far, and she wasn't about to back down now. Today would be one the next in line of big tests she'd faced, but Doc and Aria promised to stay close in case her brain when sideways. Doc was so eloquent.

She had no other choice.

As she finally went to bed, for a short sleep, the exhaustion overtaking her, she couldn't help but wonder what later would bring. But one thing was certain, she would be ready for whatever came her way.

She would face Alexandre DuBois with a story so perfect, so convincing, that he would have no choice but to believe it. And buy herself the time she so desperately needed to get the info on his organization.

CHAPTER 37

The morning sun was just beginning to rise over the rolling hills of Charlie Donovan's ranch, casting a soft golden light over the landscape. The serenity of the scene was at odds with the turmoil brewing beneath the surface, a turmoil that Charlotte O'Donovan, also known as Diamond Frost, was more than aware of. She stood on the front porch of her sprawling estate, her heart pounding as she prepared for the confrontation that was coming.

Alexandre DuBois would arrive soon. And with him, a new set of challenges that could either cement her control over the situation or unravel everything she had meticulously planned.

Inside, Aria was already at work, her fingers flying over her laptop as she prepared the final touches on the plan they had spent the night perfecting. Doc and the rest of the team were stationed in various parts of the house, ready to provide support if needed. This wasn't just another business meeting. This was war, a battle of wits and deception where the stakes couldn't be higher.

As Charlie's mind raced with thoughts of what she had to say, of the lies she had to tell, she caught sight of Alexandre's sleek black rental limo approaching up the long, winding driveway. The car moved with the slow, deliberate grace of a predator closing in on its prey.

Her heart skipped a beat. This was it. "Showtime," she whispered to herself, taking a deep breath and steeling her nerves.

Inside the house, Aria's voice came through the earpiece Charlie wore discreetly. "Remember, Charlie. We're in control here. He thinks he's playing you, but we're playing him. Stick to the story and let me handle the rest."

Charlie nodded almost imperceptibly, her confidence bolstered by Aria's calm assurance. She adjusted her posture, forcing a look of concern onto her face. She had to sell this performance. Alexandre DuBois was a man who thrived on control, on finding weaknesses and exploiting them. She had to give him something to latch onto, just enough to make him think he was winning.

The limo came to a stop, and the driver, a tall, stern-looking man, quickly stepped out to open the door for Alexandre. The man himself emerged from the vehicle with the casual elegance of someone who had the world at his feet. He was impeccably dressed, his tailored suit a sharp contrast to the rustic charm of the ranch. His eyes, however, were cold and calculating, scanning the surroundings before they settled on Charlie.

"Charlotte," Alexandre greeted her with a smile that didn't reach his eyes as he approached. "Good to see you this morning. I must say, your ranch in the morning light is quite… charming."

"Thank you, Alexandre," Charlie replied, keeping her voice steady. "I'm glad you returned. There's a lot we need to discuss."

He offered his hand, and she took it, noting the slight tension in his grip. He was testing her, probing for any sign of weakness. She met his gaze head-on, willing herself to appear as calm and composed as possible.

"Shall we go inside?" Charlie suggested, gesturing toward the house.

"Of course," Alexandre agreed, allowing her to lead the way.

As they entered the house, Charlie could feel his scrutiny on her. Alexandre was watching her every move, searching for any cracks in her armor. She had to be perfect. She had to be believable.

The living room was bathed in soft, natural light, the warm tones of the décor creating a welcoming atmosphere. Alexandre glanced around, taking in the details with a practiced eye. But Charlie knew his mind was elsewhere, piecing together the puzzle that was Charlotte O'Donovan.

"Please, have a seat," Charlie offered, motioning to the comfortable armchairs positioned near the large windows that overlooked the ranch, tea or coffee on a table between them.

Alexandre took his time before sitting, his movements deliberate and measured. Once he was seated, he turned his full attention to her, his expression one of polite curiosity. "You mentioned last night that there were things you wanted to clarify. I'm all ears."

Charlie took a seat across from him, her mind racing as she prepared to deliver the performance of a lifetime. She knew Alexandre had discovered more about her past, more than she had initially revealed. But that had been added to the plan as well. All outside contingencies. She needed to draw him in, to make him believe he was uncovering her secrets on his own.

"I want to be completely honest with you, Alexandre," Charlie began, her tone carefully measured. "There are things about my past that I've kept private, things that I'm not particularly proud of. But I think it's important that you understand why I've made the choices I have."

Alexandre leaned forward slightly, his interest piqued. "I'm listening."

Charlie took a deep breath, allowing a hint of vulnerability to creep into her voice. "Before I became Charlotte O'Donovan, the businesswoman you know today, I had a different life. I was... involved in the nightclub scene, but not just as an owner. I was a performer. I went by the name Diamond Frost."

Alexandre's eyes gleamed with interest. "Diamond Frost. The name sounds familiar."

Charlie nodded, her expression one of regret. "It should. Diamond Frost was well-known in the gentlemen's club arena. I ran... run the clubs as Diamond Frost, stripper turned club owner, it was the only way I could turn things around."

"And did it work?" Alexandre asked, his voice smooth but probing.

Charlie allowed herself a small, bitter smile. "It did, but it came at a cost. I was drawn into a world I wasn't prepared for, a world that involved people like Gabriel Carvalho."

At the mention of Carvalho's name, Alexandre's eyes narrowed. "You were involved with Carvalho?"

Charlie shook her head quickly, her expression one of sincere regret. "Not in the way you're thinking. I attended his auctions as Diamond Frost, to get him interested in the club scene. But I was never part of his operations. He was a powerful man, and he had connections everywhere. It got to where I couldn't run the clubs without crossing paths with him. He took an interest in Diamond Frost, saw her as an asset, but I kept him at arm's length. I knew what kind of man he was."

Alexandre studied her, his gaze piercing. "So why didn't you leave?"

Charlie looked down, as if struggling with her emotions. "I wanted to, but it wasn't that simple. I had worked hard to build something out of nothing, and I couldn't just walk away. But when the opportunity came, I bought the ranch and started over as Charlotte O'Donovan. I thought I could leave that life behind."

"And yet," Alexandre said, his tone casual but laced with suspicion, "you ended up right in the middle of a sting operation here at the ranch."

Charlie nodded, her expression somber. "Yes. That was pure bad luck. I bought this property as an investment, a way to start fresh. But I had no idea what was happening on the other end of the ranch. I was planning a party, getting ready to entertain some guests when the raid happened. It was a nightmare."

Alexandre watched her for a long moment, as if weighing the truth of her words. "So, you had no idea?"

"None," Charlie replied, her voice firm. "And I've been trying to distance myself from it ever since. That's why I wanted to meet with you, to clear the air. I don't want any misunderstandings between us."

As Charlie spoke, Aria's voice came through the earpiece, calm and collected. "We're in, Charlie. His phone, his watch, and the limo. Everything's bugged. Just keep him talking."

Charlie resisted the urge to smile, focusing instead on maintaining her concerned facade. Alexandre believed he had the upper hand, but he had no idea how thoroughly he was being played.

"Thank you for being honest with me, Charlotte," Alexandre said finally, leaning back in his chair. "I appreciate your transparency. But I have to wonder, if you were so determined to leave that life behind, why keep the clubs at all? Why not sell them and walk away?"

Charlie met his gaze, her expression resolute. "Because I wanted to prove something to myself and to the people who doubted me. I wanted to show that I could succeed, that I could take something broken and make it whole again. And I have. The clubs are legitimate businesses now, profitable and clean. And look at what is happening with this ranch. I've learned my lesson. I refuse to let my past define me."

Alexandre studied her for a long moment, his expression unreadable. "You've certainly led an interesting life, Charlotte."

Charlie forced a small smile. "I've made mistakes, but I've also learned from them. And I'm not the same person I was back then."

Alexandre seemed to consider her words, his gaze lingering on her face as if searching for any sign of deceit. But Charlie remained calm, her expression sincere.

Finally, he nodded slowly. "Very well. I believe we can move forward, but I must warn you, Charlotte, I have no tolerance for deception. If I find out that you're hiding anything else from me, our partnership will be over."

Charlie felt a chill run down her spine at his words, but she kept her composure. "I understand, Alexandre. You have my word that I've told you everything."

"Good," Alexandre said, his tone firm. "Then let's put this behind us and focus on the future."

As they continued their conversation, discussing business and potential investments, Charlie couldn't help but feel a sense of triumph. Alexandre had bought the story, every carefully crafted lie. He believed he had her under his thumb, that he could control her.

But he was wrong. Charlie was in control, and with Aria and the rest of the team feeding her information, she knew exactly how to play him.

By the time their meeting ended and Alexandre left the ranch, Charlie felt relief fill her. She had survived another round, another test of her abilities. But as she watched him drive away, she knew that the game was far from over.

Aria's voice crackled through the earpiece. "We got everything, Charlie. Every word, every movement. Whoever his research person is, they've fully downloaded your portfolio and fed the information to Alexandre. He's in the dark, and we're in the clear."

Charlie smiled to herself, a mixture of exhaustion and satisfaction washing over her. "Good. Let's keep it that way."

As she turned and walked back into the house, she knew that the stakes were only going to get higher. Alexandre DuBois was a dangerous man, and the more they pushed him, the more dangerous he would become.

She would play this game to the end, and she would win. No matter what it took.

CHAPTER 38

Calista leaned back in her chair, her eyes narrowing as she stared at the screen in front of her. The dim light of the room was the only illumination, casting eerie shadows across her face as lines of code scrolled rapidly past. She had been digging through the darkest corners of the internet for hours, ever since Kit handed her the cryptic web address that Alexandre had given him. What she had found so far was both disturbing and deeply unsettling.

The website, on the surface, appeared innocuous, a high-end dating site catering to wealthy individuals. The homepage was sleek, well-designed, with elegant graphics and a sophisticated interface. But as Calista delved deeper, it became clear that there was something far more sinister lurking beneath the polished veneer.

She had encountered plenty of dark web sites in her time, but this one was different. It was meticulously coded, with layers of encryption that even she had to work hard to crack. The site's content was carefully worded to avoid any direct connection to illegal activities. The profiles were seemingly normal, filled with descriptions of affluent lifestyles, preferences for travel, dining, and exclusive events. But the deeper she went, the more she realized that the profiles weren't just fake, they were fraudulent in the most horrifying way.

Calista leaned in closer, her fingers flying over the keyboard as she decrypted the next layer of code. The faces in the profiles were all enhanced to look older, their features subtly altered to give the appearance of adulthood. But as she ran an age-regression analysis on the images, the truth became sickeningly clear, the people in these profiles were children, digitally aged to appear as adults.

"Son of a bitch," Calista muttered under her breath, her stomach churning. Whoever had created this site was a master of deception. The level of skill required to pull off such an elaborate ruse was terrifying. They had gone to extraordinary lengths to disguise the true nature of their operations, making it nearly impossible for anyone to connect the site to trafficking.

She quickly pulled up another window and initiated a deep scan of the site's server, hoping to find any breadcrumbs that might lead to the creators. Every lead she found was either a dead end or redirected her back to the same main server, which was based in a country known for its lack of cooperation with international law enforcement. Whoever was behind this had covered their tracks well.

But Calista wasn't deterred. She had been navigating the dark web for years, and she knew how to play the game. She opened a secure line and quickly typed a message to Aria, detailing everything she had uncovered so far.

Within seconds, her phone buzzed with an incoming call. Aria's voice came through, tense but controlled. "Tell me everything, Techie."

Calista launched into an explanation, her words coming fast and clipped. "It's definitely a trafficking site, but it's masked as a high-end dating service. The profiles are all of children, but they've been digitally aged to look like adults. The coding is insanely good, someone's gone to great lengths to keep this hidden. I've decrypted most of it, but it's going to take time to get to the bottom of who is operating this."

"Jesus," Aria breathed. "How the hell did they pull this off?"

"Whoever they are, they're good," Calista replied. "Really good. This isn't some amateur operation. We're talking serious professionals here. The kind that know how to stay under the radar."

"Can you find out who's behind it?"

"I'm working on it," Calista said, her fingers already flying over the keyboard again. "I've got a few leads I'm following up on, but it's going to take time. This isn't something I can crack in an hour."

"Keep digging," Aria said, her tone grim. "We need to find out who's running this site and work on shutting them down."

Calista nodded, even though Aria couldn't see her. "I'm on it."

"Charlie and I need to talk to Kit about what's happened in the last 24 hours. There are some decisions that need to be made that he's going to be involved in." Aria informed Calista.

There was a pause on the other end of the line before Calista spoke again. "Kit's out cold right now. Jane's been keeping him sedated so he can heal. That Mr. DuBois is supposed to be here tomorrow."

"We can't afford to wait any longer. No more drugs. We need him awake and clear-headed for this. If Jane has something to get him up, then do it please, now." That sounded like an order, which Calista didn't mind following, but not from an outsider.

Calista bit her lip, glancing toward the closed door of the room where Kit was resting. "I'll talk to Jane. We'll set up a meeting for 8 p.m. tonight. No sooner. Can you ready by then?"

"We'll be ready," Aria confirmed. "And I'm connecting you someone who's a devil with the dark web. He'll help us tear this site apart and figure out who's behind it."

"Good," Calista said, her resolve hardening. "Because whoever's doing this needs to be taken down. Hard."

They ended the call, and Calista took a moment to steady herself. The information she had uncovered was horrifying, but she couldn't afford to let it rattle her. Not now. There was too much at stake.

She left the room and headed down the hallway to find Jane, who was in the kitchen preparing some herbal teas and remedies. Jane looked up as Calista entered, her brow furrowing in concern.

"Is everything okay?" Jane asked, setting down the tea she was mixing.

Calista shook her head. "No, it's not. We've got a situation, and we need Kit awake for it. Aria says no more sedatives. We have a video meeting at 8 p.m., and Kit needs to be ready."

Jane's expression turned serious. "I was hoping to give him more time to heal, but if it's urgent, I'll do what I can. He'll be groggy and in pain, but he'll be awake."

"Thanks, Jane," Calista said, her tone grateful. "We need him at his best for this."

Jane nodded, already thinking ahead. "I'll have some painkillers ready that won't cloud his judgment. We'll make sure he's as clear-headed as possible."

Calista gave her a tight smile before heading back to her room. Once there, she sat down at her computer and prepared to dive back into the dark web. The site, ShadowExchange, Alexandre had directed Kit to was still her primary focus, but now she had another mission, to find out exactly who was behind it and what their endgame was.

Hours passed as Calista navigated the twisted corridors of the dark web, her mind sharp despite the growing fatigue. She knew she was playing a dangerous game. The people running this operation weren't just skilled, they were ruthless. But she also knew that if they didn't stop them, countless children would suffer unimaginable fates.

Her fingers flew over the keyboard as she followed lead after lead, each one leading her deeper into the web of deception that surrounded the site. She uncovered more profiles, each one meticulously altered to hide the true age of the children being trafficked. The language used in the profiles was carefully coded, designed to pass as normal dating site jargon but with a darker, more sinister meaning that only those in the know would understand.

It was like trying to untangle a web of lies, each thread more twisted than the last.

Calista paused for a moment, rubbing her eyes and taking a deep breath. She had to keep going. She couldn't stop now, not when she was so close to finding the truth.

A new window popped up on her screen, and Calista's eyes widened as she realized what she had found. It was a hidden directory, buried deep within the site's code. The directory contained files, dozens of them, each labeled with a different name and date. She clicked on one at random, and her blood ran cold.

The file contained images of a young girl, no older than twelve, posed in ways that made Calista's stomach turn. The accompanying text was a sales pitch, describing the girl in sickening detail and listing a price. There was no doubt now, this was a trafficking site, and the people running it were monsters.

She quickly copied the directory's URL and sent it to Aria, along with a message detailing what she had found. Aria's response was immediate: **"We'll take them down. I'm connecting my guy now. We're going to expose every last one of them."**

Calista felt a surge of elation. This was why she did what she did, why she spent her downtime navigating the dark web and exposing the horrors that lurked in its shadows. These people thought they could operate in secret, hiding behind layers of encryption and deception. But they were wrong. They were about to be exposed.

She continued to dig, her eyes scanning the screen as she uncovered more and more evidence. Each piece of information was another step closer to bringing these criminals down. And with every file she opened, her resolve grew stronger.

By the time 8 p.m. rolled around, Calista had compiled a mountain of evidence, gotten the new tech guy, Dak, completely up to date, his searches having confirmed the information Calista had located, and had enough to not only shut down the site but to trace its origins and identify the people responsible. She had also uncovered more about the site's creator, a shadowy figure who went by the alias "Merlin." Whoever Merlin was, they were a digital ghost, leaving no trace of their real identity. But Calista was determined to find them.

She logged out of the dark web and leaned back in her chair, her mind buzzing with the information she had gathered. She knew the meeting with Kit, Aria, and the rest of the team was going to be intense. They had a lot to discuss, and the stakes were insanely high.

Calista stood and stretched, trying to shake off the fatigue that had settled in her muscles. She had a few minutes before the meeting, just enough time to grab a quick bite and clear her head.

As she made her way to the kitchen, she couldn't help but feel a sense of satisfaction. They were so close to taking down one of the most sophisticated trafficking networks she had ever encountered. And when they did, it would be a victory not just for them, but for every child whose life had been destroyed by these monsters.

But there was still work to be done, and Calista knew that the fight was far from over. They were about to go up against some of the most dangerous people in the world, and they needed to be ready for anything.

As she grabbed a snack and prepared to head back to her room, Calista's phone buzzed with a message from Aria: **"We're ready when you are, Techie. Let's make this happen."**

Calista smiled grimly, they were ready. Nothing was going to stop them from bringing these bastards down. She took a deep breath and headed back to her computer, ready to take the next step in the fight against the darkness.

CHAPTER 39

The sun had barely risen over the rolling hills of Virginia when Alexandre arrived at Kit's vineyard. The early morning light cast a golden hue over the lush, well-manicured rows of grapevines that stretched out as far as the eye could see. Kit was waiting for him at the entrance to the estate, his posture relaxed, but his eyes sharp and focused. Today's meeting was as much about business as it was about feeling each other out, and Kit knew that he needed to be on his game.

"Alexandre," Kit greeted him with a firm handshake, a polite smile on his lips. "Welcome to Virginia. I trust your flight was pleasant?"

"Indeed, it was," Alexandre replied, his own smile not quite reaching his eyes. "Your vineyard is even more impressive in person."

Kit gestured for him to follow as they began walking toward the winery attached to the vineyard. "Let me show you around. We've made some improvements over the last few years, streamlined the production process, introduced some new blends. I think you'll find it interesting."

As they walked, Kit pointed out various aspects of the vineyard's operations, from the different grape varietals they cultivated to the state-of-the-art equipment used in the winery. Alexandre listened attentively, occasionally asking questions that revealed his keen business acumen. But Kit could sense that Alexandre's interest in the vineyard was only surface level, the real reason for this visit lay beneath the pleasantries.

They eventually made their way into the winery, where the cool air was thick with the scent of fermenting grapes. Kit led Alexandre through the stainless-steel fermentation tanks, the oak barrels aging their finest wines, and the bottling line that hummed quietly in the background.

"I've always believed in combining tradition with innovation," Kit said as they walked. "We respect the old methods, but we're not afraid to embrace new technologies to improve our product. It's the same approach I take with all of my investments."

Alexandre nodded thoughtfully. "It's a philosophy I can appreciate. One must adapt to survive in this ever-changing world."

Kit led them to a small tasting room where two glasses of wine awaited them. He handed one to Alexandre and raised his own in a toast. "To new ventures."

"To new ventures," Alexandre echoed, clinking his glass against Kit's before taking a sip.

The wine was excellent, smooth and rich with a complexity that spoke of careful craftsmanship. But even as they tasted, Kit knew it was time to steer the conversation toward the real reason Alexandre was here.

"I've been thinking a lot about our conversations over the phone," Kit began, setting his glass down. "About the investments you proposed, both the straightforward and the more... discreet ones."

Alexandre's eyes glinted with interest. "And what have you decided?"

"I'm intrigued," Kit said, leaning back slightly in his chair. "But I'm also cautious. My business is built on reputation, and I can't afford any missteps. I need to be sure that whatever I get involved in is worth the risk."

"Of course," Alexandre agreed, his tone smooth and reassuring. "I wouldn't propose anything that wasn't thoroughly vetted. And I understand your need for caution. Perhaps we can discuss some specifics?"

Kit nodded, and for the next hour, they hashed out various plans of action. Alexandre listened as Kit laid out opportunities for investments with his high-end unique wines, the exotic cars he had purchased, and, more subtly, in ventures that operated in the gray areas of legality. Alexandre listened carefully, asking pointed questions that showed his interest but also his hesitancy to dive in without complete assurance.

"I'll need to consider these options carefully," Kit finally said, his tone thoughtful. "I don't make decisions like this lightly. But I'll admit, the potential is... compelling."

Alexandre smiled, pleased with Kit's response. "Take all the time you need. I'm confident you'll find these opportunities to be as profitable as I do."

They continued their tour of the vineyard, discussing more mundane topics, market trends, global economic shifts, and the challenges of running a business in today's world. But Kit knew Alexandre was just biding his time, waiting for the right moment to turn the conversation to more personal matters.

That moment came at dinner.

The evening meal was served in a private dining room overlooking the vineyard, the sun setting in a blaze of color over the distant hills. The food was exquisite, showing off his personal chef's skill, and the wine flowed freely. But despite the pleasant surroundings and the excellent cuisine, Kit could feel the questions waiting to be asked.

He knew what was coming. Charlie and Aria had briefed him extensively on what Charlie had revealed to Alexandre during their meeting at her ranch. Kit was prepared... at least, he thought he was.

As they reached the end of the meal, Alexandre set down his fork and looked directly at Kit, his expression shifting from congenial to something more probing.

"Kit," Alexandre began, his voice measured, "there's something I need to ask you. And I would appreciate it if you were completely honest with me."

Kit met his gaze steadily, a slight nod indicating for him to continue. "Of course, Alexandre. What's on your mind?"

Alexandre leaned back slightly in his chair, his eyes never leaving Kit's. "I've just come from Charlotte O'Donovan's ranch. She and I had a very enlightening conversation."

Kit felt a slight tightening in his chest, but he kept his expression neutral. "Oh? And what did you two discuss?"

Alexandre's smile was thin, almost predatory. "She told me everything. About her past, about her alter ego, Diamond Frost, I believe she called it. And about her... association with Gabriel Carvalho."

Kit took a slow breath, carefully considering his response. He had been prepared for this, but it was clear that Alexandre had done his homework. Still, Kit knew he had to stay calm, to stick to the narrative they had crafted.

"I'm aware of Charlotte's past," Kit said evenly. "She's been very open with me about it. But I can assure you, Alexandre, there's nothing in her past that affects our current business dealings. Charlotte O'Donovan is a shrewd businesswoman, and whatever she did before me is her own business."

"Is that so?" Alexandre's tone was casual, but Kit could sense the sharpness beneath it. "And what about your relationship with her, Kit? I've heard you've been... quite close."

Kit forced a small smile, carefully walking the line they had established. "Charlotte and I have known each other for some time, yes. We've worked together on various projects. But our relationship is purely professional."

Alexandre tilted his head slightly, as if studying Kit's every reaction. "Are you sure about that? Because from where I'm standing, it seems there's more to the story. Especially considering how thoroughly I've vetted your life."

Kit felt a chill run down his spine, but he didn't let it show. He had expected Alexandre to dig, but the depth of his investigation was unsettling. Still, Kit knew he couldn't falter now. He had to play this carefully, give Alexandre just enough to satisfy his curiosity without revealing too much.

"You're right to be thorough, Alexandre," Kit said, his tone measured. "But I assure you, there's nothing in my past, or my present, that should concern you. I've built my business on integrity, and I wouldn't risk it by getting involved in anything... too unsavory."

Alexandre's gaze remained locked on Kit, his eyes narrowing slightly as if trying to read between the lines. "You say that, but there are whispers, Kit. Whispers about your involvement in certain... activities. Activities that might be more aligned with Charlotte O'Donovan's past than you're letting on."

Kit's pulse quickened, but he kept his expression calm. "I won't deny that I've been looking at some... unconventional ventures. But everything I've done has been within the bounds of the law, or at the very least, within the bounds of good business practice."

"And what about the whispers regarding your association with Charlotte's clubs? Specifically, the ones she runs under the name Diamond Frost?" Alexandre pressed, his tone sharper now.

Kit leaned back in his chair, maintaining a calm demeanor. "Charlotte's clubs are legitimate businesses. She turned them around from failing ventures into profitable enterprises. Yes, she took a hands-on approach, but that was part of her strategy. It's the same approach I've taken with my own businesses. We see potential where others see failure."

"And Gabriel Carvalho?" Alexandre asked, his voice a little too casual. "How did he fit into all of this?"

Kit knew this was the moment of truth. He had to be careful, precise. "Carvalho was a powerful man with his fingers in many pies. It's not surprising that he crossed paths with Charlotte during her time in the club scene. But as far as I know, their relationship was purely business. She kept him at arm's length. Again, this was before I met the woman so I don't know how deeply she was involved with him."

Alexandre watched Kit for a long moment, the silence between them stretching taut. Finally, he gave a slight nod, as if coming to a decision.

"I see," he said quietly. "It seems you've both been... careful."

"We have," Kit replied, meeting Alexandre's gaze steadily. "In our line of work, caution is necessary. But I want to assure you, Alexandre, that I value our partnership. I wouldn't risk it for anything. or anyone."

Alexandre's lips curled into a smile, though it didn't reach his eyes. "I appreciate your honesty, Kit. It's rare in our world."

Kit returned the smile, though his own was more guarded. "I'm glad we can be honest with each other. I think it's the foundation of a strong partnership."

They finished their meal with the conversation turning back to more mundane topics, but Kit knew that the real test had already taken place. Alexandre had dug deep, tested his story, and, for now, seemed to have accepted it. But Kit also knew that this was only the beginning. Alexandre was a man who didn't trust easily, and while he might be satisfied for the moment, he would continue to watch, to probe, to search for any sign of weakness.

As the evening drew to a close and Alexandre prepared to leave, Kit walked him to the door of the main house, the cool night air brushing against his skin.

"Thank you for the hospitality, Kit," Alexandre said, his tone polite but with an edge of something darker beneath it. "I'll be in touch soon to discuss our next steps."

"I look forward to it," Kit replied, shaking Alexandre's hand firmly.

As Alexandre's car disappeared down the driveway, Kit stood on the porch, watching until the taillights were no longer visible. He let out a slow breath, the tension that had coiled tightly in his chest finally beginning to unwind. He felt as weak a as newborn kitten.

He had made it through the meeting, but the encounter had left him hurting, tired, a very much uneasy. Alexandre was far more dangerous than he had anticipated, and the fact that he had vetted Kit's life so thoroughly meant that he wasn't going to stop until he had all the answers.

Kit turned and walked back into the house, his mind racing. They needed to catch Alexandre and his associates quickly, before things spiraled further out of control. As he made his way to the study, Kit knew he had to inform the others, to prepare them for what was coming. This game they were playing had just become a lot more dangerous, and they needed to be ready. He needed to gut up his injury and get on with things.

If they weren't careful, there would be hell to pay.

CHAPTER 40

Kit Thorne's eyes fluttered open to an unfamiliar darkness. His mind, still groggy from sleep, or something else, struggled to grasp where he was. He pushed himself up, feeling the cool metal beneath his hands, and blinked into the black void. The last thing he remembered was falling asleep in his own bed, exhausted after the day with Alexandre at the vineyard. This wasn't his bed.

Charlie Donovan stirred nearby, her breathing quickening as she came to. What the heck had happened. She remembered falling asleep after a long conversation with Aria and Doc. "Who's here? I can hear you breathing."

"It's Kit."

Kit could hear her soft groan, followed by the rustling of fabric as she shifted. "Where are you?" she called out, her voice unsteady.

"I'm here," Kit replied, his own voice hoarse. He reached out, finding her arm in the darkness. "Are you okay?"

"I think so," Charlie replied, though her voice held a note of uncertainty. "Where the hell are we?"

Kit didn't answer immediately, his senses slowly coming back to him. The air was thick, metallic. He could feel the walls close in around them, cold and unforgiving. He ran a hand over the wall, his fingertips tracing the ridged surface. "It feels like…a shipping container."

Charlie cursed under her breath. "How did we end up in a shipping container? I was at home, in my own bed…"

"Me too." Kit felt a knot of dread forming in his stomach as the pieces started to click together. "We've been taken."

"Taken? By who?" Charlie asked, panic beginning to edge into her voice.

Kit didn't want to say it, but they both knew the answer. "Alexandre and Gero," he said grimly. "They've found out more than we thought."

Charlie fell silent, the weight of the situation sinking in. Kit's mind raced, trying to piece together what had happened, but his memory was foggy. Whatever they had been drugged with had done its job well.

"I'm in my pajamas," Charlie murmured, disbelief in her voice. "They took us from our beds."

Kit realized he was also in his pajamas, a simple pair of lounge pants and a T-shirt. They had been taken while they were at their most vulnerable, with nothing to defend themselves.

"Check around," Kit instructed, trying to maintain some semblance of control. "There has to be something in here that can help us."

They both started feeling their way around the container, hands running over every surface. The metal was cold and smooth, the walls solid with no apparent openings other than the door they couldn't see in the dark. It was utterly barren, save for two bottles of water that they found near where they had woken up.

"Just water," Charlie muttered, frustration in her voice. "No tools, no light, nothing."

Kit sank down against the wall, his mind racing but coming up with nothing. They were trapped, with no idea of where they were or how they had gotten here. The pitch-black darkness was suffocating, pressing in on them from all sides. There was nothing to do but wait.

They sat in silence, the only sound their steady breathing. Time lost all meaning in the darkness, every second stretching into what felt like hours. Kit's thoughts turned to their teams, Aria, Doc, Calista, Jack, Jane. Would they realize something was wrong? Would they come looking? The thought brought little comfort. If

Alexandre and Gero had gone this far, they had likely covered their tracks.

Charlie shifted beside him. "Kit, what are we going to do?"

"We'll figure something out," Kit said, trying to keep his voice steady. "We just need to wait for an opportunity."

But even as he said it, he wasn't sure he believed it. They were at the mercy of two men who were known for their ruthlessness. And now, they had to figure a way out.

Finally, after what felt like an eternity, they heard the sound of metal scraping against metal. The door of the container creaked open, flooding the space with harsh white light. Kit and Charlie squinted, momentarily blinded after hours in darkness.

As their eyes adjusted, they saw silhouettes standing in the doorway, two large, hulking figures that could only be bodyguards, and behind them, the familiar forms of Alexandre DuBois and Gero Meyer.

"Good morning," Alexandre's voice cut through the silence, his tone dripping with false pleasantries. "I trust you slept well?"

Kit forced himself to stand, his muscles stiff and aching from the cold, hard floor. "What the hell do you think you're doing?" he demanded, his voice rough with anger.

"Let's just say we're taking you on a little vacation," Gero replied, stepping forward with a smirk on his face. "You've been so busy trying to ruin our business that we thought it was time you experienced it from a different perspective."

Charlie stood beside Kit, her eyes narrowed. "You won't get away with this," she said, her voice low and dangerous.

Gero chuckled, a dark, humorless sound. "We already have. Your teams think you've decided to take some time off together, flitting around the world like the rich, spoiled brats you pretend you are. They won't come looking for you, not for a while."

Kit's heart sank. He had feared as much, but hearing it confirmed sent a wave of dread through him. They were truly alone in this.

"We know all about your little operations," Alexandre continued, his voice taking on a colder edge. "The Houston rescues, New York, Los Angeles... You've been quite the busy bees, haven't you? And Charlotte... or should I say, Detective Donovan? What a surprise to learn that you've been playing double agent all this time. Tsk, tsk, little police girl."

Charlie's breath hitched slightly, cop, not FBI. The revelation hitg Kit like a punch to the gut. He hadn't known. She had never told him. But now wasn't the time for that discussion.

"We're onto you, both of you," Alexandre said, his eyes narrowing. "And we're not the forgiving type."

Gero stepped closer, his towering frame casting a shadow over them. "It's time you learned what trafficking is like from the other side," he said, his voice low and menacing.

Kit's mind raced, trying to think of a way out, but there was none. They were trapped, at the mercy of men who saw them as nothing more than obstacles to be removed.

"What is it you really want?" Kit asked, his voice steady despite the fear gnawing at his insides.

Alexandre's smile was chilling. "We want you to feel the fear that our merchandise feels. We want you to know that there's no escape, no one coming to save you. We want you to understand that you're at our mercy now, just like they are."

"And then?" Charlie asked, her voice hard. "What's your plan? To kill us?"

"Not yet," Gero replied, his tone almost casual. "First, we're going to have some fun. Then we'll decide what to do with you."

Kit exchanged a quick glance with Charlie, a silent understanding passing between them. They were in deep, and they were going to have to fight their way out of this. But for now, they had to bide their time, wait for the right moment.

"You can do whatever you want," Kit said, his voice firm. "We won't break."

Gero's smile widened, a predator's grin. "We'll see about that. People always break."

With that, he turned and nodded to the bodyguards. One of them stepped forward, tossing a bag at Kit's feet. Kit crouched down, opening it to find rough, uncomfortable clothing, a far cry from the nightwear they had woken up in.

"Put those on," Alexandre ordered. "We're going for a little walk."

Kit looked up at him, meeting his cold gaze. He knew they had no choice. Slowly, he and Charlie began to change, their movements stiff with the knowledge that they were being watched by men who held their lives in their hands.

Once they were dressed, Alexandre motioned for the bodyguards to step back. "Follow us," he said, turning on his heel and walking out of the container.

Kit and Charlie exchanged one last glance before following them out into the blinding sunlight. As their eyes adjusted, they realized they were in the middle of nowhere, a desolate, barren landscape stretching out in all directions.

This was a nightmare, but Kit knew one thing for certain, they would find a way out of this. They had to. Because if they didn't, Alexandre and Gero would make sure they never saw the light of day again.

The world was reduced to darkness again. Kit and Charlie could feel the rough fabric of the hoods covering their heads, cutting them off from everything, sight, sound, even the subtle cues of the world around them. The only thing they could discern was the rumbling of the vehicle they were in, the vibrations thrumming through their bodies as they were driven to an unknown destination.

Kit strained to hear anything that might give them a clue as to where they were being taken, a distinct sound, a shift in the road, the scent of the air, but the hoods muffled everything. He reached out mentally, trying to piece together the fragments of what he could sense, but it was like grasping at smoke. He felt a flicker of frustration and anger, both at their situation and at himself for not being able to do more.

Beside him, Charlie was similarly tense, her mind racing as she tried to stay calm. She was methodical, running through every possibility in her mind, but the lack of sensory input was maddening. All she could do was listen to the sound of her own breathing and the rhythmic bump of the road beneath them.

The drive didn't last long, though in their current state, it felt like an eternity. The vehicle finally came to a halt, and the two of them were yanked roughly out by unseen hands. Kit stumbled as his feet hit the ground, his balance thrown off by the sudden movement, causing his stitches to tear. Charlie, not far from him, felt a similar jolt as she was pulled forward, her hands bound in front of her.

They were led forward, their footsteps echoing against what sounded like a concrete floor. There was a brief pause as a door creaked open, followed by a blast of cold, damp air. The smell of mold and decay filled their nostrils, making Charlie's stomach lurch. Wherever they were, it was not a place anyone would want to spend time in.

A shove from behind sent Kit stumbling forward again, his shoulder brushing against a metal surface. He was shoved down into a narrow, confining space, and when he heard the clang of a metal door closing behind him, he knew he was in a cage. The realization hit him like a physical blow, sending a surge of adrenaline through his veins.

Charlie was shoved into a cage beside him, the sounds of metal against metal echoing in the space. Her hands scrambled along the cold bars, her breath coming in sharp gasps as panic threatened to rise. But before she could fully react, their hoods were ripped off, and the sudden flood of light, dim though it was, left them momentarily blinded.

As their vision cleared, Kit and Charlie took in their surroundings. They were in a large, dimly lit room that looked like an old warehouse or basement, the walls lined with other cages like theirs. In those cages, other adults, some bruised and battered, others with expressions of hopelessness, huddled on dirty bedding, their eyes filled with fear and resignation.

The sight was gut-wrenching. Kit's hands gripped the bars of his cage, his knuckles turning white. This was a nightmare, a twisted game that Alexandre and Gero were playing, and they were the latest pieces on the board.

The sound of footsteps drew their attention to the center of the room. Alexandre and Gero stood there, flanked by their bodyguards, smug expressions plastered on their faces. Gero, in particular, wore a smirk that made Kit's blood boil.

"Well, well," Gero drawled, his eyes flicking between Kit and Charlie. "It looks like the mighty have fallen. How does it feel to be on the other side, hmm?"

Charlie's eyes blazed with defiance, but before she could respond, Kit spoke, his voice a low growl. "What the hell do you think you're doing, Gero?"

Alexandre stepped forward, his cold gaze fixed on them both. "Teaching you a lesson," he replied smoothly. "You've been meddling in things you shouldn't have, disrupting our operations, causing problems. We thought it was time you understood the consequences of your actions."

Charlie's grip on the bars tightened, her mind racing. "You think this is going to stop us?" she demanded, her voice edged with anger. "You think you can just lock us up and we'll roll over and die? You're delusional."

Gero chuckled darkly, shaking his head. "Oh, we're not going to kill you, not yet anyway. We're going to let you stew in here, let you feel what it's like to be powerless, to be nothing more than a commodity."

Alexandre crossed his arms over his chest, his expression one of cold amusement. "The auction will take place in three day's time. By then, you'll have come to the realization that your lives are no longer your own. You'll be sold off, just like all the others."

Kit's heart pounded in his chest as rage boiled within him. "You're insane," he spat, his voice thick with contempt. "You think you can get away with this? My team, Charlie's team, they're going to find us."

Alexandre and Gero exchanged a glance, as if sharing some private joke. "Oh, I'm sure they'll be looking," Alexandre said, his tone mocking. "But they won't find you. We've made sure of that."

Charlie lunged at the bars, her hands clawing at them as she tried to reach the smug faces of the two men before her. But before she could get close, one of the bodyguards stepped forward, brandishing a cattle prod. There was a crackle of electricity, and pain shot through Charlie's body as the prod made contact with her ribs, sending her sprawling back into the cage.

"Calm down," Gero ordered, his voice devoid of sympathy. "Or we'll make this a lot more unpleasant."

Kit surged forward, his anger overcoming his sense of self-preservation. But he was met with the same response, a jab from the cattle prod that sent a jolt of agony through his body, dropping him to his knees. He gritted his teeth against the pain, refusing to give them the satisfaction of hearing him cry out.

Both Kit and Charlie lay on the dirty bedding of their cages, their bodies still trembling from the shocks. Alexandre and Gero looked down at them, their faces cold and unmoved.

"This is just the beginning," Alexandre said softly, his tone almost gentle. "You have three days to come to terms with your new reality. Use that time wisely."

With that, Alexandre and Gero turned and walked away, their bodyguards following closely behind. The sound of the heavy door closing behind them echoed through the room, leaving Kit and Charlie in silence.

Kit slowly pushed himself up, his muscles still twitching from the electric shock. He looked over at Charlie, who was doing the same, her face pale but determined.

"They're not going to break us," she said through gritted teeth, her voice filled with resolve. "We're getting out of here, Kit. One way or another."

Kit nodded, his own determination hardening as he held his side. "Damn right we are. But we have to be smart about this."

They sat there for a moment, realizing the danger of their situation. They were trapped in a cage, surrounded by others in the same hopeless situation, with no clear way out. But Kit knew one thing for certain: they couldn't give up. They couldn't let Alexandre and Gero win.

"We need to figure out a plan," Kit said, his voice steady despite the fear gnawing at his insides. "We need to find a way to communicate with each other, with the others in here. We don't know what they're planning, but we can't just sit and wait for them to auction us off."

Charlie nodded, her mind already working. "There has to be a way. We just need to find it." Then she saw his side. "It's bleeding. At least lay down and let the bleeding stop."

"It superficial. The stitches tore, but I don't think the wound opened. Damn inconvenient though. Can't let them see it or they'll use it against me."

For now, they were at the mercy of their captors, but Kit and Charlie knew that this battle was far from over. They would fight, they would resist, and they would find a way to turn the tables.

As they sat in the dark, cold room, the reality of their situation sinking in, they steeled themselves for the battle ahead. They were up against ruthless men who held all the power at the moment, but they weren't defeated yet.

And they wouldn't be. Not as long as they had each other for support.

CHAPTER 41

The atmosphere in the lodge outside Atlanta was tense, worry hanging over the room as both teams gathered. The usually vibrant space, filled with laughter, was now heavy with the absence of their leaders, Kit and Charlie. The sun had set hours ago, casting long shadows across the room, but no one had even thought to turn on the lights. The dim glow of laptops and the occasional flash of a phone screen were the only sources of illumination, adding to the sense of urgency that gripped them all.

Aria sat at the head of the large conference table, her fingers tapping rhythmically against the wood as she stared at the array of screens in front of her. She had been going over the same data for hours, looking for any clue, any hint, as to where Kit and Charlie might have gone. But there was nothing, no messages, no calls, not even a text. It was as if they had vanished into thin air, and that was what terrified her the most.

Across from her, Jane leaned forward, her usually calm demeanor strained. "This doesn't make sense, Aria," she said, her voice low but insistent. "Kit wouldn't just disappear without a word. He would've left something behind, some kind of message. This isn't like him at all."

Aria nodded, her mind racing as she tried to piece together the puzzle. "I know. And Charlie's the same way. She's careful, methodical. She wouldn't leave without a plan in place, without telling someone. Something's wrong, Jane. I can feel it."

Jane glanced at the others in the room, Calista, Zara, Sofia, Jack, all of them wore the same expressions of concern. They were all seasoned professionals, used to dealing with high-stakes situations, but this was different. This was personal.

"Have we heard anything from Marley, Izzy, or Rafe?" Jack asked, his deep voice cutting through the silence.

Aria shook her head. "They're on red alert in LA, but so far, nothing. Doc has his people searching too, and I've sent out alerts to all my contacts around the globe. If Kit and Charlie are out there, we're going to find them. But..." She trailed off, her voice catching in her throat. "But time is ticking, and we're running out of leads."

Calista, who had been working furiously on her laptop, suddenly looked up, her face pale. "I've been scouring the dark web, but it's like they've vanished. Even Dak hasn't found anything. It's like someone's wiped their existence off the map."

A heavy silence followed her words. Aria felt a cold knot of fear twist in her gut. Kit and Charlie had faced dangerous situations before, but this was different. They were up against someone who knew how to cover their tracks, someone who was playing a very dangerous game.

Six hours had passed since they'd realized Kit and Charlie were missing, and every second that ticked by only heightened Aria's anxiety. She knew the longer they were out of contact, the worse the situation would get.

Her phone buzzed suddenly, breaking the silence. It was Vicky, Charlie's friend and fellow FBI agent based in Atlanta. Aria quickly answered the call, her voice filled with concern. "What do you have, Vicky?" she asked, her heart pounding in her chest.

"I've got something," Vicky replied, her tone serious. "And it's a bit of a bombshell. Turns out, the agency had a tracking device implanted in Charlie without her knowledge, or anyone else's, for that matter."

Aria's eyes widened in shock. "What? How the hell did that happen? And when?"

"Apparently, it was a precautionary measure taken after the sting at the ranch," Vicky explained. "High-ups thought it would be wise to keep tabs on her, just in case. But the thing is, the device is dormant by default. We need someone to activate it, someone who can hack into the system and turn it on remotely. The agency doesn't need to know it's activated."

Aria's mind was already racing, considering the implications. "Can you do it?"

"Not me, but I know someone who can," Vicky replied. "Your guy Dak, he's good at sneaking in, Aria. Real good. If anyone can get that tracker up and running without the agency knowing, it's him."

Aria felt a glimmer of hope for the first time in hours. "I'll get him on it right now. Keep hunting, Vicky. Time's running out."

"I'm on it," Vicky said, her voice firm. "I'll keep you posted."

Aria disconnected the call and immediately turned to the group, her eyes blazing with the challenge ahead. "We have something. Charlie has a tracking device implanted, something none of us knew about. I'm texting Dak now, who's hopefully going to activate it. We might be able to find her, and hopefully Kit, soon."

The room buzzed with a new burst of energy, everyone snapping back into action with renewed focus. The thought of having a way to locate Charlie, and by extension, Kit, brought a much-needed jolt of hope to the team.

Jane leaned in, her voice hushed but intense. "If we can get a location on Charlie, we need to be ready to move immediately. There's no telling what condition they'll be in when we find them."

Aria nodded, already making a mental checklist. "Agreed. I want everyone geared up and ready to go at a moment's notice. Calista, keep working the dark web. If anyone tries to post anything related to them, I want to know about it immediately."

Calista gave a curt nod, her fingers flying over the keyboard once more. "I'll keep looking. And I'll keep Dak on high alert as well."

Sofia, who had been silent until now, spoke up, her voice steady and calm. "If Alexandre and Gero are behind this, they won't keep them together for long. We need to be prepared for the possibility that they'll try to separate them, or worse."

A shiver ran down Aria's spine at the thought. "We need to move fast. If we lose them..."

She didn't finish the sentence. She didn't need to. The stakes were clear to everyone in the room.

Minutes ticked by as they waited for word from Vicky. Each passing second felt like an eternity, the tension in the room high. Aria paced the room, her mind racing with every possible scenario they might face once they found Kit and Charlie. She refused to let herself think about the worst-case scenarios, she couldn't afford to. Not now.

Finally, her phone buzzed again, and she snatched it up, answering immediately.

"Vicky?" she said, her voice urgent.

"We've got it," Vicky's voice crackled through the line, filled with relief. "The tracker is active. We've got a signal. I had a friend silence it for 48 hours. That's all the time we've got."

Aria's heart skipped a beat. "And their location?"

"Sending the coordinates to you now," Vicky replied. "It looks like an industrial area on the outskirts of..." They heard a sharp intake of air from Vicky. "Holy crap! They're in LA. I'm coming to you. Get your plane ready."

"You got it," Aria said, already motioning to the others to prepare. "We'll be waiting."

She ended the call and turned to the team, her expression fierce. "We've got a location. LA, industrial area, outskirts of the city. We've got one hour to get our gear and get to the airport."

There was no hesitation. The team sprang into action, grabbing gear, checking weapons, and preparing for what would undoubtedly be a dangerous extraction.

Vicky was there in less than thirty minutes, no one asked how. And as they piled into the SUVs parked outside the lodge, Aria's mind was laser-focused on the mission ahead. She had no doubt that they were walking into a trap, Alexandre and Gero weren't the type to let anything happen without a plan. But Kit and Charlie were out there, and they were running out of time.

The drive to the airport was tense, the silence in the vehicle telling how serious the mission had become.

Five hours later, the private jet was met by Rafe and Izzy, Marley had gone ahead to stake out the port warehouse Kit and Charlie were located. Quickly and efficiently, all their equipment was loaded into waiting SUVs and the two teams were taken to a safehouse not far from the port. There, they were met by several of Doc's operatives from days gone by. But everyone knew, including the two big men, Grunt and Miguel, those older guys were not to be messed with. They had this fierceness about them that would stop a bullet.

Aria kept her eyes on the GPS, watching the coordinates, praying this was not another trick by those two foreigners. She had a bone to pick with those two men. Then Marley's voice came over the comms.

"You're not gonna believe what I'm seeing." He sounded shocked.

Marley crouched behind the rusting hulk of an abandoned truck, his binoculars trained on the warehouse across the lot. The old industrial district was a warren of crumbling buildings and overgrown weeds, the perfect place for someone to conduct illicit activities without attracting attention. But what Marley had discovered inside that warehouse chilled him to the bone.

He had spent hours surveilling the area, moving from one vantage point to another, keeping to the shadows. The warehouse was massive, with multiple entrances and windows, but most had been boarded up or blackened to prevent any prying eyes from seeing inside. However, Marley's persistence had paid off when he found a small crack in one of the boarded windows at the rear of the building, just large enough to give him a glimpse of what was happening inside.

What he saw made his blood run cold.

In the dim light of the warehouse, he could see the outlines of cages holding people. He counted at least forty men and women, all older, all looking defeated and exhausted. They were huddled on filthy bedding, their faces gaunt and haunted. Some had bruises, others looked dehydrated, and all wore expressions of hopelessness that twisted Marley's gut.

But that wasn't the worst of it.

The main part of the warehouse was being transformed into something horrific. A large ring was being set up in the center of the space, surrounded by tables and chairs that were being arranged by workers. Marley watched as the windows on the upper level were methodically blackened, ensuring that no light would escape and no one from the outside would be able to see in.

It didn't take long for Marley to realize what was happening. This wasn't just a trafficking operation. This was something much worse, some kind of fight event, where the captives were likely to be forced into brutal, deadly combat for the entertainment of a select, depraved audience. The thought made Marley's stomach turn.

He pulled back from the window, taking a deep breath to steady himself before reaching for the small earpiece nestled in his ear. "Aria," he whispered, his voice tense, "I've got eyes on the captives. It's bad, real bad."

Aria's voice crackled through the earpiece, her tone sharp with concern. "What do you see, Marley? What's happening?"

Marley swallowed hard, forcing himself to stay calm. "There are about forty people in here, all older men and women. They're being held in cages, like animals. And it looks like they're setting up some kind of fighting ring in the main part of the warehouse. I think they're planning to have some sort of event. The windows are being blackened. Security is tight, at least thirty heavily armed guards."

There was a long pause on the other end, and Marley could almost hear Aria processing the information. They knew what this meant, it meant their plans had to change, and it meant they were running out of time.

"Are Kit and Charlie there?" Aria asked finally, her voice low and strained.

"I couldn't get a clear look," Marley admitted, frustration gnawing at him. "But if they're in here, they're probably being held separately from the other captives."

Aria's sigh was barely audible, but her fear was clear. "We can't move in tonight, not with that kind of security and not knowing exactly where Kit and Charlie are. We're going to have to wait."

Marley's heart sank at her words, but he knew she was right. Rushing in without a solid plan would only get them all killed. Still, the thought of leaving Kit and Charlie in that hellhole for another day was unbearable.

"I'll keep watching," Marley said, his voice grim. "But we need to come up with a plan fast. Whatever they're planning in here, it's going to happen soon."

"Agreed," Aria replied. "Get as much intel as you can, but don't take any unnecessary risks. We need you alive to get them out."

"Copy that," Marley said, his eyes flicking back to the crack in the window. "I'll stay on them."

As the connection ended, Marley adjusted his position, trying to find a more comfortable spot behind the truck. The night was still young, and a sense of urgency gnawed at him. Every minute they delayed was a minute closer to whatever horrific event was about to unfold in that warehouse.

He continued to watch as more workers arrived, some carrying equipment, others setting up what looked like audio and video with lighting systems. This was no ordinary fight, this was going to be a spectacle, a gruesome display for the sick and twisted minds willing to pay to watch human beings tear each other apart.

The thought made Marley's hands clench into fists. He had seen a lot in his time, including illegal fights, but this was something else, staged assassination. He didn't want to think about what Kit and Charlie were going through, trapped in this nightmare. He had to stay focused, had to keep his emotions in check if they were going to get out of this alive.

Marley's mind raced as he tried to think of ways they could infiltrate the warehouse, but every scenario he ran through ended in disaster. The security was too tight, the risk too high. They needed more information, where Kit and Charlie were being held, what the layout of the warehouse was, how many guards were on duty at any given time. Without that, any attempt to rescue them would be suicide.

As the night dragged on, Marley continued to watch, his mind a whirlwind of thoughts and plans. He knew Aria and the others were working on a strategy, but time was slipping away. They needed to act soon, before it was too late.

His thoughts were interrupted by a sudden movement inside the warehouse. A group of men, heavily armed and wearing tactical gear, entered the section where the cages were. Marley tensed, watching as they moved toward the captives.

One of the men, who appeared to be in charge, barked orders, and the others began roughly pulling the captives to their feet. Marley strained to hear what was being said, but the distance and the muffling effect of the window made it impossible.

The sight alone was enough to send a cold chill down his spine. The captives were being lined up, and Marley had a sickening realization, this was a selection process. They were choosing who would fight and who might not survive the battle.

He needed to tell Aria, needed to relay what he was seeing, but he couldn't tear his eyes away from the horror unfolding in front of him. The captives were too weak to resist, some barely able to stand as they were prodded and pushed by the guards. The expressions on their faces, terror, resignation, despair, would haunt Marley for many days to come.

He had to act, had to do something, but the rational part of his mind held him back. Rushing in now would only get him captured or killed, and that would help no one. He took a deep breath, forcing himself to remain calm, even as his blood boiled with rage.

Finally, the men moved on, leaving the chosen captives to their fate. Marley let out a slow breath, his heart pounding in his chest. This was worse than he had imagined, and it was about to get a whole lot worse if they didn't act soon.

He tapped his earpiece again, his voice a low whisper. "Aria, it's Marley. They're selecting fighters. I don't know when it's going to start, but it's soon. We need to move."

There was a long pause, and Marley could almost feel the pressure of Aria's decision pressing down on her. "We can't go in blind, Marley," she finally said, her voice thick with emotion. "But I hear you. I'll get the team ready. We'll move as soon as we have a solid plan. If anything starts, let me know and we'll play it by ear."

Marley nodded, even though she couldn't see him. "I'll keep eyes on them. Just… just hurry. I think it's happening tonight."

"Stay safe," Aria said, her voice tight. "We'll be there soon. We're going to get them out."

As the connection ended, Marley hunkered down behind the truck, his heart heavy with the knowledge of what was coming. The fight was about to begin, and Kit and Charlie were running out of time.

But they weren't alone. Marley and the rest of the team were out there, and they would do whatever it took to bring them home. The night was dark, but dawn was coming.

And when it did, they would be ready.

CHAPTER 42

Aria sat in the hotel room, her eyes locked on the screens in front of her. The room was buzzing with quiet activity. They were running out of time, and every minute that ticked by without solid intel made her stomach twist tighter with anxiety. Kit and Charlie were still somewhere in that warehouse, and if they were going to get them out alive, they needed eyes and ears inside.

"Calista, Dak, I need you to focus," Aria said, her voice calm but firm as she addressed the two tech wizards in front of her. Calista was already deep in concentration, her fingers flying over her keyboard, while Dak, a wiry young man from LA, with an air of unshakeable confidence, was methodically monitoring his equipment.

"We're on it, Aria," Calista replied without looking up. "I'm scanning the dark web for any signs of a live stream or security feeds from inside the warehouse. If there's anything broadcasting from that building, we'll find it."

Dak nodded in agreement, his eyes flicking between his multiple screens. "I'm setting up a backdoor into any security systems they might have in place. If they've got cameras or mics in there and are broadcasting, we'll tap into them. I'll put a delay if possible. "

Aria's mind raced as she considered their options. They couldn't afford to go in blind, not with the kind of opposition they were up against. Marley had already reported that there were at least thirty heavily armed guards patrolling the warehouse, and now they knew that some sort of fight event was scheduled to take place tonight. That gave them precious little time to gather intel and formulate a plan.

"Good," Aria said, her voice tense. "I need to know what's happening inside that building. We can't leave anything to chance. Not with Kit and Charlie in there."

Calista nodded, her expression serious. "We'll get you what you need, Aria. Just give us a little more time."

Aria forced herself to take a deep breath, willing herself to remain calm. This was her team, her family, and they were all relying on her to lead them through this. There was no room for doubt or hesitation.

Just then, Marley pinged in, his voice urgent and grim. Aria clicked back, sensing that he had something important to report.

"What did you find?" she asked, her voice cracked.

Marley, whispering, ran a hand through his hair, his jaw clenched. "I contacted someone from my old neighborhood, asked to see if anyone had heard about anything unusual going on. He knows me as a reporter, so didn't think much of me snooping around. That's when one of the local leaders interrupted and told me about a fight event happening in tonight."

Aria's heart skipped a beat. "A fight event?"

Marley nodded. "Yeah. Apparently, it's supposed to be a big deal. The kind of event where people prove their worth, whatever that means. It's open to anyone who wants to show what they're made of, and the people in the know seem to think it's going to be brutal."

Aria's mind raced as she processed the information. "And you're sure this is connected to what's happening in the warehouse?"

Marley's expression darkened. "I'm sure. The leader mentioned something about newcomers being brought in for the event, real fighters. That lines up with what I saw in the warehouse, the cages, the setup. It's all connected."

Aria felt a cold dread settle in her stomach. "This fight event... it's not just some underground brawl, is it? They're planning something far worse."

Marley shook his head, his eyes filled with grim understanding. "I don't think it's a normal fight at all, Aria. This is going to be a bloodbath. They're going to pit those people against each other, force them to fight for their lives."

Aria's fists clenched at her sides. She couldn't let that happen. She couldn't let Kit and Charlie be part of some sick, twisted spectacle.

"Did you get anything else?" she asked, her voice tight.

Marley hesitated, then nodded. "Yeah. I had the tip checked out by some of Doc's people. They confirmed that the warehouse has been flagged as a potential site for illegal activities before, but nothing's ever been done about it. It's like the place is untouchable."

"Until now," Aria muttered, her resolve hardening. She turned to Calista and Dak, who were both still focused on their screens. "Any luck finding the feed?"

Calista's fingers paused on the keyboard, and she glanced over at Dak, who was nodding slowly, his eyes never leaving his screen.

"I think we've got something," Dak said, his voice calm but laced with tension. "There's a live feed set up on a private server. It's encrypted, but I'm working on getting in. If we can crack the code, we'll have access to whatever they're streaming from inside the warehouse."

Calista leaned forward, her brow furrowed in concentration. "I've got the backdoor ready. Once Dak cracks the code, I can reroute the feed to our equipment and monitor it from here. We'll be able to see and hear everything that's happening in real-time."

Aria felt a surge of hope. "How long?"

Dak's fingers danced across the keyboard, his eyes narrowed in focus. "Give me twenty minutes. Maybe less."

Aria nodded, her mind already shifting to the next steps. They needed to gather as much intel as possible, but they also needed a plan. They couldn't just charge in with guns blazing, not with Kit and Charlie's lives on the line.

As Dak worked, Aria turned her attention back to Marley. "We need to confirm Kit and Charlie are in there before we make a move. Can you get a better position without being seen?"

Marley nodded without hesitation. "Can do. I'll keep a low profile and get as close as I can without drawing attention."

"Good," Aria said, her voice steady. "Once we have eyes on them, we'll figure out the best way to extract them. But we can't rush this. We need to be smart."

Marley clicked off, heading back out into the warehouse. Aria hung her head, her heart pounding with a mixture of fear and dread. This was the moment of truth. Everything they had been working toward hinged on the next few hours.

The room fell into a tense silence as Calista and Dak continued their work, the only sounds the rapid clicking of keys and the occasional beep from the equipment. Aria's mind raced, formulating plans and backup plans, preparing for every possible scenario. They had to be ready for anything.

Finally, Dak let out a triumphant sound, breaking the silence. "I'm in," he said, his voice filled with a mix of relief and excitement. "I've got the feed."

Calista quickly took over, her fingers flying as she connected the feed to their equipment. The screens in front of them flickered, and then the live video appeared, a grainy, black-and-white image of the inside of the warehouse.

Aria's breath caught in her throat as the camera panned over the cages, over the people huddled inside. It was exactly as Marley had described, men and women, old and broken, trapped like animals.

But then the camera moved again, focusing on a smaller section of the warehouse, where two figures were slumped against the bars of their cages, their faces obscured by the darkness.

Aria's heart skipped a beat as she recognized them.

"Kit... Charlie..." she whispered, her voice choked with emotion.

"They're alive," Jane said softly, her relief noticeable. "Thank God, they're alive."

But as the camera continued to pan, revealing the preparations for the fight event, Aria knew their situation was still dire. They were running out of time.

"We need to find a way in," she said, her voice hardening with resolve. "Dak, keep monitoring the feed. Calista, keep an eye on the dark web for any updates. Marley's going to try to confirm their location on the ground."

Aria stood up, her mind racing as she formulated a plan. They had no time left, little to no time to get Kit and Charlie out before they were forced into that ring. She wasn't going to let them down.

"Let's move," she said, her voice strong despite her quaking insides. "We're going to get them out. Whatever it takes."

As they neared the location, the industrial area came into view, an expanse of old warehouses, rusting containers, and empty lots. It was the perfect place for a hidden operation, far enough from prying eyes but close enough to the city to go unnoticed.

Aria parked the SUV in the shadows of a dilapidated building, the rest of the team following suit. They moved quickly and quietly, weapons drawn, as they approached the coordinates Vicky had sent.

"This is it," Aria whispered, her voice barely audible as they crouched behind a stack of crates. "We're here." She clicked Marley.

Calista's voice came through the earpiece, calm and steady. "I'm picking up signals inside the building. It looks like they've been moved to a lower floor."

Aria's heart pounded in her chest as she nodded to the team. "Everyone comms check." Voice clicked from all around the warehouse. "Places and settle. Wait for my command."

The two teams slipped into the building, the sound of their footsteps muffled by the thick concrete walls. The air was damp and musty, the dim light from flickering bulbs casting eerie shadows along the floors.

As they reached the basement entrance, Aria motioned for the team to spread out, covering all angles. Signaled to the second team to enter and spread out as well. They were going to be ready for anything.

But nothing could have prepared them for what they found.

As they reached the bottom of the stairs, the sight that greeted them sent a wave of horror crashing over Aria. There, in the farthest corner of the room, were two small cages, barely large enough to hold a person. Inside those cages, Kit and Charlie lay crumpled, bloodied, and broken.

Aria's breath caught in her throat as she took in the scene. Calista inadvertently cried out. Kit was slumped against the bars, his chest exposed where his shirt had been ripped open. A deep, angry gash ran across his chest, the blood congealed but still oozing from the wound. His recent gunshot wound, which had been healing, was now torn open, the flesh raw and bleeding. His face was bruised, one eye swollen nearly shut, but what struck Calista most was the look of utter defeat in his eyes, a look Calista said she had never seen before.

Charlie was in a similar state, curled up in the small cage with one arm cradling her side. Her face was a mess of bruises, one eye completely swollen shut, her lip split and bleeding. But it was the brand above her left breast that drew Aria's gaze, a cruel, twisted mark of a bird, its wings spread wide as if it were in flight. The sight of it made Aria's stomach turn with a mixture of fury and revulsion.

As she approached the cages, she noticed the telltale signs of electrocution, small, circular burns on their skin, and the slight tremors that ran through their bodies. They had been tortured, drugged, and left to rot in this hellhole.

"Goddamn it," Aria hissed under her breath, her hands shaking with a mixture of rage and fear. She dropped to her knees beside Kit's cage, her fingers fumbling with the lock. "We need to get them out of here. Now."

Calista was already beside Charlie's cage, working quickly to free her. "They're barely conscious," she said, her voice tight with concern. "We need to move fast."

Grunt, his face a mask of barely controlled fury, stepped forward as soon as Calista had the cage open. He reached in, carefully lifting Charlie into his arms as if she were made of glass. She barely stirred, her head lolling against his shoulder, her breath shallow and labored.

Miguel, his expression grim, crouched beside Kit's cage, his large hands deftly working the lock. The moment it clicked open, he reached in, lifting Kit out with a fireman's carry, supporting his weight with ease despite the man's considerable size.

As they moved toward the stairs, the weight of what had been done to Kit and Charlie settled heavily on the group. There were no words spoken, just the silent, shared understanding that they had to get out, quickly and quietly.

But just as they reached the base of the stairs, the unmistakable sound of a battle echoed through the building. The clash of metal, the bark of orders, the heavy thud of boot, hit them instantly. They had walked into a trap.

Aria's heart sank, and she felt a cold knot of dread tighten in her stomach. "Damn it," she muttered, her mind racing as she quickly assessed their situation. They were outnumbered, and in their current state, Kit and Charlie were in no condition to fight.

"We need to get them out of here," Jane said urgently, her eyes wide with fear of their conditions. "We can't let them take them again. They won't last much longer like this."

Aria nodded, her mind working furiously. "Miguel, Grunt, get them out of the building. Use the service entrance we scouted on the way in. We'll cover your exit and meet you at the rendezvous point."

Miguel shifted Kit's weight on his shoulder, his face set in grim determination. "We'll get them out," he promised, his voice steady despite the chaos around them.

Grunt, cradling Charlie close to his chest, nodded. "We'll keep them safe," he added, his voice low and fierce.

As the two men raced up the stairs, the rest of the team moved into position, preparing to defend their retreat. The sounds of the battle grew louder, closer, and Aria knew they had only moments before they were overrun.

She signaled to the others, her voice calm and commanding despite the fear gnawing at her insides. "We hold them off here. No one gets past us."

Calista, Jane, and the others nodded in unison, their weapons at the ready. They had faced impossible odds before, but this was different. This had turned personal. Had they lost their people upstairs?

The first wave of attackers burst through the door at the top of the stairs, heavily armed and moving with deadly precision. Aria and her team opened fire, the sound of gunfire echoing through the narrow stairwell. The attackers faltered, some going down in a spray of bullets, but more kept coming, their sheer numbers threatening to overwhelm the defenders.

Aria's mind was a blur of calculations, her movements instinctive as she fired shot after shot, each one finding its mark. But for every man they took down, another seemed to take his place. The air was filled with the acrid smell of gunpowder, the walls rattling with the force of the battle.

"We're not going to hold them for long!" Calista shouted, her voice barely audible over the roar of the firefight.

Aria knew she was right. They were outgunned, outnumbered, and running out of time. But they couldn't give up, not when Kit and Charlie's lives were on the line.

"Fall back!" Aria ordered, her voice cutting through the chaos. "We'll regroup at the service entrance!"

The team moved as one, retreating down the narrow corridor, their weapons still trained on the attackers as they fought to keep them at bay. The sound of footsteps pounding down the stairs behind them sent a jolt of adrenaline through Aria's veins. They were being pursued... they couldn't stop now.

They reached the service entrance just as Miguel and Grunt emerged from the building, Kit and Charlie still in their arms. The sight of them alive, but barely conscious, fueled Aria's determination to get them out.

"Get them to the van!" Aria shouted, her voice fierce and unyielding. "We'll cover you!"

Miguel and Grunt didn't hesitate. They moved quickly across the narrow alleyway to the waiting van, the engine already running. The rest of the team fell into position, their weapons at the ready as they formed a protective barrier around their retreating comrades.

But as they reached the van, the sound of a massive explosion ripped through the night, the shockwave sending them all to the ground. Aria's ears rang as she struggled to regain her bearings, the world spinning around her. She looked up in time to see the warehouse's main entrance engulfed in flames, the attackers scattered and disoriented by the blast.

"Go! Go! Go!" she shouted, her voice hoarse as she pushed herself to her feet.

Miguel and Grunt wasted no time, shoving Kit and Charlie into the van before jumping in themselves. The rest of the team piled in behind them, slamming the doors shut just as the engine roared to life.

Aria was the last to jump in, her heart pounding as she slammed the door shut behind her. "Drive!" she ordered, and the van lurched forward, speeding away from the burning warehouse.

Doc radioed, "We got the survivors out another door. The blast was my guys creating a diversion. Did you get them?"

"Oh my God, Doc!" Calista almost screamed out. "That was insanely crazy! It worked. All present and accounted for. What about the other operatives?"

"Lost two, several with injuries, we'll meet you at the safehouse. Don't go back to the motel." His tone said this wasn't over and they had people at hotel waiting on them.

As they raced through the darkened streets, the adrenaline slowly began to wear off, leaving behind a heavy, crushing sense of exhaustion. Kit and Charlie were alive, but barely. The image of their battered, broken bodies haunted Aria, and she knew their battle was far from over.

They had gotten out, they had won a small victory. Kit and Charlie were safe, and they were going to make it through this, come hell or high water. Aria saw red and floating in that red were two men, Alexandre DuBois and Gero Meyer.

As the van sped through the darkness, Aria allowed herself a moment of relief, knowing they would have to be ready for whatever came next. They had survived this time, but the war was far from over. And the next battle would be even more dangerous.

Everyone arrived safely at their rendezvous coordinates. The two deceased operatives were honored and placed where they would be found. It wasn't honorable, but it was all they had at the moment. The silence by all present spoke volumes of how everyone was feeling.

Grunt and Miguel took their packages to a room, followed by Jane. It was going to be a long night for everyone involved. Aria and Doc thanked the men and women who had offered their assistance, Aria making sure each was compensated well. Prayers offered and the only people left were the immediate team members of Kit and Charlie.

Now it was time for healing and they would face it together. Because that's what family did.

CHAPTER 43

Alexandre sat in the plush leather chair of his private jet, the hum of the engines a distant drone in his ears. The cabin was a sanctuary of luxury, but its opulence did little to calm the storm brewing inside him. He stared blankly out the window, the clouds below illuminated by the early morning sun, but his mind was miles away, back in Los Angeles, replaying the events that had unraveled his carefully laid plans.

Across from him, Gero Meyer was a seething ball of rage, his face flushed, and his fists clenched so tightly that his knuckles were white. He had been pacing the cabin for the better part of an hour, muttering curses in a mix of languages, his temper flaring with every passing second. And when the video began to play on the screen in front of them, he stopped dead in his tracks, his anger giving way to a cold, seething fury.

The footage was grim, a picture of the failure that had befallen them. The grainy black-and-white video, streamed from the LA warehouse's security system, showed the moment their operation had been shattered. They watched as a coordinated team of operatives converged on the warehouse, their movements precise and deadly. One by one, the guards Gero and Alexandre had hired were taken down, some in quick, brutal fights, others by the silent efficiency of professional killers.

And then there they were, Kit Thorne and Charlotte Donovan, the two thorns in their side, being carried out of the warehouse by two hulking men. They were alive, battered but alive, their rescue a complete and utter humiliation for Alexandre and Gero.

Gero's reaction was immediate and explosive. With a roar of frustration, he swept his hand across the table, sending a crystal decanter of whiskey and several glasses crashing to the floor. The glass shattered, the liquid pooling on the expensive carpet like blood from a fresh wound.

"Those bastards!" Gero bellowed, his voice muted in the confined space of the cabin. "How the hell did they find them? We were careful, every detail was accounted for!"

Alexandre remained silent, his eyes still fixed on the screen, his mind working through the possibilities. It was true, they had been meticulous in their planning, covering their tracks at every turn. But somehow, Kit and Charlie's team had found them, infiltrated their operation, and rescued the very people they had intended to destroy.

"There must have been a leak," Gero continued, his voice trembling with barely controlled rage. "Someone tipped them off, or... or they have some kind of technology we didn't account for. But how? Our systems should have detected anything out of the ordinary."

Finally, Alexandre spoke, his voice calm and measured, in contrast to Gero's fury. "It wasn't a leak," he said, his tone cold and analytical. "Our security was airtight. The only explanation is that they used some kind of tracking device that our systems couldn't detect."

Gero's eyes narrowed as he turned to face Alexandre. "A tracking device? Impossible. We would have found it during the initial scans."

"Not if it was something we weren't looking for," Alexandre replied, his mind already racing with possibilities. "An implant, perhaps. Something small, subtle, designed to evade detection by conventional methods."

Gero cursed under his breath, his anger simmering just below the surface. "If that's the case, then someone is going to pay for this. We need to find out what it was, how they got their hands on the technology, and we need to make an example out of the person that gave it to them."

Alexandre nodded slowly, his expression unreadable. "Agreed. But first, we need to regroup. This setback won't go unnoticed, and we can't afford any more mistakes. We'll start by doubling down on our operations, tightening security, and expanding our network elsewhere."

He reached for his phone, his fingers moving swiftly across the screen as he sent a series of encrypted messages. "I'm contacting our lead general. I want him to start collecting as many homeless under-18 children as he can find. We'll take this fight to the streets, where it all began. We'll draw out these do-gooders, force them to reveal themselves. And when they show up, we'll crush them."

Gero's lips twisted into a vicious smile, the thought of revenge soothing his wounded pride. "They think they've won, but they have no idea what's coming. We'll drown them in their own blood."

Alexandre glanced at Gero, a flicker of something dark passing through his eyes. "This isn't just about revenge, Gero. This is about reasserting control. These people, Kit, Charlotte, their teams, they've been chipping away at our operations piece by piece. It's time we reminded them, and the world, who holds the power."

He leaned back in his chair, his mind already crafting the strategy that would lead them to victory. The plan was simple, overwhelm the streets with their presence, create chaos, and force Kit and Charlie's team to respond, scatter them. And when they did appear, and he knew they would, Alexandre would be ready.

The rest of the flight passed in tense silence, each man lost in his own thoughts, planning, calculating, preparing for the next phase of their operation. They would return to their respective countries, regroup, and strike back with a vengeance. This was a war, and they were going to win it.

As they neared their destination, Gero finally spoke again, his voice low and dangerous. "What about Kit and Charlotte? They've proven to be more resourceful than we anticipated. How do we ensure they don't slip through our fingers again?"

Alexandre's eyes gleamed with a cold, ruthless light. "This time, we won't give them the chance. We'll cut off their resources, isolate them, and then... we'll break them."

Gero nodded, satisfied with the answer. "And what about the organization they're working with? We need to find out who's backing them, who's giving them the resources to keep interfering with our business."

"I'm already on it," Alexandre replied. "I've got people digging into their connections, their finances, everything. We'll uncover their network, and when we do, we'll dismantle it piece by piece."

The plane began its descent, the ground rushing up to meet them as they prepared to land. Alexandre's mind was sharp, focused, every detail of the coming battle carefully planned out. He knew that Kit and Charlotte were formidable opponents, but they had underestimated the lengths he was willing to go to protect his empire.

As the plane touched down, Alexandre sent one final message to his lead general, instructing him to begin the collection of homeless children immediately. The message was simple, but its implications were chilling: "The streets will empty. The tears will run red."

As he and Gero disembarked from the plane, Alexandre allowed himself a small, satisfied smile. He would take this war to the streets, where it all began, and he would finish it there, too. The organization that had been a thorn in his side for too long would soon learn the true meaning of power.

But what Alexandre didn't know was that at that very moment, Kit and Charlie were already planning their next move. They had survived his attempts to break them, and now they were more determined than ever to bring him down.

The war was far from over. In fact, it was just beginning.

Alexandre DuBois was about to learn that even the most powerful empires could crumble when faced with the unrelenting force of justice.

CHAPTER 44

The atmosphere in the Atlanta lodge was tense, the people assembled angry and ready to go to the streets. The sprawling wooden lodge, usually a place of refuge and planning, had become a war room, its walls echoing with the voices of those determined to stop the potentially escalating nightmare that they feared would unfold on the streets soon.

Kit sat at the head of the large table in the main conference room, a bandage wrapped tightly around his shoulder, a reminder of the raid they had narrowly survived. Jane had done her best to patch him up, but he had refused anything that might cloud his judgment. His piercing blue eyes, though tired and bruised, were sharp as ever, scanning the faces of those gathered around him. He was a man who had faced down death and come out the other side, but he knew their fight was far from over.

Beside him, Charlie stood, her expression hard as stone, her body radiating anger. She was bruised, sore, and seething with fury, her usually elegant demeanor replaced by the raw energy of someone who had been pushed too far. The sight of the brand on her skin, a cruel mark left by their captors, had only fueled her resolve. There was no room for fear now, only the burning need to end this once and for all. Her red was similar to Aria's, but the bodies lay in their own pool of blood instead of floating.

Around the table sat both teams, every face a mix of exhaustion and anger. Marley, Izzy, and Rafe had flown in from LA, their expressions serious, their eyes reflecting the harrowing experiences they had all endured. Vicky and Manny, the Atlanta-based operatives, had arrived just hours before, slipping into the lodge quietly but bringing with them the full weight of their law enforcement expertise. Aria sat near Kit, her laptop open in front of her, her fingers ready to fly over the keys as she coordinated their next moves. Calista, Dak, Jack, Sofia, and Zara were all ready to act as soon as Kit or Charlie gave the word.

Jane stood by Kit's side, her medical bag close at hand, but even she knew there was nothing more she could do for now. Kit and Charlie had refused anything that might make them drowsy or unfocused, they needed their minds clear, their bodies ready for what was to come.

Kit leaned forward, his voice low and commanding as he addressed the room. "Because of this raid, I have no doubt that Alexandre and Gero are going to escalate their operations. They're angry, humiliated, and they're going to take that out on the people who are most vulnerable, the homeless and kids. The disappearances are going to increase, and we need to be ready."

He paused, letting his words sink in, the gravity of the situation clear in every line of his face. "We need to get the word out to the streets. Every team member with connections out there, I need you to start spreading the message. Tell them what's happening, make them understand the danger, and leave contact information so we can respond quickly if disappearances start."

Aria nodded, already sending out a virtual SOS from her laptop. "I'll get in touch with my network, start spreading the word through the usual channels. We'll make sure people know who to contact if someone goes missing."

Marley, ever the journalist with street smarts, chimed in. "I can reach out to my old contacts in the neighborhood, see if we can get the word out that way too. People trust me there, and if they hear it from me, hopefully they'll take it seriously."

Izzy and Rafe exchanged a look before Rafe spoke up. "We can hit up the shelters, get the word out to the people who are most at risk. They need to know what's happening, that this isn't just some random uptick in disappearances, it's organized, and it's deadly."

Vicky, her expression grave, added, "I'll reach out to my contacts in the FBI, see if we can get some unofficial support. If the undercovers on the beat know what to look for, they might be able to intervene before it's too late."

Manny, his voice steady and reassuring, nodded in agreement. "We'll coordinate with the local agencies, get them to start watching for patterns. Anything that looks off, we'll know about it."

As the discussion continued, a plan began to take shape, a network of contacts and informants, all working together to protect the most vulnerable from becoming the next victims of Alexandre and Gero's twisted game. It was a monumental task, but they had no choice. If they didn't act now, more lives would be lost.

But even as the team strategized, Charlie stood, her fists clenched at her sides, her mind elsewhere. The fury burning inside her was a tempest, a storm that demanded action, and she knew exactly what she needed to do. She couldn't sit here and wait while people suffered. She couldn't let the bastards who had marked her think they had won.

"I have something I need to do," Charlie said abruptly, cutting through the conversation. All eyes turned to her, and Aria's sharp gaze narrowed as she watched her friend closely.

"Charlie, what are you thinking?" Aria asked, suspicion and concern lacing her tone.

Charlie's voice was cold, every word carefully measured. "I'm going to Pop's. I need to talk to someone who might have information we can use and can help me with a little something else."

Aria's eyes flashed with anger. "Charlie, we've talked about this. No more secrets. You need to tell us what you're planning."

Charlie's eyes met Aria's, unflinching. "I will. But I need to do this first. I promise, when I get back, I'll tell everyone what's going on. No more secrets."

Aria's glare didn't soften, but she knew better than to try and stop Charlie when she was like this. Instead, she nodded reluctantly. "Fine. But be careful and keep in touch. Grunt is still your bodyguard!"

Charlie gave a curt nod, motioned to Grunt, then turned and strode out of the room, her determination etched into every step. Kit watched her go, a frown tugging at his lips. He trusted Charlie, but he also knew that whatever she was planning, it wasn't going to be easy.

As the door closed behind her, the room was left in silence, unspoken question filling the room. Kit took a deep breath, then turned back to the team.

"Let's get to work," he said, his voice firm. "We have people to protect."

The team dispersed, each member moving to their respective tasks, but the anger in the room remained. They were all on edge, knowing that the battle they were fighting was far from over.

Charlie, meanwhile, was already making her way through the streets of Atlanta, her mind focused on the task at hand. The anger that had been simmering inside her since her rescue was now a controlled burn, fueling her desire to end this nightmare once and for all.

She arrived at Pop's Gentlemen's Club, the familiar neon sign glowing in the evening light. The bouncer at the door nodded to her as she approached, recognizing her immediately. She didn't stop to chat, her focus singular as she pushed through the doors and made her way inside.

The club was already filling up for the night, the low thrum of music and conversation creating a steady hum of background noise.

But Charlie had no interest in the patrons tonight. She was here for one person.

Madison, the makeup artist, was in the back room, her hands deftly applying makeup to one of the dancers as she prepared for her shift. She looked up as Charlie entered, her expression curious.

"Charlie," Madison said, her tone friendly but guarded. "What brings you here tonight?"

Charlie didn't waste any time with pleasantries. "I need to talk to you. Now."

Madison's eyebrows shot up at the urgency in Charlie's voice. She nodded to the dancer, who quickly slipped out of the chair and left the room, leaving the two women alone.

"What's going on?" Madison asked, her voice low as she turned her full attention to Charlie.

Charlie took a deep breath, her anger simmering just below the surface. "I need information, Madison. And I know you are street savvy. There's something going on in the streets, something dangerous, and I think you might know who I need to talk to."

Madison's eyes flickered with uncertainty, but she didn't back down. "What do you need to know?"

"Everything," Charlie replied, her voice hard. "There's a network operating in this city, one I missed or a new one, trafficking people, kidnapping the homeless, turning them into victims. I need to know who's behind it, where they're operating from, and how deep it goes. And I need to know asap."

Madison hesitated, her eyes searching Charlie's face. "You're not just here as a club owner, are you?"

Charlie's expression didn't waver. "No, I'm not. And if you care about the people in this city, if you care about your own life, you'll tell me what you know."

For a long moment, Madison remained silent, her thoughts racing. Then, finally, she sighed, her shoulders slumping. "I've heard things, whispers, rumors. There's a lot of money flowing through the underworld right now, and a lot of people are getting caught up in it. But if I give you names, Charlie, I'm putting myself in the crosshairs."

Charlie's voice softened, but she didn't waver. "If you don't, you'll still be in the crosshairs. I'll protect you, Madison. You know I will. But I need that information."

Madison swallowed hard, then nodded slowly. "Okay. I'll tell you what I know. But you need to be careful, Charlie. These people... they don't play by any rules."

"I know," Charlie said, her voice low. She showed Madison the brand. Madison gasped. "If you saw me without makeup right now, you'd understand. And that's why we have to stop them."

As Madison began to talk, Charlie listened intently, every word sinking in like a stone. She knew that with this information, they could start to unravel the web that Alexandre and Gero had woven around them.

"Now, Madison, I'm going to make you famous. As soon as the girls are all settled in their evening routines, meet me in the office. I've got a job you cannot pass up. Bring your stuff with you." Charlie pointed to Madison's work area, grinning. She was feeling an adrenaline rush she hoped would last until this who affair was over.

When she finally left Pop's, the night was deep, and the air was cool against her skin. Charlie felt no immediate relief, only a feeling things might be changing soon. She had promised her team that there would be no more secrets, and she intended to keep that promise. In 24 hours, life for the two men, Alexandre and Gero would change. Charlie with the help of Kit, was going to make sure of that. Madison's skills were amazing.

Back at the lodge, the work continued, the teams coordinating, spreading the word, setting up the networks that would save lives.

Kit watched it all with a sense of pride, but also with a deep, gnawing worry for Charlie.

When Charlie walked back through the doors of the lodge, they would be ready to take the fight to the streets, to the heart of the darkness that threatened to consume them all.

The war was far from over. But with every step they took, they were closer to bringing it to an end.

CHAPTER 45

Two days later, Marley was feeling the tension of the all alert the organizations had put out. Marley's phone had been buzzing non-stop for hours, the constant stream of calls turning his usually calm demeanor into one of barely controlled anxiety. He'd always been good at keeping his cool, but this was something different. He was getting calls from contacts in LA, New York, overseas, everywhere he'd reached out to spread the word about the disappearances. And now, those same people were calling back with the kind of news that turned his blood cold.

The first call had come from his old neighborhood in LA, where the leader of a local street gang had told him in a hushed, almost frantic tone that kids were starting to vanish from the streets, more and faster than usual. The numbers were climbing at an alarming rate, and it wasn't just the usual suspects. The word on the street was that someone, somewhere, had put out a call to grab as many kids as possible, and to do it fast.

Marley had felt a jolt of fear shoot through him at that news. This wasn't just about trafficking anymore, this was something else, something far darker... revenge.

Now, as he paced the lodge's conference room, his phone clutched in his hand, Marley couldn't shake the gnawing feeling in his gut. The calls kept coming, each one adding another layer of dread to the already tense atmosphere.

His contact in New York had confirmed similar disappearances, with kids as young as ten vanishing from shelters and street corners. The authorities there were just beginning to take notice, but they were woefully behind. By the time the cops got organized, it might already be too late.

But it was the call from his contact in LA that truly rattled him. The man, a former gang leader who had turned his life around, was someone Marley trusted implicitly. And when he heard the desperation in the man's voice, Marley knew they were dealing with something unprecedented.

"Marley," the voice had said, low and tense, "I don't know what the hell is going on, but the word out here is that the trafficking rings have been contacted directly, someone high up wants kids, and they want them fast. I've never seen anything like this. People are scared, man. Even the hardest guys I know are laying low, keeping their heads down. Whatever this is, it's big. Some of my boys have gone missing just walking to school."

Marley thanked him, promising to stay in touch and to try and help find his boys, but the fear that had settled in his chest wouldn't budge. Who the hell were these people, and why were they suddenly so desperate to snatch up as many kids as they could get their hands on? The rumors were flying fast and wild, everything from black market organ harvesting to underground fight rings, but there was no concrete information, nothing that could give them a clear target.

Now, standing in front of the team at the lodge, Marley relayed the information, his voice steady but his heart pounding. He could see the worry lining their faces, the same fear he was feeling reflected in their eyes. This wasn't just a battle against some trafficking ring anymore. This was a war, and the stakes had never been higher.

"They're targeting kids, all over," Marley said, his voice carrying the weight of the news. "LA, New York, even overseas, everywhere I've made contact, people are reporting the same thing. Kids are going missing, and it's happening fast. The traffickers have been ordered to grab as many as they can. This isn't just business as usual, something has changed, and it's terrifying even the toughest people."

Aria, who had been sitting quietly, processing the information, finally spoke up, her tone urgent and serious. "Why children? What could they possibly want with that many kids?"

Marley shook his head. "I don't know. The rumors are all over the place, but nothing is concrete. Some say it's for organ trafficking, others say it's for underground fight rings, but no one really knows. The only thing we do know is that they're targeting the most vulnerable, the younger the better, and it's escalating."

Jack, who had been leaning against the wall with his arms crossed, straightened up, his expression grim. "Then we'd better get a move on. If we wait any longer, we're going to be dealing with bodies, not rescues."

Doc nodded, his face set in a hard line. "Agreed. We need to organize now, get teams in place across the country, hell, across the globe if we have to. We have to start rescuing these kids before they disappear for good. I'm rallying my operatives, they're ready and waiting."

Aria turned to Calista, who was already typing furiously on her laptop, her expression focused and intense. "Calista, get in touch with every contact we have, every law enforcement agency, every international organization. We need their support on this. We're not going to be able to do this alone."

Calista nodded, not looking up from her screen. "On it. I'll start sending out alerts now. I'll also check the dark web again, if they're moving this many kids, there's bound to be chatter. I doubt if they are doctoring photos at this point."

As Calista worked, Aria began organizing the team, her mind racing as she considered the logistics of what they were about to undertake. This wasn't just about rescuing a few kids from the streets now, this was about stopping an organized, international operation that was ramping up to dangerous levels. They needed to be strategic, coordinated, and they needed to act fast.

"We'll need to split up," Aria said, addressing the room. "We can't cover the entire country with just one team, and we can't wait for the authorities to catch up. Jack, you and Marley will handle the interior. Vicky, Manny, you're in charge of the East Coast. Izzy and Rafe, you take the west coast. Calista and Doc, coordinate with international agencies and get a global response going. If anyone has vacay time coming, now is a good time. If not, well, I'll leave that up to you, but don't burn any bridges. I'll be monitoring and managing the operations from here."

Jane, who had been quietly listening, stepped forward, her expression determined. "And what about Kit and Charlie? We can't just leave them out of this. They're going to want to be involved."

Aria's face softened slightly, but there was still a hardness in her eyes. "They're still recovering, Jane. We can't risk them getting hurt again. But you're right, we need their help. I'll brief them as soon as they're ready and see how they want to contribute."

Sofia, who had been sitting silently, finally spoke up, her voice quiet but firm. "This is going to get messy. Innocent people are going to get caught in the crossfire, and we need to be prepared for that."

Aria nodded, her expression grim. "I know. But we don't have a choice. We can't let these people get away with this. We need to stop them, and we need to do it now."

As the team dispersed to begin their respective tasks, the team members knew this would be the fight of their lives. This was a fight they hadn't anticipated, a battle that was going to test them in ways they hadn't been tested before. But they would be ready, and they were determined to protect the innocent, no matter the cost.

Marley, now alone in the room with Aria, leaned against the table, his expression troubled. "This feels different, Aria. Like something bigger is at play here. I can't shake the feeling that we're just scratching the surface."

Aria nodded, her gaze distant as she considered his words. "I know what you mean. This isn't just about trafficking anymore. There's something else going on, something we haven't figured out yet. It almost has the feel of what happened in WWII. A cleansing of some sort. I think the fact that Kit and Charlie are still alive is what caused this to escalate. It's also now about revenge. But whatever it is, we can't back down now."

Marley sighed, running a hand through his hair. "Yeah. I just hope we're not too late."

Aria placed a hand on his shoulder, her grip firm. "We won't be. We're going to save these kids, Marley. All of them. No matter what it takes."

"I haven't been on this side too much, I'm usually the information gatherer. How the heck do people gain that much power? I mean, I know how, it's just in this day and age, you'd think others would see what's happening and put a stop to it."

Aria sipped her cold coffee and leaned back in the chair she'd plopped in. "You would think, but we've become so worried about being sued if we accuse say something wrong. The dark web offers a freedom where anything goes. Our society had given too much permission to do as you please. The recourse is being ostracized."

"God, it's just unreal." Marley ran his hands through his hair. "I'd almost prefer the days when if you did something wrong, you got the crap beat out of you, and the score was settled, life went on. Now it's dragged out for no apparent reason, causing the strong to become stronger."

"And the rich, richer." Aria finished. "I think humanity has lost its civility."

Marley nodded, said his goodbyes, and that he had some things to do.

"Marley," he paused looking at Aria, "it's gonna work out. The fates won't let anything happen to the innocent. It's not written that way."

The surety in her voice was unshakable, and Marley felt a flicker of hope ignite in his chest. As Marley left the room, ready to dive back into the fray, Aria remained at the table, her mind racing with plans and contingencies. She knew this battle was going to be long and brutal, and she vowed to have every contingency plan ready.

And somewhere out there, Charlie was preparing to rejoin the fight, determined to finish what the two men had started. Kit had been in Virginia that past two days, with only Miguel. "Those two, "Aria thought, "are brewing up some major trouble. Maybe we all won't be left out this time."

The assault on the streets amped up, and as the storm gathered on the horizon, the team steeled themselves for the war ahead. They would save the innocent, even if it meant sacrificing everything they had.

CHAPTER 46

The safehouses Charlie and Kit had been having built around the country were full to capacity. Every room, every bed, every available space had been occupied by children and teenagers, many of whom had narrowly escaped being snatched from the streets by traffickers. In just a matter of three days, the situation had escalated beyond anything they had anticipated. Children under the age of eighteen were being abducted left and right, vanishing without a trace, while those lucky enough to escape had gone into hiding in the safehouses that Kit and Charlie had painstakingly constructed or anywhere they could find that felt safe.

It wasn't just the children who were seeking refuge. Desperate homeless parents, knowing they couldn't protect their children on the streets, had dropped them off at these safehouses, praying they would be safe. But for every child that found sanctuary, there were just as many who disappeared into the shadows, taken by the ruthless networks that preyed on the vulnerable. The crisis had spiraled out of control, and no one felt it more keenly than Kit and Charlie.

Organizations across the country were frantically trading information, their communications like a frantic stock market of data. Tips, leads, and intelligence were exchanged in the hope that they could stay one step ahead of the traffickers. Raids on auctions and trafficking operations were producing results, some children were being rescued, and some criminals were being captured. But for every success, there were still too many who slipped through the cracks, too many who remained out of reach.

The safehouses were their lifeline, but they were far from enough. Kit and Charlie knew they needed more, more buildings, more resources, more allies. They began reaching out to people across the country, asking for donations of usable buildings that could be converted into shelters for the homeless and at-risk children. It was a desperate plea, and the responses they received were mixed.

Some people responded with genuine concern, offering whatever they could. Old factories, abandoned schools, even large private estates that had fallen into disuse, these were all offered up to the cause. But just as many people turned their backs, their disdain for the homeless evident in their curt replies. "At least they're off the streets," some would say, as if that were enough, as if pushing the problem out of sight would somehow make it go away.

Those responses earned them a place on Kit and Charlie's watch list. These people were blacklisted, their names noted, and Kit and Charlie made sure they would regret their indifference. The situation had revealed the true nature of many, and it was a lesson none of them would forget.

Three weeks had passed since the crisis had reached its peak. The safehouses were overflowing, but the raids were ongoing, and slowly, progress was being made. Kit and Charlie had become shadows, they were out of sight but not out of mind, their names whispered among those who sought to bring them down.

Charlie had been planning something big. She had kept her cards close to her chest, only hinting at what was to come. And now, after weeks of preparation, she was ready for her big reveal.

The morning was crisp and clear as Charlie, accompanied by Madison, walked up to the lodge. The sun filtered through the trees, casting dappled shadows on the ground as they approached the entrance. Madison, the talented makeup artist who had become Charlie's trusted ally, walked beside her, her expression uneasy as she didn't know what she was walking into.

Charlie was uncharacteristically lighthearted as they entered the lodge, her steps almost bouncing with an energy that hadn't been there in weeks. Inside, the team members who had stayed behind looked up in surprise, their conversations halting as they took in the sight before them.

"It's video time!" Charlie announced in a sing-song voice, the words tinged with a playful, almost mischievous tone. The phrase was delivered in perfect French, catching everyone off guard.

Jack and Zara, who had been sitting at the far end of the room, reacted instantly. They were out of their chairs in a heartbeat, guns drawn and aimed at Madison, who froze in place, her eyes wide with shock. The room was suddenly filled with tension, the playful atmosphere evaporating in an instant.

"Hold it right there!" Jack barked, his voice sharp and commanding. Zara's eyes were narrowed, her gun steady as she took in the situation.

But Charlie, who only sounded like Charlie, only giggled, the sound unnerving in the sudden silence. She waved a hand dismissively at the guns pointed in her direction. "Oh, come on, guys. Put those things away. We're all friends here."

Jack and Zara exchanged a glance, their expressions conflicted. They knew the voice, but this was unexpected, and in their line of work, unexpected often meant danger. Jack didn't lower his gun, but his grip relaxed slightly, his eyes still locked on Madison. He looked at the woman standing in the kitchen.

"What the hell is going on?" Zara demanded, her voice low and tense.

Charlie breezed past them, completely unconcerned by the weapons aimed in her direction. "Nothing to worry about, Zara. Just a little fun before we get down to business." She made her way to the kitchen, the scent of fresh coffee drawing her in. As she reached for a mug, she glanced back at the room, her eyes twinkling with mischief. "You all might want to gather around. This is going to be good."

"I said I would tell you what my plans were when they were all in place. And the funny thing is, I was thinking it would take a couple of weeks. What I didn't know is that I had a computer genius working as a stripper because she got in trouble using her skills... inappropriately. As well, she's a makeup artist, and I don't mean beauty from within either. This face you see before you is courtesy of Madison, aka, Holly Martinque, famous French makeup artist."

Madison had been blackballed from the French movie industry when she refused to help change the appearance of young adults wanting to break into the film industry making them look older. She moved to the States, but her bosses had made sure she couldn't work anywhere. So, she lost her accent and began stripping, as close as she could get to acting and changing her appearance. Charlie had gone to her to general information one day and discovered Madison's hidden talents, including her use of the computer.

The team members exchanged uneasy looks but slowly began to converge in the kitchen, curiosity getting the better of them. Aria, who had been watching from the doorway, stepped forward, her arms crossed over her chest. She knew Charlie's voice well enough to recognize when something was up, but this was new.

"What are you planning, Charlie?" Aria asked, her tone more inquisitive than accusatory.

Charlie filled her mug with coffee, taking a slow sip before answering. "I've been busy, Aria. Very busy. And I think it's time to show you all what I've been working on." She nodded toward Madison, who had finally relaxed, her hands still raised in a gesture of surrender.

"Madison here has been helping me put together a little surprise. Something that's going to turn the tide in our favor."

"Surprise?" Jack asked, raising an eyebrow. "What kind of surprise are we talking about?"

Charlie's grin widened, a hint of the old, daring Charlie shining through. "Oh, you'll see. But first, let's get everyone in here. You've seen me, but I promise this stuff is something you're all going to want to see."

It didn't take long for the rest of the team to gather in the large living area adjacent to the kitchen, the air thick with anticipation. Charlie had taken her time, letting the curiosity build as she prepared the room for what was to come. Each member paused upon seeing this strange new woman in their midst, and it wasn't Madison.

Jack and Zara reluctantly holstered their weapons, but they remained close, their eyes never leaving Madison. The rest of the team found seats around the room, their curiosity piqued by Charlie's unusual behavior.

When everyone was finally settled, Charlie stood in front of the large screen that had been set up at the far end of the room. Madison stood beside her, a laptop in her hands, her fingers poised over the keyboard.

"All right," Charlie began, her voice taking on a more serious tone. "We all know the situation we're in. The trafficking crisis is worse than we ever imagined, and we're fighting a war on multiple fronts. But it's time we stopped playing defense and started going on the offensive."

She paused, letting her words sink in. The room was silent, every eye on her.

"We've been raiding auctions, rescuing kids, and disrupting their operations. But it's not enough. We need to hit them where it hurts, and we need to do it now."

Madison tapped a few keys on the laptop, and the screen behind Charlie flickered to life. The image that appeared was grainy, a live feed from what looked like a hidden camera. The room leaned forward, eyes narrowing as they tried to make out the details.

"This," Charlie said, gesturing to the screen, "is a live feed from one of their stash houses. We've hacked into their system, and now we have eyes on them. They keep video footage of their stash houses to monitor their captives. But that's not all."

She nodded to Madison, who switched to another feed, this one showing a different location, an underground auction house, the kind they had raided before. The team murmured in surprise, recognizing the setup.

"We've managed to infiltrate their networks," Charlie continued, her voice rising with determination. "We have access to their communications, their locations, their plans. And with this information, we're going to bring them down, one by one."

The team exchanged looks of disbelief and admiration. This was a game-changer, a chance to take the fight to their enemies in a way they hadn't been able to before.

"But that's not all," Charlie added, a mischievous glint returning to her eyes. "There's one more thing I need to show you."

Madison brought up another video, this one showing a darkened room, lit only by the glow of computer screens. At first, it seemed unremarkable, but then the image zoomed in, revealing the faces of the people at the computers.

It took a moment for the team to realize what they were seeing, but when they did, gasps echoed around the room. The people on the screen were the traffickers, the very ones they had been hunting. They were unaware they were being watched, their conversations about their next moves playing out in real-time.

"This is what we've been working on," Charlie said, her voice low and intense. "We have their faces, their voices, their plans. And now, we're going to use it all to bring them down. Madison will share with our techies the things we forgot were available to us."

The room erupted into action, the team buzzing with renewed energy and purpose. This was the edge they needed, the advantage that would turn the tide in their favor. As they began planning their next moves, Charlie leaned back, a satisfied smile on her face.

For now, they had the upper hand, and they were going to make the most of it.

As the team dispersed to begin their preparations, Charlie caught Aria's eye. The two women shared a look of understanding, a silent acknowledgment of the battles they had fought and the ones yet to come.

"Good work, Charlie," Aria said quietly, her voice filled with respect.

"Thanks," Charlie replied, her voice equally quiet. "But we're not done yet. Not by a long shot. What do you think of my new face?"

Aria nodded, knowing that Charlie was right. The war was far from over, but with the new tools at their disposal, they had a fighting chance. "Um, it's definitely different. And you had this done because..."

"I and the FBI are planning a little trip to Marseille. I've got a bad buy to catch, and a high-end call girl is just the way to do it. I'm replacing the plant already there in a week's time." Charlie stopped Aria when she saw her bristle. "Don't worry, Doc has a new bodyguard that is already on the scene and knows what I look like. The chip has been replaced with something even better, so I won't get lost or kept. You have to trust me on this."

Aria uncharacteristically sputtered but gave her doubts over to Charlie knowing what she was doing. After all, Aria had trained her, perhaps a little too well.

The lodge buzzed with activity, Charlie stepped away, her mind already turning to the next phase of their plan. The fight was just beginning, time to become a guardian to the lost.

CHAPTER 47

Kit had spent two grueling days at his Virginia vineyard, with only Miguel by his side. The two men had been holed up in a secluded part of the estate, away from prying eyes, executing a plan that Kit had been meticulously crafting for weeks. It was a risky move, one that required absolute secrecy, and the fewer people who knew about it from the outset, the better. Kit trusted his team, but this was something he needed to do with as little exposure as possible, at least until the time was right.

Miguel had been his silent partner in this endeavor, offering both his muscle and his uncanny ability to remain unflappable under pressure. Together, they had worked with a team of specialists, makeup artists, prosthetics experts, and some of the best disguise artists money could buy. By the time they were done, Kit looked nothing like the man the world knew as the powerful corporate tycoon and clandestine rescuer of trafficked children. He had been transformed into someone entirely different, and the effect was so convincing that even Miguel had done a double-take when they were finished.

Now, two days later, Kit was back in Atlanta. The timing of his arrival couldn't have been more perfect, or more ironic. He walked into the lodge just thirty minutes after Charlie had made her own grand entrance, and from the sound of it, she'd caused quite a stir. Kit couldn't help but smirk as he heard the commotion from inside, but he kept his expression neutral as he stepped through the door.

The lodge, which had been filled with excited energy, now buzzed with a mixture of confusion and anticipation. Kit strolled in casually, his eyes scanning the room, noting the raised eyebrows, the wary glances. He could sense the tension, the team on edge from Charlie's earlier surprise. And now, here he was, ready to throw another curveball into the mix.

In perfect German, his voice calm and even, Kit announced, "I'm looking for some wine that won't burn my tastebuds."

The effect was immediate. Heads snapped in his direction, eyes widening in shock as they tried to process what they were seeing. As Kit made his way to the kitchen, echoing Charlie's earlier move, two more guns joined those of Zara's and Aria's, their barrels trained on the man who had just walked in. The tension in the room skyrocketed as confusion and suspicion swirled around him.

"What the hell!" echoed around the room as the team reacted to this new twist. Zara and Aria's eyes narrowed as they kept their weapons trained, every muscle in their bodies taut with readiness. They were prepared for anything, but this was beyond anything they had expected.

Charlie, who had been enjoying her coffee with a smug grin, looked up at Kit as he approached. Their eyes met, and for a moment, the room was silent, the air thick with the unspoken connection between them. She knew great minds thought alike, but this was uncanny. Then, Kit's gaze traveled slowly down her body, taking in the transformation that had clearly taken place.

They say great minds work together even when they're apart, and in that moment, it was clear that Kit and Charlie were operating on the same wavelength. Both of them had undergone drastic transformations, turned into completely different people with the help of prosthetics, makeup, and the skilled hands of experts who knew how to craft new identities from nothing.

The silence was broken by a low chuckle from the corner of the room. It started with Miguel and Grunt, who had both been present for Kit's and Charlie's transformation, and soon the laughter spread through the room like wildfire. One by one, the team members realized who was standing in the kitchen, Kit and

Charlie, their fearless leaders, looking nothing like themselves and everything like two people who were about to raise hell.

"What... the... hell?" Jack muttered, shaking his head in disbelief as the laughter died down, replaced by a stunned silence.

Kit smirked, his eyes gleaming with amusement as he poured himself a cup of coffee, completely unfazed by the earlier tension. "What can I say? I like to keep things interesting."

Charlie snorted, her grin widening as she leaned against the counter, crossing her arms over her chest. "Interesting is one way to put it. But I'm guessing you didn't do this just for fun."

Kit shook his head, his expression turning serious. "No. This is part of the plan. A necessary step."

Aria, who had lowered her gun but still looked suspicious, stepped forward. "Okay, I'll bite. What's the plan, Kit?"

Kit's expression hardened, his jaw tightening as he set down his cup. "We're going after Alexandre and Gero. But we're not just going after them here, we're going to their countries. We're taking this fight to them."

The room fell silent again as Kit's words sank in. It was a bold move, one that would take the fight directly to the enemy's doorstep just like Charlie had mentioned. But it was also incredibly dangerous, and the team knew it. They had seen firsthand what Alexandre and Gero were capable of, and now Kit was proposing to go into their territory, on their terms.

Before anyone could respond, Charlie spoke up, her voice cutting through the tension like a knife. "Kit's right. This isn't about playing defense anymore. We've been reacting to their moves for too long. It's time we took control of the game."

She looked around the room, meeting each person's gaze with unwavering determination. "I didn't go through this transformation just to hide. I did it so I could get close to them, infiltrate their networks, and bring them down from the inside. They won't see us coming, and by the time they do, it'll be too late."

The weight of her words settled over the room, the seriousness of what they were proposing hitting everyone at once. This wasn't just a rescue mission, this was an all-out assault on the heart of their enemy's operations.

Aria was the first to break the silence, her voice calm but firm. "This is a huge risk, Charlie. You know that, right? We're talking about going into their territory, playing by their rules. One wrong move, and..."

"We know the risks," Kit interrupted, his voice steady. "But this is the only way to end it. We can't keep reacting to their moves. We have to force them into a corner, make them desperate. And when they're desperate, that's when they'll make mistakes."

Zara, who had been listening quietly, finally lowered her gun completely, a slow smile spreading across her face. "It's dangerous as hell. But I like it. It's about time we turned the tables."

Miguel nodded in agreement, his expression serious. "I'm in. Let's make them regret ever messing with us."

One by one, the team members voiced their agreement, the tension in the room shifting to a focused determination. They knew the risks, but they also knew that this was their chance to end it, to stop Alexandre and Gero once and for all.

As the team began discussing the logistics of the plan, Kit and Charlie exchanged a look, a silent understanding passing between them. They had been through hell and back, but they were ready for whatever came next.

And this time, they were taking the fight to their enemy, on their terms.

Charlie's eyes gleamed with the same determination that had carried her through countless battles. She straightened up, her posture radiating confidence. "We'll need to be smart about this.

No more running blind. We've gather intel, we're ready to make our moves, and hit them where it hurts the most."

Kit nodded in agreement, his mind already working through the details. "We'll use every resource we have, contacts, tech, everything. Sounds like Charlie has an in and one of their clients has a son that is being groomed to take over the business. We'll be attending the same function, just on opposite sides. This isn't just about taking them down any longer... well it is, but it's about sending a message. They think they're untouchable, that they can do whatever they want. It's time we showed them how wrong they are."

Aria, who had been silent for a moment, finally spoke up, her voice filled with a quiet acceptance. "I'll coordinate from here. We'll need constant communication, updates on every move. If anything goes wrong, we pull out immediately. No unnecessary risks. The feeds we've got are amazing and from both countries. I want Madison on the team, Charlie. Even if she works from your club. She's a definite asset."

Kit and Charlie both nodded, knowing that Aria's caution was necessary. This wasn't a game, they were about to back walk into the lion's den, and one misstep could cost them everything.

As the team continued to discuss the plan, a sense of unity filled the room. They had all come together finally, and they were ready to do whatever it took to bring down Alexandre and Gero.

But as the laughter from earlier faded, replaced by the serious tone of the conversation, there was an unspoken understanding among them all, this was their final stand. The stakes had never been higher, and failure was not an option.

Kit and Charlie had come through too much, fought too hard, to let it end any other way. They would see this through to the end, no matter what.

And when it was all over, they would make sure that Alexandre and Gero never had the chance to hurt anyone again. Charlie had a death to settle, a brand to make her own, and law or not, it would be settled before she returned to the States. The team dispersed to begin preparing for the mission ahead. Kit and Charlie remained in the kitchen, their expressions serious as they discussed the finer points of their plan.

But even as they strategized, there was a flicker of something else in their eyes, something that spoke of the bond they had forged through their shared capture, the trust that had been built over their LA incident.

This was their fight, and they were ready to face it together.

CHAPTER 48

The following week was a whirlwind of activity and tension, the team on high alert as they prepared for what could be their most dangerous mission yet. The video feeds that Madison had managed to hack into were nothing short of a goldmine, providing the team with a constant stream of information. Every move that Gero and Alexandre made, every conversation they had, was being watched, recorded, and analyzed by the team. Madison, their newest tech genius, shared her methods with Calista and Dak, teaching them how she had managed to bypass the security protocols and gain access to the feeds without detection.

As they monitored the dark web site that Calista had been monitoring, they noticed a significant uptick in activity. It was subtle, the kind of thing that could easily be overlooked by someone less experienced. But to this team, it was as clear as day, something big was happening, and the traffickers were preparing for it.

Their investigations had led them to a hidden villa, a place that both Gero and Alexandre had purchased together. Their mistake. It was nestled on a picturesque piece of land just outside Brighton, disguised as an active horse farm. From the outside, it looked idyllic, a place of wealth and privilege where the elite could indulge in their equestrian hobbies. But what lay beneath the stables was something far more sinister.

The villa's true purpose was a well-guarded secret, known only to a select few. It was there that Gero and Alexandre held their most depraved events, auctions where human lives were bought and sold, and entertainment that catered to the darkest corners of human nature. The knowledge of what went on in that villa disgusted everyone on the team, but it also steeled their resolve to take these people out of the world. This was where the next auction was scheduled to take place, and they had no intention of letting it go forward.

Within hours of discovering the villa, the necessary team members had boarded the private jet, heading for London. Kit, Charlie, and the rest of the team were prepared for what lay ahead, their minds focused on the mission. There was no room for error, not when so many lives were at stake.

They arrived safely in London and quickly made their way to the closest safehouse near Brighton. The safehouse was strategically located, offering easy access to the villa while providing them with the cover they needed to operate without drawing attention. They set up their base, each member of the team taking on their roles with precision and focus.

The auction was set to take place in just 48 hours, and the team worked tirelessly to prepare. They monitored every piece of intelligence that came in, coordinating with their contacts in law enforcement and ensuring that every detail was accounted for.

The team received word that three rescues had taken place in the UK in the days leading up to the auction. The traffickers were jumpy, aware that something was happening but unsure of what. Tensions were high, but the gala had not been called off. Gero and Alexandre were determined to go through with their plans, unaware that they were walking into a carefully laid trap.

Kit and Charlie spent hours with their look-a-likes, perfecting the details that would make the deception flawless. The resemblance was uncanny, so much so that it was almost eerie. The call girl who Charlie was impersonating was a dead ringer, right down to the way she carried herself. Kit's double, the son of one of his close friends, was equally convincing. The two look-a-likes were briefed on every aspect of their roles, knowing that their safety, and the success of the mission, depended on their ability to sell the ruse.

Interestingly enough, the call girl and the man Kit was doubling as hit it off during their time together. They joked that they might just disappear for a few days and enjoy each other's company away from the chaos. Obviously Vogel didn't have a good relationship with his wife. Turned out good for the team. Funny how things work out sometimes, Kit thought, but he pushed the thought aside. There was too much at stake to focus on anything but the mission.

With everything in place, the team waited. They knew that as soon as Gero and Alexandre arrived in the UK, they would be notified immediately. Law enforcement officials were on standby, ready to move in as soon as the signal was given. The villa had been under surveillance for days, and every possible scenario had been planned for.

Now, it was a waiting game.

The day of the gala arrived, the air heavy with anticipation. The team was on edge, but also very ready. Every detail had been meticulously planned, every possible outcome considered. It was time for Charlie and Kit to step into their roles and blend seamlessly into the opulent world of the elite, a world where wealth and power masked the darkness beneath.

Charlie's transformation into Gisela, the high-end call girl she was replacing, was nothing short of remarkable. The team's specialists had crafted a look that was beyond stunning, yet with an edge that was both alluring and dangerous. Charlie stood before the mirror, her appearance almost unrecognizable. The natural strawberry blonde wig she wore was expertly styled into a sleek, short bob that framed her face with precision, giving her an air of sophistication while still maintaining a hint of seduction.

Her makeup was impeccable, designed to accentuate her already striking features. Smoky eyeshadow highlighted her almond-shaped eyes, making them appear larger and more expressive. Her lips were painted a deep, sultry red, the color of temptation and power. The foundation was applied to perfection, smoothing her skin into a flawless canvas that glowed under the soft light of the dressing room.

The dress she wore was nothing short of daring. It was a rich, deep emerald green that contrasted beautifully with her blonde hair. The fabric clung to her curves, revealing just enough to be tantalizing without crossing into vulgarity. The neckline plunged dramatically, offering a glimpse of her décolletage, while the back was cut low, exposing the smooth line of her spine, and a slit on the side exposed a shapely thigh almost up to her hip. The dress was held together by thin straps that crisscrossed over her shoulders, adding a touch of elegance to the otherwise seductive design. Madison had done amazing work on covering up the brand Alexandre had marked her with.

Her legs, long and toned, were accentuated by the stilettos she wore, five-inch heels that were as much a weapon as they were a fashion statement. The shoes were crafted from black patent leather, shining under the light with a subtle gloss that matched the sleekness of her dress. The heels added to her already commanding height, making her an imposing figure, even as she played the role of a mere accessory on the arm of a wealthy man.

A subtle, but important, addition was the voice modulator she wore, carefully hidden under the mask covering her face. It altered her voice, giving her the exact tone and inflection of Gisela, the woman she was replacing. When she spoke, it was with a precise, sultry French accent, her voice smooth and melodic, but with an underlying current of authority.

As she adjusted the diamond-studded choker around her neck, Charlie felt the small, almost imperceptible weight of the video device embedded within one of the diamonds. The device was linked directly to the team, feeding them real-time visuals and audio from her perspective. The earpiece, so tiny it was nearly invisible, allowed the team to communicate with her, offering guidance or warnings as needed.

Next, Kit stepped into the room, and the transformation was complete. He had been made into Dieter Vogel Jr., the replacement for the senior Dieter Vogel, a corporate tycoon known for his ruthless business tactics and sharp mind. Kit's appearance had been meticulously crafted to reflect the cold, calculating nature of the man he was impersonating.

Kit was dressed in an immaculately tailored tuxedo that spoke of wealth and power. The suit was jet black, cut perfectly to his broad shoulders and narrow waist, the fabric rich and luxurious. The jacket was double-breasted, with satin lapels that gleamed subtly in the light. His dress shirt was crisp and white, contrasting sharply with the dark suit, and the bow tie was a deep shade of charcoal, understated but elegant.

His hair, darkened by hair gel, was sleek and styled with precision, combed back to reveal the sharp angles of his face. Kit's natural eyes, a piercing shade of blue, were the most striking feature. They were intense, calculating, and alert, betraying the astute mind behind them. He exuded an air of authority and confidence, the kind of man who was used to getting what he wanted, no matter the cost.

Kit's role at the gala was that of a man seeking to fulfill a personal mission, finding a child or two for his barren wife. It was a story that had been carefully crafted to blend seamlessly with the real-life dealings of Dieter Vogel Jr., a man known for his ambition and cold practicality. The real Dieter Vogel could have cared less about his wife's issues. Kit's persona was one of charm mixed with an undercurrent of ruthlessness, a man who could smile while negotiating a deal that would ruin lives.

Like Charlie, Kit was fitted with a small earpiece and video device, the latter concealed within the lapel of his tuxedo jacket. The devices allowed the team to monitor every move, every conversation, and every face that passed before them. The team would be their eyes and ears, guiding them through the intricate dance of deception they were about to perform.

As they stood side by side, Charlie and Kit were a sight to behold, two figures of stunning beauty and lethal intent, perfectly disguised as players in a game of wealth and power. The transformation was complete, and now it was time to step into their roles.

"Ready?" Kit asked, his voice low and steady as he adjusted his cufflinks.

Charlie turned to him, her eyes meeting his with a spark of flirtiness. "Always," she replied, her voice modulated to match Gisela's perfectly.

They eyed each other appreciatively and nodded.

Miguel stepped forward, offering each of them a final check of their equipment. He was meticulous, ensuring that everything was in place and functioning as it should. When he was satisfied, he nodded to them both. "Good luck," he said, his tone serious. "We'll be with you every step of the way."

Charlie and Kit left the dressing room, their expressions calm and confident as they walked to their assigned meeting places. The team watched through the video feeds as they made their way to their respective locations, every move monitored, every detail scrutinized.

As Charlie, now Gisela, approached the grand ballroom where the gala was being held, she felt the familiar rush of adrenaline. The lights were dimmed, casting a warm glow over the elegantly dressed guests who mingled with champagne flutes in hand. The room was filled with the murmur of conversation, the clinking of glasses, and the soft strains of classical music played by a live orchestra.

Kit, as Dieter Vogel Jr., was already inside, making his way through the crowd with the practiced ease of a man used to navigating high society. He nodded and smiled as he passed by other guests, playing his role to perfection. The subtle glances of interest from the women in the room and the respectful nods from the men only added to the authenticity of his performance.

The team back at the safehouse watched intently, their eyes glued to the monitors as the feeds from Kit and Charlie's devices played out in real time. Aria, Calista, and Dak were the primary overseers, their fingers poised over keyboards, ready to intervene at a moment's notice.

"This is it," Aria murmured, her eyes narrowing as she watched the guests moving about the room. "Everyone, stay sharp. We can't afford any mistakes tonight."

Charlie moved gracefully through the crowd, her every step measured and deliberate. She was the epitome of elegance and seduction, drawing eyes as she passed. Her role as Gisela required her to be on the arm of a wealthy man, one who was well known to the others at the gala. As she reached him, he extended his arm, a charming smile on his lips.

"Ah, Gisela," he purred, his German accent thick and polished. "You look... exquisite tonight."

Charlie smiled back, the expression seductive and confident as she leaned into the man. "Thank you, Herr Mueller," she replied, her voice matching the tone and accent of the woman she was impersonating.

They walked together into the heart of the gala, their appearance together drawing admiring and envious looks from those around them. Kit kept a discreet distance, but he made sure to stay within sight of Charlie, his senses alert for any signs of trouble.

As the evening progressed, they mingled with the other guests, each of them playing their part flawlessly. Charlie, as Gisela, was the perfect companion, charming, witty, and attentive. Kit, as Dieter, was the consummate businessman, discussing potential investments and partnerships with the other attendees.

But beneath the surface, they were both keenly aware of the real reason they were there. The gala was just a front, a facade for the true purpose of the evening, the auction. The time was drawing near, and as they continued to mingle, they exchanged subtle glances, both of them ready for what was to come.

"Remember," Aria's voice came through their earpieces, calm but firm. "Once the auction starts, we'll be monitoring everything. We'll have to subdue the guards outside first before we can make it inside. This place is guarded like Fort effing Knox."

Charlie and Kit both acknowledged the reminder, their expressions betraying nothing as they continued to play their roles. The atmosphere in the ballroom began to shift, the conversations becoming quieter, the excitement thicker. The guests were ready for the auction to begin. The next few hours would be crucial.

As they prepared to take their places, Charlie caught Kit's eye, a silent understanding passing between them. This was it, the moment they had been preparing for. The next steps they took would determine the success or failure of their mission.

And with that, they moved forward, ready to face whatever lay ahead.

As they moved through the crowd, Kit couldn't help but notice the nervous energy in the air. The traffickers were on edge, but they were also arrogant. They believed they were untouchable, that their wealth and power made them invincible.

They were wrong.

Charlie moved with grace and confidence, her eyes scanning the room for any sign of Gero or Alexandre. She caught sight of them near the entrance to the stables, their expressions smug as they greeted their guests. They had no idea what was about to happen.

Kit felt a hand on his arm and turned to see one of the guests, a man with a thin mustache and a gleam in his eye. The man introduced himself as an investor and asked Kit what had brought him to the auction. Kit played along, spinning a tale about his interest in rare and valuable "commodities." The man nodded in approval, clearly pleased to have found a kindred spirit.

As they spoke, Kit kept one eye on Charlie, watching as she moved closer to Gero and Alexandre. She was calm, collected, every inch the sultry call girl she was pretending to be. But Kit knew her well enough to see the fire in her eyes, the determination to get to the two men that had caused her so much pain.

Charlie finally reached Gero and Alexandre, her sexy smile charming as she exchanged pleasantries with them. Little did they know that she had just implanted them with a tracking device. She was not losing them this time. They had no reason to suspect her, no reason to believe that she was anything other than what she appeared to be. But beneath that smile, Charlie was plotting their downfall.

The conversation was brief, and as Charlie turned to walk away, an extra sway in her hips, she caught Kit's eye and gave a subtle nod. It was time.

Kit excused himself from his conversation and made his way to the edge of the crowd, where he could see the operatives moving into position. The signal was given, and within moments, the operation was underway. As soon as the guests were in the auction area, the teams would start removing the security the Gero had hired.

The next few minutes were a blur of activity as the team moved with military precision, taking down guards and replacing them with their own.

CHAPTER 49

"*Ladies and gentlemen, esteemed guests,*" Alexandre began, his voice smooth and confident, resonating through the lavish underground chamber. The room was bathed in a soft, golden glow, the opulence of the surroundings belied the sinister purpose of the gathering. He stood at the front of the room, his tall frame commanding attention as he surveyed the audience, a satisfied smile playing on his lips.

"*It is truly an honor to have you all here tonight, in this most exclusive and discreet of settings. You have been invited because you are among the elite, the select few who understand the value of discretion, of power, and of influence. In this world, those who can wield these things without hesitation are the ones who shape the future.*"

He paused, allowing his words to sink in, the power of his message filling the room. The guests, each one wealthy and influential, listened intently, their expressions a mixture of anticipation and excitement.

"*As you know, we live in a world of increasing scrutiny. There are those who believe they can police our actions, who think they can dictate what we do, and how we conduct our business. But let me assure you, my friends, that those troublemakers, those self-righteous fools who believe they can bring us down, have been thoroughly dealt with.*"

A murmur of approval rippled through the audience, and Alexandre allowed himself a small, satisfied nod before continuing.

"*The steps we have taken to ensure the secrecy of this event have been meticulous. Our operatives have neutralized any threats, and we have employed the most advanced measures to ensure that no unwanted eyes have found their way to this place. We are, as always, several steps ahead of those who would seek to disrupt our plans.*"

He raised his hand, and the murmuring quieted, the room once again falling into a reverent silence.

"But tonight, ladies and gentlemen, is about more than just business as usual. Tonight marks the beginning of something greater, something destined to change the very fabric of our society. We are not merely trading in the present, but in the future. What we are building here, what we are creating, is a new shadow world order."

His words hung in the air, heavy with implication. The guests leaned forward, eager to hear more, their eyes gleaming with a mix of greed and ambition.

"You see, the children we present to you tonight are not just products, they are the seeds of a new era. For too long, the world has been plagued by the scourge of worthless street urchins, by children who are nothing more than a drain on society. But here, we have turned that liability into an asset. Here, we are creating a compound where these children will not just be raised, but bred, trained, and molded into the perfect specimens. The perfect kind of children for whatever your heart desires."

He allowed a pause, letting the full meaning of his words take root in the minds of his audience. The room buzzed with a dark excitement, the realization of what was being offered causing a visible shift in the atmosphere.

"In this place, these children will be transformed into whatever you wish them to be. Whether you seek a loyal servant, a skilled worker, or something more... specialized, we will provide it. The compound we are building will be the cradle of this new world, a place where we can ensure that only the finest, most obedient, and most perfect individuals are brought into existence. This is more than just an auction, it is an investment in the future. A future that we will control."

Alexandre's voice dropped to a lower, more conspiratorial tone as he leaned in slightly, his gaze sweeping the room with a knowing look. "*And the best part? No one will ever know. We have perfected our methods, and we have ensured that no one can trace these operations back to you. What we are creating here will be as invisible as it is unstoppable.*"

He straightened, his eyes alight with the fervor of a man who believed in his vision with absolute certainty. "*It is destiny for you all to be here tonight, to witness the birth of this new order. You are not just participants, you are pioneers. And together, we will reshape the world in our image.*"

With a sweeping gesture, Alexandre turned toward the large velvet curtains at the far end of the room, which slowly began to draw back, revealing a platform upon which several frightened, disheveled children stood, their eyes wide with terror. The sight caused a collective murmur of interest and excitement to ripple through the crowd.

"And now, ladies and gentlemen," Alexandre concluded, his voice booming with authority, "let the auction begin."

As the first bids were called out, Alexandre stepped back, a triumphant smile playing on his lips. He had set the stage for something that, in his mind, was unstoppable. The shadow world order was no longer a dream, it was a reality, and he would be the one to control it.

As the auctioneer began to rattle off the opening bids in a cold, detached voice, the signals from their operatives buzzed quietly in their earpieces, confirming that the rescue teams were in position and moving in.

Kit and Charlie both rose from their seats, moving as casually as they could to opposite sides of the room. Their movements were slow and deliberate, intended to draw as little attention as possible. Kit's hand brushed against the concealed gun under his jacket, the familiar weight grounding him as he walked. He was calm, but every nerve in his body was on high alert, ready to spring into action.

Charlie, on the other side of the room, slipped her hand into her clutch, fingers wrapping around the hilt of a small knife she had hidden there. The stilettos she wore clicked against the floor, each step measured. She was painfully aware of the eyes that could be watching, and she forced herself to stay relaxed, her breathing steady as she moved into position.

The excitement in the room mounted as the auctioneer's voice droned on, the bidding intensifying as the wealthy predators in the audience vied for their chosen "merchandise." Kit's jaw clenched as he scanned the room, eyes narrowing as he picked out the figures of Alexandre and Gero, standing on opposite sides of the platform.

The moment of chaos came suddenly, like a dam breaking. The doors to the lower auction room burst open with a resounding crash, and in an instant, the entire barn was thrown into pandemonium. Armed operatives flooded the room, their voices shouting commands, weapons drawn and aimed at the shocked crowd. The guests, their masks of civility shattered, scrambled to escape, tripping over each other in their desperation to flee the scene.

Amidst the chaos, Alexandre and Gero instinctively separated, each moving toward their respective exits. Kit's eyes locked onto Gero, who was flanked by his hulking bodyguard, a mountain of a man who looked more like a wall of muscle than a human being.

Kit didn't hesitate. He moved swiftly, cutting through the panicked crowd with practiced ease, his gaze never leaving his target. As he reached Gero, Kit pulled his gun from its concealed holster, the cold metal shining in the light of the room. He didn't even pause as he pressed the barrel of the gun against the bodyguard's temple, his voice low and deadly calm.

"Try something, and I'll put a hole in you big enough to drive a truck through," Kit snarled, his eyes boring into the bodyguard's. The man hesitated, his hand twitching toward his own weapon, but the look in Kit's eyes told him that it wasn't worth the risk. The bodyguard froze, his massive hands slowly rising in surrender.

Gero, his face drained of color, glanced nervously between Kit and his now-useless bodyguard. He opened his mouth to speak, but Kit cut him off with a sharp jab of the gun.

"Not another word," Kit warned, his voice a low growl. "You're coming with me."

Meanwhile, on the other side of the barn, Charlie had her sights set on Alexandre. She watched as he slipped through the crowd, his bodyguard struggling to navigate the mass of panicked people trying to flee the room. She had to act quickly. Removing her stilettos and gripping them tightly in her hand, just in case, Charlie began to move, her steps silent and precise.

She followed Alexandre through the yard, keeping to the shadows as she trailed him. The helicopter waiting at the edge of the property came into view, its rotors beginning to spin as it powered up. Alexandre was making a beeline for it, his desperation evident in the way he moved, his usual confidence replaced with panic.

Charlie needed to act fast, but she knew better than to reveal herself too soon. Instead, she grabbed a nearby rock and hurled it toward a cluster of metal tools lying against the barn wall. The clattering noise was loud and sudden, startling Alexandre and causing him to halt and look back toward the barn.

Taking advantage of the distraction, Charlie slipped through the yard, her feet moving soundlessly across the grass. When Alexandre turned back, she was already out of sight, hidden by the shadows of the large oak trees that lined the property. He hesitated, then made a sudden decision and changed direction, running toward the house instead of the helicopter.

Charlie followed, her heart pounding in her chest, her eyes locked onto Alexandre's retreating figure. She had to be careful, one wrong move, and the entire mission could fall apart. But she was determined he was not escaping, regardless of the bug he had been implanted with.

Inside the safehouse, Aria and Calista were monitoring the situation closely, their eyes glued to the feeds from Kit and Charlie's devices. The chaos made it difficult to track everything, but they were focused on Kit and Charlie, relaying information as quickly as they could.

"Kit, Charlie's following Alexandre toward the house," Aria's voice crackled through Kit's earpiece, her tone urgent. "You've got Gero, but we need to secure both of them. She can't do it on her own."

Kit's mind raced as he processed the information. He glanced down at Gero, who was sweating profusely, fear etched into every line of his face. The bodyguard was still frozen in place, clearly unsure of what to do.

"Miguel, where the hell are you?" Kit muttered under his breath, his eyes darting around the barn as he waited for backup.

As if on cue, Miguel appeared, moving with the lethal grace of a predator. Without a word, he approached Gero's bodyguard from behind and delivered a swift, brutal strike to the back of the man's head. The bodyguard crumpled to the ground, unconscious before he even hit the floor.

"About time," Kit said, a hint of relief in his voice as he and Miguel swiftly zip-tied Gero and his bodyguard together. Gero struggled, but his attempts were futile against Miguel's iron grip.

"Let's get him outside," Kit ordered, hauling Gero to his feet and pushing him forward. The two men moved quickly, exiting the barn and meeting Grunt, who had been stationed outside as part of the perimeter security. Grunt nodded in greeting, his eyes sharp as he scanned the area for any additional threats. They shoved Gero and the passed out bodyguard at two agents, noting their badges and faces, just in case.

"Charlie's headed for the house," Kit said, urgency creeping into his voice. "We need to back her up. She's going to do something stupid."

"Let's move," Miguel agreed, his tone all business.

Without another word, the three men set off toward the house, their pace quick and purposeful. Every sound amplified as they closed in on the large, dimly lit structure where Charlie had followed Alexandre.

They didn't know exactly what awaited them inside, but one thing was certain, they had to stop Alexandre from escaping, no matter the cost. And stop Charlie too, revenge is an ugly thing and can easily take over the mind. Kit's mind was focused, his thoughts racing as he prepared for the confrontation that was sure to come.

As they neared the house, Kit glanced back at Miguel and Grunt, giving them a curt nod. It was time to finish what they had started.

The door to the house was slightly open, but still a barrier between them and their target. Kit's grip tightened on his weapon as he prepared to open it, his every sense on high alert. Grunt and Miguel were right behind him, armed and ready. Kit's determination to find Charlie and capture Alexandre burned hotter than ever, fueling him as they prepared to storm the house and confront whatever lay within.

CHAPTER 50

Charlie slipped into the house behind Alexandre, her movements as silent as the shadows she stayed in. The opulent interior of the mansion contrasted sharply with the grim reality of the situation, but Charlie's focus was singular. She was hunting, and Alexandre was her prey. The voice modulator concealed under her mask kept her speech sounding exactly like Gisela, the woman she was impersonating. It was a deadly game of cat and mouse, and Charlie intended to win.

The soft click of a door closing somewhere in the house caught her attention, and a slow smile spread across her lips. She could feel Alexandre's panic, his fear, and she intended to stoke those flames until they consumed him. Moving quietly, she began to speak, her voice echoing through the halls, disembodied and haunting.

"I know you're in here," she called out, her tone playful, almost sing-song. "Come out, come out, little Alex."

There was a tense silence, and Charlie could almost hear Alexandre's heartbeat pounding in his chest, the rhythm frantic and erratic. The tension in the air was thick, almost tangible, and she reveled in it. She had him cornered, and he knew it.

"Who's there?" Alexandre's voice rang out, laced with anger and fear. "What do you want, whore?"

Charlie smirked, her eyes narrowing as she crept closer to where she thought he might be hiding. She knew she had to keep him talking, keep him on edge. The more rattled he became, the more likely he was to make a mistake.

"Such harsh words, Alex," she cooed, her voice dripping with mock sweetness. "I just want to have a little chat. I've been watching you, you know. You really thought your little auction in LA would work, didn't you? How foolish."

There was a pause, and she could almost feel his confusion, the wheels turning in his mind as he tried to piece together who he was dealing with. She heard him shift, a barely audible rustle of fabric, and she smiled to herself. He was nervous. Good.

"How do you know about LA?" Alexandre demanded, his voice tinged with desperation. "Who are you?"

"Oh, I have my little secrets," she replied coyly, her tone light and teasing. "But you're the one with the most to lose tonight, aren't you? Running, hiding like a little rat in your own house. It's pathetic, really."

"Show yourself!" Alexandre shouted, his voice echoing through the house. "Come out and face me!"

Charlie suppressed a chuckle, enjoying the power she held in this moment. "Why should I? You're much more entertaining when you're squirming. Besides, I'm having so much fun. Aren't you?"

There was no response, just the tense silence of the house. Charlie moved closer, her ears attuned to every sound, every shift of movement. She could sense him nearby, hiding, waiting for the right moment to strike. But she wasn't going to give him that chance.

"Come out, come out, wherever you are, little Alex," she taunted, her voice laced with a playful menace. "Let's play."

She continued to move through the house, her steps careful, her senses heightened. She knew Alexandre was nearby, and she was ready for him, her body tense with the anticipation of the catch.

Suddenly, there was a rush of movement from behind her, a blur of motion as Alexandre lunged, trying to tackle her to the ground. Charlie barely had time to react, her instincts taking over as she spun on her toes, evading his grasp by mere inches. The force of his missed attack sent him stumbling forward, his momentum carrying him into a nearby wall.

Charlie whirled around, her heart pounding in her chest as she faced him. For a moment, they stared at each other, the room charged with electricity. Alexandre's face was contorted with rage and fear, his chest heaving with exertion.

"Nice try, but you'll have to do better than that," Charlie said, her voice steady, cold.

Alexandre's eyes darted around the room, searching for an escape, but Charlie was already advancing on him, her movements calculated and precise. She pulled a small pistol from a hidden holster under her dress and aimed it directly at him, her finger resting lightly on the trigger.

"Sit," she ordered, gesturing with the gun toward a plush armchair in the corner of the bedroom. "Now."

Alexandre hesitated, his mind racing, but the cold look in Charlie's eyes left no room for negotiation. Slowly, he backed toward the chair and sat down, his body tense with barely controlled anger.

"Good boy," Charlie mocked, her lips curling into a smirk. She reached into her bag and pulled out a handful of zip ties, tossing them onto his lap. "Tie yourself to the chair. Nice and tight. And don't even think about trying anything, or I'll put a bullet in your skull before you can blink."

Alexandre's hands shook slightly as he picked up the zip ties, his mind racing with possibilities, but none of them good. He had no choice but to comply. With trembling fingers, he secured his wrists to the armrests of the chair, the plastic biting into his skin as he pulled them tight.

"Good," Charlie said, her tone clipped and authoritative. She tied the loose hand and took a step back, her eyes never leaving his.

"Now, we're going to sit here and have a little chat. And if you try anything, anything at all, you're dead. Understand?"

Alexandre nodded, his face a mask of barely controlled fury. He knew he was trapped, and the realization frightened him beyond words.

Charlie watched him carefully, her senses still on high alert. She knew the others would be closing in, but for now, she had Alexandre right where she wanted him.

And she intended to make the most of it.

———

Kit, Miguel, and Grunt moved stealthily through the house, their senses on high alert as they searched for Charlie and Alexandre. The house was eerily quiet, the opulence of the decor not attracting their attention like it was intended. They checked room after room, each one empty, the silence only heightening their unease.

Just as they were about to ascend the staircase, they heard voices coming from one of the rooms down the hall. Kit held up a hand, signaling for Miguel and Grunt to stop. The three of them exchanged a glance, then moved quickly and quietly toward the source of the sound.

As they reached the door, they paused, listening intently to the conversation unfolding inside. Kit recognized Charlie's voice through the modulator, but there was something different about it, an edge that hadn't been there before, a hint of something dark and dangerous.

"Let me tell you a little story," Charlie's voice drifted through the door, low and menacing. "There was a sting operation in New York a year or so ago. My operatives and I took down some major traffickers in the States, including one Gabriel Carvalho. But before we could put him away, he made sure to leave his mark on me."

Kit felt a chill run down his spine at the tone in Charlie's voice. It was controlled, but there was an undercurrent of anger and pain that was unmistakable. He glanced at Miguel and Grunt, both of whom looked equally concerned. Grunt knew the story.

"Revenge is a funny thing," Charlie continued, her voice taking on a slightly unhinged quality that sent a shiver down Kit's spine. "Gabriel got his behind bars. But I couldn't let the rescuing end there. You see, Alexandre, I'm not the woman you think I am."

Kit leaned closer to the door, straining to hear every word. He could sense the tension building in the room, the fear in Alexandre's voice as he responded, though his words were too muffled to make out.

Then, Kit heard the sound of something being removed, like fabric or a mask. There was a moment of silence, followed by Charlie's voice, now clear and unmistakably her own.

"I'm Charlotte O'Donovan," she said, her voice cold and steady. "And I could have lived with the beatings, even with the abuse you were planning for me. But you made a mistake, Alexandre. You branded me."

Kit's eyes widened in shock. He hadn't known the branding had affected her like this, about the depths of what had been done to Charlie. His fists clenched at his sides, his anger boiling just beneath the surface.

"And here's the thing," Charlie continued, her voice taking on a steely sound. "You branded me with the symbol of the phoenix, the one who dies and is reborn from the ashes. You thought you had killed me and Kit in LA, but instead, you created something you can't control. You created someone who will walk through fire to destroy the organization that destroys the lives of innocents, regardless of their birth."

Kit exchanged a quick glance with Miguel and Grunt. They were all tense, ready to burst into the room, but something held them back, the sense that Charlie needed to finish this on her own terms.

"All life, rich or poor, deserves to live," Charlie said, her voice ringing with conviction. "And now, with you out of the equation, they will. Your life is over, Alexandre, and I, Charlotte O'Donovan, will make sure that your money is used against the very thing you tried to build."

Kit could hear the truth and strength in her voice, the strength that had carried her through so much. He knew that she was in control, but he also knew that things could escalate quickly.

He reached for the door, ready to intervene if necessary, but then he heard the sound of movement inside the room, Charlie pulling something out of her bag. His heart raced as he imagined what it could be.

He pushed open the door just as Charlie stood over Alexandre, who was seated in a plush chair, his hands bound to the armrests with zip ties. Charlie had something in her hand, and for a brief, terrifying moment, Kit thought it was a gun. But as he stepped fully into the room, he realized it was a stack of papers.

"Sign them," Charlie ordered, her voice hard as steel. When Alexandre hesitated, she pulled a small knife from her belt and pressed it against his throat, drawing a thin line of blood. "No tricks, Alexandre. If you come loose, you die immediately. Now, sign."

Alexandre's eyes were wild with fear, his hands shaking as he took the pen Charlie offered. With trembling fingers, he scrawled his signature on the documents, his breath coming in ragged gasps.

"Thank you for your contribution to the poor of the world," Charlie said coldly, taking the signed papers and stepping back.

As she turned, the room suddenly filled with men in suits, MI5 agents, their weapons drawn, their faces hard. They moved quickly, taking Alexandre into custody, securing his hands behind his back as they prepared to escort him out of the house.

Charlie handed the stack of papers to Grunt, who took them with a solemn nod. "Guard these with your life," she told him, her voice leaving no room for argument.

Kit, Miguel, and Grunt followed Charlie as she strode out of the room, her shoulders set with determination. The air outside was light and airy compared to the room they just left, this part of the mission was over.

As they walked toward the exit, Kit couldn't help but glance at Charlie, who was still dressed in the provocative outfit she had worn to the gala. It was a vivid reminder of everything she had endured to get to this point, and of the strength it had taken to see it through.

They exited the house into the cool night air, and without a word, climbed into the waiting car. Charlie's composure never faltered, but Kit could see the strain in her eyes, the exhaustion that came from carrying the weight of what could have happened.

As the car pulled away from the house, heading toward the safehouse, Kit reached out and placed a hand on Charlie's arm, offering her a silent gesture of support. She didn't say anything, but the brief look she gave him spoke volumes.

When they arrived at the safehouse, Charlie immediately headed for the bathroom, her pace brisk, her expression unreadable. The door closed behind her, and Kit knew she needed time to process everything that had just happened.

Aria was in front of her computer, her fingers flying over her keyboard as she made arrangements for the upcoming meeting with UK government officials she knew was to come. She barely looked up as they entered, too focused on ensuring that everything was in place.

Kit, Miguel, and Grunt exchanged weary glances, knowing that they had a long night ahead of them. But for now, they were all just relieved that the immediate danger had passed.

As they settled in, Kit couldn't help but think about everything that had transpired, about the strength Charlie had shown, and about the road that still lay ahead. He knew that this was far from over, but for now, they had won a small victory, and sometimes, that was enough.

CHAPTER 51

Kit and Charlie walked into the elaborate conference room of the UK governmental law agency's headquarters, their footsteps echoing on the polished marble floor. Both of them knew this meeting was crucial to maintaining the goodwill between their teams and the local authorities, they might need them in the future. They were prepared to face the music.

As they entered, they were met by a group of stern-faced officials seated around a long, imposing table. The head of the agency, a man with dark hair and sharp eyes, sat at the center, his gaze fixed on Kit and Charlie as they approached. Beside him were representatives from various law enforcement agencies, their expressions a mix of curiosity, suspicion, and thinly veiled irritation.

Charlie took a deep breath, mentally preparing herself for the confrontation she knew was coming. Kit, standing beside her, offered a slight nod of encouragement. They had faced worse separately, but this was as a team and totally different. This was about accountability.

"Mr. Thorne, Ms. Donovan," the head of the agency began, his tone formal, almost cold. "I trust you understand the gravity of the situation we find ourselves in. You conducted an operation on British soil without informing us, an operation that, while successful, put numerous lives at risk and circumvented established protocols. We need to understand why."

Charlie stepped forward, her demeanor calm. "Thank you for meeting with us," she began, her voice steady. "We fully understand the concerns you have, and we are here to take full responsibility for our actions. The decision to move forward with the operation without notifying your agency was not taken lightly. It was a matter of timing and necessity."

She paused, gauging their reactions before continuing. "We had reason to believe that an auction involving trafficked children was about to take place. We located one of your undercover agents, Gisela, after following a lead, and there was no time to establish contact with local authorities without risking the lives of those children. I made the call to front for Gisela, and I take full responsibility for that decision."

The room was silent for a moment, The head of the agency narrowed his eyes, considering her words carefully.

"You understand that by bypassing us, you jeopardized not only the operation but also the lives of everyone involved?" he said, his voice firm. "We could have provided resources, backup…"

"With all due respect, sir," Kit interjected, his voice calm but insistent, "there wasn't time. The auction was imminent, and any delay could have cost lives. We had to act quickly, and we did what we believed was necessary to save those children."

One of the other officials, a woman with a sharp, analytical gaze, leaned forward. "And what of Gisela? What happened to her?"

Charlie hesitated for a fraction of a second before responding, "She's safe. We asked her to take a leave of absence until her after the operation was completed. Her cover is intact, and she is willing to take whatever repercussions or restrictions you will place on her. I stepped in to protect her identity so she will be of further use to your organization and to ensure the operation's success on our end. Filling her in on what was happening would have taken the time we didn't have."

There was a murmur of conversation among the officials, their expressions relaxing slightly. The head of the agency finally leaned back in his chair, his gaze thoughtful.

"Ms. Donovan, Mr. Thorne," he said, his tone less severe, "while we appreciate the difficulty of the situation you found yourselves in, you must understand that operations of this magnitude require coordination with local authorities. Should something like this ever happen again, you must notify us immediately. We are here to help, not to hinder."

Charlie nodded, her expression earnest. "We understand, sir. And we promise that if we ever find ourselves in a similar situation, your agency will be the first to know."

Kit nodded in agreement, backing Charlie up with a solemn expression. "We're all on the same side here. We share the same goal, protecting the innocent and bringing those who prey on them to justice."

The head of the agency seemed to consider their words, then nodded slowly. "Very well. We will move forward with this understanding. You've done both countries a great service with your somewhat, unorthodox actions."

There was a sense of relief in the room, the tension beginning to dissipate. The officials exchanged glances, and the woman who had asked about Gisela spoke again.

"Now, as for the results of the operation," she began, her tone more cooperative. "The American embassy has been instrumental in reestablishing goodwill between our agencies, and the arrests made during the auction have had significant repercussions."

She picked up a folder and slid it across the table toward Kit and Charlie. "Over thirty of the wealthy individuals captured and arrested at the auction were from European and surrounding nations. Ten were from the United States. While we have not yet located Alexandre's funds or businesses, the assets seized from the other individuals will be repurposed to support programs for the homeless, underprivileged, vulnerable populations, and the agencies helping them."

Charlie exchanged a glance with Kit, a feeling of accomplishment settling over them. They had struck a major blow against the trafficking network, and now, the resources seized from these criminals would be used to help those who needed it most.

"The funds will be used to establish foundations that will focus on education, healthcare, and creating futures for those who would otherwise be forgotten," the head of the agency continued. "What you and your teams accomplished has put a significant dent in the trafficking world. And while there is still work to be done, this is a victory."

Kit and Charlie nodded, absorbing the victory of the moment. It was a small consolation for all the horrors they had witnessed and been put through, but it was something. They had made a difference.

The meeting concluded with a final exchange of promises and commitments to collaborate more closely in the future. As they left the conference room, the tension between the UK officials and their team had eased, replaced by a mutual respect for the work that had been done.

Once outside, Kit and Charlie exchanged a look of relief. The situation had been defused, and they had managed to avoid a serious diplomatic incident. But more than that, they had reaffirmed their commitment to the fight against trafficking, a fight they knew was far from over.

As they walked toward the waiting car, Kit turned to Charlie with a small, tired smile. "We did it," he said quietly.

Charlie nodded, her eyes reflecting a mix of exhaustion and satisfaction. "Yeah, we did. And now I think it's time we get back home."

The drive to the airport was uneventful, and before long, they were seated on their private plane, heading back to the States. Aria was sitting in the cockpit, her voice came through the earpiece Charlie was still wearing, and she quickly brought her up to speed on what had transpired in the meeting.

"Good work," Aria said, her tone relieved. "We'll debrief once you're back, but for now, just get some rest. You both deserve it."

Charlie removed the earpiece and leaned back in her seat, closing her eyes for a moment. She could feel the stress slowly ebbing away, replaced by a deep feeling of relief. The mission had been successful, and now, they could finally take a breath.

When they arrived back in the States, it was clear that their operation had made waves. News outlets were buzzing with reports of the arrests and the subsequent investigations. Media from everywhere were reporting that foundations were being established across various countries, using the seized assets to help the homeless and underprivileged, those who had been most at risk of falling into the hands of traffickers.

But for Kit, Charlie, and their teams, the most important thing was that they were home. The lodge in Atlanta was buzzing with activity as team members who had stayed behind set up a barbecue to welcome them back. The atmosphere was one of celebration, of camaraderie and relief.

As the sun began to set, casting a warm glow over the lodge, the team gathered around the grill, enjoying the smell of sizzling steaks and the sound of laughter. Doc, ever the storyteller, regaled them with tales from his time spent in various locations overseas, some of which were more than a little risqué, much to the amusement of everyone present.

Charlie sat back, her plate of food forgotten for the moment as she watched her team, her family, relaxing and enjoying each other's company. It was a rare moment of peace, a brief respite from the darkness they had all been fighting against.

Kit, seated beside her, nudged her gently with his shoulder. "You know, we make a pretty good team," he said with a grin.

Charlie smiled, leaning into him slightly. "Yeah, we do. And I'm glad we're all here, together."

They both knew that the fight wasn't over, that there would be more missions, more challenges, more darkness to face. But for now, they had each other, and that was enough.

As the night wore on, the team continued to celebrate, sharing stories, laughter, and the simple joy of being together. They would talk tomorrow about the operation in the UK, about what they had accomplished and what still needed to be done.

Tonight was about family, about taking a moment to breathe and appreciate the people they had fought so hard to protect.

And in that moment, as the stars began to twinkle in the night sky, Kit and Charlie knew that whatever came next, they would face it together... as a family.

CHAPTER 52

The next few months brought a kind of settling, a quiet rebuilding of lives that had been torn apart by the darkness they had faced. Kit's team and Charlie's team slowly began to integrate, their shared purpose and experiences creating bonds that went deeper than any formal alliance. The lodge in Atlanta, which had been a temporary base during their operations, gradually became a permanent home for several of the members.

Kimmie, Doc, and Emily decided to remain at Charlie's ranch in New York state. The ranch had always been a sanctuary, but now it took on a new life as a center for the recovery and healing of trafficking victims. Nestled away from the prying eyes of the world, the backside of the ranch became a safe haven for those who had nowhere else to go. Kimmie, with her nurturing nature and infectious energy, made sure that every person who came through the gates felt like part of the family. Whether they were young or old, lost or simply looking for a place to belong, she was there to greet them with open arms.

Doc, the ranch foreman, found a deep satisfaction in his work. It was a far cry from the battles they had fought, but there was something rewarding about teaching the older kids and adults how to work on a ranch. He taught them how to care for the horses, mend fences, and handle the day-to-day responsibilities that came with ranch life. For many, it was the first time they had felt a sense of belonging, of being needed and valued for their skills. Doc's gruff exterior hid a heart of gold, and the kids quickly grew to respect and admire him, learning from his wisdom and experience.

Emily, the ever-compassionate nurse, finished her doctorate and now had the initials MD behind her name. She was a constant presence at the ranch, providing not only medical care but also emotional support to the victims. She worked closely with Kimmie to ensure that each person received the care they needed, whether it was physical healing or the slow, difficult process of recovering from trauma. Together, they created a nurturing environment that allowed the survivors to begin rebuilding their lives.

Meanwhile, Izzy, and Rafe decided to stay in Los Angeles. The vibrant, chaotic city had always been home for them, and despite the dangers they had faced, it was where they felt they could make the most difference. Marley, always traveling, made it his base of operations and would regale the groups with stories of his interviews with interesting people around the country and world.

With Aria's help, Kit and Charlie found a spacious house in LA, setting up a smaller base of operations that would allow them to continue their work on the West Coast. The house was large enough to accommodate everyone when the team from the East Coast visited, and it quickly became a hub of activity and planning.

China, who had been spending time in Mexico with her family when the UK raid took place, decided to remain in the fashion industry and live in LA, a world she had come to love. She enjoyed the creativity and the challenge of designing clothes, and her work allowed her to stay connected to the team while pursuing her passion and watch for the young women and men who were often exploited in the modeling industry. With Kit and Charlie's support, she continued to design for a clientele that valued both her talent and her integrity and every so often, sending a lost one to them for help.

Charlie, on the other hand, took a step back from her clubs and the intense operations that had defined her life for so long. The loss of Chase, the harrowing experience in LA, and the recent mission in the UK had left her exhausted, both physically and emotionally. The ranch, with its rolling hills and tranquil atmosphere, became her refuge. For the first time in years, she allowed herself to rest, to simply potter around the ranch, tending to the horses and the land that had become her sanctuary.

Mr. Holloway, her accountant and Chase's grandfather, was a steady presence during this time. The funeral they held for Chase was a quiet, somber affair, attended by only a few close friends and family. They laid him to rest in the small cemetery on the ranch, under the shade of an old oak tree. Mr. Holloway, who had quickly become a grandfather figure to Charlie, thanked her for everything she had done for his grandson. He promised that he would be around for a while to keep her straight, to make sure she didn't lose herself in her grief. And, to keep himself young.

Kit, meanwhile, found himself unable to fully step back from the work that had become his life's mission. The list of street kids that needed rescuing seemed never-ending, but with the extra help from both his and Charlie's teams, they managed to track down 95 percent of the children that had been reported missing. From the bustling streets of New York to the rural towns of the Midwest, from the hot, crowded cities in the South to the cool, quiet forests of the Pacific Northwest, Kit and his team infiltrated small trafficking operations and shut them down.

Word began to spread in hidden circles about the man who was hunting them, the Guardian of the Lost. It was a name that struck fear into the hearts of traffickers and criminals, a name that promised swift and unrelenting justice. But to the children Kit rescued, he was known by another name, Caretaker. It was a nickname that had started with one of the younger kids, a boy no older than seven, who had been terrified when Kit first approached him. But as Kit scooped him up, the boy had clung to him, finding safety in the arms of the giant who had come to rescue him.

Despite his imposing size, there was a gentleness in Kit that the kids sensed immediately. He wasn't just there to pull them out of danger, he was there to protect them, to care for them, and to make sure they had a future. The kids adored him, flocking to him whenever he entered a room, and Kit, in turn, found a deep fulfillment in their trust and love.

Back in Atlanta, the lodge became a place of both work and respite. When they weren't out on missions or planning their next move, the team members would gather at the lodge, sharing meals, stories, and laughter. The sense of camaraderie was strong, and they had become more than just a team, they had become a family.

One warm evening, the team decided to hold a barbecue at the lodge, a way to unwind and enjoy each other's company. Everyone that could, showed up. The smell of grilled steaks and roasted vegetables filled the air, mingling with the sounds of laughter and conversation. Doc, who had taken over the grill, regaled everyone with more stories from his time spent at various locations overseas, some of which were met with raised eyebrows and stifled laughter.

"So, there I was," Doc said, flipping a burger with a flourish, "in the middle of nowhere, trying to communicate with a local who spoke a language I'd never even heard of. All I had was a rusty machete and a can of beans. And let me tell you, that machete was the only thing keeping me from becoming dinner!"

Laughter erupted around the grill as Doc continued his tale, embellishing the details just enough to keep everyone entertained.

Kimmie, who was seated on a nearby bench, shook her head, grinning. "Doc, you've got more stories than anyone I've ever met. And I'm not sure how many of them are true!"

"True or not, they're damn good stories," Kit said, clapping Doc on the back.

Charlie sat quietly off to the side, her gaze drifting over the group of people she had come to think of as her own. The pain of losing Chase was still there, a dull ache that would never fully go away, but here, surrounded by her team, by her family, she found a sense of peace she hadn't felt in a long time.

She watched as Mr. Holloway engaged in a heated debate with Miguel over the best way to train a horse, while Aria, Calista, and Dak huddled together, talking in hushed tones about some new piece of tech they were excited to test out. Sophie and Zara were deep in conversation, their voices blending with the sound of music playing softly in the background.

For the first time in what felt like years, Charlie allowed herself to simply be. To enjoy the moment, the warmth of the fire, the sound of her friend's laughter. The road ahead would be long, and there were still battles to be fought, but tonight, they had each other. And that was enough.

As the evening wore on, the team continued to share stories, to laugh and to plan for the future. But tonight, the focus wasn't on missions or operations, it was on family. They had all been through so much, and they knew there would be more challenges ahead, but as long as they had each other, they could face anything.

Kit, who had been quiet for most of the evening, finally spoke up. "I just want to say, I'm proud of all of you. We've done some incredible work together, and I know we're going to keep doing it. But tonight, let's just enjoy being together."

A murmur of agreement went around the group, and they all raised their glasses in a silent toast. To the work they had done, to the work that still lay ahead, and to the family they had built together.

He walked over and sat beside Charlie, close enough to nudge her shoulder. "I never knew you went through all of that. You've come a long way. It'll take time to heal but look at the family you created." He paused, a tear choking his throat. "Not only here but with the community around the world. It takes a strong woman to do something like that."

Charlie watched the tear slide down Kit's cheek and wiped it with her thumb. "It takes a strong family to create something like this."

As the stars began to twinkle in the night sky, the team continued to celebrate, sharing food, laughter, and the simple joy of being together. The future was uncertain, and there would always be more battles to fight, but for now, they had found a moment of peace, a moment to breathe and to appreciate the people they had fought so hard to protect.

And in that moment, as the night deepened and the fire crackled softly, Kit and Charlie knew that no matter what came next, they would face it together, stronger, wiser, and more determined than ever.

EPILOGUE

And if you're wondering what happened to Alexandre DuBois' billions, let me explain.

It began with a discovery at Alexandre's Marseille estate, one that would forever change the narrative of his legacy. A young man was found there, severely malnourished and beaten, barely clinging to life. The authorities initially thought he was another victim of Alexandre's cruelty, one more nameless face lost to the horrors of trafficking. But as they carefully tended to his wounds and coaxed him back to consciousness, the truth emerged.

The young man, who appeared to be around 17 or 18 years old, claimed to be Alexandre's son. It was a shocking revelation. Alexandre had never married, never shown any interest in forming attachments of any kind. His life had been one of cold, calculated cruelty, driven by wealth and power, without a trace of love or compassion. The idea that he could have a son seemed impossible, yet here was this boy, broken and bruised, insisting that he was Alexandre's blood.

His name was Alex. It was a name he had given himself in the faint hope that one day, Alexandre might acknowledge him, might accept him as his own. But that day had never come.

As Alex slowly recovered, he began to tell his story, a tale that was as heartbreaking as it was horrifying. His mother had been the daughter of an elitist in Russia, a powerful man with more wealth than morals. She had been given to Alexandre as a gift when she was just a teenager, an unwanted burden in a family that claimed to have too many children to care for. For fifteen years, she had lived as a prisoner in Alexandre's estate, a secret kept hidden from the world.

When she became pregnant, she managed to hide it from Alexandre for as long as she could, terrified of what he might do if he found out. But eventually, the truth became impossible to conceal. When the child was born, a boy she never got to see or name, Alexandre's reaction was as cold and ruthless as expected. He handed the newborn off to one of his servants, without so much as a glance, and then promptly sold the woman who had borne his child, ensuring that she would never be seen again.

Alex grew up in the shadows of Alexandre's world, raised by the servants who had taken pity on him. He was told little about his mother, only that she had been sold, and he was to never speak of her again. Alexandre, for his part, made no attempt to acknowledge the boy's existence. It was as if Alex was a stain on his perfect, brutal life, something to be hidden away and forgotten.

But Alex held on to a thread of hope, even as he grew older and the beatings began. Alexandre's cruelty knew no bounds, and when he discovered that the boy was still alive, still clinging to the hope that one day he might be recognized, he reacted with the same violence and rage that had defined his entire life. He locked Alex in the basement of his estate, where the boy was left to starve, only kept alive by the kindness of a few loyal servants who risked their lives to sneak him food and water.

This was how Charlie found him, alone, scared, but still somehow unbroken.

When word of the discovery reached her, Charlie didn't hesitate. With the government's knowledge and approval, she flew to Marseille to be with the boy, knowing that this could be a pivotal moment in the battle against Alexandre's dark empire. She stayed by Alex's side as he was nursed back to health, offering comfort and support in a way that no one had ever done for him before.

Paternity tests were conducted, and the results were undeniable. Alex was indeed the son of Alexandre DuBois, the rightful heir to his vast fortune. But that was only the beginning. As they dug deeper into Alex's past, they uncovered the truth about his mother and her connection to a powerful Russian family. The patriarch of that family had died many years earlier, and the remaining members welcomed Alex with open arms, eager to embrace the son of the sister they had lost.

Charlie returned to the States with a new feeling of purpose. She had seen firsthand the horrors that Alexandre had inflicted on his own flesh and blood, and she was determined to ensure that his legacy would be one of redemption, not of continued suffering.

She called a meeting with both her team and Kit's, bringing everyone together either in person at the lodge in Atlanta or via video conference. Devlin, her attorney, was also present, ready to help with the legal complexities of what they were about to undertake.

Charlie began by explaining Alex's story, the harrowing details of his life and how he had survived despite the odds. The room was silent as she spoke, the unbelievable story of the young man's suffering filling everyone with sadness.

"Alex DuBois," Charlie said, her voice steady but filled with emotion, "is the legal heir to Alexandre DuBois' estate. He has stepped forward to claim it, and with that claim, he has also made a vow. He has promised to use his wealth to help others, to set up a foundation for trafficked victims, to establish education funds, and to find jobs for those who have none. And when he has fully recovered from the ordeal of the last few years, he wants to join our organization and continue the fight against the very evil that tried to destroy him."

"I had Alexandre sign over his fortune to me the night of the raid, with the intention of disbursing it around the world to victims and their families, but when Alex appeared, I knew if he became an ally, we could become a force worldwide in the fight against trafficking and his business ventures would continue to make money for this cause." She explained how she and Alex had spent much time talking about the industry that caused so many people so much pain and suffering.

There was a moment of stunned silence, followed by a murmur of approval that quickly grew into enthusiastic agreement. The team members were visibly moved by Alex's story, and the idea of having someone like him, someone who had lived through the horrors they were fighting against, join their ranks was met with unanimous support.

"We're with you," Kit exclaimed. "And we'll welcome Alex with open arms. He's been through hell, but he's survived. That makes him one of us."

Charlie smiled, feeling a swell of pride and gratitude for the people around her. They had faced so much darkness together, and yet they had never lost sight of the light they were fighting for.

The meeting continued, with discussions about how to best how to help Alex manage his vast holdings and ensure that the funds were used for the greater good. Devlin laid out the legal steps that needed to be taken, but the mood in the room was one of hope and determination. Mr. Holloway, his indelible self, connected Alex with a friend that would help him steer through the companies and holdings, ensuring the young man was not scammed in any way.

As the conversation wound down, Charlie couldn't help but reflect on how far they had come. From the depths of the shadows, they had brought a ray of light into the world, a light that would continue to shine as long as they kept fighting.

When the meeting concluded, Charlie stepped outside into the cool evening air. The stars were just beginning to appear in the sky, a reminder of the vastness of the world and the many lives that still needed saving. But tonight, she allowed herself a moment of peace, a moment to simply breathe and take it all in.

Kit joined her, his presence a comforting reminder that she wasn't in this alone. They stood in silence for a while, watching as the stars grew brighter, each one a tiny beacon of hope in the darkness.

"You did good, Charlie," Kit said finally, his voice soft but filled with admiration. "You gave that boy a chance, something he never had before. And now, look at what he's going to do."

Charlie nodded, her throat tight with emotion. "He deserves it, Kit. He deserves a chance to make a difference, to turn all that pain into something good."

"And he will," Kit replied, his hand resting on her shoulder. "We will be right there beside him."

As they stood there together, side by side, Charlie felt a deep sense of satisfaction. The battle wasn't over, not by a long shot, but they had won an important victory. And with Alex DuBois stepping forward to join their fight, they would grow stronger than ever.

From the depths of the shadows, a strong ray of light had emerged. And with it came the promise of a better future, a future where the lost could be found, where the broken could be healed, and where those who had been cast aside could finally find their place in the world.

For Kit, Charlie, and their teams, the work would continue. But tonight, they could all rest easy, knowing that the tide was turning, and that together, they could accomplish anything.

As the night deepened and the stars shone brightly above, they knew that no matter what challenges lay ahead, they were ready. Ready to face the darkness, ready to bring the light.

And they knew, deep in their hearts, that they would succeed… they were guardians of the lost.

CHARLIE'S CHILDREN: GUARDIAN OF THE LOST 2 415

According to the National Center on Family Homelessness, 2.5 million children in the United States are homeless annually, which is about one in every 30 children. This number has increased in the last decade due to a rise in homelessness among families, which is caused by factors like poverty and a lack of affordable housing.

- 50,000 youth sleep on the streets for at least six months each year.
- Up to 40% of homeless youth identify as LGBTQ.
- 13 at-risk youth die every day from assault, illness, or suicide while trying to survive on the streets.
- Almost 7% of youth, or 1.5 million children and adolescents, run away from home each year.

Babies/toddlers (0 – 5 yrs) 1.5 million
Unaccompanied youth (13 – 17) 700,000
Unaccompanied young adults (18 – 25) 3.5 million

The United Nations estimates there are up to 150 million street children in the world. No one knows the exact number because they are unknown to social services and government organizations.

Many children have run away from home or an institution to escape psychological, physical, or sexual abuse. They have no home except for the streets and may move from place to place, living in shelters and abandoned buildings.

They earn their keep by panhandling, stealing, selling drugs, and selling their bodies. With little to no education, they have no other options and those that can, take advantage of these youth.

Hotline Numbers for Reporting Potential Trafficking

1. **National Human Trafficking Hotline (USA)**
   - Phone: 1-888-373-7888
   - SMS: Text "HELP" or "INFO" to 233733 (BEFREE)
   - Website: humantraffickinghotline.org
2. **Polaris Project (USA)**
   - Phone: 1-888-373-7888
   - SMS: Text "BeFree" to 233733 (BEFREE)
   - Website: polarisproject.org
3. **National Center for Missing & Exploited Children (USA)**
   - Phone: 1-800-THE-LOST (1-800-843-5678)
   - Website: missingkids.org
4. **UK Modern Slavery Helpline (UK)**
   - Phone: 08000 121 700
   - Website: modernslaveryhelpline.org
5. **Human Trafficking Foundation (UK)**
   - Phone: 020 3773 2040
   - Website: humantraffickingfoundation.org

Hotline Numbers for Victims of Trafficking

1. **National Human Trafficking Hotline (USA)**
   - Phone: 1-888-373-7888
   - SMS: Text "HELP" or "INFO" to 233733 (BEFREE)
   - Website: humantraffickinghotline.org
2. **RAINN (Rape, Abuse & Incest National Network) (USA)**
   - Phone: 1-800-656-HOPE (1-800-656-4673)
   - Website: www.rainn.org

3. **Love146 (USA)**
    - Phone: 1-203-772-4420
    - Website: love146.org
4. **Unseen UK (UK)**
    - Phone: 0303 040 2040
    - Website: www.unseenuk.org
5. **Kalayaan (UK)**
    - Phone: 020 7243 2942
    - Website: kalayaan.org.uk

Signs to Look for in People Asking for Help that Might be Abducted.

1. **Physical Indicators**
    - Signs of physical abuse or restraint
    - Malnourishment or poor hygiene
    - Tattoos or branding that could signify ownership
2. **Behavioral Indicators**
    - Avoiding eye contact, appearing nervous or fearful
    - Seeming unusually submissive or fearful around certain individuals
    - Being unable to speak freely or having someone else answer questions for them
3. **Situational Indicators**
    - Lack of personal possessions or identification documents
    - Being in a location that doesn't fit their situation (e.g., a young child in a suspicious area)
    - Frequent movement or being unsure of their current location
4. **Control Indicators**

- Signs of control or monitoring by another person
- Restricted freedom of movement (not allowed to come and go as they please)
- Working excessively long hours with little or no pay

5. **Work and Living Conditions**
   - Living with their employer or in a place that appears overcrowded or unsafe
   - Working in an environment with high security measures (e.g., bars on windows, security cameras)

6. **Communication Indicators**
   - Lack of knowledge about their whereabouts or address
   - Inconsistent stories or unable to explain how they arrived in their current location
   - Speaking in a way that seems rehearsed or controlled

If you suspect someone is a victim of human trafficking, it is crucial to report your concerns to the appropriate authorities. Use the hotline numbers listed above to ensure the safety and well-being of potential victims.

Don't miss out!

Visit the website below and you can sign up to receive emails whenever Katlyn Rose publishes a new book. There's no charge and no obligation.

https://books2read.com/r/B-A-TUJAB-XGTFF

BOOKS 2 READ

Connecting independent readers to independent writers.

Also by Katlyn Rose

Charlie's Children
Charlie's Children Neon Shadows 1
Charlie's Children: Guardian of the Lost 2

Standalone
Starlight and Stilettos
Phoenix Rising: Thrive and Transform While in a Toxic Relationship
Chaos in the Kitchen
Moonbeam Chronicles: Witching Hour in Foxglove
When No One is Clapping for You, Clap for Yourself

About the Author

Raised in West Texas, Katlyn is a beacon of compassion, strength, and empowerment. With 35 years of marriage under her belt, Katlyn now resides on a small rural farm in Georgia, where she has dedicated her life to rescuing unloved animals, inspiring women, especially older women, to embrace their full potential, and expressing her creativity through the written word.

From a young age, Katlyn developed a deep connection with animals. Growing up in the Texas countryside, she witnessed the plight of abandoned and mistreated creatures, igniting a lifelong commitment to animal welfare. Now, on her small rural farm in Georgia, Katlyn has created a sanctuary where neglected animals find solace, healing, and a loving forever home.

Katlyn's passion for empowering older women stems from her belief that age should never be a barrier to personal growth and fulfillment. She loves guiding women on a transformative journey of self-discovery. Her support and encouragement inspire older women to embrace their unique strengths, unlock their hidden potential, and embark on new adventures with confidence and purpose.

In addition to her dedication to animal rescue and empowering older women, Katlyn finds solace and self-expression through writing. Her words flow effortlessly onto the page, capturing the essence of her experiences, insights, and the beauty she witnesses in the world around her. Through her writing, Katlyn aims to inspire others to embrace their passions, live authentically, and make a positive impact in their own lives and the lives of others.

Katlyn's life is her story of the power of compassion, strength, and the pursuit of one's passions. Through her undying commitment to rescuing unloved animals, empowering older women, and expressing her creativity through writing, she has become a guiding light for all who cross her path.

Her journey serves as an inspiration to embrace our true selves, live with purpose, and make a positive impact in the world, regardless of age or circumstance.